# come away with me

# come away with me

KARMA BROWN

ISBN-13: 978-0-7783-1832-3

Come Away with Me



For questions and comments about the quality of this book, please contact us at CustomerService@Harlequin.com.

www.MIRABooks.com

**Printed in U.S.A.**

First printing: September 2015
10 9 8 7 6 5 4 3 2 1

For Adam & Addison, the greatest loves of my life.

And to anyone who has been handed the proverbial lemons of life and made lemonade with them, this book is also for you.

Death leaves a heartache no one can heal, love leaves a memory no one can steal.

—From a headstone in Ireland

# *one*
# Chicago

# 1

Even now, the smell of peppermint still makes me cry…

# 2

We drive the dark streets a little too fast for the weather. Beside me, Gabe crunches a candy cane and drums his thumbs against the steering wheel, singing along to his favorite holiday tune on the radio.

He reaches for the second half of the candy cane with one hand and uses the other to turn up the radio. I tell him to keep his hands on the wheel, but I'm not sure he hears me above the music.

*If only he listened, if only I said it louder.*

It's 6:56 p.m. I watch the clock nervously…6:57 p.m. We're going to be late, and my mother-in-law hates it when we're late.

At this hour the sky has already turned black, a particularly depressing fact about winter in Chicago. But the twinkling Christmas lights that wind around the lampposts almost make up for it. On vacation from the law firm, with a whole six days of freedom, Gabe is in a feisty and festive mood. Plus, it's Christmas Eve and we have so many reasons to celebrate this year. He crunches the candy cane enthusiastically, too impatient to savor it. The candy's sweet, refreshing scent fills the car.

"Your mom is going to lose it," I say, eyeing the Jetta's dashboard clock. "We're going to be so late."

"Five minutes. Ten tops," Gabe says. "She'll live."

"Wonder if we will." I give him a wry glance. After eight years of being part of the Lawson family, there are three things I can count on. One, they love to eat, and dropping by for lunch generally means a six-course meal, prepared from scratch by his Italian mother. Two, Gabe inherited his love of life and unwavering positivity from his dad, which I am grateful for. And three, you never, ever, show up late to a Lawson family event...or without a good bottle of red wine.

"You need to relax, my love." Gabe takes his right hand off the wheel and rests it on my knee briefly, before sliding it up my thigh. His calloused palm—rough from sanding the antique cradle he's been refinishing, the one I slept in as a baby—scratches against my tights as it works its way along my thigh. The bottle of wine tumbles off my lap.

"Gabe!" I laugh and playfully swat at him. I right the wine bottle and place it between my suede winter boots on the floor. "Get your hand back on the wheel. If this bottle breaks, you're done for."

But he keeps his hand where it is. "Trust me," he murmurs, his smile widening. "This will do the trick."

"We're almost there," I protest, pressing my hand down hard on his, temporarily stopping its climb. "Let's save this for later, okay? When we're not late and you're not driving."

"Don't worry, I'm an expert one-handed driver," he says, inching his hand higher despite my efforts. "Besides, I don't want you going into my parents' house all wound up. You know how my mom smells fear." He turns and winks at me, and I melt. Like always.

His fingers hook the thick waistband of my tights, which sit just underneath my newly swelling belly, and I stop protesting.

*Rockin' around the Christmas tree…have a happy holiday…*

My breath catches as Gabe's fingers work their way past the waistband and into my not sexy, but quite practical, maternity underwear. I look over at him but he stares straight ahead, a smile playing on his lips. I close my eyes and lean my head against the headrest, as Gabe's hand moves lower…

Then, suddenly, too much movement in all the wrong directions. Like riding a roller coaster with closed eyes, unable to figure out which turn is coming next. Except there's no exhilaration—only panic at the realization Gabe no longer has control over the car. The tires lose their grip on the road and Gabe's fingers wrench from between my legs. I gasp out his name and brace my hands against the edges of my seat. We fishtail side to side, and for a moment it seems as though Gabe is back in control. I allow myself a split second of relief. One quick thought that being late to dinner isn't the worst thing that could happen, after all. An instant to contemplate how lucky we are.

Then, with a sickening lurch, the car swerves. The momentum is so great it tosses me sideways like a rag doll, and my head cracks against the window. Stars explode behind my eyes, mingling with the lampposts' twinkle lights and creating a dizzying kaleidoscope. I feel like I'm watching a lit Ferris wheel, spinning high in the night sky.

As our car smashes into the lamppost, steel meets steel and everything slows down. I wonder if the bottle of wine will be okay. I think that at least now we have a good excuse for being late for dinner. And I'm amazed the radio continues playing, as if nothing has changed.

After the impact comes the shriek of metal as our sturdy car rips practically in two. And still, the music plays. When the airbag explodes into my face and chest I worry I may suffocate. But then a rush of pain, deep and frightening, crushes my belly—where the most important thing to both of us is nestled—and it takes my breath away.

Seconds later, everything goes quiet.

I try to call out for Gabe, but have no air left to make a sound. With my left hand I reach out, hoping to feel him beside me. I need to tell him something is wrong. My head hurts terribly.

He'll know what to do.

But there's nothing beside me except cold, empty space.

Then I realize it's snowing inside the car.

We will not be lucky this time.

# 3

The biscotto shatters into a million pieces, the butter knife clanging against the fine china plate I'd planned to use for Christmas dinner. Back when I was looking forward to Christmas. Or to anything. Staring into the crumbs, I realize how closely they resemble my life. No one piece big enough to be satisfying; too many that even if you try to gather them all, a few will be left behind. Lost forever in the cracks.

"I don't know why you insist on trying to cut that stuff." Gabe leans against the doorjamb between our kitchen and the hallway.

"Because I only want half," I say. "Why do they have to make them so damn long?"

"So you don't burn your fingers when you dip them in your coffee," he replies, shrugging. *Obviously*, his expression adds, though he doesn't say anything out loud.

I sigh, tucking a stringy piece of dark hair behind my ear. "Why are you still here anyway?" It's two o'clock in the afternoon on a Wednesday, the middle of a workday. It's been a long time since I went to work, nearly three months. I pick up a small chunk of the broken biscotto and dip it in my coffee, appreciating the hot liquid's burn against my skin. Physical pain is good. It dulls the ache that won't leave my chest.

Gabe moves into the kitchen and sits on the empty stool beside me at the island. “I live here,” he says, his tone purposefully light. He’s trying to bring a smile to my face, I know, like he used to so easily.

The soggy corner of the cookie falls from my fingers and disappears below the surface of the coffee. “Besides, you need me,” he adds with a resigned sigh. “I’m not going anywhere.”

I look back into my mug, oily dots popping to the surface, and grab another piece of biscotto. My mother-in-law, Rosa, brought it over earlier, a whole tray’s worth, because she believes eating dilutes grief. But the cookies are Gabe’s favorite, not mine. To be honest, I don’t much care for them although I didn’t have the heart to tell his mom. Especially not now.

I put the thick, crusty cookie on the plate and pick up the knife again. Gabe raises an eyebrow but I ignore him, cutting the piece in half, once again unsuccessfully.

My mother bustles into the kitchen and I glance up at the stack of tiny folded blankets, covered in green turtles and fuzzy brown teddy bears, she holds in her arms. “What would you like me to do with these?” She looks uncomfortable to be asking the question, even though I’ve asked her here specifically to help pack up the nursery—something Gabe and I are incapable of facing alone.

“Get rid of them, please,” I say as if I’m talking about tomato soup cans in our trash bin. “Give them away or something.”

My mom opens her mouth, then closes it as she fingers the fine, muslin blanket on top of the pile—the one I imagined swaddling our son in before rocking him to sleep. “I could just put them in storage, until you’re sure.”

“No,” I say, shaking my head. The air in the kitchen is charged with tension. No one knows how to deal with me these days; I can’t say I blame them. If I could escape my body and mind, I wouldn't look back. "Give them away. Or throw them out. I don't really care, as long as they're gone."

"Are you sure?" Gabe asks. He looks sad. But I'm sure I look worse. I tuck my hair behind my ear again, smelling how long it's been since my last shower.

My mom hasn't moved. She's standing on the other side of the island and staring down at the blankets, sweeping her hands across the top one to try and straighten out the wrinkles. It occurs to me she imagined wrapping her grandson in that blanket, too.

"Get rid of them," I say with an edge this time. But I keep my eyes on Gabe, who has gotten up and is now standing beside my mom. I'm challenging him to argue. "Please don't make me say it again."

"Okay, hon, okay," Mom says, looking apologetic before leaving us to finish the conversation I don't want to have.

"I'm sorry, Tegan." Gabe's voice carries a sadness I understand but don't want to deal with.

I pick up another biscotto and put it on the plate full of broken cookie pieces. "I know," I reply, setting the knife directly in the middle of the cookie. I press down firmly and a large chunk of the biscotto flies off the plate, still intact. Finally. "But it doesn't really matter anymore, does it?"

# 4

"I've never seen you look more beautiful." Gabe is beside me on our couch. I'm looking at the collection of photos on my lap that have yet to make it to a scrapbook or album. I shuffle through the photos, stopping at one of Gabe and me in Millennium Park, in front of *Cloud Gate*, or what Chicagoans call "the Bean." In it Gabe kisses my cheek, my one foot kicked up and my hands holding the dress's frothy layers of material in a sashay move. Our image is reflected back in the Bean's smooth, shiny steel surface, along with the Chicago skyline and a slew of strangers, now part of our memories. A day I'll never forget.

"Aside from the tinge of green on my face," I say. Remembering. It's only been six months, but feels like a lifetime.

We were married at dusk, during an early September heat wave. The ceremony was on the rooftop of the Wit hotel under the glass roof, which, along with the potted magnolia bushes that were somehow in bloom despite the season, made it feel as though we were inside a terrarium. Glowing lanterns lined the aisle and guests sat on low, white couches that would later become seating for the reception. It was all much more than we could afford, me a kindergarten teacher and Gabe just out of law school. But his well-off parents insisted—and paid—so the Wit it was.

I was horribly sick at the wedding, throwing up most of the day—including right after the picture at the Bean, in a bag Gabe wisely tucked in his suit pocket, "just in case"—and only five minutes before I walked down the lantern-lit aisle. Luckily my best friend and maid of honor, Anna, grabbed a wine bucket just in time. My mother-in-law blamed the catering from the rehearsal dinner the night before, which my parents had organized. My mom, bristling at Gabe's mother's implication, suggested it was nerves, telling all who would listen I'd always had a weak stomach when I was nervous. As a child that was quite true. I did my fair share of vomiting before important school exams, anytime I had to public speak and, most unfortunately, onstage when I was one of the three little pigs in the school play. But I had outgrown my "nervous stomach," and figured I'd just caught a bug from school. When you teach five- and six-year-olds all day you spend a good part of the year ill.

Gabe was so sweet that morning. Sending me a prewedding gift of a dozen yellow roses, a bottle of pink bismuth for my stomach and a card that read:

> You've always looked good in green—ha-ha. You are my forever.
> G xo

Even sick, it was the best day of my life.

We found out a week later it had nothing to do with food poisoning, or nerves, or a virus. I was pregnant. I'd never seen Gabe happier than when he opened the envelope I gave him, telling him it was a leftover wedding card previously misplaced. When he pulled out the card, which had a baby rattle and "Congratulations" printed on its front, at first he looked confused. Then I handed him the pregnancy test stick, with a bright pink plus sign, and he burst into tears. He grabbed me and spun me around, laughing and hollering with joy, until I couldn't see straight. There is nothing like being able to give your husband, the man you've loved since the day you laid eyes on him, a dream come true.

We met at Northwestern in our first year, during frosh week. My dorm was having an unsanctioned floor crawl. Gabe, who had been invited by a friend who lived in my dorm, had backed into me coming out of the Purple Jesus room, his giant Slurpee-sized cup of grape Kool-Aid mixed with high-proof vodka spilling all over both of us. Shocked at the cold, rubbing-alcohol-scented drink sopping into my white T-shirt and shorts, I simply stared at him, my mouth open. But then we burst out laughing, and he offered to help clean me up in the women's washroom, which also happened to be the orgasm shooter room for the night.

"How apropos," Gabe said, wiggling his eyebrows at me and handing me a shot glass. I laughed again, tossing back the sickly sweet shooter.

"Thanks," I said. "That was the best one I've ever had."

While we'd been together for so many years after that, our lives intertwined, the day we were married was the day it all really began. If only we'd had more time to bask in that happiness. There was a carton of orange juice in our fridge that had lasted nearly as long.

I stack the photos back together, not bothering to wipe away my tears.

"Teg, please don't cry." Gabe shifts closer to me, but I can barely feel his touch. I'm so numb.

"Do you think I'll ever be happy again?" I close the lid on

the box of photos. Saving them for the same time tomorrow night. "I mean, really happy?"

"I know it," he says. "You're just not ready yet, love."

I touch my necklace, still trying to get used to it. It's a white-gold, round pendant, about the size of a quarter and a half-inch thick. It hangs from a delicate chain. And while the pendant was hollow when the necklace arrived, via a white-and-orange FedEx box nowhere near special enough for its cargo, it's now filled with the ashes of a broken dream.

I chose the necklace off the internet shortly after I was released from the hospital, one late night when sleep was impossible. I considered an urn, but somehow it felt wrong. That's how my grandma had kept Gramps's ashes, in an ornate brass urn on her kitchen windowsill. "Where we can still kiss him every day, the sun and me," she liked to say.

In truth, twenty-six felt too young to keep—or need, for that matter—an urn of any kind. I casually mentioned the idea of something a little more intimate to Anna, hoping she'd tell me wearing a necklace filled with ashes wasn't at all weird, but her frown and pinched look suggested otherwise. Gabe hadn't been much help, either. None of us wanted to deal with the horror, but I didn't have that luxury because it was my body that was now hollow. Empty, like my gold necklace used to be.

Gabe glances at the pendant. "You don't have to wear it all the time, you know."

"Yes, I do."

"Does it…make you feel better?" he asks, shifting sideways so he can face me straight on.

I pause for a moment. "No." Then I turn my head and look at him before quickly turning away. I don't like his look. It's a complex mix of concern, sorrow and frustration.

"I'm worried it's making things worse, Tegan."

Anger burns in my belly. The last thing I should have to

do is explain myself. Especially after what he's done to us, to me. "How could anything make this worse?" My voice is low, unsteady.

"You know what I mean," he says.

"Obviously I don't." I slam the box of photos on the coffee table and stand up so quickly I feel woozy.

"Hey, hey, Tegan," he soothes, and I know if I were still on the couch he'd reach for me. But I'm just out of his grasp, and neither of us tries to close the distance. "I want to understand. I'm just trying to help."

How do you explain that if you could, you'd cut your chest open and pour the ashes right inside so they could forever lie next to your heart? Like a blanket to smother the chill of sorrow. You can't, so you don't.

Gabe and I are the only ones who know exactly what's in the necklace. Well, us and the funeral director, who filled it at my request. Close to my heart. It's the only way I can keep breathing.

"I'm going to bed," I say. My muscles ache as I walk slowly to the bedroom, making the space between us even greater. I'm so fragile these days, paper-thin. Even though I'm only halfway through my twenties, I feel more like a ninety-year-old. Probably because for the past couple of months I've done little aside from move in a daze from couch, to bed and back.

I barely remember what it feels like to get up and get ready for work. To enjoy takeout during one of the nature shows Gabe loves to watch, to shop for shoes or bags or the very short dresses Anna likes to fill her closet with, hopeful for date nights. I forget what it's like to have a purpose that gets me up each morning.

These days I care little about what's happening beyond my four apartment walls. I don't remember what fresh air smells like, except for when Mom opens one of the apartment windows, touting fresh air as effective an elixir as anything else. The late winter chill that tickles my senses always feels good, but I don't want to feel good. Not yet. It has only been seventy-nine days. So I ask her to shut the window and she sighs, but she always does it. That's the thing about going through something like this. People will do anything to try and make you happy again; they'll give you whatever you want. Except that the thing you really want you can never have again, and no one can bring it back.

"I'll come with you," Gabe says, from behind me.

"You don't have to," I reply, although I don't mean it. As much as I am still so angry with Gabe, still full of rage and blame, I don't like to sleep alone.

"I want to."

"Fine," I say, pushing the door to our bedroom open. As I do, I glance into the guest room to my right. The door is supposed to be closed—I've been quite clear about that—but it's wide-open. Beckoning me.

The pile of baby blankets rests on the dresser, which would have doubled as a change table to save precious space in our not-so-spacious apartment. My mom must have forgotten to close the door when she left. Casting my eyes around the dim room, the bile rises in the back of my throat. Pushed up against one wall, the crib is still covered by a white sheet, with the mobile—plush baseballs and baseball bats, which Gabe had picked out as soon as we found out it was a boy—creating a peak in the sheet's middle like a circus tent. In another corner I see the cradle, which Gabe had restored beautifully, waiting for a final coat of stain. Even though we still had months to go, we had been ready for our boy's arrival.

Feeling sick, I turn away and shut the door firmly. Perhaps tomorrow I'll agree to the crib being taken apart. It will have been eighty days, nearly three months, and I know I'll soon have to accept no baby will ever sleep here, gazing with wide, curious eyes as the mobile circles soothingly overhead.

As I settle into our bed, pulling the sheets—which smell clean and fresh, thanks to Gabe, or my mom, or someone else who takes care of the things I no longer seem able to—up to my chin, I try to pretend none of it happened.

But the nightmares won't let me forget, not even while I sleep.

# 5

Anna has her hands on her tiny hips in a way that looks more cutesy than angry, despite her best efforts. Her nearly black, almond-shaped eyes narrow. "I'm not taking no for an answer," she says. I pull the duvet over my head, and weakly fight her as she pulls it down again. "You have to eat," she continues. "Lunch. I promise." She makes an air cross over her chest, eyes earnest. "Only for lunch and then you can come right back here to bed."

"Anna, stop," I say, finally allowing her to strip me of the covers. The flannel pajamas I'm wearing are rumpled and smell like they need a wash. "I don't want to go out."

She sits on the bed beside me, her lithe body barely making a dent in the mattress, and crosses her arms. "Listen, I promised your mom I'd get you to eat today so don't make me look bad, okay?" When I say nothing, keeping my eyes on the ceiling, she bends toward me and kisses me on the cheek. "Besides, Gabe would be pissed if I let you stay in bed all day. Best-friend duties and all that."

"Well, it doesn't really matter what Gabe wants, does it?" My voice is sharp, but frustratingly weak. Anna sighs, looking ready to argue some more, but then waves her hands about like she's trying to shoo a fly away.

"Scootch over then," she says. I don't move. "Come on, Teg. Scootch."

I shift my body over the foot or so she needs to lay her petite frame beside me. It forces me onto Gabe's side of the bed, which is cold. Anna's thick, silky black hair tickles the side of my face, but I don't move away. Head to head, her feet only reach the middle of my calves.

"Look," she begins, "I know the last thing you want to do is go out there. To see people all happy and shit. I get it. And I'd be exactly the same way." She rolls toward me, but not without difficulty. I've spent so much time on this mattress, wishing I'd disappear if I lay still enough, that I've left a hollow the length and shape of my body. A depression to match my depression.

She sinks her elbow into the mattress's pillow top, above the hollow, and rests her head in her palm. "But it's been three months, Teg. You've not even left the apartment. You've lost so much weight you look like a freakin' supermodel, and, no, that is not a compliment. There's a hole in this mattress so big we'll have to call the firemen to rescue you…by the way, let me make that call if we have to, okay?" Anna winks and I smile despite myself. "As your best friend, it's my job to make you do the things you don't want to do because they're good for you. I would expect nothing less from you."

It's essentially the same speech she's been giving me for the past month. She's made it her mission to get me out of my apartment for something other than a doctor's appointment—because no one else has been able to, including Gabe, my brothers or our parents—and I have a feeling she isn't going to relent anytime soon. I stare up at the ceiling again, at the small crack running from the light fixture over our bed to the corner where a cobweb dangles, swaying in the current of warm, forced air coming from the vent. If I could only shrink and suspend myself from that cobweb, out of sight…

"And as my *zu mu* always says, talk does not cook rice. So please, get out of this freaking bed, okay?" Anna is endlessly quoting her Chinese grandmother, who seems to have a proverb for any situation one could think up.

"Tegan, I love you."

"I know."

"Then let me help you. Please."

I sit up, without looking her way. "Fine."

A second later Anna and her tackle-hug slam me back into the mattress. For such a small person she really knows how to throw her size around.

There's nothing like strolling down Michigan Avenue on a sunny day. Even if it's cold enough to freeze nose hairs within seconds. People hold tight to bursting shopping bags full of treasures sure to at least temporarily make their lives better. They laugh often, debating over whether to go into another shop or stop for lunch. Their lives are full of small problems.

I used to love people watching on the Miracle Mile, but now all I want to do is escape. It's too vibrant. Damn Anna and her fucking best-friend speech. I long for the dullness of my pewter-colored apartment walls. For Gabe and my mom's acceptance—however hard-fought—that I'll leave the bed when I'm good and ready.

"Anna…" I stop in the middle of the sidewalk, like a tourist with no appreciation for the flow of foot traffic all around. "I need to go home." This must be how agoraphobics feel. The open spaces around me seem dangerous, unpredictable, and I have the sudden urge to lie down and let the gently falling snow cover me until no one can see me anymore.

Anna tries to escape the chill by snuggling farther down

into her chunky mauve wool scarf. She shivers a little then turns her attention back my way, giving me a critical look. Like she's trying to sort out how to react to what I've said. We've been friends forever. Well, for three years actually, but Anna has a way of making you feel like she's known you since the first moment you can remember.

She takes the few steps back to where I am and tugs me gently out of the way of the shoppers, who barely break stride. "Screw lunch. Food is overrated anyway," she says with a most unladylike snort—a classic Anna-ism, which helps to remind me that at least some things don't change. "Let's just get a coffee, okay?" I allow her to pull me into the Starbucks in front of us.

It's warm inside, and familiar. Both things that make me feel instantly better.

While Anna orders us coffee I grab a table near the back. I take off my gloves and lay my snow-damp wool hat on the chair across from me, knowing Anna will take the seat beside me. She has this thing about sitting side by side. She thinks it's easier to talk naturally if you aren't forced to stare into each other's eyes. She says it's a Chinese thing, even though she was born and raised in Chicago.

"Here," she says, pushing a venti cup across the table and into my idle hands. Without thought, my fingers close around the cardboard sleeve, the heat coming through just enough to make me never want to let go. "I got you a vanilla latte...with whole milk and whip on top." My regular order is a skinny vanilla latte, hold the whip. "If I can't get you to eat the least I can do is make your coffee more caloric."

She sits beside me and takes a sip from her own venti cup, which I know holds a soy chai tea latte, extra whip, then rests her other hand on my thigh. I jump from her touch, and she rubs my thigh harder. "Talk to me, Tegan." I'm grateful she can't see my eyes. "How can I help?"

"Tell me something funny."

"Funny...okay. Hmm." Anna sips at her coffee again. I wait. "Did I tell you about Caroline?" I shake my head. "No? Holy crap. You're going to die..." Anna's voice trails and she whispers, "Sorry." Sometimes I think I'll put together a spreadsheet of words people should avoid when in conversation with me. Words like *death*. And *baby*. Perhaps that's how to prevent these uncomfortable, cringe-worthy moments. But it wouldn't be for my benefit, because the truth is no words can make this worse—or better, for that matter. I put my hand on Anna's, still on my thigh, and give it a squeeze to let her know it's okay. She smiles, and I'm glad one of us feels relieved.

"Okay, so last week we had the fun fair, remember the one Principal Clayton planned for Valentine's Day? So one of the stations was face painting, like always, but this year the kids got to paint the teachers' faces." Anna, like me, is a teacher—grade four. She says kids under the age of nine give her migraines. "Anyway, they did a great job but that's not the part I think you're going to like," she says, her voice dropping for effect. "I'd gone to the little girl's room and Caroline was leaving the staff room as I was coming back in...and, well, I let her walk out without taking her face paint off! I looked right at her and smiled without saying a word!" Anna laughs, snorting deeply again. "She went on the 'L' with cat whiskers...ears—" Anna laughs so hard she's losing her breath "—and...and a bright pink nose!" The energy from her laughter is contagious, and I can't help the small chuckle that escapes me. Caroline DuPont was one of the other kindergarten teachers, and always trying to show me up with her Martha Stewart–perfect craft ideas for her class. The thought of her sitting on the train in full costume makeup applied by a clumsy five-year-old's hand did bring some light to my soul. For a moment.

Anna laughs again and I want to join her, but it's just too much work. She realizes she's laughing alone and stops. We drink our coffees in silence, and then I blurt out, "I think something's wrong with me. Really wrong."

She looks at me, surprise muddling her pretty features. "Why do you think that?" To her credit, she keeps her tone light. Perhaps trying not to alarm me. Or maybe, herself. "What do you mean?"

My voice is softer now. "I talk to him." Barely a whisper. "Sometimes it feels like he's still with me…right here…" I gulp back a sob and clutch my stomach, the pain that can no longer be blamed on physical wounds starting up again. "Like nothing happened."

"Oh, Teg." Anna clutches my arm. I see something flash across her face. Relief? "That's okay. There's nothing wrong with you. I promise."

I can see she believes it, and I'm grateful for her certainty. Even though I don't share it.

"It will get better, sweetie," Anna soothes. "But not today. Or tomorrow, or probably even months from now. But I promise you, you won't feel like this forever."

Something inside me snaps. My chair scrapes the hardwood floor noisily and Anna jolts back, the sudden movement surprising her.

"You promise me?" My voice is loud and unrecognizable to my own ears. It's filled with misplaced, toxic anger, which unfortunately for Anna, needs to be released right now. It's bubbling up in me like boiling water inside a tightly lidded pot. Straining to break the seal. I start to laugh, but without joy. "I suggest not promising me anything."

"Tegan, please sit down," Anna says, pulling on my coat's

arm with some urgency. People look our way, anticipating something more interesting than whatever is on their laptop screens or on the lips of their coffee dates. Their curiosity sickens me. Although admittedly, only months ago I would have been doing exactly the same thing.

"This will never get better. Never." I bite my lip, not to hold back my words but to feel physical pain. I learned while recovering from my surgery just how valuable physical hurt is in keeping emotional anguish at bay. But it would have to be extreme to counter what I'm feeling, because most days it feels like my insides are covered in a million paper cuts, and I've just swallowed a bottle of lemon juice.

I taste blood, and feel the rough edge of my lip where I've gone through the skin. "I lost… I lost my—" My voice cracks, and I can't make the word pass my lips. "I lost everything. I am without a future now. At twenty-six. Do you know how that feels? No, you don't. Because you still have the chance for all that."

I suppose I do, too, although not in any way that makes sense to me now. I keep going, despite the stares of the coffee-shop patrons, despite the tears that stream down Anna's cheeks, ruining her mascara.

"So, please. Please don't promise me anything, Anna. Especially something you can't control." *You see now?* I want to add. *No one can help me.*

"I'm sorry," Anna says, eyes downcast. Her voice is thick with emotion. For a second I feel guilty for making her cry. "I really thought…maybe if you could… You said you weren't ready. I'm sorry."

"What the hell are you sorry about?" I'm giggling uncontrollably even though I know it isn't the right reaction. I should be crying. Wailing. But for some strange reason I giggle, like a carefree schoolgirl.

I'm barely hanging on.

"You weren't driving the car. You always drive the fucking speed limit anyway. I wish you had been driving instead of Gabe. Maybe then... Maybe..." The giggles shift to a full-body sob, but I can't stop the words spilling from my tear-damp lips. "I hear it all the time. The crash. Have I told you that, what it sounded like? Did you know metal screams when it's being ripped apart? Like, it actually screams." Anna stands quickly, grabbing her stuff and then my arm as I sob around my words.

"Come on." Anna ushers me through the now crowded tables. There are murmurs, chairs pulling in to accommodate our quick departure. She leads me outside, into the cold air. I concentrate on breathing. In and out. In and out.

But I can't catch my breath, my lungs rejecting the air. My vision narrows to a long, dark tunnel, and I drop to the sidewalk.

# 6

I wake up in the emergency room, a bright light piercing my vision.

"Ms. Lawson? That's it, Tegan, open your eyes," an unfamiliar voice says.

"Thank God." Anna sounds like she has a terrible cold, her nose too stuffy to breathe through. Her face hovers over mine and I blink a few times. She's quite blotchy, her eyes red and swollen from crying.

"How are you feeling?" The voice belongs to a middle-aged man in muted green scrubs. He has on glasses that make him look quite Clark Kent–like. Cute and nerdy. His hands hold either side of the stethoscope hanging around his neck and he's watching me closely. I wonder if Anna notices how handsome he is. He's exactly her type—a decade older and brainy enough to have made it through medical school.

"Better, I guess," I say, my throat dry. I clear it a few times. "What happened?"

"You just dropped!" Anna says, seeming quite frazzled. Her obvious panic adds volume to her words. "Like one second you were standing in front of me, and the next you were on the sidewalk."

"Sorry. I'm okay, I promise." I hold the hand she puts on

my shoulder, and watch her fiddle with the cell phone in her other hand. "You didn't call anyone, did you?" She shakes her head, but she's a terrible liar.

"Anna?"

"It went to voice mail. Twice." I glare at her, hoping Gabe's with a client and hasn't picked up his voice mail yet. I don't need anyone else looking at me the way Anna is at the moment. "Sorry, Teg, but you scared the crap out of me."

"Has this ever happened to you before?" The doctor asks. Now I see his name, embroidered over his scrub shirt pocket. Dr. Wallace.

"No," I say, shaking my head, which feels leaden. I'm glad I'm lying down. "But I haven't been, um, sleeping well." I swallow hard. In an instant everything lands back on me, like a boulder falling directly onto my chest. I try to breathe around the heaviness. "I was in a car accident a few months ago."

"Were you injured?"

"Yes," I say without elaboration. He waits, but I don't add anything more.

"It was quite serious," Anna interjects. "She had to have surgery and was in the hospital for almost three weeks."

"What kind of surgery?" handsome Dr. Wallace asks, casually, like he's asking how I take my coffee. He looks up from the chart and waits again for a response.

It's as if someone has sewn my lips together. I can't get the words out.

Anna looks at me, waiting, too, then at the doctor. "She, uh…" Anna glances my way again and I try to tell her it's okay, she can tell him. The message must have come across despite my lack of voice, because she keeps going without taking her eyes off me. "She had a hysterectomy," Anna says, adding more quietly, "and she was just over six months pregnant at the time."

Dr. Wallace stops writing and gives me the most excellent sympathetic look. One I've seen before. From my surgeon, who cut out my uterus right after the accident, along with any chance I had of becoming a mother.

"I'm very sorry for your loss," Dr. Wallace says, and I can tell he means it. His voice is smooth, confident, yet it carries an appropriate amount of compassion. They must practice that, doctors—how to convince a complete stranger you really care in one minute or less. "You mentioned you haven't been sleeping. Any other changes to your health?"

"She's not been eating much, either," Anna offers, before I can answer "No, nothing," like I'd planned to.

"Well, that could explain why you fainted," he says. He licks his finger, which I find odd for an emergency room doctor to do, and flips over a page on the chart. I think about all the germs his hands must come in contact with during a single shift. I'd be wearing gloves, or carrying a bottle of hand sanitizer in my back pocket, but I guess he's not all that concerned about getting sick. "Also, that patch on your upper arm? Nicotine patch?"

I shake my head. "It's an estrogen patch. They also removed my ovaries when I had the hysterectomy." I say it as matter-of-factly as I can, but we all know what it means. I will never have a child. And every week, when I take off the old patch and put on a fresh one, the reminder of that makes me want to throw something, or punch someone, or collapse into a heap on my bathroom floor and never get up.

The good doctor nods, and gives me another sympathetic smile. "I'm going to do a few more tests, just to be sure there isn't something else going on, okay?"

"Thank you," Anna, my spokeswoman, says.

"You bet...sorry, I missed your name. Miss?" he asks, his smile for Anna this time.

"Anna," she says, extending her hand. "Anna Cheng."

"Okay, so if everything checks out we'll have you out of here soon. Sound good, Tegan?" I nod, and he pats my shoulder. "Just try and relax."

Three hours later Anna pushes me out of the hospital in a wheelchair—hospital policy, apparently—with a good handful of sleeping pills to get me through the next few nights until I can see my family doctor. A short cab ride later, I'm home and manage a pitiful thank-you when Anna strips me of my clothes and tucks me back into bed in new pajamas. The hollow welcomes me back like an old lover, and I settle in as Anna heads to the kitchen to make me soup and toast. A few minutes later I hear the front door open and close, and I brace myself for company, presuming Anna made that call after all.

I roll over, settling deeper in the mattress, and feel the cool comfort of the pendant as the weight of my body presses it into my skin. For a moment, I indulge my grief-weary brain a reprieve and imagine what life would have looked like if the car had spun out thirty seconds later, after the row of steel lampposts.

*If only Gabe kept both his hands on the wheel.*

*If only I stopped him from what he was doing under my skirt.*

*If only the de-icing trucks had already been out.*

I close my eyes, only then remembering I left my hat and gloves at Starbucks.

"Tegan." Gabe's voice startles me. Guess he got the voice mails.

"Are you okay? What the hell happened?"

He lies down beside me, barely disturbing the covers, but doesn't touch me. He knows me so well.

I keep my eyes tightly closed. "Let's just say I may not be welcome back at the Starbucks at Michigan and Lake."

Gabe sighs. "But you're okay. Right?"

I nod against the pillow. His voice softens. "What happened?"

"I had a fucking meltdown, Gabe. An embarrassing, who-let-the-crazy-lady-out kinda meltdown. Then I passed out on the sidewalk and ended up in the ER."

"I'm sorry I wasn't there with you. I was with a client." Gabe shifts closer to me. "I should have been there."

"You can't be here every second of every day," I say. "Anna took care of me."

"I know. I'm glad she was there," he says. His hand caresses my cheek; his fingers brush the hair back from my face. Still, I keep my eyes shut. "You need to eat something."

"I'm sure Anna will force-feed me the soup she's making. Or my mom will when she gets here in, oh, twenty minutes," I say, finally looking over at him. He's wearing my favorite suit—gray herringbone, cut perfectly for his lean, muscular body—with a white shirt and mint-green tie. "I assume she called my parents?"

Gabe shrugs and smiles. "You know Anna, she's not known for her secret-keeping abilities."

I sigh. Gabe and I often joked that the best time to share something with Anna was immediately after telling everyone else.

"I completely freaked her out," I say. "She didn't even comment on how cute the doctor was."

"Man, that is serious," Gabe says, his tone light. I smile. But a moment later, the smile drops from my face and Gabe's laughter fades.

"It's okay, Tegan. You're just not ready yet," Gabe finally says, when the silence becomes uncomfortable. "You need more time."

"That's what I told Anna." I'm weary now. I really want

to be alone. "I wish you could explain it to her. I think you could make her understand."

"She's doing exactly what you would do for her, Tegan."

I nod, rolling onto my side. I can hear Anna in the kitchen, as drawers open and close, and the microwave timer beeps. A salty, fragrant smell hits my nose and I know the boxed chicken noodle soup—the extent of Anna's cooking repertoire—is bubbling away on the stove. I hope I can get some of it down, if for no other reason than to appease everyone.

"I want to talk to you about that night," Gabe says, pulling me back from thoughts of my churning stomach. "We need to talk about it."

"No, we don't," I reply.

"It's okay to be angry with me," Gabe says. "You can't possibly hate me as much as I…hate myself." My strong husband, as broken as I am.

"I don't hate you, Gabe."

*Oh, but I'm lying to you, my love. I do hate you. You ruined everything.*

"Well, you should."

I say nothing.

"I have an idea," he says at last. "And I don't think you're going to like it, but I need you to trust me. Do you trust me, Teg?"

This is an interesting question. Six months ago I wouldn't have hesitated.

"We need the jar of spontaneity." His voice has regained its familiar positivity.

"I don't know where it is, Gabe," I say, although that's not at all true. It's on the top shelf of our closet, tucked out of sight behind stacks of unread magazines I'll never get to. "I think Mom may have tossed it when she was cleaning up last week."

"It's in the closet behind your magazines," he says.

"Okay, I'll get it later."

"I think you should get it now."

With an angry sigh, I throw back the covers and step onto the plastic footstool in our closet. The jar can't help. The jar is the last thing I need. But I grab the stack of magazines and drop them to the floor, the sound of their weight hitting the hardwood echoing harshly inside our small bedroom.

"You okay in there?" Anna calls out from the kitchen.

"Fine," I say as loudly and confidently as I can, hoping she doesn't come in to check on us. "Just dropped some magazines."

"Okay. Soup is almost ready," she says.

"Thanks. I'll be out in a minute," I call back. Then, stretching my arms, I reach for the jar, a large glass vase, really, and tuck it into the crook of my arm.

I let the vase drop onto the duvet and some of its contents spill out. "Here's the fucking jar, Gabe. What would you like me to do with it?"

"Now," he says, pausing for a moment. "Now we choose."

# 7

*Six months before the accident*

“I like it,” Gabe said, his fingers caressing my ear with a gentle grace that belied their size. Self-consciously I touched where his fingers had just been, trying to tame a stray piece of bang. “It’s different, but it suits you.”

“I’m not sure what happened,” I said. “I asked for a trim but then I thought about all the blow-drying and told her to just chop it off.” My hair, best described as the color of mud except for when the summer’s sun added golden touches, had been just below shoulder length since high school. It was my safe length—long enough to feel feminine, but not so long I couldn’t quickly blow-dry it if whatever I was doing called for more than a finger-swept ponytail. I ran a hand through it again, still surprised at how quickly my fingers moved through the now short strands.

“Actually, it’s really hot,” Gabe murmured, his hand sliding down my bare neck, to my shoulder, to my breast, where it lingered. “I bet it looks even better when you’re naked.” I laughed until his lips met mine, warm, full and soft. I sighed and pressed closer to him, letting my sundress drop to our bedroom floor after he swiftly untied the neck strap.

"Just like I thought." Gabe's eyes trailed down my body, then back to my face. "It really suits you."

Afterward we lay tangled in our sheets, and I rested my head against his chest. His heart thumped furiously.

"I have an idea," he said, his fingers tickling up and down my spine. I shivered and snuggled in closer.

"Oh, yeah?" I tilted my head back to look at him. He kissed the tip of my nose and I breathed in his scent. Sweat mixed with the woodsy smell of his deodorant. "You really do like this haircut, don't you?"

"That's not it," he said, smiling. "Although I would like you to hold that thought."

"Tell me." I settled back against his chest and closed my eyes. Contented. Happy.

"Well, seeing as we're getting married in a few months, I thought we should think about what we want that to look like."

"What do you mean? Everything's already planned."

He shook his head. "I don't mean the wedding. I'm talking about life after that."

"I already picture that all the time." I smiled. I couldn't wait for that wedding band to slide over my knuckle.

"I know we won't be able to do this right away, with work and everything, but I had this idea to create a list of all the things we want to do, the places we want to travel to," he said. "A list of experiences we can share."

"So, sort of like a bucket list?"

"Yeah, sort of," he said. "But that's kind of grim, right? More like a wish list, you know?"

I kissed him hard on the lips. Again and again, my lips meeting his teeth as he laughed. "Tegan and Gabe's wish list. I love it. Let's do it," I finally said.

"Now here's the thing." He jumped out of bed and grabbed

a pad of paper and pen from his briefcase. "We're going to write out each thing on a piece of paper, fold it up and stick it in a jar or something." I nodded, grinning. "Then when we have vacation time or feel like life is dragging us down, we'll pick something out and do that."

I laughed. Gabe was going to have his work cut out for him; I wasn't exactly spontaneous. He was the adventure-seeker, which was one reason why we balanced each other so beautifully. He pushed when I pulled.

"Okay," I said, tousling his dark brown hair, which was curling from sweat.

Gabe smiled. "You go first."

Over the next half hour we created a list of ten things, then folded the papers and put them in a giant crystal vase one of Gabe's parents' friends had sent as an engagement gift.

"So when do we get to pull our first one?" I asked, shaking the vase with some difficulty due to its weight, the little packets of paper dancing inside.

"Why not right now? Whatever it is, we'll do it after the wedding, okay? Wish number one can be our honeymoon."

"Deal!" I tilted the vase slightly so I could reach into its depths, then stuck my arm in up to my elbow and stirred the papers around.

"You pick." I took out my arm and extended the vase toward Gabe.

"Ladies first," he said, taking the vase from my hands. I closed my eyes and reached in, feeling the sharp edges of the folded paper scratch against my skin. I dug down to the bottom. I kissed the paper before opening it up.

Gabe's eyes, blue like a midwinter sky, were wide and his smile generous. I felt bubbly inside, like I'd had a glass of champagne. "What does it say?" he asked. "What are we doing?"

I cleared my throat, pausing purposefully. Gabe bounced the mattress impatiently, which made me laugh. "Come on!" he said. "Tell me."

I read it out loud, and Gabe cheered like we'd won the lottery. Then he pushed me back against the mattress. I laughed again as he kissed me all over.

"I love you more than life itself," I said.

"Ditto," he said. "You are my forever."

We cast the vase aside and tangled our bedsheets again. Then Gabe grabbed a permanent black marker and wrote *Tegan & Gabe's Jar of Spontaneity* on the vase's crystal-clear surface.

# 8

Holding the vase now, I don't feel giddy or joyful. I feel heavy, sluggish with misery.

"Pick something out," Gabe says softly. "Actually, pick three things, okay?"

"Why?" I ask, my bitterness seeping out. "What's the point, Gabe?"

"The point is life, Tegan. It's going to carry on, whether you want it to or not. And eventually you need to join back in."

"No one understands." I'm crying now. "Trust me, if there were some kind of switch I could flick I would. In a second. I want my life back, too."

"I know you do, love. I know." Gabe's voice lulls me, the gentleness of his tone washing over me.

"But even if I hop a plane somewhere far from here, I can't get away from it," I say. "I can't run away from my broken heart, Gabe. Or my broken body."

"You're right. So don't think about it as running away from something. More running toward something," he suggests. The look on my face says it all. "I know, I know. Hear me out, okay?" I shrug, keeping my eyes on the jar.

"Nothing can change..." His voice cracks and I imagine his Adam's apple bobbing repeatedly, the way it does when he tries to swallow his emotions. “Nothing can change what happened. And staying here, reliving it every moment of every day, is breaking you, Tegan. You’re disappearing on us, and I’m afraid soon there won’t be any of you left.”

I don’t say it out loud, but that’s exactly what I’m hoping for. One day I’ll simply cease to exist, like a puff of smoke. There one moment, gone the next.

“But pulling something out of that vase? It’s going to force you to live. To create a new memory. And I feel like if you can do that, just make one new memory that isn’t sad, it will be easier to make another one. Then another one. And soon you’ll have a stack of happy memories to help balance the sad ones.”

As much as I’ve committed to my disappearing act, Gabe’s words spark in me the tiniest flicker of something. I’m not sure, but it feels different. Fresh, like a clean, fluffy towel, or biting into a tomato straight off the vine.

“And there’s all that money from my parents from the wedding, just sitting in our bank account. Doing nothing but gathering a pathetic amount of interest,” he says.

“I think your parents expected us to do something a little more grown-up with that money,” I reply. Gabe’s parents wrote us a check for $200,000 as a wedding gift, surely intending it to go into a house in the suburbs. A proper place to raise their grandson.

“Who cares what they want us to do with it? I can’t think of a more perfect way to spend some of it.”

I give a small smile and run my fingers gently over the black lettering on the vase, taking care not to rub it off.

“You need a change of scenery, Teg,” Gabe says. “You’re going to lose yourself if you stay here. And I can’t let that happen.” He sighs heavily. “Besides, school’s out in a few months and then you have the summer off.” Not that I’m going back to work anytime soon. Medical leave has turned into stress leave, buying me at least the rest of the school year. "The timing couldn't be better."

"I don't know," I say. "The thought of leaving this apartment exhausts me. Getting on a plane?" I shake my head.

"We can do this," he says. "I'll be with you the whole time. And I promise not to let you snore or drool if you fall asleep on the plane." He laughs, and I feel the familiar pull of love, despite everything. "You need this, Teg. We need this."

I look at him, then take a deep breath as I dig into the vase, stirring the papers. "Three things?"

Gabe nods.

I pull out the first one and set it down on the duvet, hands shaking. It's the one we agreed on for our honeymoon. The trip we put off when we found out I was pregnant.

"Well, that's interesting," Gabe says, surprise in his voice. "Think it's a sign?"

I shrug. Maybe. Though I don't believe in that much anymore.

Reaching back in the vase, I pull out another one, and then one more. I carefully unfold the last two papers and smooth out the folds, taking my time lining up the small squares side by side.

Gabe starts humming a tune I recognize, breaking into song for the chorus. "We're leaving…on a jet plane…"

There's so much optimism in his voice, and I can't stomach it.

I put my head in my hands and sob.

# 9

*Three weeks before the accident*

I stared at the gift and chewed my lip distractedly as I tried to sort out how to wrap it. It was Gabe's twenty-seventh birthday, and I'd gone way over our agreed-upon budget for presents. We had two rules about birthday gifts: they had to be sentimental in some way, and they couldn't cost more than a hundred dollars. We started the rules way back when we were broke, just out of school and looking for jobs. At the time, even a hundred had seemed extravagant. But now that we were properly husband and wife, with a bank account a lot more flush thanks to Gabe's parents, I felt justified breaking the rule.

The guitar was a limited edition—a flame-red Gibson Les Paul. I couldn't wait for him to open it. I knew once he saw it he wouldn't care how much it cost—which, for the record, was way over the hundred-dollar limit. If only I could figure out how to wrap a guitar—and an amp—with the one roll of paper I had on hand.

Gabe would likely say he wasn't good enough yet to deserve such a guitar, but he'd been taking lessons every week with the beat-up, secondhand acoustic guitar my brother Jason had given him.

I unrolled the jumbo-sized roll of wrapping paper and laid it out on our bedroom floor. Gabe would be home soon from work, and I wanted to have everything ready. The beef bourguignon simmered on the stove, its rich, heady aroma filling the apartment, and the garlic-and-blue-cheese mashed potatoes were ready to go. I'd picked up Gabe's favorite dessert from a little bakery down the street—a meringue pavlova, piled high with clouds of whipped cream and strawberries, which looked amazingly fresh and succulent despite the winter season.

A few minutes and a lot of tape later I'd managed to wrap the awkwardly shaped present, adding a silver bow on top. There was no way Gabe wouldn't know exactly what it was when he saw it, which made me think I should have saved the paper—and my knees, from kneeling on the hardwood floor—and just gone with the bow. I grabbed another bow from the package, a red one, and stuck it to the amp, which by this point I'd wisely decided against wrapping.

The front door's lock clicked open and Gabe's voice echoed down the hall. "Teg? I'm home, babe."

I leaned the wrapped guitar beside the amp and went to greet him, shutting the bedroom door behind me.

"Hey there, birthday boy," I said, letting him gather me in his arms. His face was cold from the winter's wind, and I put my hands to his cheeks to warm them. We kissed deeply and I tightened my grip, feeling the fullness of my stomach press into him. "How was your day?"

"Just fine," he said, kissing me again. Then he bent down and kissed my belly a few times before giving it a little rub. I ran my hands through his thick, dark hair, feeling the swell of love inside me while he layered me and my protruding stomach with a few more kisses.

"It smells amazing in here," he said, finally standing. "Let me guess, beef bourguignon?" He crossed his fingers, a hopeful look on his face.

I laughed. "Yes, it's beef bourguignon. With those blue-cheese mashed potatoes you love and a special surprise for dessert."

"Sounds so good. I'm starving." He loosened his tie, his eyes carrying a playful look I recognized. "Just wondering, though. Think everything will hold for say, fifteen minutes?" He unbuttoned his shirt and pants, and was undressed before I could answer.

I looked him up and down, appreciating his well-toned body and the beautiful olive skin he'd inherited from his Italian mother. I never tired of Gabe. "Of course," I murmured, lifting my arms so he could pull my red-and-black striped jersey dress over my head. "Take all the time you need."

He swept me up in his arms and I burst out laughing, protesting I was far too heavy for such a move.

"You are perfect," he said, laying me gently on the couch. "Here...let me show you what I mean."

Sixteen minutes later we sat down to eat his birthday dinner, both of us flush-faced and relaxed. And still naked.

"This is delicious," Gabe said, his mouth full of the stewed, wine-laden beef and mashed potatoes. "You've outdone yourself."

"Hold that thought." I pushed my chair back and headed down the hall. "Now close your eyes," I shouted from inside our bedroom. "Are they closed?"

"Yup!"

I carefully held the pathetically wrapped guitar with both hands and made my way back to the kitchen. "Shit!" I said, when my fingers ripped the paper a little.

"You okay?" Gabe asked, keeping his eyes closed.

"Fine. Although I definitely should not go into gift wrapping as a career." He laughed. "Okay, now open!"

I stood naked in front of him, one hand on my hip and the other holding the neck of the guitar. "Happy birthday!"

"Holy shit!" Gabe pushed his chair back so quickly it toppled over. He didn't even bother to pick it up, but instead walked over to where I stood.

"I know," I said, teasingly. "I'm irresistible."

"I'm pretty much living out a fantasy here." Gabe's eyes were wide. He looked like a little boy who'd just discovered the toy he wanted most in the world was under the Christmas tree with his name on it. "Seriously."

I handed him the present, and let him kiss my neck, then my lips. "Happy birthday, Gabe," I said softly. "Go on, open it."

He didn't need any more encouragement. He ripped the wrapping paper off in one pull and whistled deeply. "Tegan, what the hell have you done?" He looked at me in awe for a brief moment, then back at the guitar. "It's a fucking Les Paul." He ran his hands over the guitar's edges, gently, like he had over my curves earlier.

"I know," I said, shrugging. "I decided that hundred-dollar rule was stupid."

"I can see that." His eyes were still on the guitar. Then he looked up at me. "But this is like, way, way over the budget. So you know what that means, right?"

"What?"

"It's open season on presents now," he said, winking. "I hope you can handle it."

I laughed. "Take it easy, tough guy."

He grabbed me with his free hand and pulled me into him. "This is the best gift ever," he said. "Thank you, Teg. I love it."

"You're welcome." I tilted my head up so his lips could meet mine. "You deserve it."

"Well, I don't know about that, but what do you think about seeing what this thing can do?"

"Let's do it," I said. "Do you want to get dressed first?"

"Hell, no! I've always wanted to play a Les Paul in the nude."

"The other thing you'll need is in the bedroom. It's unwrapped. I gave up." I allowed him to pull me over to the couch before he ran to our room to grab the amp.

I shivered, the heat of our lovemaking and the excitement of the present now fading. I grabbed a blanket from the arm of the couch and tucked it around me while Gabe plugged the guitar into the amp.

"Okay, hot stuff," I said. "Show me whatcha got."

He wiggled his eyebrows up and down a few times, then pursed his lips in what he surely thought was a sexy rock star face, and slammed his hand down against the strings. The room filled with an ear-splitting whine that sort of resembled music, and Gabe laughed when I put my hands to my ears. He reached over and fiddled with the amp, then moved his fingers more deftly over the strings, this time producing a sound that would certainly be called a tune.

As he awkwardly played his way through a classic rock song I recognized but couldn't name—I was the worst with remembering song titles—stopping every few notes to make a correction, I took a mental snapshot of the moment. Things were perfect. We were beyond happy, and not just because we were newlyweds. We'd been together long enough to know how we felt about one another had little to do with the shiny white-gold bands on our left ring fingers. We had good jobs, healthy families that loved us, great friends, an apartment that was on the small side, sure, but stuffed full of memories. And soon, we'd have a baby. A son.

Watching Gabe play his birthday guitar, in the nude nonetheless, I wanted nothing more than to stop time. To press the pause button and live in this moment indefinitely. Perhaps I knew deep down what was coming. Or maybe it's simply that the moment you realize just how perfect everything feels is the moment it's all about to change. In the blink of an eye, as they say.

I started to cry. Gabe, still focused on the chords, was oblivious. Until he looked up, a huge smile on his face that wilted the moment he saw the tears.

"What's up? What's wrong?" he asked, hand poised with a guitar pick over the strings. The last note reverberated through the living room. When I didn't answer right away, he lifted the strap from around his neck and put the guitar down on the ottoman. He kneeled in front of me.

"Tegan, talk to me," he said, worry creeping into his voice. "What's the matter?" Of course his concern only made me cry harder. I tried to stop, but couldn't.

"Shh, shh," he said, sitting beside me to rub my back. "Babe, talk to me. You're freaking me out."

"Sorry," I blubbered. "I'm just so...so happy."

He stopped rubbing, his hand resting in the hollow between my shoulder blades. "Huh," he said, wrapping an arm around my naked shoulders that now trembled, like the rest of me, with the release of emotion. "This is sort of a funny way to show it, don't you think?" I laughed, and then hiccupped through my tears. "I thought maybe it was my guitar playing."

"Nope," I said, wiping the tears best I could with my hands. "It wasn't great, but definitely not tear-worthy."

"Good to know," he said. "Maybe I still have a future as a rock star?"

"I wouldn't go that far," I teased, blowing my nose with the tissue I grabbed from the side table.

"So now you're crying with happiness?" Gabe shifted to the

edge of the cushion so he could turn and look at me. "This should be a long few months." He eyed my belly and raised an eyebrow.

"I know, it's so stupid," I said. "But I just had this moment where everything felt so perfect and I didn't want it to ever end."

"Well, I have good news and bad news for you. What do you want first?"

"Good news, always."

"Okay, the good news is we are going to have plenty of moments like this one. And I guarantee you I'll play you naked guitar songs even when we're old and wrinkled." I scrunched up my nose. "Oh, you just wait," he added. "This body is going to age well."

"Lucky me," I said. "So what's the bad news?"

"You'll have to put up with my terrible guitar playing for a long time yet. Don't they say you need to put in ten thousand hours to get good at something?"

"Something like that. Which reminds me, I just thought of something you can get me for Christmas."

"What?"

"Earplugs."

Gabe gave a "Ha-ha, you're funny," and then gently pushed me back against the couch cushions. His hands roamed my body, pulling the blanket off me as they traveled across my skin. My belly was noticeable now and my breasts were fuller than they'd ever been.

Pregnancy suited me, which surprised me. Before, I would have described myself as semi-body-confident, meaning I would wear a bikini to the beach but I'd spend a lot of time worrying about the padding in my bikini top and the small spare tire I carried around my narrow hips. Now I felt beautiful in my roundness, with the softness of my body. Especially when Gabe looked at me in that way. Like a goddess, about to be worshipped.

"I'd like to collect part two of my birthday present, please." Gabe carefully held his body over mine, and I shifted to the side so he could lie beside me.

"Part two?" I asked, my hand tickling over his hip bone, reaching lower...

Gabe groaned and closed his eyes. "This is the best birthday ever."

# 10

Today I have one thing to do. One task; I promised Gabe before he left for work. To call the travel agent and book flights. I told myself "first thing" in the morning, but it's almost noon and I'm still in bed.

It's amazing how one-dimensional my grief is. I am only capable of feeling numb. Even the pain, which used to be so sharp, has gone dull.

Mom's set to arrive in about an hour for her daily visit, which means fresh sheets and towels, and because it's Monday, a restocked refrigerator. She's turned Sundays into cooking marathons—as much for her freezer as ours, she claims, though I know how much she hates to cook. I'm subsisting mostly on Ritz crackers and peanut butter, but am appreciative of her effort, even if I barely touch the shepherd's pie, chicken à la king or barbecue chili—Gabe's favorite—she regularly brings over.

Anna will stop by not long after Mom, once school's out, to bring me a coffee and some gossip from work. Gabe usually leaves us alone for these visits, knowing if I'm going to confide in anyone, it will be Anna. And the phone will ring a lot. My in-laws, checking in; Dad, wondering if anything in the apartment needs fixing. He lives for a leaky tap or squeaking door these days, because those are things he can do something about, even though Gabe is pretty good with his hands, and we have a landlord who deals with such things.

I prop myself up in bed, at least considering getting up. My phone is right beside me, on my nightstand, so it's not like I have much of an excuse.

It was another crappy night of sleep. I'm sure my family and friends think all I do is sleep, which is fair enough based on how many hours of each day I spend in bed. But I'm asleep very little of that time—the nightmares make sure of it. And when I'm not lucky enough to be unconscious and dreamless, I usually lie in the dark, crying softly so Gabe doesn't hear me, and wonder what I did to deserve such suffering.

I long for small problems, like not having the money to take a five-star vacation, or not getting two seats together at a sold-out movie, or waking up with a giant pimple on my nose the day of staff photos.

Reaching for my phone, determined to complete one thing today, I jerk my hand back when it rings. A normal person would just answer it, but I'm far from normal these days. It rings five times and then goes to voice mail. I recognize the number—Rosa, Gabe's mom. I decide to listen to the message because if I don't respond there will be another call soon.

"Tegan, *amore*, I wanted to… I saw the calendar this morning." Rosa sounds strange. Like her words are strangling her. "This was supposed to be the happiest day for all of us…a blessing…" Her voice trails, and for a moment I wonder if she's hung up. "I'll try you later tonight, okay? *Ti penso, bella.*"

I frown, tapping the phone's calendar icon. What's the date? It pops up right away, big and bold across my screen. *March 27th.* I stare at it, and for a moment nothing happens, even though I now know exactly why Rosa called.

Then I stand so quickly I'm light-headed, and my phone

drops softly to the carpet under my feet. A moan escapes me, and I claw for things to keep me upright as I stumble clumsily toward the bathroom like I've had one too many. My hand finds Gabe's guitar, and a layer of dust transfers from it to my hand. It hasn't been touched since before the accident; now just another piece of furniture in our bedroom.

Today was my due date.

I can't breathe or see through my tears. The guilt of losing track of the days, of this day, socks me in the stomach like a punch. Gagging, I fall heavily to my knees in front of the toilet and vomit violently, though there's little to leave my stomach. After I'm done, I sit on the bathroom mat and rock back and forth. My hands clutch my now concave belly, which will never swell with a child again.

All I want is to sleep, to escape all this for even a few hours. I lean against the toilet's lid and get to my feet, shaky from the purging. Opening the medicine cabinet, I scan the bottles until I find what I'm looking for. The sleeping pills. I am one of those people who will suffer through a blinding migraine rather than take a pill, so the bottle is still full.

Wrapping my fingers around the small narrow bottle, I use the other hand to fill a glass with water from the bathroom sink. Staring into the mirror, I see a woman who used to care about how she looked, who others might have called pretty, whose stringy hair now hangs in front of vacant eyes, her face full of dark shadows and hollows. I don't want to be this woman anymore.

I open the cabinet again and take out another bottle, then make my way back to bed with the glass of water in one hand and two pill bottles clutched in the other.

First, I swallow the morphine left over from my surgery. The bottle is nearly half-full, so it takes a while to get them all down. I don't rush, because I don't want to throw up again. Then I put the empty morphine bottle in my nightstand drawer, tucked deeply into a box of tissues, and pop the lid of the other bottle. The label says to take one pill at bedtime, and not if pregnant or breastfeeding. No problem there. I shake out two little white pills, which I swallow easily with a sip of water. Then I take out two more, and do the same. And then, just to be sure they work, shake out the last one and down it goes. Sleep will not elude me today.

They say it was good my mom showed up when she did.

# 11

As strange as it sounds, I like being here. It's busy, which means plenty of distractions. And unless I have a visitor, there are no reminders of what has put me here in the first place.

Like any other floor on the hospital, the linoleum tiles carry black scuff marks; the beeps and bells work tirelessly to disturb even the deepest, most pharmaceutically induced sleep; and the smells of rubbing alcohol and cafeteria food permeate the air. The only difference on this floor is how one gets in, or out of, the unit: through windowless doors, with high security locks. While some might feel captive here, I feel safe.

Welcome to the psychiatric ward.

It has been just over a week since I swallowed the pills. I wasn't really trying to kill myself, despite what it says on my chart. I was simply searching for a moment of peace from the grief. I wanted to sleep without having nightmares. I was tired of the pain that lives in my chest. That's all it was. But when you end up in the ER, rushed by ambulance and barely breathing because of a bellyful of painkillers and sleeping pills, you get a good old-fashioned stomach pumping, a charcoal chaser and two weeks in the psych ward.

Also, you get to talk a lot about how you're feeling to perfect strangers.

"How are things today?" Dr. Rakesh, an extremely tall and thin man, midfifties I figure, with a musical accent, asks. His kind, chocolate-brown eyes are unblinking behind his wire-rimmed glasses, which are too small for his features. He takes a sip from the mug of tea beside him and waits. The tea's peppermint notes clog my nose, reminding me of candy canes. I don't want to think about candy canes.

Dr. Rakesh asks me this question every morning, at the beginning of our hour-long sessions. Then I hear it again, by whichever on-call doctor has the luck to be on the ward that day. Then by the nurse drawing blood to check my medication levels, by the food services delivery person and by any visitors I have. "Better" has become my response of choice. It seems positive enough, without being completely dishonest.

"Good, good," Dr. Rakesh says. "Better is what we hope for." I nod, and he smiles, displaying two rows of quite straight but yellowing teeth. Along with the tea's mint, his breath carries the sour smell of a not-long-ago-smoked cigarette.

"Do you think I can get my necklace and rings back today?" The ER staff removed all my jewelry when I was admitted. And although it seems highly unlikely I'll be able to strangle myself with my necklace, and certainly my rings pose no threat, the staff here are firm. I'll get it all back in a week when they let me out.

As I expect, he shakes his head. "Sorry, Tegan, but we can't give them to you until you're released." He sips his tea again.

I run my right thumb around the base of my left ring finger, the skin still holding a slight indentation from my engagement and wedding bands. Which makes me think of Gabe.

As if sensing the mental shift to my husband, Dr. Rakesh jumps right in. "I'd like to talk about Gabe today, if that's okay with you?"

"Okay," I say, pressing my thumb more deeply into the

skin of my ring finger. My heart batters my chest wall with sudden fury. I don't want to talk about Gabe. I don't want to think about Gabe.

"Tell me your favorite story about your husband," Dr. Rakesh says. I stare at him, and he offers a warm smile, but this time without teeth. It's a better look for him. "I'd like you to tell me something about Gabe that makes you happy."

I close my eyes, letting the anger dissipate before speaking. I know exactly which story to tell.

"We went to Maui after Gabe passed the bar exam. It was a gift from his parents," I say, eyes still closed to soak up the memory without distraction. "We had surf lessons planned for the end of the trip, but then the pig thing happened."

"The pig thing?" Dr. Rakesh asks. "I'm intrigued."

I open my eyes. Dr. Rakesh sits forward, notepad resting on one thigh. Aside from the date at the top of the page, he has only scrawled two words. *Gabe-accident.* I pull my gaze away and float back to Hawaii.

"It was the day before our first surf lesson and we decided to do the drive to Hana. Have you been to Maui?"

Dr. Rakesh shakes his head. "It's on my bucket list, though," he says.

"You really should go," I say. "It's beautiful."

"So I've heard."

"Anyway, Hana is a town in Maui that is completely isolated from the rest of the island. To get there you drive this superwindy highway, which is really only a narrow two-lane road," I say. "It takes about four hours but it's worth it. Unless you get carsick."

Dr. Rakesh raises an eyebrow. "Noted," he says.

"There are so many cool stops along the way, and one is this general store that's been there since the early nineteen hundreds." I spell the store's Hawaiian name out when he asks so he can write it down. He's good at feigning interest, no question.

"It's a family business and carries everything you could ever imagine. They also have this amazing banana bread. Like, the best banana bread I've ever had."

"Oh, I do love banana bread," Dr. Rakesh says, writing the two words underneath the store's name, and underlining them twice for good measure.

"Me, too." I swallow against the sadness creeping up. It was such a happy time. Stuffed full of buttery banana bread and boundless love. "We were getting back into the car when we heard this high-pitched squeal. But we had no clue what it was."

Dr. Rakesh shifts and crosses one leg over the other, leaning back in his chair. He rests the notepad against his knee and waits for me to go on.

"There was this tiny potbellied pig, no bigger than a kitten. A bunch of motorcycles were driving into the parking lot and the pig was freaking out because of the noise," I say. "It ran in circles, squealing, and for a second it looked like it was going to become bacon."

Dr. Rakesh grimaces slightly. "I'm a vegetarian," he says, by way of explanation.

"Oh, sorry," I say, but he waves the apology away.

"Did they stop?" he asks, leaning forward now.

I nod. "Just, and Gabe managed to catch the pig. Turns out it was the family pet. We got five loaves of banana bread as a thank-you," I say, smiling.

"Do you blame Gabe for the accident?" Dr. Rakesh asks, and I'm irritated by the way he suddenly shifts gears in what I assume is an attempt to throw off my guard.

"Yes," I respond without pause. "He was going too fast."

He writes something down, but I can't see what because

he's shifted the notepad up. "There was black ice that night, wasn't there?"

I nod. He must have seen the accident report. *Also, he didn't have both hands on the wheel because one of them was up my skirt—which I was happy about.*

"If he'd been driving the speed limit and the accident had happened, would you still feel it was his fault?"

Pause. "I don't know, but that isn't what happened."

More writing, more nodding from the sneaky Dr. Rakesh.

"I told him to slow down," I say, noting how weak my voice sounds. "But we were late for his parents' party."

"Tegan, were you trying to hurt yourself with the pills?"

I'm getting whiplash from the change in direction with his questions.

"No. I told you that already," I say. "It wasn't about that. I was still having pain from my injuries, and I was exhausted. I just wanted to sleep. That's all." I consider asking him if he's trying to kill himself with the cigarettes.

He nods, and I'm not sure how to take it. Does he believe me? Is he placating me? "I've read the accident report," he continues. "And the police seemed to feel it was exactly as it was called. An accident. It wasn't anyone's fault, Tegan. Yours included."

"Of course it wasn't my fault," I snap. "I wasn't driving the car."

"Do you blame yourself for losing the baby?"

"No." What a stupid question.

Dr. Rakesh observes me for a moment, pen poised above the notepad. "In situations like these, the mother often feels guilty for the loss of the pregnancy."

"Gabe was driving too fast," I say, through clenched teeth. "I told him to slow down."

"It's okay to be angry, Tegan," Dr. Rakesh says. "It's part

of the healing process. But at some point you need to decide if you can forgive Gabe, and yourself, for what happened."

*You don't understand this at all*, I think at him. But I keep my mouth shut. No matter how many fancy-looking degrees line his boring, almond-colored office walls, Dr. Rakesh is clueless.

"I think we're done now," I say, eyes darting to the clock behind him.

He glances at his watch. "Yes, you're right. I'll see you tomorrow. Maybe try to get outside for some fresh air today?"

I nod and push the cheap, vinyl-covered chair back. Without looking at Dr. Rakesh, I leave the room, rubbing my thumb around my ring finger, feeling the indentation again.

I take back what I thought this morning.

I hate this place.

# 12

I've only been home a few days, but between Gabe, both our sets of parents, my brothers and Anna, I feel more captive in my own apartment than I did in the locked-down psych ward. It takes a sweep of our medicine cabinet to make sure there's nothing stronger than acetaminophen and cough syrup, along with promises to check in hourly via text and phone to get them all to leave me alone, but finally it's quiet again. Aside from Gabe, who reiterates he's not going anywhere.

At my second-to-last session with Dr. Rakesh I had what he called "an important step in the right direction." Just shy of a breakthrough, I suppose, but good enough for the yellow-toothed doctor to sign the papers for my release. Of course, what he didn't realize was that it was mostly fabricated. The tears were real, but the proclamations of forgiveness I knew he wanted to hear were rehearsed the night before, as I tried to fall sleep under my overstarched, scratchy hospital bedsheets. Back in his office, I felt the way my kindergarteners must when they're trying to give me the answer they think I want, rather than the one that feels most true to them.

They released me with an antidepressant with so many side effects I'm not sure the pills are better than the depression, and two follow-up appointments with Dr. Rakesh over the next couple of weeks.

But I'm not about to forgive anyone yet, least of all Gabe.

"What are you doing?" Gabe asks, watching me pull out a large white melamine bowl from the bowels of our deep pantry. I hold it up to the kitchen's halogen lights, then wipe the dusty inside of the bowl with a paper towel.

"I'm making banana bread," I say, cracking the freckled skin on one of the squishy bananas. I glance at the recipe, the one Gabe coaxed out of the general store owner after he returned the pig, written on the back of a postcard picturing Maui's black sand beach. I continue peeling the ripe, fragrant fruit until three mushy bananas pile up in the bottom of the bowl.

The oven beeps, letting me know it's warm and ready, and I methodically drive the potato masher into the bananas before pouring in the whisked eggs and oil, and an overflowing cup of sugar. Setting the wet ingredients aside, I concentrate on the flour and baking soda, using my thumb to level the teaspoon full of soda.

"It probably won't taste the same," Gabe says. "Where are those from?"

I tilt my head to read the sticker from one of the discarded banana peels. "Costa Rica."

I measure out another half teaspoon of baking soda, which I toss into the flour mixture.

I stir the flour, soda and salt around and around with the large wooden spoon Gabe's mom gave me last Christmas, in the hopes I'd start making her Italian family's famous tomato sauce. She's chastised me continuously about my sauce spoons, reminding me the metal and plastic versions I typically use will ruin the taste.

I tried to make the sauce once, even using exorbitantly priced canned tomatoes imported directly from Italy and sweet basil from Rosa's garden, but it had none of the flavor or depth of her sauce. Gabe said I was crazy, but I was sure Rosa left a critical ingredient off the recipe card she attached to the spoon. Just to make sure I couldn't make it taste exactly like hers.

With a few quick stirs to blend the wet and dry ingredients together, I spatula-level the mixture into the pans coated with a healthy smear of butter, and set the timer. I sit at the kitchen island and pull out a magazine from the stack Anna brought over and flip the pages without commitment.

"I'm sure it will be good, even without the Maui bananas."

"Mmm-hmm," I mumble, keeping my eyes on the glossy pages without reading a word.

"I'm glad you're baking again," he says, keeping his voice light. I recognize the tone. It's the one he uses when I've had a stressful day at work, or when our neighbor's miniature dachshund howls at three in the morning and I threaten to storm over there and tell him exactly what I think he should do with the dog. "You look different, you know?"

"Do I?" I try to sound disinterested. But I'm actually curious. Different how? In a good way? Less depressed, maybe? I wonder what that looks like.

"Tegan?"

"Yeah?" I don't look up. I can't look up, because if I do, I know I'll be back in bed for days. If someone told me you could love and hate a person so completely, at the same time, I would have said no way. But I would have been wrong.

My hate for Gabe drives as deeply into my body as my love for him does. And it's tearing me in half, like my seat belt almost did when we hit that metal pole.

"Promise me you'll never do anything like that again."

"Like what?" I ask, knowing exactly what he means.

"Don't do that, okay? This is serious."

I sigh and slam the magazine shut. "Oh, this is serious? Wow, thanks, I didn't realize that."

"Stop fucking around, Tegan!" His blue eyes blaze with anger. "Do you even care what would have happened if your mom hadn't found you? Do you know what that would have done to the people who love you?"

"I wasn't trying to kill myself, Gabe. It was an accident."

"No. No," he says, voice rising. "An accident is pulling pink sheets that used to be white out of the washing machine because you forgot to double-check if those red socks were mixed in, or adding salt to cookies instead of sugar because they look the—"

"Or hitting black ice and killing our baby?" I shout, shaking with fury. I try to hold eye contact, but my rage makes it hard to focus on his face.

Gabe says nothing, his beautiful eyes filling with sadness. I turn my back and will him to disappear.

The timer starts its incessant beeping, and only then do I notice how glorious the kitchen smells. But instead of feeling comfort, the sweet smell turns my stomach. I choke back a sob and slam on the oven mitts so I can pull out the perfectly browned loaves. Gabe must have understood my wish, because when I turn to put the hot pans on the cooling rack, he's not in the room anymore.

Alone again, I sit at the island and shove handfuls of the still hot, moist bread into my mouth, barely chewing. The heat ravages my tongue and lips, but I don't stop until the whole loaf is gone. It turns out a dash of sorrow and a teaspoon of bitterness really will ruin even the best recipe.

Gabe's right. It doesn't taste the same.

# 13

"I'm sorry for what I said earlier."

I have the worst stomachache, likely from the loaf of banana bread I gorged on; I've been nauseous ever since. But it may also be the argument that's turning my guts. As much as I hate to admit it, my mom is right when it comes to my stomach. It's sensitive to nerves and anything too spicy, as well as angry words I wish I could take back.

Gabe sighs at my apology, but doesn't seem too angry. Though he really should be, after what I said. "It's okay," he says. "I know you didn't mean it."

I bite my tongue, because words I don't want to say are trying to get out.

*I did mean it.* But that doesn't change that I probably shouldn't have said it.

We're on the couch, watching television. Feeling guilty, and getting no relief from nearly an entire bottle of pink bismuth—the same bottle left over from our wedding day, coincidentally—I flip on a nature show Gabe loves and try to come up with the right words to convey my regret.

The television is muted, but on it a lion stalks a sick antelope that has been separated from its herd. At least I can't hear the antelope's screams when it realizes what's happening, left alone to try and fight off the too fast, too strong lion. I understand how the antelope feels.

"I know Dr. Rakesh thinks I'm depressed," I say, keeping my eyes on the antelope's final moments. Solidarity with the abandoned, weak animal. "But I don't feel depressed exactly. I feel…angry." I take another swill of the thick, pink liquid and grimace as it coats my throat. "Doesn't depression come after anger?"

"I can't remember," Gabe says. "Isn't depression at the beginning?"

"No, anger comes before depression. I think. Or is it depression, anger and then acceptance?" I sigh. "I have no fucking idea. But no matter what order they come in, Dr. Rakesh was pretty clear there are no shortcuts."

"I don't know about that." Gabe smiles at me. "You're one smart cookie. I think if anyone can find a shortcut it would be you."

"I don't think I'm that special."

"That's your opinion," Gabe says. "But I know you can do whatever you put your mind to, Teg. I've seen you in action, and it's pretty freakin' scary when you're committed. Like that lion." I look back at the screen, where the lion is tearing apart its prey, and grimace.

"I'm not sure that's a compliment."

Gabe smiles wider, one side of his mouth resting higher than the other, where a faint white line is the only remnant from a childhood dog bite that required two-dozen stitches inside his cheek. It's adorably quirky, his smile.

"The old me might have agreed with you," I say, tucking my knees up to my chest. I feel cold, but on the inside. No blanket or hot cup of tea can help with that. "But I don't recognize myself anymore. I'm…lost." I dip my head and let the tears fall onto my pajama bottoms. "And I'm afraid I'm never coming back."

I close my eyes and feel Gabe's hand. His fingers intertwine with mine, and his thumb gently tickles my palm. I stay very still so as not to disturb the moment.

"You will make it back, Teg," Gabe says, his tone gentle. "And I'm going to be here every step of the way. Promise."

I nod and stay as I am, the sensation of Gabe's hand pushing away some of the sadness and leaving something in its place. Something I haven't felt in months—possibility.

# 14

"Is this all you're bringing?" My brother Jason stands in the doorway of the master bedroom holding my backpack. I glance up from the customs forms I'm filling out at the kitchen island.

"Yup," I say, flipping the page over and working on the back side. "I don't need much."

"But it's like, six weeks. You used to pack a bag bigger than this for an afternoon at the beach." He chuckles, and I roll my eyes. "Looks like I'm rubbing off on you. Jase style. Nice."

"Jase style?" Connor says. "You mean a pair of boxers and a T-shirt for a week?" Connor, the youngest of the three of us, sits beside me, looking over my to-do list. "Let's hope nothing about you is rubbing off on Tegan."

I nudge Connor with my knee. "Be nice."

"Whatever," Connor mumbles, before pointing at items five through twelve, which are unchecked and range from acetaminophen to travel-sized bottles of shampoo. "Did you get all this stuff from the pharmacy?"

Connor is cautious, analytical, thoughtful and headed toward a successful career in engineering, whereas Jason, though brimming with enthusiasm and that hard to qualify "joie de vivre," seems allergic to regular employment, rules and generally being an adult. Though opposite in personality, they look so similar they're often mistaken for twins. Unlike my brothers, with their well-muscled height, eyes the color of fresh-cut grass and sunshiny good looks, I'm dark-haired and brown-eyed. I've also been blessed—as my perpetually dieting mother likes to remind me—with string-bean legs, narrow hips and small boobs.

"Mom came over earlier with all that stuff, including six freaking bottles of Pepto-Bismol." I give Connor a wry glance. "She's very committed to this weak stomach of mine."

"Can I have a bottle?" Jase asks, bringing my backpack to the front door. "Last night was a rough one." Gabe, who is a last-minute kind of packer, laughs from the couch, where he's reading a magazine. If there's one thing Jason excels at, it's being the life of a party.

"Take two bottles, Jase," Gabe says. "I think you're going to need them more than Teg will."

I push the bottles of bismuth to the edge of the island. "Here you go."

"Thanks!" Jase tucks a bottle in each back pocket of his jeans.

"Did you get all your shots?" Connor asks me, ignoring Jase, as usual.

"You make me sound like a dog at the vet!" He doesn't smile. "Yes, I got my shots."

"Some of them anyway." Gabe looks up from the magazine. I shoot him a warning glare and he shrugs. Connor isn't exactly flexible when it comes to things like this, and the last thing I feel like doing is arguing with my baby brother. He always wins. Even though he's the youngest, he's the cleverest.

"Most of them," I clarify. Connor's expression tells me "most" isn't going to cut it. "Don't worry, okay? My doctor said as long as I'm careful about what I eat and do, I'm young, healthy and sure to be just fine."

"What about the other medication?" Connor asks, carefully avoiding eye contact this time. "From Dr. Rakesh." I don't like to talk about the antidepressants, and everyone knows it. It makes me feel more depressed for some reason. Like, you feel totally fine, then someone comments on how flushed your cheeks are and asks if you're okay, and suddenly you're convinced you have a raging fever.

"In her bag already," Gabe says. "I made sure." I narrow my eyes and wish Gabe would let me handle this.

"I'm all set, Connor. Don't stress, okay?"

Connor lays the pen down on the list and sighs. "Mom and Dad are worried, Teg," he says, trying to keep his balance when Jason nudges him off the stool. He punches Jason's arm in annoyance. But Jason seems to barely register the jab as he claims the stool, pushes his blond hair off his forehead and leans forward with hands on his thighs. He shifts to avoid crushing the small bottles in his back pockets. "We're worried, too," Jason says.

"I know you are."

Gabe gets up and walks toward the bedroom. "Time for me to get packing," he says, but I know it's less about his empty backpack and more about giving me some alone time with my brothers.

After Gabe leaves I point to a small box on the kitchen counter. "Could you put that in the top of my bag, please?" Jason, who's the closest, grabs the small box of note cards and zips it into the top flap of my backpack.

My parents' concern is well intentioned but has been suffocating, an intrusion almost. And the box of already addressed note cards Mom gave me earlier, which came with a so-you-can-write-us-whenever-you-want speech, only made me feel more like an incapable child. But then Gabe reminded me it has only been two months since Mom found me unconscious in bed, barely breathing. *'Right,'* I said, pulling the note cards out of the trash.

While Jason deals with the box and my backpack, Connor reclaims the bar stool and picks the pen back up to check off the drugstore items with precise, perfect checkmarks. I resist the urge to throw my arms around him and kiss him on the top of the head, like I used to when he was little. I'm beginning to realize how useless my family has felt during these past few months. And how far away I've kept them.

"Look, I'm sorry I scared you guys," I say. Jason stands behind me and massages my shoulders with his strong fingers. I relax back against him.

"It's okay, Teg," he says, though Connor gives me a look that suggests he's not quite as ready to let his guard down.

"Honestly, it was an accident. It was a bad day pain-wise, and I just wanted to get a few hours of sleep. That's it."

Jason continues massaging my shoulders, kneading the little balls of tension that have taken up permanent residence there. "We believe you, sis." I reach my hands back to give his a quick, appreciative squeeze. "So, what else do you need us to do?" he asks.

"For the record, I didn't 'need' you two to do anything, if you remember." I tilt my head back so I can look at him. He smirks but keeps massaging. "I'm a big girl and you guys need to trust I'm going to be okay." Tough sell, I know, based on what's happened. Also, even though I'm the oldest and as scrappy as any kid who grew up with two brothers, Jason and Connor have always treated me like a rare and delicate bird. But I'm doing better now. Or at least, I'm close to doing better.

Jason holds his hands up in surrender, and then envelops me in a massive hug. He smells of some kind of coconut hair product and stale beer, likely from working at the bar the night before.

My breath leaves me the tighter Jason squeezes, and I finally wriggle out from inside the steel circle of his strong biceps and shoulders.

"What time's the flight?" Jason asks, eyeing a plate of pastries on the counter. After a questioning look from him and a nod from me, he grabs one and sinks his teeth deeply into its round, doughnutlike surface. "God, are these good," he says, mouth full of sweet dough oozing with a tangy, rich lemon cream. He takes another pastry before even finishing the first. "What are they?"

"I can't remember the Italian name, but apparently it translates to virgin's breast."

"No wonder I like them so much," he says, taking another huge bite. Connor sighs, eyes still on the list.

"Conn, you should try one. They're fucking amazing," Jason says, his mouth full.

"They really are. Rosa brought them over earlier. I suspect she's trying to fatten me up." Rosa is rail thin, probably because she spends more time pushing food on those she loves versus eating it herself. It used to bother me—the comments and frequent food drop-offs—because it felt almost accusatory, like I wasn't capable of keeping Gabe as well fed as she could. But over the years I learned that for her, food and love were intertwined—the more she pushed, the more she loved.

Jason pops the last bite of the second pastry into his mouth, and then licks his fingers. "Tell her she can bring these over to my place while you're gone."

I laugh. "I'll do that. Although be prepared, her pastries may be sweet but her judgment can be harsh," I say, then notice Gabe standing in the doorway of our room.

"Be nice," he mouths at me, eyes teasing. I smile and tilt my head, gesturing to him it's okay to come back out.

Jason shrugs. "I'm good with the tough ones. Along with handsome I'm also often referred to as charming."

Gabe laughs, and Connor snorts. "Is that what they're calling it these days?"

"That you are," I say to Jason. "Plus, if you eat a plate of her pastries in one sitting I'm sure you'll be in her good books forever."

"Truer words were never spoken," Gabe says, coming into the kitchen as I hand Jason a takeout container.

"Take them all," I say, when he starts to close the lid, two pastries still on the plate.

"Are you sure? You are looking a little skinny."

Gabe looks at me then. I'm swimming in the legging jeans I used to have to lie down to zip up, and I know what he's thinking. Skinny isn't good. Skinny equals sad.

"I prefer svelte, thank you very much," I say as much to Gabe as Jason. "Seriously, take them. And to answer your question, the plane leaves in about six hours."

Jason kisses me on the cheek, leaving a hint of stickiness behind. "You're the best, love ya."

"Love you, too." I hug him again. Then I hug Connor, who holds my face in his hands and kisses me on the forehead. The way my dad does. "Be good, you two," I say.

"Ditto," Connor says.

Jason salutes with his free hand. "Always am," he says with a smile that suggests otherwise.

Gabe says his goodbyes, promising my brothers he'll take great care of me like always, then heads off to take a shower.

I walk Connor and Jason to the front door, holding it open for them with my foot. "Come back in one piece, okay?" Connor says with worried eyes. My mother's eyes.

"Of course," I say, standing in the open front door as my brothers make their way to the stairwell.

Jason turns before heading down the stairs after Connor and holds up the takeout container. "Seriously, tell Rosa I'm available if she needs me to eat stuff while you're gone."

"I will." I wave and start to shut the door.

"Tegan!" Jason calls out.

I poke my head back into the hall. "Yeah?"

"Have fun, kiddo."

"That's the plan," I reply with as much enthusiasm as I can.

We wave at each other and I shut the door. For the hundredth time since booking the tickets, I try to convince myself I'm ready for this.

# 15

An hour later I share a tearful goodbye with Anna, complete with a bag of my favorite treat, caramel cheese popcorn, from Garrett Popcorn. The first, and only, time I convinced her to try the sweet and cheesy concoction she gagged so hard she vomited on the sidewalk outside the shop, which only proves how much she loves me. She also gives me a book for the plane she promises won't make me cry, with an inscription of one of her grandmother's famous proverbs on the inside cover—*a book is like a garden carried in the pocket*—which neither of us really get but pretend to be inspired by. After she's gone, I change into my travel clothes of black yoga pants, a hoodie and tennis shoes, and sit on the couch. The airport limousine should be arriving in fifteen minutes, and my stomach feels sour. Maybe from the popcorn. Probably from everything else.

"What's up, buttercup?" Gabe asks when I let out a deep sigh, scanning the tickets in front of me. The destinations are in the order we pulled them out of the jar.

"Is this a mistake? I'm not sure about the order." I frown, flipping through the three itineraries. My fingertips leave faint neon-orange popcorn dust smudges on the papers.

"The order's fine. You're just nervous."

"Of course I'm nervous," I say, frustrated to have to admit

it. "This feels fast. I don't know if I'm ready." I hold my fingers against the pendant, and it presses into my bony sternum. "I don't know if this is going to work. I don't know if—" My voice breaks as a sob catches in my throat. I take a deep breath before going on. "This is going to sound crazy, but maybe I don't want to get over it." I'm relieved to finally say it out loud. "Do I really want to feel better? To move on? Because… because…" I stop, gasping against my sorrow.

"Because you're afraid you'll forget?" Gabe's voice is soft, understanding.

I nod, sucking in air. "What if I forget how much I loved… how much I love—"

"You won't," Gabe says, interrupting me. Determination floods his voice. "I won't let you."

I breathe out through pursed lips and focus on his words. "Thank you." I rest my head back against the cushioned couch and close my eyes. "I love you, Gabe."

It's the first time in four months I've said those words.

# *two*
# Thailand

# 16

Almost twenty-four hours after leaving Chicago, with a short layover in Frankfurt—from which I was still trying to get the stench of cigarette smoke out of my hair—our plane is minutes away from touching down on the runway at Bangkok's Suvarnabhumi Airport. I keep my eyes shut, enjoying the few moments that exist between dead sleep and consciousness. Despite my exhaustion and having spent two days on airplanes with nothing to do but sit and wait for time to pass, sleep has been hard to come by. Especially because of Gloria, our seatmate on the left.

She introduced herself in the airport's bathroom mirror while I brushed my teeth before takeoff, and as luck would have it, she ended up right beside me for the entire flight. She's a single mom, late forties, with a generous smile and a wild mop of red hair that consistently reaches beyond her seat and into my face. She works for some travel company in Chicago I've never heard of, and is on her way to a conference in Bangkok.

I try to be polite, listening to stories and looking at pictures of her son, who has just been accepted to college, and her cat, that she's incredibly stressed about leaving behind, seemingly more so than her son. Gabe chuckles in my other ear, because this is what always happens.

I'm a beacon for the talkers. It's as if I have a flashing sign that reads, "I want to hear all your stories, especially about your pet or disgusting medical issue!" No matter where I am, whether on the "L" train or walking through a shopping mall or sitting at a picnic bench in the park, the talkers flock to me. "It's your eyes," Gabe says by way of explanation. "You have curious eyes."

My eyes, the color of milk chocolate and maybe a little close together, have never seemed special enough to entice such attention. Plus, despite my "curious" eyes, Gabe is by far the more social of the two of us.

"Wake up, sleepyhead," Gabe whispers. I smile but keep my eyes shut. "The fun's about to start."

I crack open one eye and glance out the window. It's early morning in Bangkok, and a beautiful one at that, the sky just hanging on to the last of the sunrise.

"Gorgeous, isn't it?" Gloria asks, leaning into me to look out the window. I shift slightly to get out of the way of her hair. "I love Bangkok. The energy is palpable, you know? You're going to have a great time."

"That's the plan," Gabe and I say at the same time, and Gloria smiles at us and pats my arm.

"I love seeing young people heading out on adventures," she says. "One of the reasons I adore my job so much. There's nothing like your first time…in Thailand, that is!" She winks. I laugh, forgiving her for her hair and loose tongue.

"How are you feeling, love?" Gabe asks, as I shift Anna's book off my lap. I still haven't cracked the spine, but I had good intentions to.

"I'm looking forward to washing the plane off my face." I rub my hands over my eyes and wipe out the crusty sleep.

"Here," Gloria says, nudging me with her arm. She holds out what looks like a baby wipe. "I swear by these. Got them in Japan last time I was there. They smell strange but your face will thank you."

"Thanks," I say, taking the moist, white disposable towel and holding it up to my nose. I have no idea what the scent is, but it's not entirely terrible, just odd. I shrug and wipe my forehead, then my chin and nose.

"Make sure you wipe it around your eyes," Gloria says, doing just that. "It has some sort of tightener that will make you look ten years younger. Not that you need that. But this old face certainly does."

"You know it's probably filled with bird-poop essence or something like that," Gabe whispers. "Apparently the Japanese are fond of their bird-dropping facials. Superexpensive." I wipe around and around my eyes while Gloria watches, hoping he's wrong.

"Ah, that's better, don't you think?" Gloria asks. "Feel like I've slept all night."

Just then the flight attendant walks by, handing out hot towels as we taxi down the runway toward the terminal. I grab one for myself and Gabe, but he waves it away.

"No, thanks. I like the plane's grit. Makes me feel like an authentic traveler."

"Whatever you do, don't use this on your face," Gloria says, unrolling her own towel so it's a flat square. I look at the towel in my hands, hot and steaming, and see the row of people across from ours all doing just that—pressing the hot towel to their faces.

"Why?" I ask Gloria, thinking it's probably because then I'll wipe away the very expensive bird-shit essence I just rubbed around my eyes.

"Trust me," she says, using her towel to wipe a spot of tomato sauce off her pants. We had lasagna for dinner, which was better than expected. "They're really low-quality towels."

I stifle a laugh. Looking at Gloria, with her denim leggings with exposed threads and long-sleeve cotton shirt that seems to have lost its shape many washes ago, I think that her caring about the quality of an airplane towel seems out of character.

"Thanks for the tip," Gabe says, and I just smile at Gloria. But she doesn't see it, as she's still scrubbing at the spot on her pants.

"Listen, if you need anything, anything at all while you're here, call me," Gloria says a few minutes later, after she's packed up her magazines and bottled water from her seat pocket. "I'll be here for the rest of the week, and know Bangkok like the back of my hand." I take the business card she holds out and murmur my thanks, though I'm certain we'll never call. The cabin is full of rustling and action, as we get ready to deplane. My heart flutters and my legs are unsteady when I stand.

"Relax, love," Gabe says. I take a deep breath. "Besides, if Red gets even a whiff of anxiety from you, we'll never shake her." I laugh loudly. Gloria turns and gives us a big grin.

"Sounds like I don't need to tell you this, but have fun," she says. Then she steps into the aisle after the other passengers filing out in a line.

"You, too, Gloria. Nice to meet you," I reply, stepping out behind her. I turn my head to the side to avoid her unruly hair, which seems to have doubled in size since takeoff.

"I hope we've seen the last of that hair," Gabe whispers, and I chuckle, amazed at how normal this all feels. I wonder how long it will last.

# 17

Bangkok is an assault on my senses. The noise. The smells. The chaos. The heat. God, is it hot.

The guesthouse is a thirty-minute drive from the airport, according to the map search I did at home. But that apparently doesn't take into consideration the morning traffic, or that our driver, a weathered Thai man whose head barely clears the taxi's headrest, seems determined to get us lost.

"Shanti House, do you know it?" I ask, for the third time. The driver keeps turning to look at me, as if waiting for me to give up this silly English-speaking thing and solve our problems.

"It's near the river?" Gabe asks, but the driver is just shaking his head, not understanding a word. Then we start a game of charades, Gabe and I using our arms and hands to try and mimic fast-moving water while repeating the name of the guesthouse, him continuing to shake his head, hands up in the air. I resist shouting at him to keep his hands on the wheel, because every time he takes them off my anxiety level rises. Also, I'm not feeling great, a combination of lack of sleep, choking exhaust and being in the wayward taxi that is making my heart beat so fast I'm light-headed. I've barely been in a car since the accident, and this ride is more than I bargained for.

"Show him the map," Gabe says, when I sit back hard against the sticky hot seat and sigh with frustration, trying to calm down.

"The map is in English." The stress is making my voice less than kind.

"Show him anyway," Gabe repeats, his tone matching mine. "At least you can point to the river. Think that's a better plan than trying to mime flowing water, don't you?"

"Here…I have a map…" I say to the driver, grabbing the handle above my window when the cab brakes hard. My heart beats as furiously as hummingbird wings and my palms are instantly clammy.

I feel around behind me again even though I know no seat belt will materialize. The taxi speeds up once again and narrowly misses a *tuk-tuk* carrying what appears to be three generations of a family—far too many people for its small size. Dust swirls around the three-wheeled motorcycle car and its passengers, who hang out all sides of the dilapidated mode of transportation.

I relax my grip on the handle and fold the map as neatly as I can, as if that will help anything. The cab swerves, the driver hitting the gas then the brakes, and my travel-weary stomach protests.

"I'm sure he's going to be impressed with your origami skills," Gabe says, and I look down at the small square of map in my hands. "Wrong country, you know that, right?"

"Shut up," I reply, though I have to smile. Diffusing tension has always been one of Gabe's greatest skills. I shove the map forward over the cracked seat back, its vinyl surface grimy to the point of looking like it's been painted black on purpose, and point at the large *X* that marks the guesthouse's location. The driver takes the map from me, and to my horror keeps his eyes on it while flipping the small square around and around, clearly trying to get his bearings.

"Uh, would you mind keeping your eyes on the road?" He doesn't appear to hear me. I stretch forward, gripping the grimy seat and hooking an elbow over it to keep my balance in the speeding taxi. "Look, there's the river." I point to the squiggly blue line on the map.

"I'm sure he knows where the river is, Teg."

I ignore Gabe and stick my finger onto the point I'd marked with the *X*. "See?" I say, tapping my finger against the map. I wish he'd just stop the cab, pull over for a minute. Fear begins to give way to rolling nausea from the taxi's jerky ride. The pungent scent of dying flowers, from the jasmine garland hanging from the taxi's rearview mirror, also doesn't help.

"Carsick?" Gabe asks, when I close my eyes and put my head down on my elbow. When I open my eyes, I see the cab driver glancing at us nervously. The map is on the seat beside him, forgotten. All around us cars jump in and out of lanes, narrowly missing each other and the bicycles and *tuk-tuks* attempting to share the road. I catch a glimpse of my face in the rearview mirror, and see why the driver looks worried. I'm a strange gray-green color, the skin around my mouth white as snow.

"Pull over," I say, but only half of it comes out because my voice cracks. All the driver hears is "over," and his eyes dart to mine in the mirror but he doesn't slow the cab.

So I do the only thing I can think of. I take my hands and mime a flowing stream of vomit out of my mouth. That does the trick. He wrenches the wheel and we come to an abrupt stop at the side of the road, somehow avoiding getting hit by the relentless stream of traffic.

As the airplane lasagna, and seemingly everything else I've put in my stomach in the past day, splatters onto the roadside,

Gabe keeps repeating, "You're okay, almost over..." the way he used to in my early morning-sickness filled days of pregnancy. While I try to catch my breath and settle my stomach before getting back in the car, the driver stops another taxi and shows him the map. Five minutes later we're on our way again, and ten minutes after that, we pull up in front of the guesthouse.

In all the online reviews I read, Shanti House was described as "serene," an "oasis inside bustling Bangkok," and that's exactly what it is. Tucked toward the end of a nondescript street that is gloriously quiet, the guesthouse is unassuming from the front, blending into the other run-down buildings nearby. Rows of shoes, mostly flip-flops and well-worn sandals, line a mat at the front step of the guesthouse, and a few patrons sit barefoot just inside at the open-air patio, enjoying breakfast.

I slip off my tennis shoes, my socked feet tingling with the freedom, and step inside. A few travelers glance up from their bowls of yogurt and fresh fruit, and smile. They're all quite tan, their features carrying the relaxed look of a perpetual holiday. The smells of cardamom and something floral waft through the space, where tiki lights hang in rows. Somewhere nearby water trickles in a comforting rhythm.

"This is awesome," Gabe says.

I nod, taking in a deep breath. "I'm going to check us in." I put my backpack on the ground beside an empty table, and Gabe takes a seat. The guesthouse proprietor turns out to be an expat Aussie named Simon, who came to Bangkok for a short vacation and never left. Over a breakfast of muesli and a succulent plate of fruit, I learn this story is fairly common around these parts. I sip a "must have" Thai iced coffee, falling instantly in love with the sweet, cool beverage fragrant with spice and rich with condensed milk.

"So what brings you to Thailand?" a young woman with long blond dreadlocks held back by a bandana asks. She's sitting at the table beside us, and introduces herself as "Vera," no last name. Her blue eyes sparkle against well-sunned, freckly cheeks. She looks happy, in a way that makes me jealous.

"Vacation," I reply, taking another sip of my drink.

"It's a travel wish list sort of thing," Gabe adds.

"That's cool," Vera says. "How long are you here for?"

I hold up two fingers as I swallow another sip of liquid heaven. "Two months?" Vera's boyfriend asks. At least I think he's her boyfriend, the way they're wrapped around each other yet still managing to eat breakfast.

This time I laugh. "Two weeks."

"Not enough time, love," Simon says, as he deposits another round of iced coffees to the table. "Thailand isn't like a vacation to Mexico. It takes time to enjoy her properly."

"How long have you been here?" I ask Vera and her table companion.

"Eight months," she says.

"Three years," her boyfriend chimes in, snuggling deeper into her.

I try to hide my surprise, and Gabe gives a low whistle beside me. They both look about our age. It's crazy to imagine what life would be like if we had spent the past few years traveling around Thailand, rather than working and starting a "proper" grown-up life in Chicago.

I can't stop staring at Vera's feet, browner than the rest of her except for where the sandals straps have shielded her skin from both grime and sun. It looks like she's wearing bright white sandals, even though her feet are bare. Her legs hang over her boyfriend's, her toenails a cotton-candy shade of pink. Even her toenails look happy.

"I think you'd look superhot in a pair of Tevas," Gabe

whispers in my ear, and I drag my eyes away from Vera's joyous feet. "Think of how freeing it would be for that weird toe of yours." I giggle softly, wiggling my big toe inside my sock. I broke it in high school, after a failed attempt to join the school's track team that proved once and for all I wasn't a natural athlete. The toe still isn't straight.

Talk turns to the "must do" things in Thailand, as well as what to avoid, and I pull out one of my mom's note cards to jot it all down. Belly full of Thai coffee and muesli, I am alert and satiated. And not just because of the food and caffeine. Chicago is very far away, and though the sadness clings to my edges like tiny rows of magnets, I feel here I can breathe more deeply.

"Love your necklace," Vera says, reaching for the gold pendant. "Where did you get it? Is there a picture inside or something?" My heart hammers and I quickly push my chair back, so I'm out of her reach.

"Oh, thanks," I say, flustered. "Just off some website. Can't remember the name."

"Too bad," she says, seemingly oblivious to my discomfort. "If you remember, let me know. I love it."

I smile and promise I will. Then I excuse myself, find the bathroom just past the restaurant, lock the door and cry.

# 18

Ten minutes later I come back to the table, self-conscious about my puffy red eyes, but grateful for my sunglasses. I try to get back into the conversation, but I can't concentrate.

"You all right?" Gabe asks quietly. I shake my head, though no one else seems to notice I'm no longer participating in the conversation.

"Think I'm going to head to the room," I say, standing up and swinging my backpack over my shoulder. "I'm feeling pretty wiped out after the trip."

"Nice to meet everyone," Gabe says, standing up beside me.

There are waves from around the table, and Vera jumps up to give me a hug. She holds on tight, saying how happy she is to meet me, and though it makes me uncomfortable, I wait until she releases me a little before I pull away.

But sleep eludes me when we get into bed, under the patchwork quilt that's too warm for the day's temperature. Sounds of a street coming to life stream through the open window, and the sun beats down onto the double bed so I throw back the covers with a sigh.

Plus, Gabe and I are fighting. Actually, he'd probably say I'm trying to pick a fight. Maybe so. It's hot, I'm tired and the combination is making me miserable.

"I'm not telling a total stranger what's in the necklace," I say, my voice a bit loud for the thin walls of our room.

"I never suggested otherwise." Gabe's voice is calmer than mine, though slightly exasperated. "Very tanned Vera doesn't need to know any of that."

I sigh, and his smile fades.

"So what are you saying?" I ask. Gabe always has a point to make. It's one of the only things that irritate me about him. Likely because he's often right.

"Part of what you need to figure out on this trip is how to talk about what happened. It will come up, probably when you're not expecting it, and hiding in a bathroom isn't always going to be an option."

"Yeah, you're probably right," I say, nodding vigorously. "Do you think I should get it put on a T-shirt? Maybe on the back, so people don't need to see my face and feel even worse when they read it."

"Tegan—" Gabe begins, but I interrupt him.

"Shut up, okay?" Even my voice sounds tired. I lean on the windowsill and let the warm air tickle my face. "You don't get to decide how I handle this. How I deal with what's inside this necklace is up to me, and me alone. Got it?" I try to control my anger, knowing it's misplaced but caring little.

"Yeah. I got it," Gabe says, his voice clipped.

Part of me wants to apologize, to blame the heat and the long flight for being selfish. For assuming how I feel is paramount. But I don't. And he doesn't, either, which irrationally makes me even angrier.

For a couple that barely used to fight, we're not off to a great start.

# 19

*Seven and a half years before the accident*

Gabe and I had been dating six months, three weeks and four days before we had our first fight. It might seem odd to know down to the day, but I was a calendar girl. I blamed my dad for the compulsion to keep track of everything from laundry day, to what I was making for dinner, to the status of my relationship. Dad was meticulous in his planning, and I'd grown up comforted by the knowledge that there would be clean socks on Mondays, Fridays were reserved for pizza and family game nights, and Sundays meant Dad's homemade burgers and Mom's macaroni salad.

But mostly I noted how long it took us to have our first fight because it seemed like it might never happen.

And then came the Easter Bunny.

We were lying in Gabe's bed, barely moving because even the slightest shift against the pillows made our crushing headaches scream. The previous evening's house party had been a haze of beer, vodka, sodas and, unfortunately, Jägermeister shots. Sipping water, I stressed internally about our afternoon plans.

I had met Gabe's parents once before, when they stopped

by his place unannounced a couple of months earlier. When I heard the front door open, I thought it was Gabe's roommate, returning from his own night of debauchery. But then Gabe's parents walked into the living room, where I sat on the couch in a pair of Gabe's boxers and a T-shirt, looking completely disheveled. While his dad seemed amused to find me there, his mother not so much. Gabe came back from the bathroom a couple of minutes later, which unfortunately allowed for awkward small talk between me and his parents, and while the entire experience left me flustered and whining about first impressions, Gabe was unconcerned. "I'm a big boy," he said with a laugh. "I'm allowed to have a girl sleep over."

Needless to say, I hadn't yet been invited to his parents' home.

"How long until we have to leave?" I asked, squinting at my watch as the numbers swirled together. I swallowed hard and shielded my eyes with one hand from the sunlight streaming through the threadbare curtains. "I feel like such crap." I knew I should have stopped after the vodkas.

"We have about thirty minutes before we have to get serious," Gabe said, his smile crinkling his eyes. One day those crinkles would turn to permanent wrinkles, and watching him, I realized just how much I still wanted to be around to see that change. Before Gabe I wasn't sure I was the marrying type. In fairness, I was only eighteen—far too young to be thinking about much aside from school, being out of my parents' place and how to get alcohol despite the age on my driver's license.

I snuggled back into Gabe's chest, letting the rise and fall of it lull me back to sleep.

"Tegan?" Gabe shifted and my head rolled off his shoulder.

"What?" I was groggy and disoriented, having been nearly asleep.

"Here, watch something and try to stay awake." He handed me the remote to the television. "I'm going to hop in the shower first, okay?"

"M'kay," I said, sitting up cross-legged. I switched the channels and yawned, the shows barely registering. *News. Sports. Infomercial. Infomercial. Weather. Infomercial. Infomercial.* "Oh, the bunny parade is later today," I said, stopping when I recognized images of the annual parade on the local news station. "My dad used to take us every year."

Gabe turned around in the doorway, towel over his shoulder and bathroom bag in his hand. He looked amused. "You've got to be kidding me."

"What?" I asked. I stood gingerly. My stomach protested, but not too seriously. I shimmied into my jeans, noting how much harder it was to get the zipper up this morning. Booze bloats. Awesome.

"The 'bunny' parade?"

I laughed. "What? That's what we called it," I said, huffing a bit as I worked to get the button on my jeans done up. Dammit. The dress I had planned for dinner didn't allow for bloating. "The Easter Bunny at the end throws chocolate eggs and plastic eggs filled with little stickers. So fun."

Gabe eyed me critically, but still with a smile. "Tegan, you do realize there's no such thing as the Easter Bunny, right?"

"I've heard that before," I said, finally getting the button done up. I was going to have to rethink my outfit. I needed something stretchy for sure. "But I refuse to believe it. That furry little guy is as real to me as you are." I winked before pulling my sweater over my head. Even though the bathroom was just next door to Gabe's room, after the incident with his parents I always got fully dressed first. Running into your boyfriend's parents—or his roommate, for that matter—in the hall wearing only a T-shirt felt like a one-night-stand kind of thing versus a girlfriend serious enough to be invited over for Easter dinner.

"Look at all those kids. Suckers." Gabe snorted.

"Oh, come on," I said. "Be nice. They're just excited."

He pointed his toothbrush at the screen, where children with giant smiles sat on their dads' shoulders, and lined the sidewalk eagerly clutching pastel-colored baskets and wearing bunny-ear headbands. I could almost smell the fresh, buttered popcorn and diesel fumes from the floats' exhaust. "I'm going to tell my kids straight up. No Easter Bunny." He tapped his toothbrush in the air to emphasize each point. "No tooth fairy, either. And definitely no Santa Claus."

"Gabe Lawson!" I said, hands on my hips. "You will do no such thing." I heaved an overly dramatic sigh. "What's wrong with you this morning? Where's your sense of childhood wonder?" I smirked, and expected him to laugh or admit he was being irrationally grumpy. But he wasn't smiling. He looked determined, and irritated. *What the hell?*

"Especially not Santa Claus," Gabe continued, oblivious to my attempts to lighten the mood. "It's a shitty thing to do, to lie to your kids about something that's basically a giant marketing ploy to sell stuff."

I paused, unsure which direction to take the conversation. On the one hand, I could just give him a kiss, shove him out the door and tell him to hurry up in the shower. Diffuse the tension. On the other hand…

"I really want to believe you're joking right now, but I'm getting the feeling you're quite serious," I said, crossing my arms over my chest. I was never good at letting things go. That trait I got from my mom, who on a daily basis for nearly an entire year brought up the one—and only—time my dad forgot to turn off the outdoor water valve before the first freeze, resulting in burst pipes and ankle-deep water in our basement.

"I am very serious," Gabe said. "I won't dupe my kids about some big fat man in a red suit who flies around the world in one night delivering presents that still have price tags on them. It's Parenting 101, Tegan. Once you lie about one thing and your kids find out, they'll never trust you the same way again." I didn't like his tone. It carried a hint of judgment I'd heard before, but never directed my way.

"I don't think you can blame Santa Claus for trust issues between parents and their kids," I said, my irritation swelling. "Besides, when did you become an expert in parenting? I didn't think they covered that in your prelaw classes."

"I didn't see it on your class syllabus, either." Gabe crossed his arms over his chest to match my stance.

"At least I'll be trained to work with kids," I said, my voice rising. For a moment I wanted to laugh at how ridiculous this was, the two of us facing off over Santa Claus, not to mention fictional children, but I wasn't about to give Gabe the satisfaction. "Besides, your kids are more likely to be ruined by your less-than-nurturing gene pool." We both knew what, and whom, I was referring to. Gabe had commented once, after meeting my parents, how his mother had many great qualities, but being warm and fuzzy with her children wasn't one of them.

Gabe's jaw tightened. "You know, it takes a lot more than a teaching degree and Santa stories to be a good parent," he said, his tone biting.

I wished I was better with quick and witty comebacks,

but in that moment his words and anger deflated me, and I couldn't think of a thing to say.

So we stood like that for another thirty seconds, neither of us moving or saying a word. Then the Easter parade promo came back on the television, the sounds of cheering kids and a marching band filling the room.

"I'm going to have my shower now," he finally said. "But I'm really looking forward to hearing more great parenting advice from you later." If there were one thing that pushed me over the edge, it was a sarcastic taunt.

I pushed past him and made my way to the front door. He followed close behind. I shoved one foot so hard into my boot the lining bent in half under my sole. I didn't bother fixing it, even though it made it hard to walk.

"Just so you know, I plan to 'dupe' my kids," I said. "About the Easter Bunny. And Santa. And the tooth fairy. Hell, I'm even going to start making new shit up. Like maybe a full-moon fairy? Or a back-to-school gnome that brings pencil crayons and new books the night before school starts." I rustled about the front hall, moving faster than felt comfortable in my current hungover state.

"You're just going to leave?" Gabe asked, watching me put my coat on but making no move to stop me.

"Yup." I stepped around him and opened the front door, disappointment filling me with uncomfortable warmth. "Excuse me."

"Tegan, come on," he said, grabbing my arm with his free hand. "You're being childish. It's just a stupid tradition."

"It's not stupid." I pulled away and walked backward through the front door. It was cold outside, and I wished I'd taken the time to button up my coat.

"Give me a minute and I'll drive you." He shivered in the cold air.

"I think I'd prefer to walk," I replied, my tone as icy as the steps I carefully maneuvered my way down, limping slightly due to my ill-fitting boot—falling on my ass at this moment wouldn't help things. "These are the things that really matter, Gabe." My voice was high and stretched thin. I blamed the booze still circulating in my system, but I was close to tears.

"The Easter Bunny *really* matters?" He watched me walk down the last of the steps, farther away from him. Then he shook his head. "Whatever," he muttered. "I'll pick you up outside your place in forty minutes."

For a moment I considered shouting, "Don't bother!" but instead all I said was "Fine." Then I seethed all the way home, my hands and ears numb with cold by the time I got back to the dorm, and a blister on my big toe from rubbing against my boot liner. While I showered, pulled on my nylons and dress, then put a quick coat of soft pink polish on my nails, I mumbled all the things I wished I'd said in the moment. And I wondered how I could date someone who would never dress up as Santa Claus on Christmas morning for his kids.

The Lawsons lived in the Chicago suburb of Park Ridge, where houses were big and landscaping was impressive. Trying not to be intimidated by the grandeur of his childhood home, I shifted restlessly beside Gabe as he rang the bell. Neither one of us had said anything on the ride over. Both too stubborn to speak first.

Nerves frayed, I was just about to break down and ask if I looked okay, when the door opened and we were swept inside. Which is when I realized this wasn't just dinner with Gabe's parents. Seems his entire extended family was invited, too. I clutched the potted Easter lily in my hands, wishing I'd bought the cut tulips instead when I saw two other lilies on the front hall table, and put a big smile on my face. I tried to ignore how Gabe walked in ahead of me, like he was already prepared to leave me behind.

Less than a minute after walking through the front door I had a glass of red wine in my hand—"I know this goes against the rules, but we're Italian," his dad had said, handing me the wine. "Or at least my wife is, and according to her you drink red wine from birth!"—and Gabe's dad was leading me around the living room, which was overstuffed with relatives.

"You have a beautiful home, Dr. Lawson," I said, between shaking hands with two of Gabe's uncles, an aunt and a pimple-faced teenage cousin who was a tad too enthusiastic with his cheek kisses.

"Thank you. We're happy here," he said. "And please, call me David. Dr. Lawson is the name I use when I'm playing cardiologist." He winked and smiled, and I smiled back, feeling more relaxed. Though Gabe was dark-haired and olive-skinned like his mom, he really looked quite a bit like his dad. Strong jaw. Dimpled cheeks. Well-arched eyebrows framing light blue eyes. Except I had a feeling Dr. Lawson would be okay with the Easter Bunny. He just seemed the type. A surge of righteousness filled me again, and I shot a frosty glance at Gabe, who didn't notice, as he was preoccupied with his nieces and nephew.

"And this is where the magic happens," Dr. Lawson, David, said, once we got to the kitchen, which was filled with stark white and glass cabinets and black granite, and smelled better than any other kitchen I'd been in before. And in the center of it all, stirring two pots at once with graceful hands, was Gabe's mother.

I was struck again by how beautiful she was. When Gabe had mentioned his Italian mother who was never without a wooden spoon in her hand or homemade tomato sauce on her apron, I pictured someone quite different than the woman who stood in front of me. Perhaps the jovial, rotund, Italian mama with the black-haired buns on either side of her head from the picture on the jar of pasta sauce my mom bought in bulk at Costco. His mom was wearing an apron, but it was spotless. Her hair fell halfway down her back, in thick, shiny voluminous waves. She was tall and narrow, all sharp angles, except for her lips, which were full like Gabe's were. Behind her red-framed glasses that offered the only pop of color to her black pantsuit, her eyes took me in. I stood still for a moment, waiting for a signal I'd passed the test. Seeing as last time we met I was dressed in only a T-shirt and her son's boxers, I expected tonight's outfit would be more up to her standards.

"*Benvenuto*, Tegan. How nice to see you again," she said, her Italian accent shining through. She wiped her hands on a nearby tea towel before coming over to where I stood in the doorway of the kitchen. After a somewhat awkward embrace and two air-kisses, one for each side of my face, she held me at arm's length. "I love this dress. It's perfect on you. *Magnifico.*"

"Thank you, Mrs. Lawson," I said. "And thank you for inviting me today. Your home is stunning."

"Oh, call her Rosa," David said, adding, "Mrs. Lawson is my mother's name!" He chuckled, I said okay, but I knew that wasn't likely to happen. Especially because it didn't look like Gabe's mother agreed with her husband. After a few more minutes of small talk we left Mrs. Lawson to cooking her meal for the masses, and I sat in the only empty seat left in the living room, which unfortunately happened to be on the couch beside Gabe. I sipped my wine, which was not going down well thanks to the night before, and tried to look comfortable.

A cry went up in the room when Gabe's sister, Luciana, switched the television from basketball to the Easter parade. "Ah, come on, Lucy!" Gabe protested.

"Stop your whining," she said, turning up the volume. Lucy, a family practice physician, was thin and statuesque like her mother, though blonde. Which I suspected, based on the rest of her family's coloring, came from frequent salon visits. "I promised the kids they could watch the parade."

The groans from the adults in the room were met with a cheer from the gaggle of kids seated in a semicircle in front of the television set, where brightly colored floats carrying waving Easter-themed characters drove slowly across the screen. Lucy was nearly fifteen years older than Gabe, and had three kids—two girls and a boy.

"Sometimes it's hard to believe we're related," Gabe said to Lucy, before joining the kids on the floor. She laughed and told him to get over it and grow up. I decided right then I loved his sister.

After stuffing myself with the traditional Italian meal Gabe's mom prepared—fried eggs filled with cheese, roasted fava beans and peas, asparagus risotto, braised lamb with artichokes, lasagna and a bread-like fruit cake shaped like a four-leaf clover—I went outside to get some fresh air and watch the kids kick a soccer ball around. I shivered in my thin wrap dress when the breeze picked up.

"Here, take this." Gabe's voice surprised me. Soon his jacket and the leftover warmth the material held from being on his body covered my shoulders.

"Thanks," I said, still watching the kids.

"I guess it had to happen eventually."

"What did?"

"Our first fight." Gabe leaned on the deck railing and twisted to look up at me.

"I guess so," I murmured. I wasn't quite ready to make up yet.

He sighed and looked out over the expansive lawn, where the kids laughed and ran between patio stones and garden beds. "I'll do it," he said. "I'll lie to our kids."

My stomach jumped. "Our kids?"

He turned so he was leaning back against the railing, facing me. He smiled, and the eye crinkles got me, again.

"Santa Claus. Easter Bunny. Tooth fairy. Full-moon fairy. Whatever. I'll do it," he said. "But I'm going to have to draw the line at the back-to-school gnome. Okay?"

I threw my arms around his neck and kissed him. "Okay," I said, relieved to be able to let go of the anger I'd been carrying around all day. Grateful to him for giving in.

"I'm sorry for what I said before," Gabe said, his voice softening as he pulled me closer. "You're going to be a great mom. The best." He kissed me on the nose, and I melted into him further.

"Thank you. And I didn't mean it, either. About the gene-pool thing."

He laughed. "You actually may have a point there," he said. "You've met my mother, right?" He raised one eyebrow, and I kissed him again.

"So, are you ready to go back inside?" he asked. "It's time for dessert."

"That wasn't dessert? That clover cake?"

"It was a dove," he said, laughing. He laced his fingers through mine and tugged me toward the door. "And nope.

That wasn't dessert. Welcome to Easter dinner with the Lawsons!"

I grumbled about being so stuffed one more bite might be the end of me, but let him lead me back inside. I managed a piece of ricotta-and-orange cake and a coffee, the whole time imagining when it would be our kids running around outside, waiting for the elaborate Easter egg hunt Gabe had spent hours putting together.

# 20

Somehow, despite the heat and the unfamiliar sounds of Bangkok at night, I manage to get a half-decent sleep. It's still early, the sun up but slung low in the sky. I'm in the restaurant checking my email on one of the communal laptops while Gabe sleeps, and enjoying a few minutes alone while I try to cool off. Even though I've had a cold shower, my skin is already slick with sweat again.

The shiny, metallic laptop stands out against the rest of the decor—dark wood furniture and a hand-sculpted statue of a Buddha in prayer, set against large ferns growing out of clay pots and a small pond teeming with goldfish. The guesthouse is basic. The toilet is literally a hole in the ground with two footsteps to mark direction—I would soon learn this was what all Thai washrooms are like—and yet feels exotic thanks to the ornamental wood, greenery and soothing sounds of flowing water. If I close my eyes, I can almost be in the waiting room of a spa back home. Almost.

"Thanks, Simon," I say as he places a second Thai coffee beside me. "I think I might be addicted to these. I may never leave." I sip the sweet, icy coffee and murmur my appreciation. "Consider yourself warned."

He smiles and claps his hands together. "Perfect! Works every time."

I push the laptop to the side, inviting him to sit with me. I'm happy to ignore my inbox for a moment, full of anxious messages from my parents, Anna and Connor, despite the four emails I sent letting them know all is okay. Only Jason seems unconcerned, offering up the name of a bar in Chiang Mai that I "have to visit," and a reminder to stay away from the "wacky tobacky." As if that even needs mentioning, here where only a hint of the green, leafy stuff could land you in jail indefinitely. Besides, the one and only time I smoked pot I ended up eating an entire bag of frozen French fries, straight from the freezer, and then falling asleep.

"So, how long have you been here?" I ask Simon.

"Here, like as in Shanti House, or here as in Thailand?"

"Both, I guess."

"Ten years in Thailand," he says, shaking his head as if not able to believe it himself. A long blond curl settles over one eye and he brushes it aside. He's very attractive, and seems to have the personality to match. I imagine the traveling women who stop at Shanti House, and probably some of the men, too, like spending time in his company. "And I've been running this place for seven. I took it over from a mate of mine who decided Indonesia was his next calling."

"Wow, that's a long time," I say, mentally calculating his age. It surprises me that he's likely in his midthirties. He looks younger than that. "What made you stay?"

"Ah, that's a good question with a short and a long answer." He smiles wide. "Which version do you want?"

"How about the short version first, then the long one," I reply. "You've got a captive audience here, as long as you keep these coffees coming."

"You got it," he says, brushing at the rogue curl again.

"Okay, so the short version is I came here for 'vacation—'" his fingers curl into air quotes around the word *vacation* "—which was really me escaping from taking over the family business from my dad. Then I stayed for a girl."

I raise an eyebrow and take another sip of my coffee. "A girl, huh?"

"Which brings me to the long version." Simon runs a hand through his thick, wavy hair. "She was Thai, and the most beautiful bird I'd ever seen." He shifts in his chair and sighs. "Her name was Sumalee, and she was a graduate student at the university. She was almost done her master's in business administration. Smart girl," he says, pride in his voice. "Anyway, I was a bit bored of the Khao San Road nightlife scene by this point, so a friend and I crashed this local wedding." He laughs. "We were the only non-Thais there, and after my friend passed out in a corner, I think Sumalee took pity on me."

Simon points to my almost empty glass. "Another one?"

"I think I better take a break," I say, holding out my hand so he can see the slight shake. "Is there a lot of caffeine in these?"

He nods. "A lot."

"Good to know." I take of sip from the so far ignored glass of water, which has little bits of tangy lemon pulp floating in it. My cheeks constrict with the shift from sweet to sour. "Okay, so you crashed the wedding, your friend passed out and you met Sumalee. Then what?"

"Well, she was there with her family. It was her cousin's wedding. She spoke amazing English and we just hit it off. One of those times where you think about serendipity, you know?"

I nod, thinking back to the night I met Gabe.

"So we were having this pretty intimate chat, knee-to-knee kind of stuff," he says. "Then my friend finally regains consciousness and comes to sit with us at the table, and when

I introduced him to Sumalee, he opened his mouth and… threw up everywhere." Simon's laughing so hard he has tears in his eyes, and I'm having a visceral reaction at the thought of being a part of that scene.

"Oh, my God," I say, cringing. "I would have died of embarrassment."

"I know, right?" He wipes his eyes with the back of his hand. "But Sumalee was amazing. Got the hotel staff to quickly clean it all up and then organized a ride for us back to the hostel. She came over the next morning, with breakfast and a gorgeous smile. I was smitten from that moment."

"She sounds pretty amazing."

Simon's eyes are slightly out of focus with the memory. "We fell in love," he says. "Fast and hard. I would have followed her anywhere. But turned out where she was going I couldn't go." Then his face changes, a darkness settling across his features. It's a look I recognize all too well. I wish I could take back the question, because I don't want to know what happened to her. I have a feeling I'm not going to like how the story ends.

All of a sudden the heat of the day blankets me, and I feel light-headed. I press the icy glass against my wrist, a trick Gabe learned from his high-school baseball coach. Apparently it's a quick way to bring down your body temperature. It seems to help a bit, and I feel less dizzy.

"I'm so sorry," I murmur because I'm not sure what else to say. I keep my eyes downcast to avoid Simon's expression.

"Ah, that's okay," he says. "I have a really lumpy head under this hair. Bald is not a good look for me. And this body would be lost under one of those monk's robes." I glance up at him as he pats his abs, smiling.

"Oh…sorry…what?" I stammer. "I thought you meant she was, like, gone." I flush, mortified I'd jumped to conclusions.

His eyes widen. "Oh, shit, you thought I meant she was *gone* gone?" He cuts the air with his hands, twice, like he's erasing something. "No, no, nothing like that. Sorry, mate. I really should watch how I put things." He chuckles and with relief, I join him.

"She became a Buddhist nun," Simon explains.

"You're right. That would have been hard to follow," I say. "What made her decide to do that?"

"We met this woman when we were in Chiang Rai on vacation, a Thai woman who became a nun after some thirty-five years as a lawyer. For whatever reason, Sumalee couldn't get that woman out of her head. And once she graduated, she gave up everything and joined her." He shrugs. "She broke my heart, but I didn't want to go back to Australia. Thailand was my home, so I stayed."

The restaurant is starting to fill, so after a few more minutes Simon heads off to take breakfast orders. I watch as he greets his guests, laughing easily and giving hugs and claps on the back.

I take one last sip of my coffee, log out and put the laptop back without answering the emails. Then I head back to the room, wishing the sadness of my story was simply a misunderstanding, too.

# 21

As instructed, I wear a long skirt that grazes my ankles and a thin, long-sleeve white cotton shirt. Even though the midday heat will reach unbearable temperatures, women cannot have exposed skin when visiting places of worship in Bangkok.

"I look like I belong in a traveling circus," I say, glancing down at my ensemble. The peasant skirt is old, from the last time they were in fashion, and has sparkly embellishments sewn into the length of its deep plum, crinkly fabric. It swishes around my legs when I walk, billowing out with the movement. "Or at best, I look like a hippie."

"It's perfect," Gabe says. "You'll fit right in with Vera."

"Ha-ha." I tug at my shirt to pull it down over the skirt as much as possible. "Speaking of Vera, better get going. She said it's best to get there early." I check my watch. "It's almost six fifteen."

"Ready whenever you are."

I clasp the pendant around my neck and tuck it under my shirt, giving it a gentle pat under the soft fabric. "Let's go," I say, grabbing my small backpack that holds sunscreen, a hat, the Thailand travel book and a camera.

Five minutes later I'm adding bottles of water and a bag

of pineapple and watermelon slices courtesy of Simon to the backpack, and we head out of the guesthouse to find a *tuk-tuk*.

"Even though *tuk* means cheap in Thai, the taxis are actually way cheaper. And a hell of a lot more comfortable," Bruce, Vera's boyfriend, says with a laugh. In my opinion, with his wild afro and retro Beatles T-shirt, he looks nothing like a Bruce—a name I associate more with golf shirts and Top-Siders. As if anticipating my next question, he adds, "But you haven't lived until you've taken a Thai *tuk-tuk* ride. Trust me."

I'm nervous, remembering the family crammed into the *tuk-tuk* on the cab ride to Shanti House. It seems like a less-than-smart way to travel in a city full of chaos and kamikaze driving.

"Also, backpack goes on your front and keep the straps inside the car," Bruce says as we walk toward the main road. "Bloody motorcycle thieves are fast."

"It's like a freaking adventure movie here," Gabe says. "I love it."

"That makes one of us," I mutter.

"Sorry?" Vera asks, turning around and walking backward so she can see my face.

"Thanks for the tips," I reply. I'm grateful Vera and Bruce offered their tour guide experience and don't want to give away the truth; I'm about as adventurous as a senior citizen switching up coffee shops.

"You got it," Vera says, catching back up to Bruce and linking her fingers through his. "We're going to have a blast." They kiss deeply without breaking stride or tripping on the uneven road, which is pretty impressive.

The first *tuk-tuk* driver we come upon speaks reasonable English, and offers his services for what seems like a very low rate. Bruce and Vera wave their hands at him, saying "No thanks" over and over, and keep walking. I smile uncomfortably at him as I pass, thinking of the family he probably has to feed.

"What's wrong with that one?" I ask, trying to keep up with Vera's long-legged strides.

"Biggest *tuk-tuk* scam in Thailand," Bruce says. "They offer to drive you around for next to nothing, if you agree to go into a few shops along the way."

"So they get kickbacks from the shops," Gabe says, and Vera nods.

"They know the shop owners?" I ask.

"Exactly. Usually family members," Vera says. "Or business relationships. They get things like gas coupons if their fares go in and look around."

Apparently the next driver isn't in to the scam, or at least wants the fare more, because Bruce motions for us to get in and after some uncomfortable positioning and shifting, we're on our way.

"Most of these cars are made for two passengers at best," Vera shouts from the front seat, over the noise of the motor. "But I've seen as many as eight people riding in one!"

I clutch the bar in front of me with one hand, while using the other to keep my backpack tight against my chest, and offer up a small prayer for safe travels. I wish Gabe were beside me, but Bruce sits between us in the back. With a lurch we're off, and my fingers instinctually grip the bar even tighter. The roads are packed with taxis and other *tuk-tuks*, along with a few brave souls on scooters and bicycles. Thick exhaust clogs my nostrils and throat and I cough, which leaves me with a layer of grit on my lips and teeth.

"All good?" Gabe leans around Bruce to check on me and I nod, not wanting to open my mouth again to the barrage of grime and dirt that swirls around us. Vera and Bruce point things out to us along the way, somehow managing to stay upright inside the *tuk-tuk* without hanging on to anything.

As we pass beautiful temples, called "Wats," covered in ornate gold and with intricate designs on every surface, I'm compelled to pull out my camera a few times. But each time I do the *tuk-tuk* veers around another car or pothole or pedestrian, and I need both hands again. A postcard will do just fine, I think. And I almost lose it when the driver takes his hands off the wheel at one point to bow in prayer fashion at a small golden shrine we whizz past.

"Whoa!" I shout, clutching Bruce's arm, which is the closest thing to my free hand.

"It's okay," Bruce says, placing his other hand over my white-knuckled one. "He's just giving a *wai* to that shrine back there."

"What's a *wai*?" Gabe asks.

"That's the customary Thai greeting. You'll see it a lot," Vera says. "Really important to the Thai people."

About ten minutes later we make it to our first stop and I tumble out of the *tuk-tuk*, grateful to have my feet on the ground again. While Bruce talks with the driver, making sure he'll stick around until we're done, Vera gives us some history on the temple.

"It's called Wat Benchamabophit, or the 'marble temple,'" she says. "The name actually means temple of the fifth king, and it's probably the most visited site in Bangkok."

Sure enough, despite it only being just before seven in the morning, there are quite a few tourists walking around. Even though it's so close to the road, the grounds surrounding the temple are peaceful, full of well-manicured shrubs and flowering bushes. As we walk up the gray stone walkway toward the Wat, which seemed to glimmer in the early morning light, Vera continues playing tour guide.

"It was designed by King Chulalongkorn's half brother, Prince Narai. They started building in 1899, at the request of King Chulalongkorn, who was the fifth king. He spent some time in training as a monk here, before the coronation, and his ashes are buried under one of the Buddha statues inside."

My hand goes to my neck at the mention of ashes, and my fingers gently play with the pendant.

"Is it common to see so much marble on temples in Thailand?" I ask. The Wat is an impressive display of marble slabs, columns and statues, with ornate gold details around the doors and windows, and along the layered, sloping rooflines.

"Good question," Vera says. "The prince and the king were both fond of Italian design. So the front of the temple, along with the pillars, and those two lion statues on either side?" Vera points to the statues that flank the entrance of the Wat, and Gabe and I follow her finger and nod. "Those are made of Carrara marble imported from Italy."

"Another cool thing is that the windows inside the temple are stained glass," Bruce adds, having caught up to us. "That's really unusual to see in Thailand."

The closer to the Wat we get, the more entranced I become. Every time my eyes sweep over a part of the temple, I notice something else. The intricacy of the gold awning over the entrance stairs. The glossy, bright red color framing the windows and doors. The perfect symmetry between the columns, and the way the marble slabs and golden window frames layer away from the front of the temple, like an opened fan. The sharp peaks of the roof, rising and dipping with each section of the temple, like ocean waves along the horizon.

"Beautiful, isn't it?" Gabe whispers.

"It's breathtaking," I say.

"It really is," Vera agrees. "I've been here more than a dozen times, and the feeling is always the same. Like I'm seeing it for the first time."

We pay our entrance fee of twenty *baht*, which is less than one American dollar, and make our way to the courtyard, where Bruce promises something "fucking mind-blowing." As we cross the gleaming marble that lines the courtyard, I hear it. The mingling of multiple voices coming together to make one consistent sound.

Though I can't understand the words, the rhythm of the chanting is melodic and pulls me closer, from somewhere deep in my gut. The doors are open to the inside of the temple, where dozens of bald monks wearing tangerine-orange robes sit in rows, their legs bent to the side on the deep red carpeted platform. Their backs are to us, feet hiding under their long robes, and as they chant they bow in unison to the massive golden Buddha statue at the front of the room.

I'm overcome.

Dropping to my knees on the carpet behind the praying monks, I close my eyes, listening to their melody. Gabe, kneeling beside me, whispers, "These are the moments, babe. These are the memories that will fill that space." I nod and open my eyes, blinking a few times to move the tears away so I can see everything clearly.

The shock of the slap against my bare feet makes me gasp, and I look back to see an old monk in glasses walk by, his orange robe swishing around his legs and his hands on the ends of a long rope sash around his waist. He doesn't look at me, and I wonder if it was simply his robe that caught on my feet, which now sting a little.

But then I notice Vera and Bruce laughing, hands over their mouths to stifle the noise. "What?" I ask, keeping my voice low.

"Your…feet…" Vera says, trying to control herself. "Your feet…are…"

"You just got schooled by a monk who's half your size and at least four times your age," Bruce whispers, chuckling. He twists and gestures at something behind us.

Then I realize what they mean. The way I kneeled down made my bare feet point directly at one of the revered Buddha statues behind me. Simon explained yesterday that feet are considered the lowliest and dirtiest part of the body, so to be careful to never point them at someone, and especially not toward someone's head. "And for the love of all things good, never ever point your feet at a religious statue," he said. "That's the fastest way to piss the Thai off." I was so caught up in the moment, I forgot to tuck my feet up underneath me like is customary in Thailand. And clearly the monk, and his rope sash, was not pleased with my lack of courtesy.

"Move your feet, Teg, he's coming back," Gabe whispers, and I quickly move them to the side. "Look at you," he continues in my ear, as the monk does another pass without touching my feet this time. "Breaking rules and pissing off the monks. That's my girl."

The laughter bubbles inside my belly and I know I'm not going to be able to keep it in. We quickly leave the chanting monks and make it back to the courtyard before I lose it, laughing so hard tears roll down my cheeks in unstoppable streams. People stare at us like we're crazy, or drunk, but I don't care. I clutch at my stomach and try to catch my breath. It has been a long time since I've laughed this damn hard, and I don't ever want to stop.

It's late, and we've just gotten back from our tour of Bangkok. Along with the Wat where my feet were slapped, we were blessed by a monk with a lily flower dipped in whatever the

Thai version of holy water is; saw the giant reclining Buddha and the Golden Buddha; ate pad Thai Bruce claimed was the best in Bangkok; and booked the Chiang Mai leg of the trip with a travel agent, who also happened to be a local mechanic and taxi driver. In the past few days I've really come to respect the Thai people: they make everything beautiful, from their temples to their food, and are certainly industrious.

"What a day," Gabe says.

"What a day," I agree. I lie in underwear and a tank top under the bedsheet, watching the palm shaped ceiling fan make lazy circles. I start to laugh, thinking of the monk again.

"I love that sound," Gabe says, lying down beside me.

"What? Me laughing?" I keep my eyes on the hypnotic fan.

"Yes."

"Me, too. I need to do more of it." But a familiar heaviness settles onto my chest, almost as if the weight of the pendant around my neck triples. I pick it up in my fingers and move it back and forth along its chain.

"You will. This was a good day, Tegan. A really good day."

"Yes, it was," I murmur, eyes blinking heavily against sleep.

"Sweet dreams, love," Gabe whispers, his fingers tickling my palm before taking hold of my hand.

"Sweet dreams." I leave my hand in his and allow my eyes to close and stay shut, and a minute later I'm sound asleep.

# 22

I sigh, and rest my forehead against my fingertips. With the other hand I start writing.

Mom & Dad—

Okay, it's a start. But I only have ten minutes until I have to be downstairs for the taxi. This letter needs to get written, because I know its arrival in my parents' mailbox is directly tied to my mother's peace of mind. And stressing her out any more than I already have just seems cruel. I sigh again, and Gabe sits beside me on the bed. I keep my eyes on the blank note card, but feel him watching me.

"I'm waiting for inspiration," I say. "I hate writing letters. You know that." I run my hand over the note card, brushing away a few crumbs from the potato chips I'm calling breakfast. "What's wrong with email?" I grumble.

"Your mom and dad just want to know you're okay," Gabe says. "That's all you really need to write."

"Right," I say, pen poised back over the blank card. "I'll just tell them I'm okay."

"Because you are, right? You're doing okay?"

"I'm doing surprisingly okay."

"Good. Then tell them that," Gabe says. "And I'll stop talking so you can get it done. It's almost time to go."

I take another stack of the oily chips and crunch into them, and then start writing again, balancing the book that's acting as a table against my crossed knees

How are things at home? Everything is good here. Bangkok has been amazing so far. Full of energy and beautiful architecture and all sorts of bizarre customs. Did you know it's considered bad luck to get a haircut on a Wednesday, so all the barbershops close? No one is sure exactly why, but it apparently has something to do either with a king who used to summon all the barbers to cut his hair on Wednesdays, or that Wednesdays were for growing crops, not cutting them down.

It's a different world here for sure. But they definitely know how to make a coffee worth getting up for. Dad, you would love the coffee here. I'll try to make it for you when I come home. The guy who runs Shanti House, Simon, gave me the recipe so I can bring you to the dark side with me.

Met a couple of other travelers, "real" travelers, like ones who are probably never going back home again kind of travelers—don't worry, Mom, I promise I'm coming home—who like to play tour guides in their "spare" time, and we visited a few different Wats, what they call temples of worship here, all over Bangkok. I even got my feet slapped by an old monk! File that one under experiences I never thought I'd have.

Heading to Chiang Mai today so I need to make this letter short. I'll write you a longer letter on the train ride, which is about twelve hours. But the scenery is supposed to be worth the trip. If I can find a half-decent connection I'll send you a few pictures.

Tell Connor thanks for the inflatable pillow and the bug spray—I've been using both a lot. And tell Jase I'm staying away from the "wacky tobacky"—and before you get mad at him for even mentioning it, don't forget he's just looking out for me. In the way only Jase can.

Love to all—Tegan xo

I start folding the letter then as an afterthought, open it back up and write a postscript at the bottom.

I'm doing okay. I'm taking my medication and think it's really starting to help. Love you both. See you soon.

I fold the letter quickly and put it into one of the self-addressed envelopes from my mom, licking it shut. Simon told me he'd take care of mailing it for me, so I tuck it under my arm and grab my backpack with the other hand.

"Ready?" Gabe asks, his backpack already on.

"Yup." I hoist one of the backpack's padded straps over my shoulder. "Let's go."

"I'm going to miss it here," Gabe said.

"Me, too." I take a last glance around the simple yet comforting room that has been home for the past few days.

Vera, Bruce and Simon, who gives me an iced coffee to go, are waiting to say goodbye in the lobby. I feel surprisingly emotional when Vera gives me a very tight hug, making me promise to stay in touch. I know that means a few emails will be exchanged, perhaps a couple of photos, then we'll simply become vague yet nostalgic memories to one another. Regardless, I take her hug gladly and Simon snaps a picture of us on my phone, so I won't forget her crazy dreadlocks and rosebud lips.

"Thanks for getting up, you guys. You didn't have to," I say, giving Bruce a hug. He looks like he's just tumbled out of bed, which he probably has since it's only five thirty in the morning.

"Of course we did," Bruce replies, smiling through a yawn. "We've shared Thip Samai pad Thai. That binds us as forever friends."

I grin, and he hands me a folded piece of paper. "As promised, all the must-do things in Chiang Mai. And get that Thai massage, okay? At least one."

"Promise." I tuck the paper into the top of my backpack.

"Don't forget," Bruce adds, holding up a hand. "If it's hot, eat the lot. If it's cold, you're gold, and if it's—"

"In between, flee the scene," Gabe and I say in unison, and I give Bruce a high five. "Got it." Bruce said he's never had food poisoning in Thailand, which he attributes to the what-to-eat mantra he learned from a fellow traveler years before.

"Any other last-minute tips?" I ask.

"Well, you know the shoe thing," Bruce says, referring to the Thai custom to always remove your shoes before entering someone's home, "and from personal experience, the foot thing." We all laugh, remembering the monk. "Don't touch anyone's head, that's considered rude, and definitely no nude sunbathing." Bruce winks. "They're really not into that kind of thing."

"Refrain from nudity, got it," Gabe says, laughing.

"Oh, and I learned this the hard way when I first got here—" Vera gives us a wry smile "—but under no circumstances should you refer to someone's baby as 'cute' or 'adorable.'"

"Why not?" I ask.

"Apparently they think if you say a baby is cute, the evil spirits will snatch it away," Bruce says, yawning again and giving his unruly hair a rub. "They give their kids nicknames like 'Moo,' which means pig, or 'Looknam,' which is Thai for mosquito larvae."

"You've got to be kidding me," I say.

"Moo?" Gabe shakes his head. "Can you imagine if we did that back home?"

Vera laughs. "Consider yourself warned."

Simon motions to the front gate, where a taxi has pulled up. "I hate to break up the party, but you better get going."

"You're right," Gabe replies, and I glance at my watch.

"Thanks again for this." I hold up the take-out coffee cup. "You read my mind."

"You're very welcome." He kisses me on the cheek and gives a tight squeeze. "And Alice is expecting you, so just give this address to the taxi driver in Chiang Mai." Simon arranged a room at his friend's guesthouse after he saw the place I booked online, which he claims is overpriced and, worse, makes terrible coffee.

"Much appreciated," Gabe says.

"She'll take good care of you," Simon adds. "Hers is the best guesthouse in Chiang Mai. You'll love it."

After another round of hugs, it's time to go. Bangkok is still in the dark, the streets fairly quiet. In contrast, the train station is bustling with what seems to be an equal split of backpack-laden adventurers and locals. Despite the language barriers it's easy enough to the find the train, which is weathered, with scratched paint and dented metal here and there. But the vinyl-padded seat is more comfortable than it looks. Although I'm not sure if I'll still think so after a dozen hours.

Thankfully I'm facing forward, as I can't imagine my stomach would do well riding backward all the way to Chiang

Mai. Across from me is another bank of seats, empty for now, and I rest my feet on the edge and shimmy lower until I feel a groove in the lumpy padding.

Zipping open the top of my backpack, I pull out an envelope. It's crumpled, which doesn't really matter, but I try to smooth it out regardless.

"Hard to believe we're here doing this, right?" Gabe sits beside me on the vinyl-padded seat.

I nod, releasing the flap from the envelope. "I know. I thought it was going to be a really long time until we got here." *It should have been much, much longer.*

"I know what you're thinking, Teg, but don't."

"How can I not?" I open the note. "This wasn't supposed to be our story." I try to keep the bitterness out of my voice but fail. The shifts in emotion still surprise me. Or perhaps it's more how rapidly I can go from feeling okay, even able to laugh at a joke, to being sad and enraged. I feel like a ship in the middle of a wicked storm—the side-to-side sway extreme and alarming.

"No, it wasn't." Gabe sighs deeply. He leaves it at that, which is likely wise.

Running my fingers over the black inked letters on the note, I shiver. When we wrote this wish, after Gabe saw it on one of his nature shows and insisted it had to go on the list, I never believed it would really happen.

"Remember what you said to me when I wrote that one down?" Gabe asks.

I don't respond, just continue tracing the letters with my index finger. The train starts moving, slowly at first, and I tuck myself a little lower in my seat, but still high enough to be able to watch everything go by out the dusty window.

"After you told me how mean you thought it was, to make animals do that..." Gabe begins.

"And you promised me they are well taken care of," I say. "And they like doing it...although I have no idea how you know that for sure."

"Yes, after that you said, 'It's like going halfway around the world to see something I get to see every day at work.'" Gabe laughs.

"Well, it's true." I let the corners of my mouth turn up in a smile. "Their skills are about on par."

"I think the elephants might be offended to hear that," Gabe says. "That they only paint as well as a five-year-old? Geesh."

My smile widens as I think of the kids in my class. After the accident they sent a giant handmade "Get Well Soon" card, with their names scrawled in large lowercase letters on every space not occupied by a picture of a flower, butterfly, dog or fire truck. It feels like years rather than months since I've been in the classroom. I barely recognize that life anymore. It was so easy, so free of real problems.

Coming back to the train, to the note, I read it out loud. "'Buy a piece of art painted by an elephant...in Thailand.'"

"It's going to be awesome," Gabe says, excitement filling his voice. "I even thought of the perfect spot to hang it at home."

"Where?" I ask, my eyes trying to adjust to the fast-moving greenery outside the window, now that the sun has risen. Feeling off-kilter by the staccato movement, I rub my eyes and rest my head back against the seat.

"In the hall, right next to the light switch at the front door."

"Why there?"

"Because it will be the last thing you see before you leave, and the first thing you see when you come home," Gabe says. Then he softens his voice. "And it will remind you that if an elephant can hold a paintbrush in its trunk and create a work of art, there isn't anything you can't do."

"Huh," I say. I take a sip from the bottle of water on my

lap. "Is that the best you've got?" I ask, taking another swig of the water. "Because…it's pretty lame."

"Lame?" Gabe feigns insult. "Not nice, Teg, not nice at all."

I shrug. "Just thought you could do better."

"Is that a challenge?" he asks, and I'm reminded of our early dating days. When every conversation was peppered with little jokes and quick-witted jabs, the ultimate goal to produce a laugh as often as possible. Back when we were giddy with the possibility of what we could become to each other.

"Fine, it can go in the front hall," I say. "But only because that wall has always been too bare."

"I'll take it," Gabe replies, his laugh deep and full, his eyes crinkling. The sound of his laugh ignites warmth deep in my belly, and I curl my arms around myself protectively, trying to keep it there.

# 23

The train ride is long, but uneventful. After a meal of fragrant red curry and jasmine rice, a handful of plastic wrapped, triangular-shaped candies with the consistency of gelatin and an odd flavor, and two ice-cold Singha beers that taste like the lush landscape outside—crisp and green—I fall asleep, my head resting against the window. I wake once, when I hear voices shouting to look outside, and see a large pack of monkeys through the train's windows. The monkeys run beside the train and hang from nearby trees, and I wonder for a moment if I'm still asleep and dreaming.

It's dark when the train arrives at Chiang Mai station, the air still warm but not sticky and cloying like in Bangkok. Being farther north now, the air smells different. Less inhabited and hectic, like country air after spending too long in the city.

The taxi ride to the guesthouse is quick, and I only grab the handle over the window once, when another car darts in front of us, bumpers somehow missing each other. The driver lets out a string of Thai words I can only assume are of the cursing variety, and pounds on the steering wheel. I clutch the handle with both hands to keep from flying into the front seat.

"Chicago traffic is going to seem like nothing after this," Gabe says, sounding a little nervous.

"Seriously." I lift my pack back onto the seat from the floor, where it tumbled with the jerk of the car. I loop my fingers through the straps and let go of the handle. "These drivers must have nine lives."

As promised, Alice is up waiting and is as lovely as Simon said. Though I expected someone closer to Simon's age, Alice looks to be in her midsixties, with pronounced wrinkles across her face that almost seem like they've been carved with a fine hand and artistic vision. Her blue eyes are bright, as if tiny lights shine behind the irises, and her hand is smooth, dry and warm when she takes my own.

"Welcome to Alice's Guest Lodge," she says, her arms opening in a welcome gesture and her wrinkles deepening with her smile. "I imagine you want to get some sleep so why don't I show you to your room and we'll catch up in the morning?"

"Thank you," Gabe says. "It was a long day."

"Those trains aren't the best for sleeping, are they?"

"It wasn't too bad." I shrug against the arm Alice has wrapped around my shoulder, guiding me through the door. She lets her embrace drop, and I hope she doesn't think I'm trying to shake her off. It felt nice, having her arm around me like that. She reminds me of my mom, though she's at least half a foot taller and graying, whereas Mom still likes to pretend her brown hair doesn't come from a bottle. "Better than I expected, to be honest."

"Good, good," Alice says, walking ahead of us and pulling a key out of her pocket. She bends over slightly to put the key in the lock, and with a swift turn and click, the door opens. The room is small but cozy, with a light duvet covering the bed, which is flanked by two narrow nightstands. There's also a wooden desk and chair against one wall, and a window seat stacked high with pillows, some with whirling, colorful tie-dyed fabric and others bearing embroidered Buddhas and crown-wearing elephants. I take a deep breath and smell oranges, along with a sharp, herbal scent I can't quite place.

"Tea tree oil," Alice says. "We only clean with natural oils here, which means nothing toxic for the environment and lovely smelling rooms for our guests." She smiles and waves her hand in a beckoning motion. "Come in, come in."

"This is perfect," I say. "Thank you." The bed calls to me and I yawn, trying to hide it behind my hand.

"You're tired," Alice says. "I'm going to make up a small plate so you can sleep on a full stomach, sound good?"

"Sounds perfect," Gabe replies, and I nod.

"Be back in a jiffy."

"She's awesome," Gabe says, after Alice shuts the door behind her. I murmur in agreement. "She sort of reminds me of your mom."

"I know, right?"

"Are you missing home?" Gabe asks.

"Not exactly." I say, but I don't elaborate. I both miss home and loathe the idea of being back there, trapped in an apartment full of reminders I have no capacity to deal with. Like the silver baby rattle from Gabe's parents I found when I was packing, stuffed in the back of my linen closet and still in its box.

I dump my backpack into the chair and walk around the room, poking my head into the washroom. "Oh, my God!" I step back out quickly.

"What? Is it a bug?" Apparently the bugs get bigger the farther north you go in Thailand, and giant cockroaches are as commonplace here as the black houseflies that invade our Chicago apartment every spring.

"There's an actual toilet," I say, laughing. "Like a real flushing one!" I've never been so happy to see a porcelain bowl in all my life. "Simon was right. I love this place."

After using the fancy toilet, I go sit on the window seat. I push the delicate woven blinds to the side and gaze into the blackness beyond the window.

"What are you thinking about?" Gabe asks.

"What's out there," I say, keeping my eyes on the darkened window.

"Adventure! Excitement! Painting elephants!" Gabe's enthusiasm makes him sound like a sports announcer, or a big-top circus ringmaster.

I smile, and let the blind fall back to cover the window. "The damn painting elephants," I say. "This had better be worth it."

"It will be," Gabe murmurs. "I promise. It will all be worth it."

*That's what I'm counting on.* I lie on the bed and put my hands behind my head, sighing as my body relaxes into the duvet. Gabe lies beside me and the familiar feel of his body next to mine helps me relax further.

Though I don't say it out loud, I think about how I'm starting to feel like myself again.

# 24

It starts in the most beautiful, magical way. Gabe, running his hands and warm lips over my naked body. I quiver with his touch, my body jumping to attention with the knowledge of what's coming next. It has been so long…so long…and I want nothing more than to have his mouth consume me, and for us to become one again.

Then, as dreams do, the slideshow changes and I'm standing in front of our closet mirror in our Chicago bedroom wearing a pristine white bathrobe, Gabe's hands around my burgeoning belly. His eyes close and his breath is warm against my neck. He smiles. I smile back, even though somehow I know he can't see it. I stare at my belly pushing out the robe's fluffy fabric, at the beauty of what it means. And then I'm suddenly filled with inexplicable sadness and my smile melts away. I begin to sob. It's ugly, and I don't want to watch myself in the mirror, but I do.

Gabe doesn't move. He stays as he is, hands around me and releasing slow, warm breaths against my neck as I shake. This goes on for a while, Gabe standing still and me sobbing in his arms. It's as if we're having two separate experiences.

A moment later, the robe slips off and my naked body is on full display in the mirror. Gabe's hands have dropped away at some point, and now I see something is very wrong. My stomach is flat, with an angry red line running across it just above my pubic bone. The incision is new, I can tell. The medical staples glint in the light. In horror, I watch as the staples begin to release, one at a time, hitting the mirror with the force and leaving small, bloody marks on its surface. *Pop. Pop.* Gabe's eyes remain closed, his breathing even, the strange half smile still on his face. *Pop, pop, pop,* the staples go.

Blood starts to pour from the incision. I'm now wide-open, bleeding onto our hardwood floor, and my no longer white robe is lying at my feet.

At some point during the chaos, Gabe disappears.

I open my mouth to scream, but no sound comes out.

"You don't look great," Gabe says. "What's the matter?"

We've been awake for a while, but I'm still feeling off. Shaky, unsettled. Like a too tightly strung guitar string, one strum away from snapping. Looking in the bathroom mirror I see what he does. Face pale, with gray circles under slightly puffy eyes that are more red than brown. Lips dry and chapped, pressing together in a tight line.

"I'm just worn-out." I pinch my cheeks, making bright red circles that fade soon after.

"We don't have to do the elephants today, Teg," Gabe says, frowning. "You could just rest."

"I had a crappy sleep, that's all."

"You tossed and turned a lot. Bad dreams?"

"No." *Yes.* "Nothing like that."

He pauses. "Do you want to talk about it?"

Damn, he knows me too well. I've never been a good liar to begin with, but Gabe can always tell when I'm not being honest.

"Not really."

"It might help," he says. "Maybe I can be like your sand-man, sprinkling good dreams—"

"Gabe, stop." Frustration seeps out of me. How can I explain this rush of hot anger is all because of a bad dream? That's not rational. Plus, I've realized I'm not doing as well as I want to be, as I keep saying I am. A breakdown feels like it's one nightmare away. "I don't want to talk about it, okay? It was nothing. Just a stupid dream. Drop it."

"Fine." He's exasperated, but tries to rein it in. "I'm just trying to help."

"I don't want to do this right now," I say, lowering my voice. Trying to change my tone. I close my eyes and rub them hard enough that I see stars for a few moments when I open them again. "I need a few minutes to get ready, okay?" I start arranging my small bag of toiletries, looking for the bottle.

Though I don't look at him, I know he's hurt at my not-so-subtle dismissal. "Okay," he says. "I'll just… I'll be back in a bit."

Once alone, I snap open the top of the prescription bottle and shake out one little pill.

"I'm going to prescribe you Ativan along with the anti-depressant," Dr. Rakesh said at our last appointment, when I told him about the trip. "It's an antianxiety medication and works fairly quickly. But follow the dosage instructions and don't drink alcohol or drive while you're taking it. It's a short-term fix, but many patients find it helps when they're feeling anxious."

The tiny pill disintegrates under my tongue, leaving a chalky feel in my mouth. Dr. Rakesh said it would take about twenty minutes to start working, and that while I would mostly feel like myself, I would also feel calmer.

The water is hot and soon steam fills the small bathroom. Normally when I shower, I try to get in and out as quickly as I can. I don't like being naked because it's the only time I can't hide my scars. And looking at them, or running my soapy hands over them, never fails to depress me. For one thing, they remind me of what I lost in the accident, and I try not to think about that. But it's the permanency of what they mean that haunts me, that makes me feel like a failure.

I can't do the one thing my body was intended for. And even though I would tell anyone else in my situation it simply isn't true, this makes me feel like less of a woman.

So I try to avoid my scars.

Turning off the water only five minutes later, I grab a bath towel and wrap it around myself, wondering when Gabe will come back.

# 25

I'm not sure if it's the Ativan or the hot shower, but by the time we arrive at the Maesa Elephant Camp I feel better.

In fact, anyone watching me—squealing as I try to stay in the *howdah* basket carriage on the elephant's back, and laughing with delight every time she takes a banana from my hand—would assume I'm a carefree twentysomething on a romantic holiday; my biggest worry finding a job when I get back to the real world.

"What did I tell you?" Gabe asks from behind me. I squeal again and try to shimmy backward to avoid sliding down the elephant's large head as she ducks to grab some grass. My hands clutch at her skin, which is thick, leathery and covered in long wiry hair.

"This is freaking awesome!" I say, patting her head. "Good girl, Mali. Want some sugarcane?" As if understanding me, she tosses her trunk up and holds it there like a vacuum hose, curling it around the piece of sugarcane I hold out. She unfurls her trunk and pops the cane in her mouth, chomping as she lumbers along the trail.

Bin, Mali's *mahout*, what the Thai call the elephant's caregiver, gives a thumbs-up and a toothy grin as he leads her through the knee-deep stream. We pause in the middle of the river and Mali sprays water all over herself. Which also means we get drenched in the process. I sputter and wipe water from my eyes, laughing with Gabe all the while.

After an hour the ride is over, and I give Mali's dry and dusty skin a few more rubs once I dismount from the *howdah*. I can only reach just below her ear, she's that tall, but then she bends her head and nuzzles her trunk into my hand.

"Thank you for the ride, Mali." I caress her trunk with both hands.

"She's beautiful, isn't she?" Gabe says. "Those eyes…it's like she can see right through us, you know?"

Mali's lids blink, as if in response, her lashes long and plentiful. "Thanks, Bin," I say. "That was the best elephant ride I've ever had. Really, the only one I've ever had, but I'm sure it will always be the best."

"You welcome! She like you," Bin says, giving us another thumbs-up. "You watch the show?"

"We wouldn't miss it," Gabe says.

"Can't wait." I smile at Bin, and give Mali another few pats on her trunk.

"Good, good." Bin walks Mali around in a circle to turn her around so she's ready to join the group of elephants getting ready for the show. "Start in ten minute, okay?"

"Oh, wow, Gabe," I say, breathing deeply. The air is fragrant with greenery and fresh elephant dung. "This place is amazing."

"I don't want to say I told you so, but…"

"It's okay, you can." I close my eyes and take in another deep breath. "You were right, again."

"I know," Gabe says with just the right amount of cockiness. "We should probably get seats."

I glance at the large dirt arena some twenty feet away. A circle of rustic wooden benches that are quickly filling with other tourists surrounds it. Gabe starts walking toward the arena, but I don't follow.

"Gabe, wait."

"What's up?" He turns back and raises one eyebrow. It gives him a somewhat comical look, which makes me smile.

"Thank you."

He pauses, his eyebrow dropping back to its regular place on his face and his eyes lighting up. They are the most beautiful color of blue. Like a perfect, cloudless sky. "You're welcome."

"Ready?" he asks, extending his hand.

I take it. "Ready."

The elephants parade and paint, holding brushes in their trunks and dipping into pots of colorful paints their *mahouts* have in their hands. The audience cheers, as blank canvases soon become masterpieces with flowers, trees and Thai landscapes.

"That's the one I want," Gabe whispers, and I know exactly which one he's talking about. It's a self-portrait, done by a male elephant named Phaya. It looks like modern art, with plenty of white space surrounding the deep red lines that outline the elephant's profile. It's only partially colored in with red paint, which almost appears to be an artistic decision versus one due to time constraints. Once the painting has dried and been rolled into a cardboard tube, it's time to leave and head back to the guesthouse.

I lean back against the taxi's sticky vinyl seat and smile, remembering the feeling of riding on Mali's back. "I'll never forget today," I say. The driver glances in the rearview mirror, perhaps wondering if I'm trying to get his attention, then thankfully gives his focus back to the road.

"Me, neither." Gabe sounds so happy it almost makes me cry.

"What should we do with the note? From the jar?" he asks. "I feel like we need to burn it or something, to make it official. Our very first list item, checked off."

I turn to stare out the half-opened window, watching the strange and beautiful Thai landscape whip by. Traffic noise fills the taxi along with the wind's whistle, which carries with it a cornucopia of smells—everything from exhaust, to fragrant jasmine, to hot asphalt. "I took an Ativan today," I say, my voice soft, then add, "I'm sorry." Though I'm not sure what I'm sorry about, exactly.

Gabe pauses for a minute before responding. "That's okay. You have nothing to be sorry about."

"I know." Though I feel almost compelled to apologize again, for apologizing.

"You know, one day you're going to walk by that elephant painting on the wall and smile. A big goofy smile," Gabe says. "You won't think of all the terrible things that happened before that painting. You'll just remember this amazing day, when you watched an elephant paint a picture of himself under the Thai sunshine."

I start to cry, but my tears dry quickly with the breeze—leaving fine rivulets in the dirt already layered on my skin.

"If that's what you need to be able to enjoy these moments, Tegan, then take the damn pills. Take them every day if you have to, okay?"

"Okay."

The taxi slows and pulls up to the guesthouse and I see Alice, flying out the front door with a look on her face that makes my stomach drop.

# 26

"Tegan, I am fine, sweetheart, just fine," Dad says, his voice gravelly. He clears his throat a couple of times. Something beeps incessantly in the background, and I can hear Mom's voice close by.

"Richard, I want to talk with her when you're finished."

"You are not fine!" I wipe a shaking hand across my forehead. "You had a heart attack, Dad."

I'm on an old-school rotary phone in Alice's office, which is essentially an open-air room that looks out onto the back of the guesthouse's property. It has a thatched roof, an old computer that takes up most of the surface of the simple teak desk, plus two wooden chairs and a small filing cabinet. There are two framed pictures on the wall behind the desk, a photo of Alice and three small blonde girls whom I assume are her grandchildren, and a Maesa elephant painting of a rubber tree.

I transfer the bulky handset to my other ear, my palms slick with anxious sweat. I can't believe how stupid it was to leave my cell phone behind today, carelessly tossed onto the bed's covers before walking out the door. I think about what could have happened, and press my lips tightly closed to prevent the sobs trying to escape me. I need to be strong. It's my turn to be strong.

"A mild heart attack," Dad repeats. "I'm only going to be in the hospital for a day or two, then I'll be home and your mother will take good care of me."

"Did you call Gabe's dad?"

"Yes, yes, he's been here. Don't worry, Tegan. Everyone is taking excellent care of me."

"I'm flying home tomorrow," I say, my mouth set in a tight line.

"You will do no such thing. I will not have you coming home for this."

"Well, guess what, Dad? You don't get to decide, okay?" I'm starting to unravel, my voice high-pitched and weak, my lips trembling. *Hold it together, Tegan.*

"Janet, tell our daughter I'm okay, will you? She's trying to tell me she's coming home." There's a shuffling sound, my mom's voice muffled by something, then she's on the phone.

"Your dad is okay, Tegan. We don't want you to come home."

"You sound tired, Mom. Are you okay?" I glance at my watch—6:07 p.m., which means it's only six o'clock in the morning in Chicago.

"It's been a long night, but yes, I'm okay. And so is Dad. The doctors said he was very lucky. It was mild and there's been no damage to his heart." Mom lets out a long sigh I recognize as her stress sigh. I've heard it a lot over the past six months. "The boys are both here."

"Can I talk to Connor?" I ask, crying now but trying to keep her from hearing it in my voice. I don't want my mom worrying about anyone but Dad, and I know Connor will tell me straight up if I need to come home.

"He and Jason just left to get some breakfast, but I'll tell them you said hello," Mom says. "Are you taking your medication?"

I close my eyes. "Yes, Mom, I am taking my medication," I reply. "Please, don't worry about me. I'm fine. It's Dad we need to focus on. I really think I should come home."

"You stay put, sweetheart. I promise I'll call if anything changes. There's nothing you can do here, though I love you for offering to come home," she says. "Now, tell me. What adventures did you get to today? Thailand is somewhere your dad and I have always wanted to visit."

I know they don't want me coming home because they're afraid. This trip is supposed to be the catalyst to getting their old Tegan back, the one who loves her life and sees positivity as a basic life skill. *This trip is going to heal her,* they probably whisper to each other at night before they fall asleep.

Gabe sits with me quietly while I give my mom a few details about the elephant camp, trying to infuse some energy into my voice. It's a good effort on my part, and Mom sounds less stressed by the time we get off the phone ten minutes later.

I hang up but don't move, still staring at the grounds beyond the office. The low shrubs and greenery are beginning to lose their vibrant color with the fading sun. Soon it will be dark again.

"What do you want to do?" Gabe asks.

*I want to go home. I want to make sure my dad is really okay. I want to see Anna. I want to go back three hours, so I can feel happy again.*

"I have no idea," I say. "They really don't want me coming home." Part of me is upset my mom was so quick to turn down my offer, which is ridiculous because I'm sure any one of them would switch places with me in a second.

"Your dad is tough," Gabe says. "You get that from him, you know."

"That's what I'm worried about. If he has his way he'll be back at work the day after they release him." Dad is a partner at a small accounting firm, and loves his job more than I think is normal for someone who has been working for that many years.

"Your mom won't let him leave the house," Gabe says. "Because she's even tougher than your dad."

He's right. I imagine my mom handcuffing Dad to the sofa table and barring the doors if she has any inkling he might try to do something other than rest.

"Do you still feel like going out? We can stay here if you want."

Chiang Mai's market is on the agenda for the evening. I'm not sure I'm up for it, but the thought of staying here isn't all that appealing, either. It's too quiet. Which means I'll have too much time to think.

"Not really, but let's go anyway. I just want to let Alice know everything is okay, and then I'll hop in the shower."

Gabe smiles and I close my eyes, clutching tightly to the pendant around my neck.

"Do you really think he's okay?" I ask, lip quivering as I think about the what-ifs.

"I do," Gabe says. "Now, let's make sure you're okay, too."

# 27

Chiang Mai's Night Bazaar is exactly as Vera and Bruce described: crowded, frenzied and electric—the air buzzing with the frenetic energy of vendors making deals and shoppers moving from stand to stand. Smells, some delicious and now familiar, and some less so, mingle from stands that look as though they were built that afternoon, with scraps of wood and threadbare fabrics.

The market stretches along Chang Khlan Road, the outdoor vendors practically set on top of one another, and other more established-looking shops line the interior of a low-rise building. Seems here you can get everything and anything, from unbelievably cheap knockoff T-shirts, watches and purses, to golden Buddha statues, jeweled figurines and richly embroidered textiles, along with enough cheap food to fill hungry bellies on budgets.

Backpackers are everywhere, mixing with the locals like oil and water. The Thai bustle from shop to shop, often as families, with young kids in carriers on their backs. They buy vegetables and fruit, plus meat, fish and eggs, which have probably been sitting out all day in the hot sun as is customary here. The travelers, by comparison, sip bottles of beer and casually stop at the stands selling batiked sarongs and carved wooden elephants. They also frequent the "fast-food" stands, which serve up noodles in small cardboard containers and overcooked mystery meats on sticks. There's a particularly rowdy bunch of young men and women at one stand, daring each other to eat the salted, roasted grasshoppers and deep-fried bamboo worms considered a delicacy.

"Want to get a drink?" Gabe asks. I do. The night air in Chiang Mai has cooled significantly, but a cold drink still sounds good. I'm feeling more relaxed, though still stressed about Dad. Mom promised to call if there's any sort of update and I check my phone every few minutes, just to make sure it's working despite the unpredictable cell service.

Sipping my Singha beer, I walk into one of the shops. Inside are figurines and lacquerware dishes, along with rows of textiles hanging like freshly washed laundry from ropes strung end to end along the shop's ceiling. It's the kind of place I could spend an hour in, and the sort of place Gabe is ready to leave after a minute.

I finger the fabrics and walk around alone, Gabe having disappeared as expected into a menswear shop next door. The silky material caresses my shoulders as I move through the shop. A batiked sarong catches my eye, and I stop to admire the pattern. It has small robin's-egg-blue flowers with midnight-black centers covering its surface, along with white vines and pale green leaves that intertwine from flower to flower. I immediately think of Anna, and know it will be perfect for her. Blue is her favorite color.

"Batik is a good buy here," a voice says. "Same with the lacquerware stuff. But skip the Thai silk. It's fake. If you're looking for good silk, head three doors to the right."

A young Thai man, perhaps in his early twenties, comes to stand beside me.

"Do you work here?" I ask, then realize he likely doesn't

if he's telling me to take my *baht* elsewhere. Also, there's no hint of an accent.

"Nope," he says with a laugh. "I'm from Baltimore."

"Oh, sorry, I thought..." I trip over my words, uncomfortable with the assumption.

"I am Thai, so don't worry," he says, a wide smile coming across his face. "But I was born and raised in the US." He holds out a hand. "I'm Pete."

"Tegan." I shake his hand. "I'm from Chicago."

"So Tegan from Chicago," Pete says, "what brings you to Chiang Mai?"

By now I should have a good answer to this question. But I suddenly feel nervous, and the words lock in my throat. Pete seems to notice my discomfort, and changes the subject.

"Listen, I'm meeting a bunch of friends at the Red Lion just outside the market—"

"The Red Lion?" I say, remembering Jason's email. "I know that place. My brother told me I had to go there."

"Then your brother must have been to Chiang Mai before. It's a great place."

"Actually, no, but he has this knack for knowing the best bars in every tourist destination," I say with a smile.

"You're welcome to join us if you want?" When I don't respond right away, Pete puts a hand on my arm in a way that is comforting, not concerning. "I promise, I'm a nice guy."

"Oh, it's not that. I'm married." I hold up my left hand and my gold and diamond bands sparkle under the bulbs.

"Cool," he says, nonplussed. "So is he here with you?" Pete glances around.

"Fabric isn't really his thing," I reply, shrugging my shoulders.

Pete laughs. "Fair enough. But the offer still stands. Why don't you find...?"

"Gabe."

"Gabe," Pete continues, "and both of you come join us?"

"Thanks, Pete." I know full well that's not going to happen. I'm not in the mood for a bar night with a bunch of strangers at the moment, no matter how friendly. "I'll see if he's up for it."

"Nice to meet you, Tegan," Pete says, heading out of the shop. "And don't forget, the Red Lion. Hope to see you there later."

"Got it," I say. "Thanks and nice to meet you, as well."

"Who was that?" Gabe asks, walking back into the shop just as Pete walks out, and obviously catching the last of our conversation.

"Pete from Baltimore." I tug on the blue sarong until it slides off the display. "I'm going to buy this for Anna, then I'd like to get something to eat."

"Sounds good to me. What are you in the mood for?"

"I thought pad Thai and a side of grasshopper might be good," I joke, walking deeper into the shop to pay for the sarong. I pick up two sets of lacquered bowls for our parents, one with brilliant red flowers painted on a glossy black background, and the other covered in gold and black swirling designs, and take everything to the counter at the back of the store. After paying what the shop owner asks, my purchases are wrapped in paper and presented to me in a plastic bag.

"You could have negotiated, you know," Gabe says. "I think it's pretty much expected."

I wait until I'm out of the store before saying, "It's hardly any money. Why try to bargain when I can afford to pay what they're asking?" I imagine the shop owner needs the money more than me, though that might be a sweeping generalization on my part. It's possible he makes a very good living with his shop, even with all the well-practiced tourists looking to save a few bucks.

"Say what you want," Gabe says, his tone teasing. "But I think it's mostly because you're a bit of a rule follower."

"That's not true," I reply, zigzagging around the waves of people walking past. "I've broken plenty of rules. Plenty."

"Name one."

"Well..." I think hard.

"See? Told ya," Gabe teases. "Rule follower extraordinaire."

"I pointed my feet at that statue in Bangkok!" I say. "That was definitely a rule I didn't follow."

"Ha!" Gabe exclaims. "True, but you didn't mean to do it. So it doesn't count."

I frown, slightly irritated. Who cares if I'm not all that adventurous or willing to break a rule or two?

"Fine. Dare me to do something."

"No, no, no," Gabe says with a shake of his head. "Nope. I'm not falling for that."

"Seriously, dare me. I'm all about trying new things these days in case you hadn't noticed."

Gabe pauses for a moment, and I nervously wait to hear what he's come up with.

"Okay," he says, "I dare you to eat one of those roasted grasshoppers."

I gulp, stopping a gag in the process. *A grasshopper?* That's not adventurous; that's plain crazy.

Gabe laughs at the look on my face. "You don't have to, Teg. I'm just teasing you."

Without another word I stride over to the insect vendor and order a mixed bag—two roasted grasshoppers nestled on a bed of deep-fried white bamboo worms, with charred green onion bits scattered throughout. I'm fairly certain this will not end well, but I'm not stopping now.

The group of backpackers has moved on at this point, but

in their place stands two couples, who suddenly become my cheering section.

"Go! Go! Go! Go!" they shout, pumping fists as they do. I shudder as I pick up one grasshopper by a leg, a two-inch-long bamboo worm caught in the grasshopper's wing.

"Perfect," Gabe says. "A two-for-one deal." I know he thinks I'm not going to do it.

But as I stare at the insect, roasted golden brown, I consider exactly how to do it. If I try to nibble at it or take a small bite, I'll likely vomit before even the tiniest bit gets down.

So I pop the whole thing in my mouth, treating the scenario like ripping off a Band-Aid. I close my eyes and chew furiously, trying to ignore the grasshopper leg that catches between my front teeth. I'm surprised, though, at the taste. Having never eaten an insect before I have no idea what to expect. My mouth is full of crunchy, salty bits, not dissimilar to very crispy pieces of fried chicken that have been cooked in onion-flavored oil. If I don't think about it being an entire grasshopper, I have to admit it's not all that bad.

"So?" Gabe asks, close to my ear to be heard over the cheering group of travelers, which has now grown.

I swallow a couple of times, and gratefully take the bottle of water the laughing vendor opens and hands to me. I fill my mouth with the lukewarm water and swish out the last bits of grasshopper. "Tastes like chicken," I say, smiling.

Everyone whoops and hollers and laughs, and I chuckle along with them, taking a few more sips. Turns out grasshopper aftertaste isn't all that great. After Gabe turns it down and says, "Are you nuts? No way," I hand my plate of bamboo worms to one of the guys in the group who has just accepted a dare from his friends, and wish him luck.

It's perhaps the craziest, most spontaneous thing I've ever

done, and I can't wait to tell Jason about it, knowing what a kick he'll get out of it.

"That was beyond awesome," Gabe says, a huge grin still on his face. "You are my hero."

"Thanks." I finish the water and put the bottle in a nearby trash can. "I can't believe I did that."

"Me, neither!" Gabe says. "For the record, I never would have eaten one leg of that grasshopper. Even if you dared me. Never."

"I didn't think so," I say, smiling wide. "Guess I win this one, huh?"

"Top prize to you, my love. Top prize."

I close my eyes when we kiss, in the middle of Chiang Mai's Night Bazaar. Softly. Deeply. The way we used to just before falling asleep in our darkened room, when I would find his lips by touch if there wasn't enough light to see his face.

Afterward, as I walk from vendor to vendor picking up a few more trinkets to bring home to my family, I run my fingers over my lips, still feeling Gabe's mouth on mine.

# 28

"Oh, god..." I groan, clutching my stomach, which feels like it's turning inside out. "The grasshopper...I shouldn't have eaten the grasshopper."

Gabe winces. "Babe, I don't think it was the grasshopper. I'm betting the bottle of water was what did it."

I moan in response as another cramp clenches my guts. Everything hurts. I feel hot and light-headed. And sick. So, so, sick.

"I'm going to throw up again," I mumble, scrambling off the bed and just making it to the toilet in time. If there's one silver lining, it's that this happened here, where there's actually a toilet bowl to get sick into. I can't imagine being this ill and having to deal with only a hole in the ground. The thought makes me heave harder, and I just keep telling myself it will be over soon enough. Gabe murmurs supportively and I try to focus on his voice.

"Think we should get Alice up?" Gabe asks, his voice betraying his worry, once I've made it back to the bed. I shiver uncontrollably, clutching at the thin duvet and tucking it up under my chin. "You might need a doctor."

"I don't need a doctor," I mumble, teeth chattering. "It's just food poisoning. Or water poisoning, I guess. Besides, it's—"

I glance at my watch on the side table "—only three in the morning. She'll be sound asleep."

"She won't care, Teg. You're in rough shape and I'm not sure I'm okay with letting you ride this one out." I feel his caress on my sticky, hot forehead—combined with the soft breeze from the ceiling fan above, it feels wonderful. "You look terrible."

"Geez, thanks a lot." I attempt a laugh. Gabe doesn't join me. "I'll be okay. I can't believe how stupid I was. Bruce said to never drink a bottle of water I hadn't opened myself. Stupid."

"Speaking of water, think you can get a little down?"

"I doubt it will stay down." I grimace at the thought of putting anything inside my tornado-like stomach. "But I'll try."

I crack open the lid on the bottle of water Alice left on the bedside table, grateful for the sound of the plastic tabs snapping as I do. After a small sip, I put the bottle back on the table and lie back against the cool pillow.

"Did Connor pack you anything for an upset stomach?"

"Oh, I'm sure he did," I say. "And after I go throw up again—right now—I'll check." I quickly push the duvet off my fiery body and run to the washroom.

I spend most of the night running to the bathroom, then collapsing back into bed, and by the time the sun rises, I'm exhausted. I feel like my body has been used as a punching bag, and I'm weak with dehydration. At some point in the night Alice hears me—likely during one of the particularly violent dry-heaving sessions that come after my stomach is long empty—and takes over as nursemaid. I'm grateful for the cool compresses she presses to my feverish head, the flat soda—she heated it on the stove until it lost its fizziness, then let it cool, just like my mom always did when I was sick as a child—and her motherly touch.

There are also rehydration salts that Connor packed in my toiletries bag, and along with those and some ginger tablets from Alice, I mercifully stop vomiting around six in the morning.

Luckily the train back to Bangkok isn't leaving until later in the evening, so I have a full day to recoup. I can't imagine getting on a train at the moment; things are delicately balanced inside my body, with my stomach ready to protest again at even the slightest hint of too much motion.

"It was probably the water," Alice says, wiping my forehead again with a cool cloth. "To save money some vendors will take old bottles and fill them up with tap water."

"I should have known better."

"You weren't thinking clearly, which was my fault really," Gabe says. "I did dare you to eat that grasshopper."

"That damn grasshopper." I sigh.

"What grasshopper?" Alice asks, wringing out the cloth in the bathroom sink.

"Oh, you should have seen her," Gabe says. "She showed that grasshopper who was boss!"

I roll my eyes. "It was at the night bazaar," I explain, swallowing against a wave of nausea at the thought of the grasshopper leg between my teeth. "I ate one of the roasted grasshoppers, and a bamboo worm, too."

Alice laughs as she comes back into the bedroom. "You are a brave one, Tegan. I've been here for over twenty years and have yet to try a grasshopper. Crickets, yes, but there's something about the grasshoppers." Alice shudders. "Even when you pull off the legs and wings, they still—"

"Wait, what?" I ask, sitting up to take the glass of soda from her. I have a small sip, the dark, syrupy sweet liquid coating my tongue and throat. "I didn't take the wings off. No one told me I was supposed to do that!"

"Well, you didn't really give anyone a chance, did you?" Gabe says. "You were a woman on a mission."

Alice starts laughing, but tries to hide it behind a cough. Gabe joins in, and I chuckle weakly.

"You're supposed to take the wings off? And the legs?" I hold my stomach and pout. Alice nods, and Gabe tries to stop laughing. "Well, I guess I'm even more of a badass, then, aren't I?"

"Think you're up for a little something to eat?" Alice walks over to the door, resting her hand on the knob. "I'm going to make myself some breakfast."

Gabe nods and murmurs his thanks, but the thought of food makes me have to close my eyes and take a few deep breaths.

"Maybe just a piece of dry toast for you, Tegan?" Alice asks. I nod, giving her a weak smile before she closes the door behind her.

"Fuck," I groan, my stomach muscles screaming from the night of sickness. "I can't believe I ate grasshopper wings when I didn't have to. And legs. I'm going to be pulling bits of grass-hopper leg out of my teeth for the next few days." I resist the urge to gag. "Okay, I have to stop talking about grasshoppers."

"Just wait until Jase hears about this," Gabe says.

"Let's leave out the part of me throwing up half my body weight, okay?"

"Yeah, that does bring your street cred down a bit."

"Exactly," I say. "Especially because I didn't have a lot of it to begin with." I lean back into the pillows, letting their softness wrap around my aching head. "It sucks this is going to be the last memory I have of Thailand. Grass—" I pause, putting a hand to my mouth. I clear my throat, tasting bile. "Grasshoppers and all-night vomiting."

"Well, we still have one more day in Bangkok," Gabe says,

"so as long as we stay away from fried bugs and water bottles and showing off, you should be good."

I close my eyes, which feel gritty and sore.

"Why don't you try to sleep? I'll be here when you wake up."

"Okay," I reply, and moments later I'm sound asleep.

# *three*
## Italy

# 29

*Four months before the accident*

I peered inside the large, stainless steel pot I'd bought for the occasion and frowned at the sauce bubbling away inside.

"Does it look right?" I grabbed a soupspoon from the drawer. "It doesn't look right to me."

"It smells amazing," Gabe said from the bedroom, where he was getting out of his running clothes.

I dipped in the spoon and brought it to my lips, blowing on the ruby-red tomato sauce a few times before tasting it.

"Can you come and taste this?" I shouted to Gabe. He came out of the bedroom, stark naked.

I raised an eyebrow. "You couldn't have put something on first?" I said, my tone teasing as I took in his post-run, sweaty and well-defined body. I especially loved his legs—they were lean and muscled, and I liked to joke that he'd look better in my heels than I did. "How am I supposed to concentrate on making this meal for your parents when you're tempting me with all that?" I waved the ladle around, pointing it at his midsection area, splattering a few spots of deep red sauce onto the counter.

Gabe grinned and took the spoon I handed him. "It's hot,"

I warned. He dipped it into the sauce, standing back a little to avoid getting any of it on his bare skin, and put it right into his mouth.

"Ah, ah, ah!" He opened his mouth in an attempt to cool the sauce burning his tongue. "Shit, that's hot!"

"Didn't I tell you?" I said, laughing. "So, what's missing?"

He took another spoonful; this time giving it a couple of quick blows first. "It's really good, Teg." I gave him a look, which basically said he better be telling the truth. "Honestly, it's not missing anything. My mom will be impressed." I thought that might be a stretch but I appreciated him saying so. "I'm going to hop in the shower now, okay?"

I nodded and gave the sauce a stir, trying to calm my nerves. Rosa was an amazing cook; food loved her touch. That was the best way to explain it. She was born and raised in a small Italian town on the Amalfi Coast called Ravello, and whether she was cooking a traditional Italian feast or poached eggs, everything she made tasted like success. My mother, on the other hand, was a decent cook but we never had anything fancy growing up. Dinner was usually some kind of chicken or beef, with potatoes or rice on the side and either an iceberg lettuce salad or steamed carrots and broccoli, and my dad's pizza on Friday nights. Cozy and predictable, that's how I described the food I grew up with, whereas the menu at Gabe's house always carried an exotic look and flavor. So to say I was feeling out of my element making Rosa's famous tomato sauce was an understatement.

The recipe was simple: ripe plum tomatoes, onions, olive oil, salt-and-pepper and a handful of basil leaves. I wasn't sure how many a "handful" of basil leaves was, so I counted out ten from the giant bunch I'd bought at the market, and stuffed them in my hand to see if that felt like a good handful or not.

But for some reason, despite the simplicity of the recipe and me following it to the letter, it just didn't have the same flavor. It also seemed a tad darker than Rosa's sauce, and a little thicker. I sighed and gave it another stir. The Lawsons would be arriving in an hour and there was still so much to do. Including for me to get cleaned up and dressed, I noted, looking down at my sauce-splattered tank top and pajama bottoms. For not the first time, I wondered why I hadn't simply chosen a meal I knew how to make with my eyes closed. Like the baked chicken, double mashed potatoes with bacon and chives and ice cream from a tub my mom whipped up most Sunday nights. Also, we were having a late summer heat wave and between the brownouts that kept making our air conditioner go off, and the stove and oven running full tilt, I lamented my dinner choice again. I should have gone for cold potato salad and barbecue chicken.

Bending over, I glanced into the oven. The lemon cake, a traditional Amalfi Coast dessert and another Rosa specialty, was starting to brown ever so slightly on top. At least it looked like hers, filling the Bundt pan nicely and emitting its sweet lemon fragrance into the kitchen. Noting there was another fifteen minutes until the cake had to come out, I started taking off my tank top as I made my way to the bedroom. Might as well get ready now. I'd wear the new black wrap dress I bought with Anna last week, because even if sauce splattered on me, it wouldn't be noticeable. Gabe was just getting out of the shower, and the steam had started creeping into the bedroom.

I wriggled out of my pajama bottoms and was about to undo my bra when I felt Gabe's hands, still damp and warm from the hot shower, circle my waist from behind.

"Mmm," he said, nuzzling into the back of my neck. The hair on my arms stood on end as his nose tickled the sensitive spot behind my ear. "Want some help with that?" He undid the clasp on my bra then turned me around.

"Oh, hello there," I said, feeling the full length of him press up against me. "Fancy meeting you here."

He bent his head toward me and gently licked a spot just below my collarbone. I shivered, and tilted my head slightly to the side to allow him better access. "You have a little something there," he said, his breath hot against my skin. "Tomato sauce. Delicious."

I laughed. "We don't have time for this." I tried to pull away, but Gabe held me tight and smiled.

"Your parents…the cake…"

"Not so fast. You have a little more right…here…" His tongue moved lower. "And here…"

"I doubt I got any *there*," I said, though I stopped resisting. My breath caught as he made his way down the front of my body, until he was on his knees. He looked up at me grinning wide, his eyes mischievous.

"I think you should let me worry about that," he said. So I did. Twice.

Dinner was a success. Rosa graciously told me the sauce tasted just like her mother used to make, and Gabe's dad had two helpings. The lemon cake was the highlight of the meal, if I do say so myself, even if it didn't rise as much as it was supposed to.

"It's all in the pan," Rosa explained, while I bemoaned the somewhat stout cake. While I cut slices of the warm yellow dessert and plated them, she drizzled lemon syrup over each piece. The simple syrup was made of fresh squeezed lemon juice, water and sugar, and cooked until fragrant and thickened. As she drizzled, she explained it was wise not to use a nonstick pan, which I had, and commented—with disdain, I might add—how North Americans are so committed to their nonstick kitchenware. "And the weather," she continued, looking out the windows in our apartment's living room. Rivulets of water streamed down the glass, giving the city lights a distorted appearance. "Heat is good, but the rain can make a *bella torta* go poof!" She brought her hands together in a clap, as though squishing a spider.

After dessert, I made espresso in the stove-top moka pot Gabe's parents had gifted us when we moved into the apartment, and tried not to grimace as I sipped mine. Yes, I loved coffee, but in the way that those who really loved coffee would say was practically sacrilegious—with cream and one sugar, in a take-out cup.

Once Gabe's parents left, we tackled the mound of dishes I'd created.

"I don't know how your mom does it," I said, eyeing the pots, the stacks of tomato-sauce-covered plates, the bowls overflowing with emptied mussel shells and the dessert plates, sticky with lemon syrup and crumbs.

Gabe laughed and rolled the sleeves of his lavender button-down shirt. "Practice," he said. "Or as my dad would say, she has an excellent sous chef."

He looked so good in the shirt, the color highlighting his eyes and making them almost indigo in the dimmed light of the living room. I felt a flush, remembering our predinner warm-up, and considered leaving the dishes until the morning so we could finish what we'd started.

But the moment was broken when Gabe reached over the pile of dishes to turn on the water in the sink, and in the process, knocked the haphazardly stacked bowls off the counter. With a crash, our kitchen floor was covered in shards of white ceramic, mussel shells and an oily sheen from the lemon fennel broth the mussels had been simmered in.

"Shit!" Gabe said, turning off the water and standing statue-still so as not to step in anything with his bare feet.

"At least this happened after your parents left," I said, laughing as I retrieved the broom and dustpan from the hall closet.

Gabe crouched down and picked up big pieces of the broken bowls, tossing them into the garbage under the sink.

"What a mess," he muttered, starting to gather the mussel shells in his hands.

"Leave it."

He looked up at me quizzically, one eyebrow up, his lips still slightly stained from the red wine at dinner. "What? I'll just grab the big stuff and then use the broom."

"Those shells aren't going anywhere." I untied the knot at the waist of my dress and began unwrapping the fabric ties until my dress was open. I shrugged it off my shoulders and kicked it to the side. Gabe's eyes wandered from my face down my body, and back up, and the confused look changed to something else. He grinned and wiped his hands on the nearby dish towel. In one quick jump he'd cleared the broken bowls and shells and then reached for me.

"Oh, no, you don't," I said, taking a step back. I stood there in my black bra and thong underwear, and he groaned.

"No fair."

"I think some of that sauce got on your clothes." I pointed to his chest. He looked down at his pristine shirt, then back at me with a grin.

"I think you might be right," he said, unbuttoning the shirt. "I'd better get it off."

"Mmm-hmm," I murmured. "We don't want it to stain."

Gabe watched me as he took his shirt off, followed by his pants. They lay in a heap at his feet.

"That's better." I beckoned with my fingers. "Now, come here."

He lunged at me and I laughed, then squealed as my feet

left the ground. He kissed me, softly at first and then deeper, as he started walking us toward the bedroom.

"The bed is too far away," I said, coming up for air.

He burst out laughing. "Yes, those eight steps will take way too long," he said, but he changed direction and a moment later, we were on the couch in the living room. The same couch we sat on not half an hour before chatting about the things you do with your soon-to-be in-laws: the weather, our jobs, the next family gathering, our imminent wedding.

"This is better," I said, rolling over so I was on top of him.

"Agreed. I like the view."

I unclasped my bra and let it drop to the floor.

"Now," I said, bending down to kiss his lips, then his neck and chest, and moving one hand lower until it found what it was looking for. His breath caught in his throat, a sound coming out of him that let me know he approved. "Where were we?"

"I'd love to take you to Italy one day. To Ravello, where my mom grew up."

Everything was cleaned up, and we'd finally made it to bed. It was almost midnight. "I'd love that, too," I said. "It sounds like a beautiful place."

"It is," he said, nodding. "There's nowhere like it. And the food…it's to die for."

"If your mom's cooking is any indication, I believe it."

He rolled on his side and rested his head into his hand. "You did an amazing job with dinner tonight, Teg. No, really. I could tell my mom was impressed."

"Your mom is polite." I gave him a sideways glance. "It wasn't a bad effort, but it definitely didn't taste the same as your mom's." I snuggled into him, forcing him to lie on his back. He rested an arm around my shoulder and I found the nook I'd been looking for. "I'd love to learn how to cook authentic Italian dishes, like, really authentic. Maybe I could take a class?"

"I'm sure my mom would be happy to teach you."

"I don't think that's a good idea," I said. "I don't want her to know just how much I really suck."

"You do not suck." Gabe nudged me with his shoulder to get up. "But I do have an idea."

"What?"

"The list. Let's add it to the list." He got out of bed, then returned a moment later with the small notepad I kept in the kitchen to write grocery lists on and a pen.

"An authentic cooking class in Ravello, Italy," he said out loud as he wrote it down. "For Tegan," he added.

"Wait, you're not going to do it with me?"

"No, ma'am. Besides, my mom taught me all her secrets years ago."

I gaped at him, and he nodded and smirked.

"So now you tell me?" I swatted at him. "If I'd known that I would have made you do all the cooking."

He winked. "Exactly."

"Well, I love the idea," I said. "Learning to cook in Italy is so much better than some class in a dingy, fluorescent-filled kitchen here in the city."

Gabe folded the sheet of paper and dropped it into the glass jar that sat on our dresser. It was about half-full, and I wondered how we'd find the time to accomplish everything.

As if reading my mind, Gabe glanced back at the jar. "The good news is we have our whole lives to work on this list."

"True. But let's not wait until we're gray and need new hips to do these things, okay?"

Gabe pulled his pajama bottoms up as high as they would go, rib level, and then tied the drawstring tightly to keep them there. He rolled his shoulders forward and shuffled slowly toward me, like an old man. "Will you still love me when I lose my waist? And my teeth?" He wrapped his lips over his teeth and smiled. I burst out laughing.

"Forever and always." I pulled him to me by the drawstring's knot. "Even if I have—"

"Ouch!" he said. "How does any man wear his pants like this?" He grimaced and pulled out of my grasp, tugging at the navy-blue-and-white-striped cotton pants until they rested low on his sharp hip bones. "Ah, so much better."

"As I was saying," I said, standing up on the bed so I was facing him. I put my hands on his face and crouched slightly so our lips were even. Then I gave him a few quick pecks. "Even if I have to blend all our food once you lose your teeth, I promise to love you—" I kissed him again, holding my lips to his longer this time "—and feed you forever."

# 30

"It's...stunning," I say, breathless with the exertion.

"I know," Gabe replies. "A little slice of heaven."

Heaven. I gaze out over the landscape, covered with jagged rock faces and layered rows of lush, ripe lemon and olive trees as far as the eye can see. I touch the pendant around my neck, lifting it off my skin where it's stuck with sweat. It's hard to believe we're here. That I'm not still in our Chicago bed, trying to sleep, trying to forget, trying to breathe around the heavy pain that I carry around like a bowling ball inside my rib cage.

The ocean, a blue azure that stretches out from all sides, is dotted with boats—a few small fishing craft, coming in after the morning's haul; a ferry boat on its way to Capri; and a monstrous cruise ship docked at the shore, waiting for its passengers to return from their hustled day trip into the cobblestoned streets of Amalfi, carrying hand-painted ceramic olive dishes, or bottles of Limoncello, or some other memento to prove they were here.

The hike up to the ruins of Torre dello Ziro, which was a fortress in the late 1400s, is particularly arduous, with steep, craggy rock steps and a harrowingly narrow path that snakes around the cliff's edge. But as I stand in the ancient stone ruins, I have no fear despite the thin metal post that's clearly meant to be a railing but would be no more effective than a fraying rope at keeping hikers from falling off the ledge. I don't fear death the way I used to. The way I probably should.

Weak from months of inactivity, my thighs seize up the moment I stop climbing. I rub at them, taking in deep gulps of the ocean-scented air, and look around.

"I can't believe this is where your mom grew up." I open my arms wide and spin around in a circle, somewhat clumsily thanks to my overworked legs.

"Careful there," Gabe says as I spin around another time, my muscles relaxing now that I'm moving again. "The Italians aren't known for making safety a top priority." I ignore him, standing right up against the railing and cupping my hands to my mouth. I shout, "I love Italy!" then stay still to listen for the echo, laughing when I hear it come back faintly with the breeze.

The Amalfi Coast is straight out of a travel brochure. The homes are stacked into the hills like LEGO blocks, whitewashed with rust-colored clay tiled roofs, which contrast the greenery of the lemon and olive trees. The fruit trees, mostly covered in black netting to protect them, grow in beds that stretch along the hills row after row, each one higher than the next, like a staircase up the mountainside. Bright yellow lemons and clusters of ripening green and black olives hang from the branches, making it clear why this part of Italy is famous for its lemon-infused cuisine and olive-based dishes. Low clouds hang over the cliff top across from us, its peak hidden in a billowy white mist that looks like meringue.

"It's crazy to think this used to be a castle," I say, running my hands along the rough, crumbling stone walls as I walk into what used to be the lookout tower but is now only a circle of stones about six feet high. "And that we're allowed to be this close to it, you know? Back home something like this would be behind a Plexiglas wall." I peer at the sea below through a hole in one of the stones. "So much history, just sitting here."

"It's actually amazing there's anything left at all," Gabe says. "They certainly don't make things like they used to. Can you imagine any part of our apartment building still standing hundreds of years later?"

"Maybe that dungeon of a parking garage." I rest my chin into the rough stone and press my face deeper into the hole. From this vantage point it almost feels like I'm floating, with nothing but blue seas and wispy clouds ahead. Though I don't want to pull back, a wave of vertigo makes it necessary so I can regain my bearings.

I sit on one of the rocks that had at some point tumbled from the wall, and open my small day pack. The breeze tickles the back of my sweaty neck. After a couple of sips of water, I reknot my ponytail higher and tuck the ends into the elastic. "That's better," I murmur, brushing a piece of loose hair to the side and sliding it behind my ear. Pulling out the travel book I brought for this part of the trip, I easily turn to the section on hiking, thanks to the pink Post-it note on which I wrote "Trails."

"You can take the teacher out of Chicago, but you can't take the teacher out of the girl," Gabe says with a laugh. "Or something like that."

"Yeah, I don't think that's how it goes," I reply, keeping my eyes on the page. I run my index finger down the page, trying to find the section on the fortress's history.

"It says it was built in 1480, and the queen who lived here… Queen Giovanna d'Aragona…" I pause, reading a few more lines. "Oh, that bites. She was beheaded here." I make a face and look around. "Wonder where that happened?" I shiver despite the warmth of the day, trying to imagine what it would have been like to live at a time and in a place where beheading was a legitimate risk.

Going back to the page to read the next few lines, I hear voices coming up the path. A woman who looks about my age walks through the tall grass lining the path and heads toward us. Her pale blond hair lays tight to her head in a French braid, and she's holding the hand of a man who is perhaps the tallest person I've seen in real life. Like, pro-basketball kind of tall. They sneak in a couple of kisses, him bending way down to reach her mouth, and then she pulls on his hand again.

"Come on," she says with a British accent. "Almost there, you lazy lug." He laughs and lets her lead him farther up the path.

"Oh, hello," she says, when she practically trips over my feet. "Didn't notice you there."

"Don't worry about it." I bend my knees to get my feet out of the way, then think it might seem rude if I don't stand up, like Gabe does.

"Beautiful up here, isn't it?" Gabe says, brushing dust off the butt of his shorts.

"This is beyond gorgeous." French braid girl takes a deep breath and looks around. In her very short shorts and tank top, she looks to be in amazing shape, her petite legs tan and muscled. She's also barely winded. I tug self-consciously on the midthigh-length running shorts I'm wearing for the first time, even though I bought them a few months before the wedding when I decided to get serious about exercise. I also realize, as I pull at my shorts, I haven't shaved my legs since the day before the elephant camp in Chiang Mai. Luckily, there's a lot else to look at up here aside from a stranger's stubbly shins.

"Would you mind taking a picture for us?" the young woman asks, putting her sunglasses atop her head. She shields her eyes, brown like mine, and gives us a smile.

"Of course not." I drop the travel book into my backpack and take the small camera from her, putting the strap over my wrist. "Anything I need to know about this?"

"Just point and shoot," the tall man says. "Jump on, love." At that the woman giggles and jumps onto his back, in piggyback fashion, so their heads are at the same height.

"That's a great shot." Gabe takes a few steps to the left, pointing over a lower portion of the stone wall. "Just make sure to get that view of ocean in the background if you can."

I stand on the rock I was previously sitting on, to be sure to get a little of everything in the shot. A few clicks later, I hand the camera back and the woman quickly scans the photos.

"Brilliant, just brilliant," she says, showing the last one to the man. "You look even more gorgeous in Italy."

He kisses the top of her head, then her lips, where he lingers for long enough that I wonder if I should look away. "You, too, love."

"Sorry, we're honeymooners." She smiles at her husband, and he leans down for yet another kiss. After she pulls away, finally, she taps her temple and looks at us with widened eyes. "Oh, how rude of me. Would you like a picture, too?"

"That would be great," Gabe says, heading toward the stone wall.

"Uh, sure, okay." I hand over our camera and then lean against the section of wall that's low enough to see the ocean beyond, beside Gabe.

"Colin, why don't you take this one?" the woman says, giving her husband the camera. "I'm so short I might only get you from the knees down." She laughs.

"Ready in three…two…one…say 'Vino!'" Colin's finger is poised over the shutter button, and he crouches slightly to line up the photo.

"Vino!" Gabe and I say in unison, smiling wide.

"Lovely, lovely," Colin says, glancing through the viewfinder. "Okay, one more. Smile big!"

Colin takes one more picture then hands me the camera. I thank him and am about to introduce myself when a group of khaki-wearing tourists arrive, with professional-looking cameras hanging heavy around their necks, and wearing those utility shorts where the pant legs zip off. They tilt the brims of what appear to be matching Tilley hats and gaze about, speaking an unfamiliar language and offering smiles as they walk past our little group. They smell of sweat and beer.

"Best be going if we plan to make that tour," Colin says to his new wife. "We're doing a Limoncello factory tour later this afternoon," he adds by way of explanation, taking her small hand in his larger one.

"Time to get bloody drunk after all this exercise!" she says with a laugh. They link fingers and wave goodbye with their other hands as they head back down the path.

I sigh and take a last look around, the spot no longer feeling as magical now that there's so much company to share it with.

"Ready to go?" Gabe asks.

I nod and pack up, then sling the backpack's straps over my shoulders, grateful it's all downhill from here.

# 31

After the hike it's time for lunch—a hand-tossed Margherita pizza with fresh tomato sauce, basil and melting buffalo mozzarella—in the little seaside town of Atrani, after which I feel sufficiently ready for the serious climb back to Ravello. It's not all that far, maybe two miles, but it's straight up.

Ravello, a small town that's surprisingly sophisticated and elegant with its architecture, boutique hotels, cobblestoned streets and high-end artisan shops, is far up the mountain and has breathtaking vistas of the Mediterranean. Gabe's mom suggested we stay in Hotel Villa Maria, a charming boutique hotel whose dining patio sits directly on the cliff's edge, giving diners unprecedented views of the hills and villages down below.

Putting one foot in front of the other on the first dozen or so of the hundreds of stone steps that lead out of Atrani and toward the trail to Ravello, the pizza and beer slosh uncomfortably in my stomach.

"I told you the rocket salad was a better idea," Gabe says, when I complain. The curiously named "rocket salad" is actually a simple arugula salad with fresh chopped tomatoes, but at the time I felt far too hungry for a salad.

"I should have skipped the beer." I stretch my arms over my head and lean back to give my stomach some more room to digest my large lunch. "And that pistachio gelato." Though I was wary of trying ice cream made from green pistachio nuts, I promised Gabe's dad I would. He told me it was traditional to this part of Italy, and delicious. And he was right—creamy and sweet, with a hint of saltiness, it's become my new favorite thing.

"You should never skip gelato while in Italy," Gabe says. "Come on, let's keep going. You'll burn it off in no time."

With a groan I go back to climbing the stairs that wind through the hill, counting as we go to try and distract myself. *Eighty-six. Eighty-seven. One hundred and fifty-one. One hundred and ninety-three.*

My breathing speeds up along with my heart rate and I realize again just how out of shape I am. I feel especially pathetic when an old woman, who is as round as she is tall, climbs past me with both hands holding overflowing grocery bags, barely breaking her stride. About fifty steps ahead she stops and sets her bags down, putting a key into the lock of a large wooden door that has bars across its front, before disappearing inside.

This staircase that leads from Atrani up the hill is lined with similar front doors, every fifteen feet or so. Some are wood, some a combination of wood and metal, but most are without windows. There's also dozens of stray cats that call this staircase home, nibbling on fish bones and pieces of stale bread put out by the residents.

I stop counting when I reach stair number two hundred and thirty, because I need to focus on making my legs continue the climb. They burn, and my breath comes fast and painful in my lungs. I have a searing cramp in my side from the heavy lunch and exercise.

"Not too much farther now," Gabe says, and I silently curse him as I look up and see nothing but stone stair after stone stair stretching beyond, with no end in sight.

But sure enough, around two more bends, the stairs mercifully end and are replaced by a rock-riddled dirt path that's still steep, but easier to climb.

Many of the homes along the path are literally built into the hillside, some with clay tile patios that hold bicycles, wooden crates of grapes and, in a few cases, a scooter or motorcycle, which seem to be the preferred modes of transport on the Amalfi Coast's winding, narrow highways. Laundry billows in the breeze from wires strung between upper-floor windows, whose wooden shutters are all wide-open to let the outdoors in.

"It's all so, I don't know the words...*old-fashioned* maybe?" I say. "Except for those." I point at another scooter, shiny apple red, which is parked in the short, cement-block-lined driveway of one of the homes.

Gabe chuckles. "It's not really old-fashioned. Traditional?"

"Traditional," I repeat, pausing at the top of the dirt path to take a sip from my water bottle. "That's more what I meant." It's so hot now, the midday sun beaming down from a cloudless sky that I roll my shorts up another two inches and take off my socks.

"You're going to regret that," Gabe says pointedly at my now sockless feet, which I'm busy trying to shove back into my dusty, sweat-damp sneakers. My feet seem to have grown a size in the heat, and don't want to go back into my shoes.

"I'll be fine," I say, getting my shoes back on with some difficulty. I tie the laces, double knotting them for good measure. "Another half hour or so you think?"

"Imagine so."

Just then a goat bleats loudly and I jump. "Holy hell!" I put a hand to my chest, my heart hammering. "That scared the shit out of me." The goat, which appears on the other side of the path, pushes its head forward and bleats again.

"That is one pissy goat," Gabe says. The goat takes a few more steps until it's on the path, standing directly in front of me.

"Take it easy, buddy," I say, looking at the goat warily. "Can goats bite?" I ask, keeping my eyes on the goat.

"I'm sure they can," Gabe says. "But they only have front teeth on the bottom I think, so it probably won't do too much damage." Looking at the goat, with its yellow and black eyes and long, scraggly white beard, I'm not so sure. It looks mean, and none too pleased with me.

"Move it, goat," I say, in the firmest voice I can muster. The one I use in my kindergarten classroom. "Shoo!"

"Yeah, I don't think it's too interested in what you have to say," Gabe says, when the goat ignores me and instead of moving out of the way, grabs a mouthful of grass from the edge of the path. Its jaw slides sideways as it chews, slowly and methodically.

I take a step toward it, hoping it will get skittish and take off, but instead the goat puts its head down and runs straight at me.

"Oh, shit!" Gabe says as I shriek and jump off the path, my bare legs getting scraped by the thorny bushes and tall grasses.

"Gabe, do something!"

"Like what?" Gabe's laughing, which irritates me to no end. He notices. "You're doing just fine. Besides, I think this goat's bark is worse than its bite." He gives me a wink and points up the path to the goat that now seems most interested in the patch of grass it stands in.

"Thanks for nothing, funny guy." I stumble back onto the path and quickly put more distance between the goat and me. I look over my shoulder a couple of times, the goat still standing in the middle of the footpath but seemingly oblivious to us now.

I turn and walk backward a couple of steps. "You know, you'd be perfect in roti," I shout to the goat. "I'd sleep with one eye open if I were you."

The goat stops its chewing, stares our way, then breaks into a run again. Which causes me to shriek again. Gabe howls with laughter but I ignore him, too focused on scampering up the last few feet of the footpath to where it ends at the paved roadway that leads to Ravello. Gabe, ahead of me, reaches out a hand and I grab for it, shaky and clumsy from the influx of adrenaline. Once I'm safe at the top of the footpath, I look back and see the goat has simply run over to where another goat is standing, partially obscured by the wooden stakes and tall plants in a vegetable garden. Seems I was never in danger of an Italian goat bite, after all. The goats take turns dipping their heads into a plastic bucket that presumably holds something more interesting than the path's grass, and I scowl.

"Damn cheeky goat," I mutter, looking both ways on the road before crossing. A small Fiat and two scooters zoom by, then it's safe to cross. On the other side the footpath continues, with a small sign on the rock. The sign is painted on a blue ceramic tile, bordered with delicate yellow-painted flowers. It reads Ravello and has an arrow pointing up the path.

"I think it's good we live in the city." Gabe is still chuckling. "You're not exactly Dr. Doolittle."

"Shush," I say. "That goat had it in for me."

But then I start laughing, too, and soon can't stop. Tears stream down my cheeks and I have to crouch to the ground to avoid losing control of my bladder. A few people walk by, staring curiously at the scene, and I wave them on and give a thumbs-up sign that I'm okay, still laughing too hard to get a word out.

I think maybe I should go back and thank the goat. Then I

decide a goat bite will really kill the mood, so instead I shout, "Thank you, you stupid goat!" as loudly as I can, then dissolve into another fit of laughter. All the while, Gabe laughs right alongside me.

"Do I ever need a shower," I say as I step through the front gate of the hotel. "I stink!" I'm already fantasizing about the hot water and lemon-scented soap the hotel makes on-site.

"I didn't want to say anything, but..." Gabe raises an eyebrow and I laugh easily. Even though my muscles are shaky from the hike and my heels are covered in painful blisters from my decision to go sockless, I'm energized. I'm happy to be here. This day has felt like an ice-cold glass of sparkling soda when all you've had to drink is lukewarm tap water.

The lobby, with its warm peach walls, gray-and-white tiled floor and dark wood furniture, is fairly empty and a nice reprieve from the blazing heat outside. A giant ceiling fan works hard to keep the space cool and fresh.

"Oh, Mrs. Lawson, we've been trying to get ahold of you." The hotel's concierge beckons me over to his desk. He puts his glasses on and looks down at a stack of papers in front of him as we walk over.

I sit at the chair he motions to, my sweaty thighs sticking to its leather cushion. I shift and the cushion makes an embarrassing squeak. "What is it?" I resist the urge to explain the noise was from the cushion, and not me.

"The chef has had a death in the family," he begins, tilting his chin to look over the rim of his glasses.

"Oh, that's terrible." The smile drops from my face.

"Very sorry to hear that," Gabe says.

The concierge nods, then taps his pen against the paper on top of the stack. I stare at him, at his tapping pen, and wait.

While it's certainly sad news for this woman, I'm not sure what any of this has to do with us.

"Yes, well, because of this we're going to have to cancel the cooking school for the next week while she's away."

Now I get it.

The cooking school. The wish list.

A strange mix of dread and fury fills me, and my cheeks flush. I lean forward in my seat and the cushion squeaks again, but this time I don't care. "You can't cancel the cooking class," I say, my voice low and wobbly. Any feelings of happiness I had moments earlier disappear.

The concierge looks at me sympathetically. "I understand how frustrating this must be, to have your vacation plans change, but if you give me a moment—"

I stand up so quickly the concierge starts. "I don't think you do understand." My words permeate the small lobby. I feel sick, very aware of the pizza in my belly, but I don't sit back down.

"Tegan, take a breath." Gabe's voice is soft, soothing and in such contrast to my own tone.

I put my hand up, ignoring him, and turn my focus back to the concierge. He looks confused and tries to speak but I interrupt him again. "This is the only reason I'm here, do you understand that?" I'm embarrassingly loud, and the tears stream fast down my cheeks. The concierge rises from his chair and takes off his glasses, a strained half smile locked on his face. I know I should listen to him and Gabe—who are saying that everything is fine, to calm down, take a breath, have a seat—but I don't.

Half an hour ago I would have said that today was a good day.

But one good day isn't enough to leave a dent in the fortress of sorrow I've built up.

I'm not better nor am I healing, despite my protestations otherwise. My rage-fueled grief is still so close to the surface. A tiny nick—this time in the form of a canceled cooking class—is all it takes to unleash it, and with a sense of panic I realize I don't know how to tuck it away again.

"You can't cancel the cooking class. You can't. I've paid for it in full." I dig frantically through my day pack until I find my cell phone. "You sent me a confirmation number. I have it here…just give me a second…" With shaking fingers I type in my password, and my phone's screen jiggles to let me know I got it wrong. I swear and punch in my password a second time. Again, the screen jiggles in response. I'm nearly hysterical now, and can feel the stares of the other guests in the lobby, of the staff behind the front desk. "This class is… it's the only thing that matters."

The cooking class was supposed to help my wounds scab over, to help staunch the flow of blood slowly killing me. Without it, I might as well hike back up that Italian mountain and step boldly over the useless railing.

I wish there were some way to explain this to Gabe, and to the concierge, without sounding melodramatic at best, crazy at worst. But I can't find the words. Sobbing, I try my password a third time.

"I'm sorry," Gabe says to the concierge, trying to diffuse the situation. He's watching me carefully. "We've had a… It's been a difficult time."

For his part, the concierge seems to have recovered from the force of my outburst, and gives us a kind smile. "Please, have a seat. You're clearly upset and I'd like to help."

"I'd rather stand." My teeth chatter. I feel strange, like my head is floating above my body. Hollowness settles over me, like something has sucked out my insides leaving little more than bones and skin. I clutch the back of the chair in front of me, and Gabe steadies me from behind.

"It's okay, babe," Gabe says. "It's going to be okay."

The concierge is watching me with concern. "We will fix this. Please, sit. Let me get you a glass of water." He gestures to someone behind me, and a moment later a glass of ice water appears, a semicircle of lemon floating on top.

In truth I'm not sure I can stand much longer, so I take a seat and accept the tissue the concierge hands me. My breath catches as I try to get ahold of myself, and my body shakes in rhythm with my chattering teeth. "This was really important to me," I say, wiping my eyes with the tissue.

"I can see that," the concierge replies. He has kind eyes, and I feel badly for how I've behaved, though he brushes aside my apology when I offer it. "I'm the one who's sorry. I should have started with the news that I've found another class for you to attend." He reaches a hand out to pat mine, which is clutching the edge of his desk, my knuckles whitening from the pressure. I relax my body and take a deep breath. The shaking subsides somewhat.

"Francesca's Cooking School is only a short walk from the hotel. Luckily they had a cancellation and I've booked you in for tomorrow," he says. "Of course, the hotel will cover the cost and we'll refund you for the class you've paid for here."

"Thank you," I say, balling the damp tissue in my hand. Gabe rubs the spot between my shoulder blades, and the tension starts to dissipate. "I appreciate that."

"Of course, of course." He hands me a fresh tissue. Then he leans toward me, elbows resting on his desk. "Now never repeat that I said this, but trust me when I tell you Francesca is the best," he whispers. "And not just in Ravello, in all of Italy, if you ask me." He winks and sits back in his chair.

"Here's everything you need for the class." Glasses perched

back on the bridge of his nose, he hands me the paper on top of the stack. “Again, I’m sorry for the inconvenience and the confusion. I know you’ll enjoy Francesca and her class.”

Once back in the room—with its white plastered walls that yesterday felt clean and fresh, and now feel stark and cold—I head to the bathroom to take a shower. I’m physically spent from the hike, and emotionally frayed from the incident in the lobby.

“Are you okay?” Gabe asks. We both know I’m not, but I don’t feel like getting into it just now.

“Yes,” I say, hoping he can tell from my tone I’m not interested in discussing it.

“Are you sure?”

“Gabe, I really need to take a shower.”

There’s a pause before he says, “Sure. I’ll be out here.”

I shut the bathroom door and turn on the taps, making the water as hot as I can. I shimmy out of my shorts and tank top and gasp when I step into the streaming water, the heat intense. It’s painful, but I don’t change the temperature. The water coats my skin, changing its color from a light bronze to a bright, angry red.

I’ve held it in as long as I can. Water still running, I open the glass door and lean over the bidet—luckily right beside the shower stall in the small bathroom. My body heaves and I vomit, my pizza lunch gone from my stomach in an instant. After I’m done, I get back in the shower and kneel down under the hot, cascading water, my arms wrapped around my stomach to cover the scars.

# 32

"Yee-ouch," I say, trying to walk around the room without limping. I slide off my beige espadrilles and look at my heels, which are covered in angry, bubbled blisters.

"At least you outran the goat," Gabe says. "I'm sure socks would have slowed you down. I'd take blisters over a goat bite to the ass any day." He's been trying hard to keep the mood light and breezy since yesterday's lobby meltdown, and while I'm still feeling its effects, I'm grateful for the reason to laugh.

"Very funny," I say.

"I'll be here all day." He takes a deep bow.

"Good to know." I smile and then grab my backpack out of the closet. "Do you think I can wear flip-flops to the class? The note said closed-toe shoes." I dig around through the pack for the rubber sandals I know are in there somewhere. "Where the hell are they?" I sigh with frustration, but then my fingers find the sandals buried deep at the bottom of the pack.

Gabe waves a hand like he's trying to get rid of a pesky fly. "Forget the note. That's for clumsy people who don't know how to work a ladle. You, my love, are not that person."

"Maybe so, but it's right here," I say, reading the paper the concierge had given me. I point at the last paragraph. "'Wear comfortable clothing and closed-toe shoes. Aprons and all supplies will be provided. Bring your appetite!'"

"Well, if a lame rule is more important than your comfort, go right ahead and wear the shoes."

I slide into the black flip-flops and sigh, this time with contentment. "Oh, so much better." I take a few quick strides. "Screw it, I'm wearing these. At least my dress is long so you won't really see them."

"Good call," Gabe says. "Comfortable and fashion-aware." I roll my eyes. "Now go forth and learn to cook all the things. That's why we're here, after all."

A lump forms in my throat. "That's not the only reason," I say, then wonder why I always do that. Force us back there, instead of looking forward. For whatever reason, as illogical as it is, I'm afraid to stop focusing on the accident. On all that was lost.

"I know, Tegan. But let's not think about all that right now, okay?"

I nod, putting one arm through the strap of my small leather purse so it lies across my chest. I adjust the yellow-and-white herringbone striped sundress that hangs to the floor so it's not bunched up, and tie a pashmina scarf around the purse strap. "See you soon?" I ask as I grab the key card off the table by the door along with three sealed-and-stamped envelopes—one for my parents, one for Gabe's parents and one for Anna—and slip everything into my purse. "I think it's over around four."

"You bet," Gabe says. "See you when you're back."

I take the back stairs from our room to avoid the lobby, still feeling embarrassed by my outburst. The walk from the hotel to the cooking school is short, and maneuvering the cobblestones makes me grateful I chose the flip-flops in the end. The streets bustle despite the early hour. Tourists enjoy frothy cappuccinos and delicate pastries in outdoor cafés as they pore over travel brochures and maps. Store owners open their shops, their displays spilling out onto the cobblestone to catch the attention of the passing tourists. And locals with empty bags stand in line outside the fishmonger's storefront, waiting to choose tonight's dinner from the morning's fresh catch.

Two restaurants, a church and a lookout point that offers an incredible panorama of the Amalfi coastline border Ravello's pedestrian square. Walking through the square, I drop the envelopes into the postbox near the lookout and take a few pictures of the view, thinking how much my parents would love it here. I've spoken with them on the phone a few times since Dad's heart attack, and also with Gabe's father, who reassured me that my dad was doing very well. Anna had also sent a flurry of emails in the past few days, detailing dates one through four with Samuel, her latest crush.

All the correspondence makes me miss home, and at the same time, feel thankful for the distance. Because I know if I were at home, in our apartment full of memories and suffocating sadness, I'd still be stuck in bed while everyone else carried on like normal. Here, though, I have moments of intense pain when I open my eyes and realize none of it was a bad dream, but I also look forward to what the days will bring. Possibility exists here.

A few minutes later I arrive at my destination and ring the doorbell, a quick flurry of nervous excitement filling my belly. I'm not sure if I'm anxious about the actual cooking part, or the fact that out of three things from the jar, this is stop number two. After today, the trip that is supposed to be my salvation is more than half over.

The cooking class is run out of a private home, a 250-year-old house that looks out over the ocean. It's surrounded by gardens, where everything from clusters of cherry tomatoes, pumpkins, rosemary, basil and Italian parsley grows, along with bright yellow and pink flowers I've never seen before, and bushes of wild capers. Even though I'm five minutes early, it seems most of the rest of the class is already here. The other seven participants are wearing white aprons sporting Francesca's Cooking School and standing around the decently sized and surprisingly modern kitchen, with granite counters and an industrial-looking range. The room is filled with excited chatter and plenty of amazing smells. I hang my purse on a hook by the front door and tie an apron around my waist.

"Welcome," the younger of two women bustling around the kitchen says to me when I come to stand at the island with the others. "I'm Gianna, but everyone calls me Gia." She holds out her hand and I shake it.

"Nice to meet you. I'm Tegan."

"Thank you for coming to Francesca's Cooking School, Tegan. We're thrilled to have you with us today," she adds, smiling brightly. Her English, though accented, is excellent. She introduces me to her mother, Francesca, who speaks no English but is, from what I understand, the creative genius behind the cooking school and the recipes. Gia explains she leads the class while her mother does the cooking demonstrations.

During the ten minutes or so of group introductions, we learn Francesca has been cooking since she was a young girl, and about some of the rich and famous visitors she's cooked for over the years. While we listen to Gia explain how it's all going to work, we nibble on sweetly glazed lemon cake and sip cappuccinos, and I think of Rosa, imagining her life here, surrounded by such beauty and perfection. I understand her better, being in Ravello—much like what happened when I learned we were having a son. It helped me appreciate that her at-times challenging intensity had little to do with me, and everything to do with her fierce love for Gabe.

Some participants scribble notes as Gia speaks, one takes pictures of every surface in the kitchen and others, like me, simply enjoy the cake, coffee and atmosphere.

"Now, first things first," Gia says. "The basic tomato sauce. My mother—"

"Bloody hell, Colin," comes a woman's voice from behind us. "I told you it started at nine, not nine thirty."

The group turns to see the latecomers, and I'm surprised to recognize them. It's the newlyweds from Torre dello Ziro.

"Oh, hi!" she says to me. Then she slaps her husband's arm and points. "Colin, look who it is."

There's an awkward moment as the rest of the group looks between us, and I self-consciously wave back and say, "Hello again."

Gia comes around the island and hands them aprons, commenting about how with Colin's height it might be more like a baby bib, which draws a laugh from the group. Colin and his still nameless bride tie on their aprons and come to stand beside me.

Her blond hair is now in a high ponytail rather than a French braid, and she's wearing a white sequined tank top and denim skirt that only falls midthigh. She really does have amazing legs.

She sticks out a hand. "We didn't meet properly last time. I'm Becca," she says. "And this is Colin."

I shake her hand, then his. "Tegan," I say. Gia starts back up, so Becca leans in closely. "You here alone?"

I nod and whisper back, "My husband stayed at the hotel."

"Lucky bugger," Colin says out of the corner of his mouth, and Becca smacks him again.

I smile then turn my attention back to Gia, who's explaining that for the tomato sauce, the garlic should never be chopped but added to the oil whole, and that burnt garlic ruins a sauce, so to watch it closely. Whole, skinless plum tomatoes, harvested from the family's crops and preserved the summer before, are added and crushed into the garlic and oil. Then comes a handful of basil—I now know what a good handful of basil looks like—a generous pinch of crushed red pepper flakes and about two cups of ripe cherry tomatoes, all from the family's garden. As the deep red aromatic sauce simmers, Gia offers a few more tips.

"Now this is the basic tomato sauce, which we'll use today for our eggplant parmigiana," she says. "Here in our home, we make a large batch of this sauce on Saturday and use it for the rest of the week on pastas and pizza."

I take the spoon Gia hands me, blowing a couple of times on the sauce as per her suggestion, and then pop the spoon into my mouth. Flavors explode on my tongue—tangy tomatoes that carry the faintest hint of freshly turned earth, a subtle bouquet of basil and garlic, and a tickle of heat from the chili flakes. It tastes nothing like any sauce I've made at home, even with imported Roma tomatoes from the authentic Italian grocery shop not far from our apartment in Chicago.

"Good, good, right?" Gia asks as the group murmurs its appreciation, more spoons of sauce being handed out. "The secret is in using the best, freshest tomatoes you can, and adding, as Mamma says, *'un pizzico di amore,'* or a 'pinch of love.'"

Through the next few hours we learn about how traditional Italian cooking is done with very few ingredients, but always the freshest, and most locally available options, like the olives, lemons, tomatoes and buffalo mozzarella cheese this region is famous for. We taste all the herbs and vegetables, in their raw and cooked states, as we prepare the dishes on the class menu—Farmer's spaghetti, with cherry tomatoes, garlic and black and green olives; delicate and lemony white fish with capers; and eggplant parmigiana, which comes out of the oven puffy and golden brown, thanks to the smoked provolone that covers the layers of thinly sliced eggplant.

Gia and Francesca plate the meals for our lunch, and Gia's husband, Aberto, treats us to a tour of the gardens and explains why this part of Italy has ideal growing conditions: a combination of sun, mountainous rain and ocean breezes. We also tour the family's winemaking production, and see how they smoke their own cheeses.

Church bells from the nearby square let us know it's four o'clock, and we're escorted back to the large rustic dining table on the patio. Under a vine- and flower-covered arch, we enjoy the meal we've prepared, along with bottles of the family's homemade red wine. Unlike other homemade wines I've had in the past, this one tastes expensive and goes down so smoothly I'm three glasses in and feeling a bit light-headed before the second course is even served.

"So, how long have you and…what's your husband's name?" Becca asks, twirling the fresh pasta noodles onto her fork.

"Gabe."

"Right. How long have you and Gabe been married?" She pops the forkful of pasta in her mouth and her eyes open wide. "Oh, fuck, this is good," she mumbles around the spaghetti.

"A year in September," I reply, taking a large gulp of wine to force back the catch in my throat.

"Ah, so you're still newlyweds, too," Colin says, clinking his wineglass to mine.

"I guess so." I take another large gulp of the wine.

"It's only been two weeks for us, but so far, so good." Colin smiles at Becca. "She's a real cracker and I'm never letting her go."

"Even though it almost didn't happen." Becca points her fork at Colin and raises an eyebrow.

Colin laughs. "True enough," he says, wiping his mouth

with the linen napkin in his lap. "I royally fucked up the proposal."

Becca laughs, taking another bite of the spaghetti and reaching over to dip her crusty ciabatta bun into the dish brimming with murky green-tinged olive oil. She's already eaten more than Colin and I combined, and I have no idea where she's putting it.

"Why?" I ask, because it seems like they're waiting for me to do so. "What happened?"

Colin and Becca exchange a look. "You tell it," she says.

"No, you go ahead, love," he replies.

Becca puts her fork down and leans forward on the table. "I told him all along, 'I want to spend the rest of my life with you, you crazy bugger, but I will not say yes to anything without a ring on this finger.'" She sits back and nibbles on an oil-soaked hunk of bread. "So five years to the day we started going out, and yes, I waited five fucking years for him to finally come to his senses..." Colin grabs her cheeks gently with his mitt of a hand, and kisses her on her smiling lips. "We had a big night planned with friends in London, and he was acting all crazy, so I knew something was up. Plus," she says, chewing a few times and swallowing, "it was our first-date anniversary, so I had a feeling."

She turns and grins up at him, and I smile politely at the two of them, wondering how long the story might drag out. Something's brewing inside my gut that has nothing to do with the food, and I decide more wine—lots more—will help smother it. I go to take another sip from my glass and realize my glass is empty. Colin reaches over and refills it.

"Anyway, to make a long story short, by the end of the night we were good and sloshed, and it was time to head back on the Tube. And this finger?" Becca holds up her ring finger, upon which rests two bands—one plain gold and the other with three large diamonds set on top. "Still bare.

"So finally we get home, and I'm fumbling around trying to find the keys to our flat," Becca says.

"And she's giving me shit," Colin adds, gesturing his thumb towards Becca. "Because I'm not helping."

Becca nods, sipping from her water glass. "I turn to give him more grief, and there he is, on one knee in front of me." She smiles wide, showing teeth with a purplish hue thanks to the wine.

"It was going brilliantly," Colin says. "Exactly how I planned it, so she'd be surprised. And then—"

"And then." Becca puts a hand on his arm to stop him. "He held the ring out and started to ask me, and…he dropped the fucking ring."

Colin starts laughing. "It rolled right into the bloody sewer grate."

My eyes open wide. "Seriously?"

"Yup," Becca says, nodding. "Gone! Rolled right into a giant pool of shit."

"Shhhhh," Colin says, laughing but noticing the rest of the table's reaction to her loud voice and words.

"Well, it did!" Becca exclaims. She leans forward again, so I do, too. "No way was I saying yes without a ring. And definitely not with a shitty ring. Who would? So I yelled at him some more…"

"She went a tad mad, she did," Colin adds.

"Of course I did." Becca shrugs. "What woman wouldn't have a meltdown in that situation? Right?" I nod, draining my glass again. Colin is quick to fill it back up. "So after I finished beating on him with my bag and telling him exactly what I thought of his shitty proposal, I went inside the flat and left him on the front step."

"You didn't!" I'm laughing now, tipsy and thoroughly entertained by my dinner companions.

She nods, eyes wide and sincere. "Yup. I told him to come back when he had a proper ring."

"So I did," Colin says. "The next day as soon as the shops opened I went and bought her that gorgeous, not-shitty ring that's on her finger, and proposed again."

"And I said yes," she says. "Of course, what the stupid lug didn't know was that I would have said yes to a plastic ring." Colin shrugs and Becca stares at him adoringly.

My stomach clenches and I turn my attention back to my pasta, which is now cold.

"How about you?" Becca asks. "How did Gabe do it?"

I wipe a few small drops of wine from the edge of the glass and smile.

# 33

*Eleven months before the accident*

"I think I'm going to stay home tonight," I said as loudly as my hoarse voice would allow. I cleared my throat a few times. "I really feel horrible." I ran the water at the kitchen sink until it was warm, then filled a tall glass and added a tablespoon of salt, stirring it until the salt dissolved.

Gabe came into the kitchen from the bedroom just as I was gargling the salted water, and leaned back against the counter, waiting until I spit it out.

"Gah, that's so gross," I said with a grimace.

"Throat's not feeling better, huh?" He rubbed my back as I took another gulp of the water, working hard to fight my gag reflex.

I gargled again, nearly gagged again and then spit into the sink. With a "nope, can't do any more of that" I dumped the rest of the lukewarm, salty water into the sink. "Lucy said this should help, but I think I prefer the sore throat." I swished my mouth out with some cold, unsalted water, then collapsed on the couch.

"How about a cup of tea?" Gabe crouched behind our kitchen island. Pots and pans banged while he searched for the kettle, which we only used when my mom was over or when one of us was sick.

I shook my head. “No, thanks. Every time I swallow it’s like I ate a mouthful of razor blades,” I said, my voice cracking. “It’s probably strep. Anna had it two weeks ago and it’s been making its way through the staff.” I cleared my throat again and winced. “Why don’t you just go without me? I’ll likely be in bed by eight anyway.”

“Oh, no,” Gabe said, sitting beside me on the couch and dragging my feet on to his lap. “For one, it’s Scotty’s breakout night, and two, you are not leaving me alone with Anna and what’s his name. No way.”

We were headed to a local pub in our neighborhood, where we often spent Saturdays with a group of close friends. It was the pub’s first amateur talent night, and Scott, Gabe’s best friend from law school, was performing his first ever stand-up comedy routine.

As well, Anna was currently dating a business major she had met at her gym; he was nice to look at, but at just twenty-one—we were, of course, only twenty-five, but somehow the four-year span was a significant gap at this stage of life—he was annoyingly confident for someone who couldn’t legally drink beer until a few months ago.

“First of all, Scott only really cares that you’ll be there,” I said. “And secondly, *his name* is Chad and Anna told me he likes working out, and running, too, I think. You can talk about that.” I wrapped my hands around my throat as I swallowed, giving Gabe the most pathetic look I could muster, which wasn’t hard based on how I was feeling.

“Forget it, sickie. You’re going even if I have to drag you there.” He glanced at his watch and gave my legs a couple of taps before shifting them off his lap and getting up. “Up you get. I’m going to grab you copious amounts of painkillers, unfortunately only over-the-counter ones, though, that I'll crush into a spoonful of honey if I have to, then you're getting dressed."

"Fine," I croaked. "But I'm not going to talk to anyone, and we're leaving early."

"You're such a drag when you're sick," Gabe said with a wink. "Drugs coming right up, m'lady."

I laid my pounding, feverish head back against the couch and tried to imagine how I was going to make it through the night.

I made one final attempt to stay in my pajamas by calling Anna while Gabe hunted for the acetaminophen, and tried to convince her to tell Gabe he should leave me at home. But she was equally unsympathetic and equally determined to get me out that night.

"It's been ages since we went to the Flying Fork together," she whined. "You are not bailing."

"I think 'ages' is a bit melodramatic," I said. "But it's been 'ages' because *you* were sick for two weeks, remember?"

"You'll be fine," she said distractedly.

"Of course I'll be fine," I grumbled, tucking the phone between my ear and shoulder and standing to fold the blanket. Clearly I wasn't going to need it tonight.

"Teg, I gotta go." Excitement bubbled into her voice. "He's here. See you in twenty, okay?"

Twenty-five minutes later I sat in one of the well-used, wooden captain chairs at the round table we always occupied, and wrapped my navy blue crocheted scarf tighter around my neck. It was early February, and I'd basically been cold since the first snow in December. Tonight was worse, which likely meant my fire-lined throat was making my fever rise.

Anna and Chad arrived a couple of minutes later, then Scott and his girlfriend, Harper, sat down. Finally, Cass, a good friend of Anna's from high school, and James, another work friend of Gabe's who had a serious crush on Cass, filled out the rest of the chairs.

Everyone waved and said hi as they removed hats, gloves and heavy coats, before ordering a round of drinks. While our group drank beer and martinis, I sipped from a cracked mug of lukewarm tea, feeling quite sorry for myself. You should never order tea, or coffee, at a bar. It was terrible.

The small, dimly lit stage at the front of the bar, normally used for a local band that played the Flying Fork on Saturday nights, tonight held only a stool and a microphone.

Scott and Harper came around the table and over to where Gabe and I sat, and Scott gave me a huge kiss on the cheek, while Harper and Gabe hugged.

"You nervous, Scotty?" Gabe asked, clapping Scott on the back.

"Not a bit," he said, smiling wide. Scott had smooth, caramel-colored skin, thanks to his Indian mother, and deep blue eyes courtesy of his Californian dad. The combination of the two made it hard to call him anything but beautiful. "How about you?" he asked, winking at Gabe.

"What does he possibly have to be nervous about?" My voice could barely be heard over the background music and bar patrons. The place, as usual, was packed. "Except for what revenge his sick girlfriend might be plotting for dragging her to a freezing cold bar where they serve crappy tea."

"Whoa, Teg," Scott said. "You do not sound good. You should be in bed."

Harper, who was as fair as Scott was dark, but equally stunning, nodded. "You should definitely be in bed, Tegan."

"Thanks, guys." I turned to Gabe. "You see?"

"She's tough," Gabe said, smiling at me. "Don't worry. After Scotty does his thing I promise I'll take you to bed."

He wiggled his eyebrows, eliciting a laugh from Scott, an eye roll from me and a sympathetic look from Harper.

"Men," she said. "Always thinking with their other heads."

I laughed, then gave a dramatic fake sob while I held my hands to my throat.

"Poor baby," Gabe said, kissing my forehead. "Oh, man, you are warm. I probably should have tucked you in and left you to a night of having complete control over the remote."

"It's okay." My voice cracked again. "But right after Scotty is done, promise?"

"Promise," he said.

The energy in the pub picked up as the owner, a young guy we only knew as "Sully," took the stage and tapped the microphone.

"Hey, everyone," he said, and the room cheered back a hello. "Okay, so I know we usually do live music on Saturdays here at the Fork, but we're trying something new tonight. I'm calling it 'So you think you're hot shit?'" Everyone laughed, and a few whistles pierced the room. "It's an amateur talent night, and we have a great lineup, starting with one of our regulars, Scott Tramsworth." Sully put a hand to his brow and tried to see into the crowd. "Scotty, where are you, buddy? Get up here and do your thing." There were claps and more cheers, especially from our table, as Scott made his way up to the stage.

My stomach flipped nervously for him as he took a seat on the stool and adjusted the microphone. Gabe put his fingers in his mouth and let out a loud whistle, and Harper clapped and blew kisses toward the stage.

"So, thanks, Sully," Scott began, and everyone cheered some more. "I have a joke for you guys, just to get things warmed up. Wanna hear it?" The cheers increased in intensity.

Scotty nodded and put a hand to the microphone. "Now

keep in mind, I'm a lawyer not a comedian, okay? Be nice." Whistles and hollers filled the room and, with a smile, Scott sat on the edge of the stool. "Okay, so, here goes. A horse walks into a bar, and the bartender says—" he paused for effect and the room hushed "—'why the long face?'"

Silence. I cringed and, embarrassed for Scott, looked at Harper instead of the stage. She just sat there, trying to hide a laugh behind her hands. A few chuckles could be heard throughout the room, along with the sounds of drinks being consumed to fill the uncomfortable silence.

"I can see that one wasn't superpopular with this crowd," Scott said, getting off the stool. "The good news for you guys is that I'm not actually doing stand-up tonight." He held up a finger, asking for a moment, and walked off the stage.

I leaned toward Gabe. "What's he doing?" I asked.

"No clue," Gabe replied. From the other side of the table Anna gave me a questioning glance, looking as perplexed as I felt. I shrugged and turned back to the stage.

A few seconds later Scott walked back into the middle of the stage, this time holding a guitar in his hands. "Hey, that looks like your guitar," I whispered to Gabe, noticing the sticker on its back—deep purple with a white outline of Willie the Wildcat, Northwestern's mascot. "What's he doing with your guitar?" I hoped for Scott's sake he wasn't planning on following up that terrible joke with a musical interlude.

Scott held the microphone in one hand and the guitar's neck in the other. "Gabe? Gabe Lawson? Wanna come up here and save me from this tough crowd?" This got a few laughs, and Scott pretended to be offended. "Oh, so you laugh at that? Wow. Good luck to you, my friend," he said to Gabe, who had just come up onstage to stand beside Scott.

I sat with my mouth open, wondering what the hell Gabe was doing up there. Had he decided to play something for amateur night? He had been practicing a lot lately, usually while I did my classroom planning at night, or while I watched one of the dramas he couldn't stand and typically ruined for me with his running commentary.

"Thanks, man," Gabe said, taking the guitar from Scott and sitting on the stool. Scott slapped him on the back and came back to our table, where Harper gave him a kiss.

"What the hell, Scotty?" I said. "What's he doing?"

"Just wait," Scott replied, a huge grin on his face. He kept his eyes on Gabe. "Just wait."

I looked back at Gabe, who had put the strap over his shoulder and was strumming a few bars. He looked up from his guitar and adjusted the microphone. "First, thanks, Scotty, for helping me out by telling the worst joke I'm sure any of us has ever heard," he said, laughter filling the room. "Now I can pretty much do anything and look like a rock star." There was a lot of clapping, but I was too confused to join in. Glancing around the table, I realized everyone else knew something I didn't. They were staring at me and smiling, all except for Anna, who was crying big fat tears as she held her clasped hands to her heart.

"And thanks to Sully, who helped me set this all up. There is no amateur night, you'll all be happy to know," Gabe said, strumming the opening bars of a song that sounded familiar. "I wrote this for my girlfriend, Tegan, and she's here tonight." He stopped strumming and put the pick in his mouth, pointing with one hand out into the dark room, toward our table. "Somewhere out there," he said, talking around the guitar pick.

"She's right here!" Scotty shouted, jumping up and pointing at me while people swiveled in their seats to get a look. I slid a little farther down in my chair, my heart beating fast.

"She's crazy sick, but she's here anyway," Gabe continued.

"Which is good, because even though this song is going to be short, and trust me, once I start singing you'll be happy about that—" Gabe smiled wide, continuing to strum the guitar "—these are the most important words I'll ever say." Now the room was quiet, except for the sounds of Gabe's guitar, and his voice, which was clear and sweet, even if it would never win him any kind of talent contest.

*"Promise me your heart...and I will carry it with mine...*

*"Promise me your body...I will worship for all time."*

He hummed a few lines of the melody and then started singing again.

*"Promise me your mind...and it will carry us away...*

*"Promise me your soul...I will feed it every day."*

Then, still strumming the bars of the song that I now recognized as the one that streamed softly from behind the closed door in our bedroom all those nights, Gabe got off the stool and walked down the stage's stairs, heading toward our table. I held my breath; my heart was going to burst right out of my chest.

Soon he was in front of me and it was just the two of us. Him humming the song's melody, and me, tears streaming down my face as he watched me, smiling. He locked his eyes on mine and sang me the last two lines, in a smooth, sure voice.

*"Promise me your love...and I will let mine flow...*

*"Promise me your hand...I will never let it go."*

He handed the guitar to Scott, who then passed him a small black box. Gabe stood in front of me for a second longer, then got down on one knee and opened the box. Even though I knew what was nestled on the black satin inside, I had no clue what it looked like because I didn't take my eyes off Gabe's face.

"Tegan Jane McCall," Gabe said. "Will you marry me?"

There wasn't a moment of hesitation. "Yes," I squeaked out, my voice nearly gone. I was crying and laughing at the same time. "Yes, yes, yes!" The room erupted with my answer, and Gabe stood and pulled me to my feet, pressing his mouth to mine so hard our noses squished together and our foreheads banged.

I leaned into him, then just as quickly, pushed him away. "Wait, stop," I said, my voice barely a whisper now. "You're going to get sick!"

"So worth it," he said, and kissed me again. "So very worth it."

The next morning I woke up without any sign of a voice, and covered head to toe in a splotchy red rash. Gabe immediately texted his sister, Lucy, despite my begging him not to, telling him it was Sunday and I could wait a day until she was back in the office. "What's the point of having a doctor for a sister if I can't text her twenty-four seven?" he'd asked, laughing as he tugged his phone out of my hands after I'd snatched it away from him. "Besides. I'm her baby brother, which means she's always happy to hear from me."

He sent her a picture of the rash and a list of symptoms, along with another picture of my hand, complete with engagement ring. Lucy texted back almost immediately:

Looks like Tegan has scarlet fever...and a husband-to-be. Tell the to-be Mrs. Lawson to stay in bed, and welcome to the family. Congrats to you both! xo

Even with the antibiotics Lucy prescribed for the strep throat and the mandated bed rest that Gabe and my mother enforced annoyingly well, it took me almost a week to feel like myself again. But I didn't care, because I had a ring on my finger—a beautiful platinum band filled with sparkling diamonds—and a promise from the man I loved more than anything else in the world.

# 34

It's not until I walk out of the cooking school and try to maneuver the uneven cobblestone street that it occurs to me I might be drunk. I try to remember how many glasses of wine I had. Four? Six? I turn toward Colin to ask how many times he filled up my glass, but I do it too fast and my head spins.

"Whoa, Tegan." Colin grabs my arm when I trip over a stone that protrudes slightly higher than the rest, my flip-flop twisting sideways. Good thing he does, otherwise I might have ended up on my face and I'm not sure I would have had the ability to get up. "All right there?"

"Thanks," I say, the alcohol numbing any embarrassment I might feel at falling into a stranger's arms.

"So what do you ladies say?" Colin asks as we make our way into the pedestrian square. "Fancy another drink?"

Becca puts her hand up and I say, "At least one more!" which makes them both laugh. Becca links arms with me and we make our way to an empty table, where I plop down into one of the steel chairs gracelessly. I feel warm and fuzzy around the edges.

Over two more glasses of wine, we chat about our jobs—Becca is a graphic designer and Colin's in finance—and the differences between living in Chicago versus London, and make ambitious plans to meet back in this very spot for a bottle of wine every year.

I think I might have stayed there all night, with my new best friends whose last name I didn't even know, if they didn't break the spell.

"Too bad Gabe didn't catch up with us," Becca says. "I'm sure Colin would have appreciated another male perspective, especially with all that shoe talk." She winks at Colin, and he grins back. At the mention of Gabe, a small shock moves through me, and the warm feeling disappears.

"Yeah, I'd better get back to the hotel." I clumsily pull out a handful of euros from my purse. "It must be late."

Colin pushes the bills back into my hands. "Nope, this one's on us." I thank them both for the drinks and the company. "Apologize to your bloke, would you, for us kidnapping you this evening?" Colin says.

"I will, I will." I stand up and promptly tilt sideways, catching myself hard on the edge of the table with my elbow. I swear and rub at my tingling arm, then hold tight to the table's top while I take off my flip-flops. "Think I'll do better without these," I say, tucking the rubber sandals under one arm. Colin and Becca ask me if I'll be okay getting back to the hotel—I assure them I will—then link hands at the table and order another bottle from the ever-present waiter. I wave at them over my shoulder as I make my way back to Villa Maria, weaving through the busy streets barefoot.

But the closer I get to the hotel, the more the happy, free-floating feel from earlier fades. Numbness replaces it, with a familiar edge of darkness I wish I could ignore. Back at the hotel I find my way to the room and at first don't think Gabe is there. It's dark aside from a few streams of lamplight coming in through the window from the garden below. Then he clears his throat.

"Fuck!" The sandals drop to the floor. I flick on the overhead light and try to catch my breath. "You scared me."

"Where were you?" Gabe asks. He's sitting in the armchair in the corner, his arms crossed on his chest. He does not look pleased.

"Sorry." I wrestle with my purse to get the strap over my head. I'm loud and clumsy. Definitely overdid it on the wine, but I'm hoping I don't look as drunk as I feel. The purse's buckle gets caught in my hair and I swear as it pulls painfully. I finally get untangled, and sit on the bed. "That couple from the hike, Becca and Colin?" I say, my words coming out with difficulty. "I had a drink with them after the class."

Gabe's quiet for a moment, and then in the silence I let out a burp, which makes me laugh. I fall over onto the bed.

"You're drunk." Disappointment laces his words.

"So what?" I flip over onto my stomach and rest my head in the crook of my bent elbows. Eyelids heavy, I try unsuccessfully to stifle a yawn. "It was fun."

"I thought we agreed getting drunk was not a good idea right now, especially with your meds."

It's irrational, but it irritates me the way he shortens the word *medication*. Like they're old friends or something. "We?" I raise my head to look at him. I'm too dizzy to hold it there, so I let it drop back down again. "You must have decided that was for the best," I murmur. "*We* did not agree to anything."

I am not a good drunk, if there is such a thing. Of the half dozen or so serious fights I've ever had with Gabe over the years, at least five of them happened after too many drinks. A little booze relaxes me and turns me into "fun" Tegan; too much makes me mean and weepy. Two things I do not need in my life at the moment.

"Besides, I took the stupid pill early this morning. I'm sure it's mostly worn off by now."

"What about your patch?"

I crack open one eye and twist my head to look at my bare shoulder. *Shit.* I forget to put on the new patch this morning. "No problem, I'll do it now." I roll off the edge of the bed, somehow landing on my feet.

Stumbling a little I search for my backpack, where I keep a Ziploc bag full of my extra patches. "Ah, there you are." I bend over to grab the pack, which is leaning against the armoire. It's only when I go to lift it up onto the bed that I realize it's upside down; everything inside falls out around me. "Oops," I say, giggling as I look at the contents strewn across the tiled floor. Pack of gum. Balled-up athletic socks. First-aid kit, courtesy of Connor. Chapstick and sunscreen. A pen, the cap chewed. Two and a half bottles of pink bismuth, zipped into a plastic bag. The box of cards from my mom. The book from Anna, which I have yet to read.

"The patches are in the bathroom, on the counter," Gabe says.

Hands on my hips, I swivel toward him and nearly lose my balance. "That would have been good information, oh, say, two minutes ago?"

Annoyed, I crouch down and drag my arm across the floor, gathering everything into a sloppy pile. I'm about to start tossing stuff back into the pack, but then freeze when I see the envelope sticking out of the book.

I had forgotten I packed it—tucking it into the middle of the book Anna gave me—at the last minute before heading to the airport. My fingertips grasp the edge and I pull it out of the book's pages, clutching the white greeting-card-sized envelope to my chest. Closing my eyes, I take a few deep breaths, willing myself to stop the tears that come so easily thanks to the wine.

The envelope is crumpled, the glue on its flap long gone

and the tape now barely holding it closed, grungy with dirt and lint from the inside of my pack. I won't open it now, though I feel a desperate urge to, as I don't want Gabe to know what it holds. But I don't have to open it to picture the paper inside, folded into small squares so as to fit in the too-small envelope, with the words "Merry Christmas to my husband. Love you forever, T xo" scrawled across its top in gold-flecked ink. I never gave it to him, never had a chance. And now, after the accident, there's no point.

Gabe crouches behind me, a hand on my shoulder to try and turn me around so he can see for himself that I'm okay. I jump at his touch, but I resist him. "Tegan, what's going on?" Gabe asks, his voice sharp, which makes me cry harder. Dropping his hand from my shoulder, he sighs and I want to tell him I'm fine. To remind him a few tears are perfectly normal when I drink too much wine. I'm about to say we should just go to bed when he swears under his breath but loud enough for me to catch it, and says, "See, this is why you shouldn't be drinking so much. It just makes you sad."

The anger bubbles up inside me.

"Well, dear husband of mine," I say, sliding the envelope back into the book's depths. Then I stand to face him. "You're right. Like always." Gabe sets his mouth in a firm, straight line. "But guess what? Everything makes me fucking sad. So I might as well enjoy some good Italian wine while I'm here. Because let's be honest. None of this was my idea." Too drunk to stand, I sit on the bed and wrestle with the scarf until it's unwound from my neck. With a sigh I lie back against the pillow.

Gabe is unrelenting. "I'm worried about you, Teg," he says, coming to the side of the bed to stand over me. "That you'll do something again, like before—"

"Like before, when?" I ask, bitterness seeping into my voice.

I keep my eyes on the ceiling. "You mean with the pills? For fuck's sake, how many times—"

"Tegan, stop."

"No, you stop, Gabe." I lift my head from the pillow and the whole room spins. For a moment I'm sure I'm going to throw up, but then the nausea passes. I sit up against the headboard, thankful for its sturdiness behind my back, and turn toward him. "What do you think I'm going to do? Try to off myself with the best fucking red wine I've ever had? Or maybe I'll use this scarf? Wrap it around and around and around my neck, and then tie it to the balcony and jump? Or maybe I'll go take my chances with that goat again." I laugh, bitterly, and Gabe grimaces. "The pills were an *accident*. How many times do I fucking have to tell people that? Re-lax."

"I know it wasn't an accident, Tegan."

His words hang between us, and the anger boils over.

"Who cares what you think!" I try to stand up on the bed, but my legs collapse under me. Gabe reaches out to keep me from falling and I smack his hand away. "Do not touch me."

My fury builds and it's all I can do to keep from slapping his face—which carries a look of deep sadness and a touch of fear. "None of this would have happened, would be happening, if you hadn't…if you'd been…" My eyes are hot and full again. "You ruined everything for us, Gabe." I point a shaking finger at his chest. "*You* did this."

"Enough!" Gabe shouts, and I jump in surprise but stay on my knees facing him. "It was an accident, Tegan. Did *you* see the black ice? Do you think I wanted any of this to happen?" His voice rises, unstable with anger and grief. I ball a fist to my mouth and try to hold back the moan that wants to come out, but I don't turn away. I want him to see exactly what he's done to me, what he's done to us. Sobs wrack my body but he doesn't reach for me like I expect him to.

"You are so goddamned selfish," Gabe says. "As if you're the only one...the only one who lost something." He buries his face in his hands for a moment before looking back at me, eyes red and wet. "Well, fuck you, Tegan. He was my son, too."

Despite his harsh words, I could be kind—should be kind—because I understand what intense sorrow can do to a person. How it can turn them into someone they don't recognize. At the very least I don't have to make things worse than they already are. But I'm too full of thick black anger to care about anything or anyone else.

I calmly take my hands away from my mouth, quivering head to toe, but leaning toward him so that our faces are only inches apart. As I lock eyes with him, I realize we can't come back from this. We are both broken, likely beyond repair.

And that understanding makes me hate him even more.

"You're right, Gabe. This isn't just about me. But you left out one important detail." My shaky legs are barely holding me upright, but I spread my knees for balance and grip the headboard tightly. "Our son is dead, and only one of us is to blame for that."

His jaw clenches, and for a moment I'm not sure what he'll do, what he'll say. But then he breaks eye contact and sits back down heavily in the armchair, leaving me swaying unsteadily on the bed, all alone and jacked up on adrenaline, ready for a fight no one else is interested in having.

"By the way," he says with an emotionless tone that lands harder on me than his anger did. "You forgot your necklace today. On the side table." My eyes snap to the dark wood surface of the nightstand and sure enough, there's the necklace. I took it off to shower and forgot to put it back on. Shock fills me, then a deep sense of guilt.

I forgot to put the necklace on.

And I have no idea what that means.

★★★

A few hours later I wake to a splitting headache and a dark room. As I lie there, head pounding and stomach sour with wine, I piece together the events from earlier. Relief floods me as I place a hand to my collarbone and feel the necklace, back where it belongs.

"Tegan?"

At first I give no response. Then the pause feels too long. "Yeah?"

"I'm sorry."

The silence drapes over me, and I feel claustrophobic and too warm. I push down the covers, realizing then I'm still in my sundress. Unsure exactly how to say everything I want to, I settle for the only word that comes to mind. "Okay."

"I...I don't want to fight with you."

My eyes start to adjust to the darkness, and I stare up at the ceiling, willing myself not to cry. I want the anger to come back, because it protects me from the sadness.

"Okay," I say again, and clench my fists tightly as I roll away from him.

# 35

*One day before the accident*

"So, what do you think?"

Anna's mouth hung open. "Wow," she said. "Wow, it's… really something."

We were on Christmas break from school, heading out shortly for the gift we gave each other every year—a mess of Indian food and the cheesiest horror movie that's playing, since Gabe would never watch those with me—but I said I had to show her what I was giving Gabe first. "I can't wait for you to see it," I'd told her, suggesting we do coffee at my place first. "I've really knocked it out of the park this year."

She turned the crystal cube, about the size of a box of tea, over in her hands, holding it close to her face. Her silky black bangs dropped into her eyes and she brushed the hair aside, keeping her other hand tight on the crystal. "It's pretty heavy, huh? How much did this cost?"

I grinned—my back to her so she couldn't see my face—as I went to the kitchen to get the coffee carafe. Even though I told everyone I was only drinking decaf now that I was pregnant, including Gabe, who set out my prenatal vitamin every morning in an egg cup, alongside a glass of milk, it was a lie.

Only Anna knew the truth, because I knew she'd never judge me for something as mundane as caffeine. I was on my third cup of the day.

"It wasn't bad actually. Hundred and fifty, I think?" In truth, it had only cost about forty bucks, but I knew a little exaggeration was needed here.

Her lips snapped shut and she nodded vigorously, her ponytail bouncing. She placed the cube down on the coffee table between us. I hid my smile behind my mug, and watched as she poured cream into her coffee. "No, no, not bad at all," she said. "Though I have no clue what these sort of things cost, but that seems totally reasonable."

I picked up the crystal and held it carefully between my palms. "Gabe's going to be so surprised."

"No doubt about that." Anna took a big gulp of her coffee and averted her eyes. "I wish I could be here to see his face."

I had planned to drag things on longer, but couldn't hold back the laugh that burst from me at the look on her face. She was notoriously terrible at hiding her emotions, or her sarcastic tendencies.

"What?" she asked, adding, "What did I say?" when I couldn't stop laughing even long enough to catch my breath. Tears streamed down my cheeks and I started to hiccup.

"Ou-ouch," I said, the hiccup cramping my diaphragm, which was starting to get squeezed by the baby.

"Easy there, preggers, you're going to shake that baby right out of you," Anna said, cringing when another loud hiccup escaped me. She put her hand on my belly, and I covered it with my own. "Do you need some water?" I shook my head, holding my breath to try and quell the hiccups. "Next time I see my *zu mu* I'll bring you some candied tangerine peel. Best thing for hiccups. Seriously, it works," she said, seeing my reaction. I was nothing if not a skeptic. "Don't mess with my *zu mu*'s remedies, okay?"

"They're gone, I think." I took a deep breath and when nothing happened, took another one, followed by a sip of my coffee. "All good."

"Okay, so what did I miss? What's so funny?"

I leaned back against the throw pillows on the couch and raised an eyebrow. "Anna, you know me better than anyone. Do you really think this is what I'd choose to give Gabe for our first Christmas as a married couple? Really?"

"I don't know!" Anna threw her hands up and tucked her tiny legs under her butt. "I mean, I hope not, but you've got all those hormones swirling around inside you. Plus, you're growing *a penis* in there." She pointed at my belly and I laughed. "I can only imagine what that does to a girl."

I picked up the crystal cube and tried to keep my face neutral while I studied the hologram image inside. It was a laser-engraved picture of our first ultrasound, with the words *Daddy's Little Prince* floating just below it. "It really is hideous," I finally said, grinning.

"It really, really is." Anna nodded, and then we both burst out laughing. "Question, though. Have you considered he may actually like it?"

I stopped laughing and stared at her. I shook my head. "Not possible. You're looking at it, right? It's…kind of creepy, no?"

Anna shrugged. "To an *über*excited and emotional dad-to-be, which we both know Gabe is, it could be seen as sentimental."

I chewed the inside of my cheek, looking critically at the crystal. "Shit. You may have a point there." It was possible my practical joke could backfire. "Still, I'm going ahead. I'll just have to risk breaking his heart when I tell him it's going straight to his sock drawer." Anna grinned and drained her coffee, and I put the crystal back into the box. I'd wrap it when I got home from the movie.

"So what's the real gift? It better be something really good."

"It is," I said, getting up from the couch. "Give me a second." In my master bathroom I opened the drawer where I kept the tampons and pads—a drawer I hadn't needed for a few months and one I knew Gabe would never rifle through—and pulled out a white plastic cylinder. Back at the couch, I handed it to Anna and sat back down. She rolled it around in her hands, looking for a clue on its nondescript surface, then looked back at me. "How sweet, Teg. You got him a plastic tube. You really are the best wife *ever.*"

I swatted her and told her to open it. She laughed and popped off the plastic cap on one end, peering inside the tube. My heart beat a little faster, imagining Gabe's reaction when he opened it two days from now, on Christmas.

Anna gently pulled out the paper inside and unrolled it. I watched her eyes as they took in what I'd written across the top of the page—*Merry Christmas to my husband. Love you forever, T xo*—before scanning the rest of the page. A moment later her eyes welled up, and she sniffed a couple of times. "Oh, Tegan. This is beautiful."

"So much better than a crystal hologram, right?"

"*So* much better," she said, looking back at the paper. "Who wrote this for you?"

"Scotty's friend, Adam. He's a music teacher and a musician on the side apparently. He wrote the music, and we worked on the lyrics together. I thought Gabe could learn it on the guitar and then sing it to this little guy when he's born." I rubbed my belly, never tiring of the feel of its firm roundness under my hands.

"He's going to love it, Teg," Anna said, nodding vehemently. "It's perfect."

"Thanks." Taking the sheet music from her, I rolled it up tightly and fed it back into the plastic cylinder. The song was part lullaby, part love song, and I couldn't wait to give it to him. I glanced at my watch. "We'd better get going."

"He's going to bawl like a baby, I hope you know." Anna took our coffee mugs over to the kitchen and put them in the dishwasher.

"That's the plan," I said, packing up the crystal and hiding it behind a stack of old magazines in the bookcase.

Anna pulled on her coat, then wrapped her arms around me and tucked her head under my chin. "Fuck me, you two are way too adorable." I smiled, and returned the hug. "Seriously, I don't know how much more I can take."

"Sorry," I said over my shoulder as I made my way back to the bathroom. "I'll try to consider your feelings next Christmas, okay?" Then I hid the gift back in the tampon drawer before we headed out for dinner.

# 36

"Tegan?"

I whirl around, shocked to hear my name.

"Ah, *buongiorno*! I thought that was you." Gia, of Francesca's Cooking School, stands in front of me. Her arms are heavy with bags of all shapes and sizes bursting with groceries, but she looks like carrying them is no burden at all. "Are you staying here? In Amalfi?"

"Uh, no," I splutter. I'm fuzzy with my hangover, and have a throbbing headache from the wine, not enough sleep and last night's fight with Gabe. "I'm—well, we're staying in Ravello."

"Are you going inside?" Gia cranes her head up the wide stone staircase, which leads to the famous Amalfi Cathedral. I was actually considering it, but am not sure what I'm supposed to do once I get inside. Aside from the ceramic Nativity scene my mom puts out on the fireplace mantel every Christmas—as a child I broke the baby Jesus figurine, which mom replaced with a fabric-wrapped cork—religion isn't exactly something my family pays attention to.

"I was thinking I'd get a coffee first," I reply, though that wasn't really the plan, either. I didn't have a plan when I got in the taxi this morning, other than escaping Ravello or, more specifically, the hotel room and Gabe. I've been standing at the bottom of the cathedral steps for nearly a half hour, alternating between regret for last night's fight that I instigated and being annoyed with myself for feeling guilty. Also, I can't avoid the profound disappointment; the cooking class was amazing, everything I hoped it would be, but the subsequent fallout with Gabe? Two steps forward, two steps back. However, getting into all of this with Gia seems ill-advised, because I don't trust what I might say right now.

"I have a bit of a headache," I say, wishing for not the first time this morning I'd skipped drinks with Becca and Colin yesterday.

"Best cure for a headache is a strong espresso," Gia says. "At least one, but two is better." I grimace and rest a hand to my stomach, and she laughs. "Trust me. Come, come." I offer to carry a few of her bags but she waves me away. "Aberto is picking me up in twenty minutes, so I'll join you."

Beside the church steps, in Amalfi's pedestrian square known as Piazza del Duomo, is a white marble storefront with scalloped canvas awnings. The name *Andrea Pansa* is carved into the marble above the door, and inside a half-dozen people line up in front of a glass case full of pastries. The smells of coffee, chocolate and fresh-from-the-oven sweetness waft out the door, and I take a deep breath. Gia puts her bags down on one of the cushioned outdoor chairs and gestures for me to take a seat. "I'll go and order for us. We drink cappuccinos in the morning, but you'll start with an espresso first," she says. "Okay?"

I nod and then fumble clumsily with the zipper on my purse, trying to get to my wallet. "Please, let me pay."

"No, no, no," Gia says, already heading inside. She's back a few minutes later, a tiny espresso cup in one hand. She says the waiter will bring out our cappuccinos and pastries shortly. "If you see my mother don't tell her I stopped for breakfast here," she adds with a wink. "She'd have a thing or two to say about that."

"I won't." I smile, then take a hesitant sip of the espresso. The liquid is hot, but it's not as bad as I remember. In fact, after another two sips I'm enjoying the strong flavor. I take another sip and Gia smiles at me, gesturing with her hand as if to tell me to drink up.

"Mama thinks it's overpriced here," Gia says, unwrapping the silk scarf from around her neck. It amazes me how stylish everyone is here, especially so early in the morning. If you run out to get a coffee on a Saturday morning in Chicago, sweatpants, sneakers and a ball cap are perfectly acceptable. "And she's probably right, but I don't like to give her the satisfaction by admitting that!" Gia laughs, and I drain my espresso cup.

The waiter brings out our cappuccinos, beautifully frothy and rich, and two pastries that look more like dessert than breakfast. "This is an Italian's breakfast," she says to me before murmuring, *"Grazie"* to the waiter, who is dressed in a white tux jacket and bows slightly before leaving our table.

"It's a beautiful place," I say, looking back at the patisserie, where the line continues to grow. "And this is probably the best cappuccino I've ever had, thank you." I take another sip, the dark coffee under the foam burning my lips ever so slightly.

"It's been here since 1830," Gia says. Then she lifts her plate, where an icing-sugar-dusted pastry in the shape of a large clamshell, with delicate layers of pastry leaves lining its top, sits in the center. "And they make the best *sfogliatella*, in my opinion."

"What's it filled with?" I bite into the buttery, flaky pastry, and my teeth sink into something sweet and thick.

"Orange ricotta cream," Gia says, taking a bite of her own pastry.

"Delicious," I say, and we eat in silence for a minute, the sounds of morning in Amalfi filling the air.

"When I was younger I used to eat one of these every morning," she says, using her black linen napkin to wipe the fine layer of icing sugar from her lips. "But no amount of stair climbing allows for that now."

I notice a constant stream of locals, mostly young, moving in and out of the patisserie. Looking around, I realize tourists occupy the majority of the tables. "Does no one sit down here to eat?" I ask.

"Not usually," she replies. "Breakfast in Italy is a cappuccino and pastry at the bar. You catch up with friends for a few minutes, eat and drink, then go on your way."

"Have you always lived here?" I ask.

"Yes, aside from a few years at La Sapienza." I raise my eyebrows and nod like I know what that is. "Roma's state university," she adds. "I took architectural design. Then I moved to England for a year to learn English. Then—" she pauses, finishing her cappuccino "—back to Ravello to help with the school. What about you? Always in America?"

I nod. "I'm a kindergarten teacher, back home."

"A teacher!" Gia says. "I should have guessed. You have that way about you. Curious, yet an excellent listener."

I have a mouth full of pastry, so I give a closed-mouth smile of thanks at the compliment.

"Are you traveling alone?" she asks casually enough, though I'm sure she's noticed my wedding rings already. Gia doesn't seem to miss much.

"Um, no," I reply, feeling awkward. The coffee cup slips from my hand and clangs noisily onto the plate below. Luckily nothing breaks. "Sorry, I'm all thumbs today." I wipe up a bit of spilled coffee with my napkin. "I'm married." Then I realize that doesn't exactly answer her question. "He's back at the hotel." The hostility of the night before still clings to me, and I'm glad I don't have to deal with Gabe right now. Though a few hours of sleep and this headache have dulled my anger somewhat, it still burns deep in my gut.

She nods politely but doesn't say anything.

"I had a lot of wine to drink last night, and, well, there were words..." I trail off and shrug. The words weren't the problem, of course. But that's not something I want to get into over coffee and pastries with a virtual stranger. However, my clichéd excuse seems to explain everything to Gia.

"Ah ha!" she says, clapping her hands together. "Say no more, say no more. I have been married for twenty-two years. I understand that wine can make a passionate woman even more so." She winks at me. "How is your head now?"

I think about it for a moment, and realize the nauseating pounding has turned to only a dull ache. "Much better."

She smiles and stands up, so I do, too. "Well, I'm sure Aberto is waiting for me." She embraces me, and the scents of rosemary, garlic and lavender linger after she lets me go. "This has been nice," she says.

"Thank you so much for the company," I say, adding, "and for the coffees and pastry. I'm glad I have a walk ahead of me to burn that breakfast off."

Gia laughs and pushes her chair in. "You're lucky you're still young," she replies.

Once she gathers her bags she stops to look at me for a moment, and I feel suddenly exposed. Like she knows there's something important I haven't mentioned. "If you're looking for a beautiful place to say a few words, walk to the right of the cathedral's stairs there." She points into an alley that seemingly disappears under the church. "You'll see two small doors with stained glass inside them. It's right in the tunnel, only a few feet. You can't miss it and I know it's open today."

"Thank you."

"*Ciao*, Tegan," she says. "It was very nice to run in to you again. I hope you'll come back and visit us again."

"Same to you, Gia. I hope so, too."

A minute later I realize another couple is waiting for a table at the hopping patisserie, so I take a last sip of my cooling cappuccino and gather my things. Walking in the direction Gia pointed, I soon find myself in front of the doors she described. The padlock is open on the iron barred doors, which are colorful with stained glass inlaid between the rods, and I push one door inward. Inside, rows of candles illuminate the very small space, which only holds a few rows of pew-like benches facing pictures of religious deities. I am the only one there, but sit down at the back. The candles flicker softly, and I hear faint music coming from somewhere close by.

The wooden bench is uncomfortable, much like other pews I've sat on the few times I've been to church. Weddings and funerals, that's pretty much the extent of my churchgoing experience—though I did go with the Lawsons the Christmas before last, which was nice if not strange. I shift around on the bench, uncomfortable and trying to sort out what, if anything, I want to say. I know many find comfort in the idea of God, but I am not one of them. In my view once you're gone, you're gone. But I wish I believed something different, now that I'm the one needing comfort.

I lay a hand against my pendant and close my eyes, hoping that brings me closer to an answer. I let out a deep sigh, waiting for something to come into my mind.

The giggling is soft and at first I think it's coming from the tunnel. I open my eyes and turn around, expecting to see someone at the door, but no one is there. Then it gets louder, and I realize it's coming from the front of the room. A second later a very young couple—late teens, I guess—stands up in front of the rows of candles. They are quite disheveled, cheeks flushed and eyes only for each other. Holding hands, they whisper *"scusi, scusi"* to me as they walk quickly past, the tunnel filling with their laughter as soon as they exit the room.

I can't help it. I start laughing, too. I apologize to no one in particular, as the room is empty once again, and leave. I wonder if Gia has any idea this beautiful haven of worship is also a place where lovers worship each other.

If I were looking for a sign, I decide this is it.

Walking slowly back through the tunnel, which is carved right out of the rock but feels modern with painted white walls and fluorescent lighting, I feel the final vestiges of the hangover leaving me and a clarity taking its place.

If I want to make this work, I have to spend less time focusing on everything I lost that night and more time figuring out how to live without it. And though it's still skittish and unfamiliar, forgiveness has begun to peek out from the dark, devastated corners of my soul.

# 37

I chew a cuticle hanging from my thumbnail and wait while the phone rings, switching to an unoccupied bank of seats at a nearby gate in search of a quieter spot. Our departures gate is noisy, the tinny sounds of flight announcements coming through multiple speakers mixing with the shouts of rambunctious, bored children playing tag while their parents ignore them with cell phones and other devices. I cover my other ear and turn toward the massive windows facing the tarmac as the phone rings a sixth time. I'm about to hang up when someone finally picks up.

"H'lo?"

"Hey," I say, confused. "Jase, what are you doing answering Mom and Dad's phone? Is everything okay?" My heart rate picks up as I imagine what might be wrong.

"Everything's good, Teg." Jason sounds relaxed, as usual. "I'm just keeping Dad company while Mom's out. And I'm kicking his ass at Monopoly. You should see all the hotels I have going on." He exhales a few quick times, and I know he's pretending to polish his knuckles. "Just call me Jason Trump from now on."

"Go easy on Dad," I say, with a frown. "You know how competitive he gets when he's losing at Monopoly."

"Who said I'm losing?" Dad asks, now on the line. "It's all about strategy. Jase may be winning right now, but he's going to end up eating humble pie."

"Nice try, old man," Jase says, laughing. "You'd better not be messing with my properties in there."

"Just you worry about the coffee being hot," Dad replies.

"I hope it's decaf," I chime in.

"It is, don't worry," Dad says. "And it's so good to hear your voice! We've really missed you."

"Miss you guys, too." I sigh deeply and then wish I hadn't. I don't want Dad to worry about me any more than I know he already is. "But I'll be home soon enough."

"So how's Italy?" Dad asks lightly, thankfully ignoring the sigh.

I lean back against the lounge's seat. *How's Italy?* Beautiful. Unforgettable. Complicated. Draining. Delicious. Refreshing. Disappointing. Full of memories—some lovely, some… not. I settle for simple. "Italy is spectacular."

"Your mother loved your last note, by the way. She's going to be sorry she missed you," Dad says.

"Where is she? I'm surprised she left you alone."

"Hey, he's not alone!" Jase says.

"You know what I meant." I roll my eyes at his petulance.

"She's at the store likely filling the cart with anything she can find that's green, leafy and low-fat," Dad says, sounding irritable. "Oh, and don't forget it must also taste like dirt…or worse, taste *healthy*."

Jason snorts. "The heart attack didn't get him, but the kale just might."

"She's doing exactly what she should be, Dad," I say. "We

need you around for a long time yet, so eat your kale and shut up about it, okay?"

"Yes, ma'am," Dad replies, and I can hear the smile in his voice. Picturing him, with his salt-and-pepper hair, and the scar on his forehead from a childhood run-in with a brick wall that makes him look tougher than he is, makes me homesick. A brief wave of panic settles in my belly as I consider again what might have happened if Dad hadn't been so lucky. I resist the urge to blurt out that I'm going to change my flight and come home instead.

"So what do you have on the agenda today?" he asks as if sensing my vacillation and pushing me past it. "Please tell me it involves some kind of pasta slathered in melted cheese, or a cold beer overlooking the Mediterranean...oh, oh, or one of those Italian bun things Rosa makes." He sighs. "I dream about those, you know."

"Yeah, the nuns' boobs are really something else," Jason says, and I hear some rustling on the phone. "Here you go, Dad. Your black, organic, fair-trade, small-batch-roasted, bird-friendly, decaf, no-fun coffee has been served."

I laugh as I imagine Dad's face. Likely in a grimace, as his usual coffee order is double cream, triple sugar. "Why even bother?"

"Habit," Dad replies. "It's one of the only things I can have from life before my ticker went on the fritz. And you probably won't believe me, but I actually like it black now." He takes a noisy sip, and I hear him blowing on the clearly hot coffee. "Now I know what coffee is supposed to taste like." I know exactly what he means.

After a few more minutes of catching up on life back home and filling them in on where we're headed, the airline makes an announcement that the flight from Rome to Los Angeles, our layover destination, is boarding. I hastily say my good-byes and ask Dad to pass my love on to Mom and Connor.

"Will do, sweetheart," Dad says. "But just before you go—"

"I'm okay, Dad. Honestly, I'm doing fine." I only half believe this, but I hope my tone sells it sufficiently.

"Okay, then," he says. "You sound good to me, and if you say you're okay, I believe you. Have a great flight and call us when you get there or your mother will worry."

"I will," I say, knowing Dad is the one who will worry most. "Love you."

"Love you, too, sweet Tee."

I hit End Call and head back to our gate.

"How are things back home?" Gabe asks.

"Good. Mom was at the store so Jase was there with Dad. Obviously she's not leaving him alone, which is exactly what I'd expect," I say. "I'd be surprised if she even lets him go to the bathroom without supervision."

Gabe chuckles. "How did your dad sound?"

"Really good. Energetic. Though none too pleased with my mom," I say. "Seems she's shoving him full of kale every chance she gets. And he's drinking his coffee black now, if you can believe it."

"Going to have to tell Mom that." Gabe smirks. "She'll be so proud."

There's a lull between us as the airline announces preboarding instructions. Though I'm unsure of where things stand between Gabe and me—the fight still so fresh—I remind myself of the promise I made back at the cathedral. To keep my eyes forward. To focus on the future. A wave of anxiety and anticipation fills me, and I pull the note with our final destination out of my jeans' back pocket. I unfold it along the creases and read it again.

"So, are you ready to get back on American soil?" Gabe asks as I fold the note back up into a small square.

"I am." I throw my day pack over one shoulder and tuck the paper square, on which is written *Hang ten in Maui*, back into my pocket. "Here we come, Hawaii."

# *four*
# Hawaii

# 38

The hula girl on the bus dashboard waves as her hips sway side to side with the movement. I make a mental note to find a similar dancing hula girl for Dad, knowing he'll love it. Mom probably won't, and will likely suggest it's better suited for his desk rather than their luxury car's dashboard.

We're packed into a shuttle bus, six of us plus the driver, on our way to the hotel in Waikiki. The air is heavy with floral notes from the leis we wear around our necks, a welcome to Hawaii gift from our driver, Rudy.

"Real flowers." I touch one of the petals—white with a starburst of hot pink spreading through it. "So pretty."

"I think the men lucked out," Gabe says, and I glance at the glossy, deep brown circle of nuts in the men's leis. "These will last forever."

"What are those nuts called again?" I ask. "I can't remember the name. Think it starts with a *k*..."

"*Kukui* nut," Rudy replies. "The ones on the leis are made of the shells, though. The nuts are used for all sorts of things. Like ink for tattoos," he continues, turning out of the airport and onto the highway that leads into downtown Waikiki. "And *kukui* is also used in the condiment *inamona*, which you need to make good poke."

"What's 'poh-kay'?" asks one of the passengers, a middle-aged man with a large belly and small eyes behind glasses that turn to sunglasses with direct sunlight. Currently the lenses are halfway shaded. He sounds Southern, though I can't quite place exactly where from.

*"Poh-keh,"* Rudy repeats, correcting the man's pronunciation, "means 'cut or slice into pieces' in Hawaiian, and it's basically cubes of raw fish or seafood, mixed with sauces and spices, and small bits of vegetables." Rudy opens a cooler by his feet without taking his eyes off the road. "Water, anyone?"

The group murmurs "yes, please," and Rudy passes waters back from the cooler until we all have a cold bottle in our hands. The surface of the plastic bottle is wet from being in the ice, and I rub it against my shorts to wipe the condensation off.

"Poke is one of our traditional dishes," Rudy says. "If you get a chance to try it while you're here, you definitely should. Where are you all from?"

We go through our hometowns, and Rudy says he's never been to Chicago but would love to, if only it didn't snow there. I laugh, and suggest he visit in the summer, when temperatures can reach fried-egg-on-the-sidewalk levels.

"Maybe I will," he says. "Here we are folks, the beautiful Moana Surfrider."

We pull into the semicircle driveway of the hotel, which, with its large white pillars at the entrance and bamboo fans, feels majestically colonial. There are tall palms lining the driveway, and an open-air lobby with plenty of white cushioned seating and polished marble floors.

Gabe whistles as we walk inside. "This is pretty sweet."

"It's gorgeous," I say, and an older woman standing beside me nods in agreement.

"Isn't it, though?" Her green eyes, rheumy but still bright, turn our way. "This is my third stay here, and my twelfth visit to Hawaii." Her hand shakes slightly as she accepts the champagne-style glass, a welcome drink, from the hotel's manager. "Thank you." The manager smiles at her and bows his head before handing me a glass. The older woman takes a long sip and sighs happily. "How about you? Is this your first trip?"

"Second visit." I take a sip of the drink. It's fruity and red, and something sharp sparkles across my tongue.

"But definitely not the last," Gabe says, having turned down the drink. He generally sticks to beer, or red wine if he's visiting his parents.

"You'll be hooked after this trip." She holds her glass up to mine and murmurs a "cheers." "That's what happened to me and Wyatt, my husband. We came to Hawaii for the first time on our honeymoon, fifty years ago now, which makes me quite old." She laughs, sipping her drink again. "We were just kids, but thought we were so, so wise."

I wonder where Wyatt is, and hope he's merely in the washroom or dealing with their luggage, though I sense that's not the case. We move forward, closer to the front desk, as a couple ahead of us finishes checking in.

"Wyatt passed eight years ago," she continues as if sensing my question. "I've been coming here on our anniversary ever since. I feel close to him here."

"I'm…sorry." Tears spring to my eyes, and a choked sob—loud in the high-ceilinged lobby—escapes me, which surprises me as much as it seems to the woman and Gabe, who look at me with concern. Mortified, I turn my head and dab at my eyes with the napkin from my drink.

"That sounds like an excellent way to honor his memory," Gabe says, keeping his eyes on me. I envy that he always knows what to say at difficult times. When he mouths, *You okay?* I nod and give him the most reassuring smile I can.

"Thank you," the woman says. "He was a good man." Then

she raises an eyebrow. "Not perfect by any stretch. Oh, no. Not my Wyatt. But a good man. And he loved this island."

"I can certainly understand why." I'm relieved at the change in topic. "Even the air smells unbelievable here."

"It's amazing, isn't it?" Her green eyes go wide. "It's like we've landed right in the middle of God's favorite flower garden."

I smile at that, and then we're at the front of the line and the woman excuses herself to check in. I sip the last drops of my drink and hand it back to a uniformed man with a tray.

"Well, I'm off," the older woman says, key card in one hand and a refreshed glass of welcome punch in the other. "Hope to see you again soon."

"Same," Gabe replies warmly.

"Enjoy the rest of your trip," I say.

"You, too!" She waves as she heads down the hall toward the bank of elevators. "Thank you, young man," she says to the bellhop who follows her, pulling a small suitcase behind him. "I certainly could do that myself but you're far too handsome to say no to."

I laugh, and Gabe and I wave back to her before she turns the corner to the elevators.

"I hope I have her attitude when I'm her age."

"It's only been five months, Tegan," Gabe says, hearing what I didn't say. "Give yourself a break."

I nod, then step forward to check in.

After a hike up Diamond Head mountain, where it's so windy tourists' hats fly off at an alarming rate, and a quick tour of the shops in the market across from the hotel, I decide a swim to wash the heat and grime off my skin is a good idea. Heading down to the hotel's beachfront, I lay my towel out on a beach chair and open the book Anna gave me, the envelope now resting safely in a pocket in my backpack. I smile reading the proverb she wrote on the inside cover, and think I should call her later. I miss her.

Gabe rests a light hand on my bare knee, the way he does when we lie side by side in bed at night. I put my sunglasses on and read the first few pages of the book. A thriller, with heart-pounding twists and no cry-worthy scenes, as Anna promised. But the sounds of families frolicking and boats buzzing by make it hard to concentrate.

"I'm going for a swim," I say, dog-earing my book's page.

"You go ahead," he says, sleepily. "I'm just going to stay here for a bit."

I pull off my terry cloth sundress and put it on the beach chair along with my sunglasses, then walk closer to the water's edge. The gentle waves tickle the tops of my feet and ankles, sending pleasant shivers up my legs. Digging my toes deep into the sand to the cool, wet layer below the surface I gaze out over the ocean, which is littered with colorful kayaks and paddleboats that tourists rent by the hour. A parasailor glides through the sky, the rainbow parachute billowing behind him. It looks a lot more peaceful up there than here on the beach, where things are crowded and chaotic, especially close to the water. Parents sit in umbrella-topped beach chairs, reading magazines and books or catching up on sleep while their children squeal as they run in and out of the surf, many with bright orange floaters on their arms.

The sun warms my shoulders and I adjust the straps of my black one-piece bathing suit. I used to only wear bikinis, mostly because I thought one-pieces were reserved for women in the next stage of life—either mothers who wanted to hide the collateral damage of multiple pregnancies, or for older women, like my mom, who felt two pieces were only appropriate for those under the age of thirty.

Now I wear a one-piece because of the scars.

"How's the water?"

I turn and see a young woman beside me. She's in a white-and-purple-striped bikini, with a soft belly and breasts that seem ready to burst from the small triangles of fabric that cover them. In her arms is a tiny baby, wearing a onesie meant to look like a baseball uniform and a floppy sunhat covered in baseballs and the words *Little Slugger.*

"It's warm," I say, smiling at her. "How old?"

"He's nine weeks tomorrow." She snuggles her face into her baby's, which still looks more old man than chubby cherub. He obviously has yet to gain his baby fat. "Aren't you? Aren't you, my little monkey? Oh, now now, Momma will stop, no tears, sweet pea." The babe in her arms protests as she nuzzles him, giving a few little mews, but then just as quickly falls deeply asleep against his mother's bare skin.

I can't take my eyes off the baby.

Our baby would have been close to the same age.

It could have been me standing with my feet in the ocean while holding our baby boy, wearing my favorite emerald-green bikini, my belly still soft and my breasts full of milk. Gabe smiling at us from the beach chairs, snapping a dozen photos of the same moment—pictures we would later force on everyone, our hearts bursting with love and pride. I wouldn't even notice my lumpy, post-pregnancy body in the photos, having eyes only for our sweet baby.

I wanted to call our boy Harrison, though Gabe's reaction to the name had been less than enthusiastic…

"Harrison?" Gabe had said. "Really?"

"Well, it's a family name, on my dad's side," I said. "Besides, I like it. It's a good strong name. Harrison Gabriel Lawson."

"You know what will happen, right?"

"What?" I grabbed the duvet cover out of the laundry basket. Gabe took the one end and we folded it into a neat square.

"We'll spend the first four years of his life calling him 'Harrison' and telling everyone there's no nickname," Gabe said, helping next with the fitted sheet. "Then on his first day of school he'll come home and he'll be 'Harry' from that point on."

"I think you're being a bit dramatic. And I sort of like Harry."

Gabe paused, golf shirt partially folded, and stared at me. "You do not."

I laughed. "I do! I think it's adorable. Look at Prince Harry. He's really grown into that name."

"Sweetheart, every name sounds better when it has 'Prince' in front of it," he'd said.

I shake my head, ridding myself of the memory and coming back to the beach. The woman with the baby is waiting for my answer to a question I didn't hear.

"Sorry, what did you say?"

"Are you here on your honeymoon?" she asks, gesturing to my left hand, where the diamonds shine with the sunshine.

"Yes," I say, because it's the easiest answer. "We're headed to Maui tomorrow morning."

"Congratulations! We were supposed to get married this summer, then this little guy decided to come along first." She runs a finger over his cheek, and her face fills with a love that is both familiar and yet mysterious. "But I wouldn't change a thing. He's perfect. Yes, you are, my little man. Yes, you are!"

She looks up, her blue-gray eyes connecting with mine. I try to keep my own guarded, so she won't see what I'm really thinking.

"Are you trying to quit?" I give her a blank look. She points to the estrogen patch on my upper arm. "I saw the patch. My fiancé started wearing one as soon as Jack here was born."

I simply nod. Let her presume my biggest issue is trying to quit smoking.

"Do you plan on having kids?" she asks, in the clueless way someone who has never been forced to question motherhood does.

"Yes," I say, again because it's entirely easier than any other answer I can give.

"Such a blessing. I hope to have four, but we'll get married first. Plenty of time for making babies!" I smile politely before looking back out over the ocean.

"Well, guess I better feed this little guy and get him out of the sun. Enjoy the rest of your honeymoon. I've heard Maui is amazing."

"Thanks," I reply. "Enjoy the rest of your trip, as well."

She heads back up the beach, where she sits under an umbrella and takes off her bathing-suit top. She covers up with a light blanket once the baby is latched on, then smiles and says hello to people walking by. Clueless. Happy. The envy is suffocating, and I turn away.

I take a deep breath and watch the waves lapping the shore, wishing for a way to hide under the crystal-blue water rolling gently toward me. I walk into the water until it's up to my thighs, take the deepest breath I can, and dive under the surface. After gliding through the water for a few seconds, I take another deep breath and then fan my arms upward to move my body deeper. Once my toes touch the sandy bottom, I cross my legs and let my breath out, which allows me to sink to the ocean floor. I sit there until my lungs scream for air.

Breaking the surface I gulp in another breath, then do it again, sitting on the bottom as still as the water's wavy momentum will allow. Again and again, I take in air and disappear back under the waves to sit on the ocean floor, where no one can find me. Then a young guy swims up to me as I break the surface for a fourth time, asking me if I'm okay.

I say I am before swimming back to the beach.

# 39

*Two and a half years before the accident*

The scream that filled the air was a happy one, but still caused Gabe to jump beside me. I chuckled and patted his bent knee as he glanced about wildly, shaking off sleep, sunglasses hanging off one ear.

"What the hell was that?" Gabe asked, rubbing at his eyes. He looked annoyed and rumpled as he tried to come out of his slumber.

"No idea." I squinted and put a hand over my eyes as I scanned the beach. "Oh, over there." I pointed to where the commotion was coming from, about twenty-five feet down the beach. "Looks like someone is having too good of a time. How dare she." I winked at him as he followed my finger with his still-sleepy gaze.

A young woman, late teens probably, in a teeny-tiny bikini shrieked with joy as an equally young man wrestled her into the blue water. The ocean was warm this time of year, so the drama had more to do with flirting than the temperature of the water. After she popped up, sputtering from being dunked, he gathered her into his arms and kissed her passionately. You could see her practically melt into his body, arms and legs encircling him, and they spun around, creating their own current in the shallow water.

"Kids these days." Gabe huffed and then lay back with a grin. He crossed his hands over his tanned and muscled chest, shining with sunscreen and sweat. It was hot in Maui. The kind of hot where even naked felt like you were wearing too much.

"Yes, at twenty-four you're oh-so mature," I said, laughing. "You're just jealous." I leaned over and kissed him hard on the mouth, tasting salt on my lips as I pulled away. He pulled me back forcefully enough to tip my beach chair, which sent me tumbling onto his body. I slid a little, our oiled-up skin providing a slick surface. He hung on tightly and I could feel every part of his body through his swim trunks.

"Mmm. Now they're the ones who are jealous..." he murmured in my ear as he tickled my sensitive lobe with his tongue.

I laughed and snuggled in. Gabe reached an arm around me and plucked the pink hibiscus from my drink, tucking it behind my ear. "You are so gorgeous," he said. I kissed his neck. Then my mouth found the hollow of his throat, and I let my lips linger there for a moment. It was one of my favorite spots; just shallow enough for my lips to fit in perfectly.

"I can't believe you brought us to this terrible, terrible place." I leaned back slightly and crossed my arms against his chest. The sun warmed my back and I sighed contentedly.

"I know, right? The beach. The ocean. The sun. The absolute perfection of these..." He held up his drink, a sort of Hawaiian rum punch served in a hollowed-out coconut shell, and took a long sip. The pink-hued liquid made its way up the white plastic straw. We were already on round two, and it was only just noon. "What will I ever do to make it up to you?"

"You can start by getting me another one." I sipped up the

last of my drink and handed the green coconut shell to him. "Then you can promise me we'll come back every year. This is officially my happy place. I wish we never had to leave." I sighed contentedly.

"Done," Gabe said, trying to balance the coconuts in one hand.

I gestured to the coconuts. "This might have to be it for now if we're going to snorkel today." The booze was getting to me. My cheeks were hot, warmed from the inside rather than the sun, and I felt sleepy, like I was just sinking into a nap, or just waking from one.

Gabe jumped easily off his chair, the extra weight and size he carried making him more immune to the alcohol. "Up you get," he said, grabbing my hand with his free one and tugging on it.

I protested for a moment, but then gave in and let him pull me up. "Why?" I said, pouting a little. "I was comfy."

"Because, my love, I fear I have gotten you drunk." Gabe placed the coconuts on the plastic table between our beach chairs. "And I need to know if it's time to go take advantage of that, or sober you up a bit for snorkeling."

I laughed and stumbled a bit as I walked through the shifting sand, letting Gabe pull me away from the beach chairs. I adjusted the top of my bikini, then put my hands on my hips. "How are you going to determine that?"

"Simple sobriety test, of course," he said. He backed up a dozen steps, drawing a line in the sand with his fingers as he did. "If you can walk this line without falling off it, you can have another drink before going snorkeling."

"And if not?" I stepped forward to where the line started and settled a foot on either side.

Gabe shrugged. "If not, you can have another drink and we're going back to the room for the afternoon."

"So, this is really a win-win situation all around?"

"Well, we are on vacation courtesy of my dad's credit card," Gabe said. His parents had paid as a congratulations to Gabe for passing the bar exam. "Why do anything that isn't win-win?"

"Fair enough," I said, then lost my balance and stepped off to the side of the line.

"Oh, this is worse than I thought." Gabe shook his head and pretended to look concerned. "Seems like maybe you're going to need two drinks."

I positioned my feet again, then took two steps forward, holding my arms out as I did.

"Wait!" Gabe shouted, from his end of the line. "You're doing it all wrong. Man, it's like you've never been given a roadside sobriety test or something."

I giggled but held my position, waiting for the next set of instructions.

"Okay, so you hold your arms out, just like you're doing," Gabe said. "But then you have to touch your nose...like this..." he said, demonstrating by bending one elbow so his pointer finger landed on the tip of his nose, then putting that arm back in position and using the next arm to do the same. "All the way to the end of the line."

I started walking again, my fingers alternating to touch my nose, which I managed to get nearly every time.

"Wait!"

I sighed. "What? What now?"

"Close your eyes while you do it."

I gave him a look. "I obviously can't walk in a straight line with my eyes closed."

"Well, then that's our answer," Gabe said with a sigh. "Drink, then straight up to the room. I really thought you had it in you."

I narrowed my eyes before closing them. I put one foot in front of the other, continuing to touch my nose with my fingers. When I felt Gabe's hands encircle my waist, I opened my eyes.

"So, how did I do?" I asked, looking behind me.

Gabe just pointed to the line, which was about three feet to my right.

I burst out laughing and turned back to kiss him. He had the same idea, but somehow we were just slightly out of sync and his chin connected with my nose. Flashes of light burst in front of my eyes and shocking waves of pain moved across the bridge of my nose.

"Oh, fuck." Gabe held my face with both hands and lifted it up. "Are you okay?"

I just laughed, even as I felt the blood tickle my upper lip. Then I tasted it, metallic and warm. "How's your chin?" I asked, seeing a red mark forming under the scruff.

Gabe grabbed a wad of napkins from under the coconut drink and pressed them against my nose, pinching it as he did.

"Ouch! Not so hard." The napkins muffled my voice.

"Sorry, sorry, sorry," he said, wincing. "Are you okay? It's bleeding a lot." He took away the napkins and frowned at how much blood had seeped into them, his face going pale under his tan. He was quite squeamish when it came to blood, which I thought was adorable. "If I broke that gorgeous nose of yours, I'm going to—"

"Gabe. I'm fine," I said, taking the napkins and folding them over to a fresh, white spot. I sat on the beach chair and leaned forward, pressing the napkins to my nose again. "It's not broken. See? Barely bleeding anymore."

"Are you sure?" Gabe looked stricken.

"Trust me," I said, my voice nasally. "I grew up with two brothers. I've had a broken nose before." I smiled and glanced over at him. "Maybe you've just helped me straighten it back out again?" He kissed the top of my head.

"I think you've earned that next drink."

"On second thought," I said, "screw the drinks." I stood and let him wrap an arm around me, my body tingling where his hands touched my bare skin. My nose was throbbing but the tingling spoke louder.

"I like the way you think," he said, his voice soft and deep. I wished we were already in our room, with my red-and-white-striped bikini on the cool tiled floor. "We'd better get off the beach before we teach those kids a thing or two."

I could never have known that almost three years later I'd be back on the same stretch of beach, trying to decide if walking into the ocean and not coming back out was crazy...or the perfect solution.

# 40

I open the fridge and sigh. I can easily whip up an omelet or a fruit salad thanks to the condominium's full kitchen setup, but I have no desire to cook or eat anything. I'm not sure if it's the jet lag, or the nightmares that are happening nearly nightly again, but I'm too tired to even pour myself a glass of orange juice. Breakfast seems an insurmountable task.

"Want to go out?" Gabe asks as I move items around in the fridge. Whoever was tasked with stocking the condo's fridge was either in a rush, or didn't care. Likely the latter. The jug of milk is stacked on top of the bread, which has been squished down to half its original size, and the eggs, yogurt and cheese have all been tossed into the vegetable crisper. Plastic containers of fresh-cut pineapple and coconut lay sideways in the fridge's door, and leaking pineapple juice has left a sticky residue.

"Okay," I say, rearranging the dairy on the middle shelf and putting the fruit in the crisper. The lack of order is making me crazy. I can barely concentrate on anything else. "Just let me finish with these eggs and then I'm ready." I take out the carton and carefully place each egg into its own slot in the door's holder, tossing two already broken shells into the trash.

Once I have the fridge in what I consider proper order, I

grab the orange juice and pour a glass. We never have orange juice at home, even though I love it, because oranges give Gabe hives. Or so he says. But I've never questioned it; seems silly to argue about something as ridiculous as fruit.

"Why don't we go find a breakfast spot?" Gabe says as I step out onto the lanai.

"I doubt anything is open yet." It's still very early in the morning, the sun up now but only just. I sit in one of the white plastic chairs and set the glass on the table. Taking a deep breath, I try to settle the jangling inside my chest. I feel unsettled here, despite the beauty of Maui.

I take a hesitant sip of the juice and watch as a pod of dolphins jump through the water in front of the condo. Normally I'd be on my feet, leaning far over the balcony's railing to get a closer look, squealing with delight at seeing the wild dolphins. But this morning, it's all I can do to lift the glass of juice to my lips. The contentment and tiny hints of happiness I felt in Italy are gone, and I wonder what's changed.

"Tegan?"

I need to respond to Gabe, but I can't seem to hold on to a single thought for more than a second. *What were we talking about?*

"Sorry, what?"

"What's up? You seem far away today."

"I didn't sleep that well," I say, though I can tell he doesn't believe that's the whole story.

"I'm sure you'll feel better after you eat."

I'm not so sure. The juice has turned my stomach, and the thought of putting food in there as well is unappealing.

"Come on, let's go for a walk and see what we can find," Gabe says.

"I don't think I'm up for it right now. Maybe I'll just go back to bed for a bit."

"Why don't you take an Ativan?" he suggests. "That seemed to help last time."

"Because I don't want to take a pill every time I feel off," I snap. Gabe doesn't respond, and I immediately feel guilty. "Sorry, I'm just tired. I don't need drugs, I just need to sleep."

"Maybe you're coming down with something?"

"Maybe," I reply. "Probably just jet lag, though. Think I'll go back to bed for a bit, okay?"

"Whatever you need to do, Teg. No problem."

I get up, leaving my nearly full glass of juice on the table, and walk through the sliding glass door. In the bathroom, I rummage through my toiletries bag until I find the bottle of Ativan. Even though I don't want to admit it to Gabe, I know I need the pills. I've been taking them almost daily since the cooking class incident in Italy, but they don't seem to be helping much anymore.

Popping the lid, I place a pill under my tongue and let it disintegrate, watching myself in the mirror. I actually look better than I feel. Unless you look closely at my eyes. They don't look right to me, though I can't quite put my finger on why.

"We can go out later, if you're feeling up to it," Gabe says from the bedroom.

"I'm sure I'll be fine after a rest." I take another glance in the mirror. To look at me, you would never know what a disaster I am on the inside. My hair is shiny and bouncy, thanks to the humidity and salty ocean breeze. My cheeks are freckled, and my chest and shoulders bronzed. I look healthy. Young and vibrant. Except, again, for my eyes.

I lean forward until my nose touches the mirror. My vision goes blurry as my brain tries to settle on an image, like a camera lens working hard to autofocus.

"You all right?" Gabe asks, from outside the bathroom door.

This question, one he asks me multiple times a day, now feels like a formality. And so I give my stock answer.

"Yes." I move slowly away from the mirror until my vision is sharp again. "I'm fine."

After rinsing the pill's chalky, bitter residue from my mouth with a glass of water from the bathroom tap, I head into the bedroom. Lying down on top of the covers, Gabe settles in beside me and looks at me questioningly. I give him the most comforting smile I can, and it occurs to me I never should have come back here. Maui was so full of happy memories—back from a time when life was all about possibilities and our biggest problems were Gabe's busted ankle and canceled surf lessons.

I decide to talk with Gabe about looking into flights when I wake up; I'm pretty sure I have to get out of here, or I might break into too many pieces to put back together again.

# 41

This time the Ativan doesn't work at all. When I wake up, I'm more exhausted than I was before. Sweaty, listless, and my mouth is Sahara Desert dry—a side effect of the pill. And even though I have nothing more than a sip of orange juice in my stomach, the thought of eating anything makes me feel sick.

I try to get out of bed, my bladder demanding attention, but it feels like the mattress has a magnetic force keeping me tight to its surface. Shifting an arm—tingly with pins and needles from being trapped under my body—I glance at my phone when it pings. A reminder pops up on the screen and I swear out loud.

Surf lessons start in an hour.

Everyone else who signed up for the class will be on vacation. Happy and excited, with visions of hang tens and waterlogged bragging rights to take back home. I don't know how to qualify what this is exactly, this trip, but it feels like the furthest thing from a vacation. And I can't stop thinking about the young mother on the beach in Waikiki, the one with that sweet, perfect baby in her arms. It could have been me, should have been me. Sadness and jealousy mingle inside me, ripping through what's left of my emotional stability.

Even though I've never said it out loud, I've been hanging

on to this idea that Maui would be the place where I'd feel better. Like, really start to feel better. Maui was supposed to be my salvation.

But now there's a very real chance I may pee the bed because I can't get out of it, and I'm not sure what I'm supposed to do about that. And the worst part is I can't bring myself to care about any of it.

"Gabe." My voice is hoarse. "Gabe," I say, a bit louder.

"Wha'?" he murmurs, from close by.

"I can't... I don't think I can go," I whisper, trying not to disturb the calm.

"Go where?"

"Surfing. I don't think I can go."

Gabe is alert now. "Why not? That's why we're here."

"I know, it's just that..." I start to say I'm not feeling well, that I must have picked something up on the plane, or that I have cramps, whatever, but I don't have the energy to follow through on the lie. "I don't want to." I close my eyes and hold my breath.

I'm not sure what I expect Gabe to say, or what I want him to do about it all, but when he says, "No," my eyes open in surprise.

"No?" I repeat, still lying there even though my bladder says, *Get the hell out of bed or suffer the consequences.* I squeeze my legs together tightly.

"No, Tegan, we're going."

"Gabe, you don't get it. I'm—"

"You're what?" Gabe no longer sounds relaxed. "What is it?"

Thrown off by his abruptness, I close my mouth and shake my head. I'm not used to this Gabe, and I'm not sure how to react.

"I can't get out of bed." There, I've said it. And I know that now I've admitted it, he'll say all the right things. He'll ask the questions that force me to tell the truth, and he'll take care of me. *I understand, love. We won't do anything you don't want to do,* he'll say, his eyes understanding, his embrace warm and safe. *We can stay in this bed until you're ready to get up, or until the day our plane leaves. Whatever you need.*

Except this time he doesn't say any of those things.

"Of course you can get out of bed, Tegan," he replies. His voice takes on a particular tone, like he's speaking to a child. The old me would snap at him for being condescending, one of his only character flaws, but I say nothing. He keeps going. "You may not want to, but you absolutely *can*. And if you don't start paying attention to that difference soon, none of this is going to change. You're never going to feel better."

I wait for the wave of anger to take over. I much prefer feeling something, especially when it's not the cloying layers of sadness. But no matter how hard I try to elicit that burn in my chest, it doesn't come. "Fine," I finally say. "I *can* get out of bed. And you're right, I don't want to. I don't want to go and smile and laugh and pretend I give even one shit about surfing. *Can* you understand that, Gabe?" I'm shaking, and pull the covers up to my chin. "I am not going to just 'get over' any of this, no matter how many miles I put between me and that stretch of road. There is no real happy for me anymore. I've accepted that. So why can't you?"

"I understand how you feel," Gabe says, more softly now, but with frustration building in his voice. "I get what it's like to feel as though—"

"How can you possibly understand how I feel?" Still, no anger. My voice is flat, my movements sluggish. I want to jump out of bed, to pummel him and tell him to shut up, but it's all I can do to sit up. "I wish every day that a hole will open underneath me so I can drop into it and never come out.

I wish I didn't have to live through that moment each morning, where I lie in bed and wonder, just for a second, if it was all a bad dream. I wish your parents had never invited us to that party. I wish… I wish you had…" I press my lips together to keep in the unkind words, and exhale through my nose. *You promised, Tegan. You promised to keep your eyes focused ahead.*

A moment of silence hangs between us, the air charged with my words and unfinished thought.

"I wish things were different, too, you know," Gabe finally says, his voice thick with emotion. "I wish so many things, Tegan. So many things, all the time." He starts to cry, and it makes my chest hurt. "I wish we hadn't been late for the party. I wish I'd taken the busier roads, so the ice might have been melted down." He sobs the last part out, and I try desperately to keep my lips together so my own grief doesn't explode out of them.

The reality of what has been lost is too much to bear, and even though I've been trying desperately to convince myself I'm recovering, that life could maybe, just maybe, go on, I realize it never will. Not really. "I wish I hadn't ruined our lives, your life," Gabe continues. "But you know what I wish most of all? I wish…"

And then he says the thing that nearly rips me right open. "I wish I'd had a chance to be his dad."

# 42

*Three years before the accident*

"I just don't get this," I said. "This woman gave birth in a bathtub because she had no idea she was pregnant." I held up the magazine, where a picture of a young dark-haired woman smiled, a small, sleeping baby in her arms. "How does that even happen?"

Gabe squinted at the page, then shook his head and laughed. "I have no idea," he said. "That's a whole new level of not being self-aware." He ladled a scoop of batter into the cast-iron pan, where melted butter bubbled and browned.

I went back to reading, every now and again saying, "Seriously?" or, "Well, that should have been your first clue..." as I read through the story.

"I love how indignant you get when you read those magazines," Gabe said, leaning back against the counter. The kitchen was filling with smoke from the pan along with the heady scent of deep-fried butter.

"I don't know where they find these people." I flipped a few more pages, then wrinkled my nose. "You may want to open a window. It's getting smoky in here."

Flipper still in hand, Gabe pushed off from the counter and

opened the living room window. It was snowing outside, but the cold air was refreshing.

"I think five is a good number," Gabe said, flipping the thin, golden pancake in the pan we only used for this purpose. It was Saturday, and for the first time in what felt like months, we didn't have anywhere we had to be, so Gabe was making me his famous Dutch pancakes.

"Five what?" I'd moved on to another story, one about making your own sunscreen, and was only half paying attention to Gabe.

"Kids," Gabe said.

I looked up from the page. "Five?"

"Don't look so surprised," Gabe said with a laugh. He flipped the thin, crêpe-like pancake onto a plate beside the stove and ladled more batter in the pan. The smell was making my stomach growl. "You know I'd love to have my own hockey team."

"So you've said." I put the magazine down on the coffee table and went to sit on a stool at the kitchen island. Gabe grabbed the coffee carafe and raised his eyebrow.

"Yes, please," I said, pushing my nearly empty mug forward. He filled it three quarters of the way and then added the coffee cream I liked. A vanilla one so sweet it almost turned the coffee into liquid dessert. "But five?" I blew on my coffee, which was hot despite the long pour of cream. "Remember, I'm the one who has to push them out. This body would never be the same again."

Gabe flipped the next pancake onto the plate, which was now stacked high. He turned off the heat and tossed the batter bowl into the sink. "I would do it for you if I could," Gabe said. I gave him a look, and he chuckled. "Okay, I'd at least split it with you." I smiled over the lip of my mug, picturing a time when Gabe would make Saturday morning pancakes for our kids, teaching them how much butter needs to go in the pan and the exact right way to use your wrist when whisking the eggs, just like his dad had taught him.

"Aw, so sweet," I said, taking a pancake and laying it flat on my plate. "Of course, it would mean a lot more if you actually could give birth, but still."

"I can't help it if I don't have the right equipment." Gabe took a pancake for his own plate. I poured a long line of syrup on our pancakes, then we rolled them up using our fork prongs until the pancakes formed long tubes.

"You're getting good at that," Gabe said, taking a bite.

"I learned from the best," I replied. "It's all in the way you fork it."

There was a pause, then we both burst out laughing. A piece of my pancake flew out of my mouth and landed on the island.

"Damn, girl," Gabe said, once we'd caught our breath. "I can't take you anywhere."

I shrugged, still laughing, and took another bite of pancake.

"Fine," I said, once I'd swallowed. "Five it is. But we'd better start soon. I'm not getting any younger, you know."

"Yeah, at twenty-three you're nearly over the hill." He tried to keep a serious face. Then he tossed down his fork, which clattered against the plate. "Easy," I said, cringing. I imagined cracks in the still pristine, white dinner plates we bought when we moved in together a month ago.

"Don't worry, these are indestructible. IKEA said so." He wiped his mouth on his napkin, then tossed that down on the plate as well and jumped off the stool.

"It's probably a good idea to get practicing," he said. I smiled, and cut off another piece of pancake, ignoring his hand as it snaked up my leg. "My schedule is wide-open today," he added, trying to get me to forget my breakfast.

I nudged his hand aside. "Pancakes first," I said, dredging

a piece through the pooling syrup on my plate. I popped it in my mouth and blocked his hand, again.

Gabe looked amused, if not mildly disappointed. He sat back down and with a shrug, took another pancake. "But I'd like to remind you, if you think these are good?" He held up the rolled pancake with his fork, and pointed it toward the bedroom. "You should see what I can do in there after a pancake breakfast."

"Oh, don't worry," I said. "I have every intention of putting your skills—all your skills—to the test."

He gave me a look, the bite of pancake halfway to his mouth with syrup dripping down to the plate.

"Fine," I said with a resigned sigh. I got up and put my plate in the sink. "Pancakes can wait."

Piece of pancake uneaten, he put down his fork and grabbed me around the waist.

"Let's see what you've got," I murmured, pulling him close. We kissed, the remnants of syrup making our lips sticky. He tasted like warm maple sugar, with a hint of coffee. "You taste good," he said. I smiled and his lips found my teeth. "Even your teeth taste amazing." I laughed, letting him drag me to the ground.

"Here?" I asked, the nubby wool rug scratching against my back.

"It's perfect, really," he said, settling his warm body over mine. "This way I can break for bites of pancake every now and then. To keep up my energy, of course."

He bent to kiss me again and I craned my neck toward him, so our mouths met in a hard and clumsy, but very satisfying way. And even though my belly was full of vanilla-flavored coffee and probably one too many pancakes, and the carpet was leaving indentations in my back that would take a while to go away, and Gabe's weight on top of me meant I might either lose my breath or the pancakes, or both, I wouldn't have changed a thing.

# 43

Things are worse, if that's even possible, and I really haven't gotten out of bed for the past day. I put the Do Not Disturb sign on the door and sleep for nearly twenty-four hours straight. I ignore my phone when it rings, twice, and keep the blinds closed.

I have vague memories of Gabe, nearby each time I awaken, though we haven't said a word to each other since the morning before. But my silence isn't because I'm angry. I try hard to muster up the fury I felt in Italy; the self-righteousness I had about what happened. And while a spark is still there, it feels smothered, like throwing wet sand onto the burning embers of a campfire.

The clock on the bedside table tells me it's just after midnight. Gabe isn't in the bedroom, and I try to decide if I'm glad to be alone right now or not. I drag myself out of bed and go to the bathroom, turning on the light. I shut my eyes tight against the sudden brightness, the pain shooting deep in my head as my eyes try to adjust. With one hand held to my eyelids, I sit to pee, then stand to wash my hands. I squint and turn on the water, letting it warm up a bit, and catch a glimpse of myself in the mirror over the sink. If I had more energy, I might have gasped at my reflection.

My dark hair, stringy with oil from being unwashed for three days, clings to my face, which is translucent and pale. There are dark purple circles under my eyes, and my lids look puffy and veiny, like I'm suffering from a nasty case of seasonal allergies. Deep cracks line my dry lips, and bits of dried blood dot the cracks. Even my cheeks appear hollower, probably because I'm dehydrated and haven't eaten in almost two days.

I look like death.

I wash my hands, still staring at myself in the mirror, and then splash water on my face. My lips sting with the cracks and my skin feels like sandpaper. Stumbling back to bed, exhausted from the effort, my heart beats fast as I lie still under the covers.

I have to do something.

Or I'm not going to make it home from Maui.

Turning on the bedside lamp, I pick up my phone with shaking fingers.

I find the number in my contacts list and hit the call button. "Hello?" Of course she's up. Her kids are early risers and she's always at the office well ahead of her patients.

I open my mouth to speak but nothing comes out.

"Hello? Hello?" she says again.

Afraid she might hang up I clear my throat and try again. "Lucy?"

"Tegan? Is that you?"

I start to cry.

"Tegan, are you okay? What's wrong?"

"Things are a mess." My voice cracks. I clutch the phone tightly to my temple so it doesn't slip out of my hand. "I don't know what happened. I was fine, or at least okay only a couple of days ago." I wipe my dripping nose on the sleeve of the cotton shirt that I've been in for two days, and try to stop crying. "I think I'm losing it, Lucy. Like really losing it this time."

"Tegan, it's going to be okay," Lucy says, and she sounds so sure of herself I almost believe her. "I'm glad you called me. We'll figure this out, okay?"

I nod, and then remember she can't see me. "Okay," I say.

Over the next fifteen minutes Lucy manages to get everything out of me. Well, almost everything. I hold back the part about what happened with Gabe, about what he said, because she doesn't need to know any of that. Hell, I wish I could erase it from my memory.

"You shouldn't be alone right now," Lucy says, sighing deeply. I hear the concern in her voice shift to something else, something aching, and I want to stop her before she gets angry with Gabe for leaving. I've dished out more than enough anger for all of us. Luckily she lets it go, focusing back on the reason I called.

"What antidepressant did Dr. Rakesh give you?" she asks.

"I can't remember the name of it."

"Can you get the bottle for me?" I go into the bathroom and pull the bottle out of my toiletries bag. "Lexapro," I say, reading the label. "Ten milligrams a day."

"Hmm," she says. "We might just have to up your dose a bit. Has it been working okay until now do you think?"

"I, um, I..." I begin. I swallow hard before whispering, "I haven't been taking it."

"Sorry, what did you say?"

"I, uh, haven't been taking the pills."

"Since when?" Lucy's tone is serious now. "You can't just stop an antidepressant, Tegan, it's really dangerous."

"I haven't...taken it at all. Like, ever."

There's silence on the other end, though only for a moment. "Tegan—"

"I know," I say, a little too loudly. I take a deep breath to try and calm myself down. "I know it was stupid. Dr. Rakesh only agreed to the trip because I told him I'd take the medication. I lied. I told everyone it was helping…" Lucy stays quiet on her end. Letting me confess without interruption. "I thought I could handle everything without it." I look at the bottle again, full of white, oblong pills that rattle around inside with the shaking of my hand.

Lucy's all business now. "Listen, I'm going to call Dr. Rakesh and then call you right back, okay? Sit tight."

"Where am I going to go?" I ask, giving a short, weak laugh.

"Hang in there, sweetie," she says. "In the meantime get yourself something to eat, please. Or at least some juice, okay? We're going to sort this out."

After hanging up, I shuffle into the empty kitchen and pour another glass of orange juice, wondering briefly where Gabe could be this late at night. My throat resists the juice at first, closing as I try to swallow, which makes me choke until the acidic, pulpy juice comes out my nose. After getting the worst of it out with a few blows into some tissues, I sit in the living room and drink the whole glass, one sip at a time. I'm starting to worry. It's not like Gabe to leave me for so long. Especially not when I'm…like this.

I wake to the phone ringing and a kink in my neck from falling asleep upright. It's Lucy, and she and Dr. Rakesh have a plan. I'm to start the Lexapro tonight, and call Dr. Rakesh first thing in the morning. She also suggests I take an Ativan, which is fine along with the Lexapro, as long as I don't drive or drink anything stronger than orange juice. She says it will help me sleep.

Gabe comes back as I'm ending the call.

"That was Lucy," I say, shifting the now empty glass between my cold, shaky hands. I get up slowly, pain shooting through my neck and shoulders, and walk back to the kitchen.

"Why were you talking to Lucy? Is everything okay?"

"With her, yes." I pour more juice and pop the lid off the pill bottle. "With me, not so much."

"What are you taking?" Gabe asks.

"Lexapro." I shake out one pill and place it on the table. "It's the antidepressant Dr. Rakesh prescribed." I swallow the pill, feeling it stick a little in my still dry throat. I gag, and take another sip of juice to get it down.

"Did you get more than one bottle? That one looks full."

"No, it's the same bottle. I lied, Gabe. I haven't been taking the medication."

"Tegan, what the hell?" He shouts it out, frustration in his voice.

"Trust me," I say, wiping tears from my eyes. I take it as a good sign I can actually produce tears now. It means I'm no longer as dehydrated. "There's nothing you can say that I haven't already thought."

"It's almost like you don't want to feel better." Gabe's voice is still loud. Angry. Stressed. "You told everyone you were taking your meds. Our families agreed to this because *you promised* you'd take care of yourself."

"I know, I know. I'm sorry. Please, Gabe, stop yelling at me. I can't take it."

Gabe sighs, and thankfully lowers his voice. "I don't want to yell at you," he says. "But I can't believe you would do something so stupid. Don't you get it, Tegan? If something happens to you..." He stops, like he forgets what's supposed to come next. I want to ask him, *What? What happens if something happens to me?* But instead, I cap the bottle and head back to bed, hoping he'll follow me.

# 44

An hour later I'm still awake, wondering why Gabe didn't follow me to the bedroom and why I didn't ask him to. Then I remember Lucy said to take an Ativan as well, to help me sleep. I get the bottle from the bathroom, take out a pill and put it under my tongue, then with a critical look at my greasy nest of hair, consider taking a shower. But the thought of how much effort that will take, regardless of how great it might feel, makes me reconsider. Instead, I methodically run a brush through my long, stringy hair. I count the brushstrokes as I do, and when I reach a hundred, I stop and put the brush down.

By the time I'm done brushing, I can feel the Ativan starting to kick in; the edges around my consciousness are becoming blurry. But as I'm about to turn out the light and head back to bed, something stops me. My necklace. I don't know what makes me consider it at this moment, but once I let my eyes settle on it, I can't take them off of it.

Hanging from its delicate chain, the pendant rests a few inches above where my cleavage would start, if I had big enough breasts to create any sort of cleavage. The necklace has become such a part of me now I barely notice it against my skin anymore.

Reaching behind my neck I unclasp it and hold it in my

hands, running my fingers around the smooth rounded edges. My fingers rest on the tiny screw at the bottom of the pendant, the hole through which the ashes were delicately funneled in. The funeral home explained the process to me, making sure I understood just how little of the ashes could actually fit inside the pendant. They also told me I could do it myself, if I wanted to, and had instructions on a printout for at-home filling. I simply nodded at this, and asked them to go ahead and do it for me.

I hold up the pendant, so I have a good view of the screw. It's white gold, like the rest of the necklace, and tiny; about the size of a screw used to hold the arm on a pair of sunglasses. I take my fingernail to see if it will fit into the very narrow slot running the length of the screw. It does, and a thrill runs through me. My heart starts to beat faster as I take my nail and very gently at first try to turn it. Nothing happens, and the screw stays in place.

But something is happening inside of me.

I want to get the pendant open.

I want to hold the ashes in my hands.

No, I *need* to hold the ashes in my hands.

Just for a minute I tell myself, then I'll put them back inside the pendant somehow.

More determined now, I turn on the bathroom fan, lock the door and start the shower. I don't want to be interrupted. Taking out my tweezers—a travel pair, so they're quite small, with sharp pointed ends—I pull the ends apart, until the metal gives way and bends. Using one end, I wiggle it into the screw's slot and start to twist. It's still not working. But I keep trying, becoming more and more frantic.

I'm crying now, and the tears drop onto the pendant I'm holding very close to my face.

"Come on, come on, come on," I whisper, working furiously. The tweezers keep slipping, and I have tiny nicks on my thumb from where their sharp ends have punctured my skin. "Come on!" I shout in frustration when the tweezers slip out again. I wipe my eyes with my arm, take a deep breath, then try one more time. I think I feel something shift, and I wiggle the tweezers so hard that when they slip out of the screw this time, the jerk causes the pendant to fall from my hands. It clatters into the bathroom's porcelain sink.

"No!" I shout, hands grabbing clumsily at the falling necklace. I manage to stop it before it goes down the drain, just, and for a moment hold my hand there against the pendant, feeling the coolness of the sink on my palm. My heart races, and my breath is ragged as I imagine what could have happened.

The necklace could have slipped right down the drain, which probably would still have been okay as the hotel likely has a plumber who could have fished it out. No, that isn't the worst thing that could have happened. If my final attempt at opening the pendant worked, just before the necklace dropped, those precious ashes—all I have left—would have scattered into a cheap, hotel bathroom sink. That would have been their final resting place.

Taking a deep breath and making sure the shaking in my hands is controlled, I drag the pendant up the side of the sink until it pokes over the edge, then I grab it with my other hand and hold on tight. I close my eyes and rest the pendant against my lips for a moment, apologizing for so many things, then clasp it around my neck again.

It's only as I'm falling asleep that I remember the funeral director telling me the screw is held in place with bonding glue, so it will never fall out.

# 45

The next few days pass much like ones do when you're recovering from a bad flu. I sleep a lot. I eat as much as I can stomach. I finally finish that book Anna bought for me. I manage to shower every day, and even go out for a walk on the beach with Gabe on day three. The surf school is very understanding about my unfortunate case of "food poisoning," and offers to move the registration to the following week, our last week in Maui. I take the Lexapro. I end up taking my rings off because I've lost so much weight they slip around my fingers, and I'm terrified I'll lose them. But my hand feels too bare, and it makes me nervous to see the rings lying in the bedside table's drawer, so I put them on my necklace chain, where they hang beside the pendant.

I spend a lot of time on the phone with Lucy and Dr. Rakesh and Anna and my parents—though I downplay the situation somewhat for Mom and Dad. I'm pretty sure if not for my dad and his heart attack, my parents would be on a plane within the hour. Dad in particular is disappointed I let things go on so long and get so dire, and that makes everything just a little bit worse for a while. Mom doesn't cry, like I expected, and I'm grateful to her for that. And Anna threatens more of her *zu mu*'s remedies, along with promising that if I come home in one piece, she'll share a bag of Garrett's popcorn with me. It's a relief to tell them the truth. And even though I'm ashamed, and feel awful for the worry and stress I've caused, things don't seem quite so hopeless anymore.

There's also a lot of talking with Gabe.

It's sort of like being sequestered during jury duty, or at least how I imagine that would be. When the door closes we're on opposite sides; three days later, when the proverbial door opens again, we have reached a consensus.

I will not lie anymore about how I'm doing.

I will take my medication as long as I need to.

Gabe won't leave me, no matter what I say or how long it takes me to get my head on straight again.

I finally admit that he's right; the pills were not an accident like I've been telling everyone. I didn't plan it, but once I had the bottles in my hands, I realized how easy it would be to just slip away. A gentle parting of ways with the world. Aside from telling me he forgives me, he says little at this admission, having known the truth all along despite my protestations.

And so I forgive him for being behind the wheel that night, because in truth, it could just as easily have been me.

I will remember how much I love him.

I will allow him to love me back.

We will finish what we came to Maui to do, and then it's time to go home and figure out what comes next.

# 46

“There are change rooms inside if you need them, but most people just put on their wet suits right here,” Sara, the quite young and quite tanned surf school assistant, tells us. We’re standing on the beach just outside the school. The sand is still a bit cool and damp thanks to an overnight rainstorm. But the sky is cloudless and the sun is starting to warm things up. Sara hands out the wet suits, very quickly sizing each of us up as she grabs the black, neoprene suits off hooks against the wall of the building.

“Thank you.” I take the one she hands me. There are eight of us in the class, the youngest one looking to be early teens and the oldest in her sixties. There’s one awkward moment when one of the group, a woman in a gold string bikini who is clearly middle-aged but trying to pretend she isn’t, takes her wet suit and frowns at it, holding it up against her. She’s very slight, except for her chest, where breasts that Jase would callously describe as “fully loaded” cry out for attention.

“Um, excuse me,” the well-endowed woman says to Sara. “I don’t think this is going to fit.”

The man beside her adds, “She just had ’em done for our one-year anniversary.” He smiles proudly, and gestures at his wife’s balloon-like breasts.

"Oh, dear God," Gabe whispers. "Wonder what she'll get next year?" I try not to laugh.

"Congratulations," Sara says to the couple with only a tiny whiff of sarcasm tempering her cheery tone. It's unclear if she's talking about the anniversary, or the enhancements. "Don't worry, these suits are quite stretchy. It should fit just fine."

Everyone starts taking off their clothes, revealing bathing suits and swim trunks underneath, which makes me realize I didn't get the what-to-wear memo. Even Gabe already has his swim trunks on.

"Shit, I didn't put my bathing suit on yet," I whisper.

"Just go inside and change," Gabe says. "She said they have change rooms."

Sara is in front of me again. "Do you need a change room?" she asks.

I nod, feeling like the kid who wore ripped jeans instead of a fancy red dress to the school's Christmas concert. "I didn't realize I was supposed to change ahead of time."

"No worries. Go on in and pick any room. We won't be starting for another ten minutes or so."

"Thanks," I say, and she smiles and moves on to check on everyone else.

"I'll wait here," Gabe says. "I want to see if Mrs. Gold Bikini gets that suit zipped up." I laugh and shake my head, heading inside with my wet suit and backpack.

I push open the door and bells jingle, announcing my arrival. I'm hit by a blast of cool air and a dizzying array of brightly colored T-shirts and board shorts, and row after row of wet suits. There are surfboards hanging from the ceiling, and though the shop is packed to the brim, it's bigger inside than it appears from the beach.

"Hello?" No one appears with the door's chiming, so I glance around trying to find the change rooms myself. I see three open curtains in front of small rooms toward the back of the shop.

I pick the first one, and the curtain doesn't slide easily along the pole from which it hangs. But I tug on it as hard as I can to at least get it mostly closed. There's a five-inch gap on one side, but it's the best I can do and I don't want to miss any part of the class, so I hang up my wet suit on the hook and open my backpack. Once I have my bathing suit out I quickly take off my shorts and T-shirt and am about to unhook my bra when the curtain door opens.

"Oh!" I'm standing in only my bra and underwear. I'm too shocked to even try and cover myself.

"Oh, God, I'm sorry." For a moment we stare at each other, then he wisely averts his eyes and tries to pull the curtain back across the pole. "I didn't think anyone was in here. I… Shit, I just thought someone had left the curtain half-closed." In his haste to get out of there, he tugs the curtain so hard the pole pops out on one side and the whole thing crashes down onto him.

"Shit!" he yells, trying to untangle himself from the massive piece of fabric. I grab my T-shirt and throw it back on, and almost have my shorts zipped up by the time he's wrestled the curtain off. He holds one hand over his eyes until I tell him it's okay, I'm fully clothed again.

"I am so, so sorry," he says, then sees I'm laughing, which makes him laugh, as well. He holds out a hand. "I'm Kaikane Edwards, and while I'd like to say I'm just a board waxer here and have that excuse my pathetic behavior, I have to admit I own the place." His smile lights up his face—cheesy to put it that way, but it really does. He has black-brown eyes, and skin the color of wildflower honey—silky amber—I presume from his heritage, and not just plenty of days in the sun.

"Nice to meet you, Kaikane." I shake his outstretched hand.

"I'm Tegan. Tegan Lawson. And I stupidly forgot to change into my suit before coming here." I shrug and laugh nervously, wondering how much he saw before he turned his head. The scars on my abdomen are still quite pink, especially set against the pale skin of my stomach, which hasn't seen the sun in well over a year.

"Ah, you're Tegan!" he says, recognition flashing across his face. "Hope you're feeling better? Food poisoning is the worst when you're on vacation. Was it Charlie's, down on the beach? I've had quite a few students tell me they got sick from eating there. Bad shrimp burrito, apparently."

"Not Charlie's or a shrimp burrito," I say. "But thanks for the tip."

"No problem." He smiles wide again. "And you can call me Kai. I think we've probably reached that level of familiarity now, don't you think?" He points at the curtain, and I blush a little.

"Fair enough," I say. "I think I'll move to the next room and try this again."

"Of course." He steps aside. "And I promise I won't touch the curtain this time." I think I see his eyes rest for a moment on the patch on my upper arm. I've been trying to switch up the locations, because one of the annoying side effects is an itchy rash. And even though it's so obvious on my arm, here where the heat makes tank tops and bathing suits the only tolerable clothing, the skin there seems to fare better than other parts of my body.

"It's not a nicotine patch, if that's what you're thinking," I blurt out. For whatever reason, I don't want him to think I'm a smoker.

"Oh, okay," he says.

"I had an accident a few months ago, a car accident," I continue, all the while telling myself to just shut up. "They had to… I had a… I have to wear this now." I stumble over my words, and my face flushes. Why the hell am I telling him any of this? He seems to be wondering the same thing, but thankfully doesn't comment on my confusing, useless and unsolicited explanation.

"Well, I'm glad you're okay now," he says with a smile. He lifts the pole up and slides it back into place so the curtain hangs again in front of the change room. Then he points at my necklace. "You'll also want to take that off. We have lockers here so you don't need to worry. You can get a lock from Sara."

"Right," I say, though I have no plans to take it off. "Do I really have to? It's just that…well, this necklace never comes off."

He shrugs. "It's up to you, but I'd recommend it. The waves are really powerful, and trust me," he adds with a wink "you are going to spend a lot of time with those waves initially. I'd hate for you to lose it."

I try to look nonchalant, though I'm feeling anything but. "Okay, I'll take it off. No problem."

Kai smiles. "I'm going to head out there now. See you in a few?"

"Thanks, I'll be right out."

After changing into the wet suit, which smells like it's been sweated in by a thousand people before me and never washed, I grab a lock from Sara and place my necklace carefully in the small locker. My neck feels bare, uncomfortably light without the pressure from the pendant and rings, and I quickly zip up the suit to cover the bare spot.

When I come back out to the beach, everyone is grabbing their surfboards and heading down to the water's edge. We have dry-land training first, which involves learning how to stand up and balance on our boards.

"Everything okay?" Gabe asks.

I nod. "All good." I wrap my hands around the board and carry it down the beach to meet up with the rest of the group. "Except that these wet suits are disgusting." I'm trying to breathe only through my mouth.

Over the next thirty minutes we practice going from lying on our stomachs, to jumping up into a crouched position on the board, and back down again.

Kai catches my eye and smiles.

"I think he's sweet on you," Gabe whispers in my ear between practice jumps.

I just shake my head and roll my eyes.

"He's not smiling at anyone else like that," Gabe says, though there's no jealousy in his voice. He's never been the jealous type. It's one of the things I appreciate most about him, even though he has no reason ever to be jealous.

Despite all that's happened, there will never be anyone else for me.

I return Kai's smile and then go back to lying on my board.

# 47

Though I spend a lot of time trying to keep the ocean out of my lungs, it doesn't take long before I fall in love with surfing. And I'm not half-bad at it, either. By the fourth day, with only one day of class left, my arms no longer burn from the paddling and my feet consistently find the board's sweet spot so my weight is balanced enough to get a decent ride.

Of course, the trickiest part is figuring out which wave is the best one. Apparently there's a whole system to counting the waves, but I haven't sorted it out. Each class, Kai and Sara sit on their boards, legs dangling in the water and eyes scanning the coming wave crests. Then when they yell, "Go, go, go!" we all lie flat and start paddling to get ahead of the wave. With a quick snap, we jump to our feet and stay crouched for a second, getting our balance, then we stand with knees and elbows softly bent, and try to stay on our boards as long as possible.

Today has been a good day, and I seem able to stay on my board longer than anyone else, except for the teenager who is so good I'm sure he's lied about never having surfed before.

"He's young," Gabe says as we sit on our boards waiting for our turns, watching as the teen coasts past us effortlessly.

"I'm young!" I say, and Gabe laughs.

"True. I was just trying to make you feel better."

I wipe water out of my eyes, then sneeze three times in a row thanks to a nose full of saltwater from the last fall. "You okay?" Kai yells across the waves, and I give him thumbs-up.

"See?" Gabe says, a teasing tone to his voice. "Told you."

"Stop it. He's just checking in. You know how dramatic my sneezes are."

"Mmm-hmm," Gabe murmurs.

We're still a good distance out from shore, and I'm ready to catch another wave. I look behind me, maneuvering my board so it points toward the shore, and paddle my arms in the water to try and stay steady. Then I wait. For fun, I count the waves, but when I hear Sara yelling, "Go, go, go!" I lose my count and just start paddling as quickly as I can, taking a few deep breaths to pace myself.

Placing my hands flat on either side of the board, I jump up to my feet, feeling a deep stretch in my stomach muscles as I do. Then I crouch, waiting until I feel balanced and for the wave to pick up my board. Suddenly, it's like I'm flying. I hear a lot of hollering and know I've caught a good one. I feel it, too. It's easy, my board gliding on top of the wave, the wind at my back.

I have no idea what happens, but I go from shouting with the thrill to being pulled quickly under the strong waves. My ankle strap tugs painfully on my leg as I tumble around in the churning water, like a lone sock in a washing machine. I hold my breath and try to stay calm. I know I have to wait for the swirling water to pop me back up above the surface, but the panic inside me starts to build and I'm not sure how much longer I can hold my breath. As I struggle I hit something, and there's a sharp pain in my elbow. But a second later my head breaks the surface and I take in a deep, grateful breath.

Glancing around, I try to figure out where I've ended up.

I'm about twenty feet closer to the shore than I was when I started paddling, and see a few other surfers from my class nearby, who must also have had a great ride.

My elbow burns as I pull myself back onto my board. Once I'm straddling the surfboard, I twist my arm to get a closer look. The wet suit only reaches partway down my upper arm, and there's a wide, fiery red scrape running across my elbow. It looks a lot like road rash and I wonder what I hit.

"That was an amazing ride, Tegan!" Sara says, the first one to reach me. "You okay?"

"Thanks, I think so. I hit my elbow on something."

"Let me have a look," Kai says. Everyone is paddling toward where we're floating on our boards, as the class is getting ready to catch one more wave before we end for the day. Sara moves back to count the waves and help the rest of the group get ready, and I twist my arm again so Kai can see it.

"What happened?" Gabe asks, paddling his board up beside me.

"I scraped it on something when I went under the last time." I wince, the burning intensifying. It's definitely painful now.

"Ouch," Gabe says. "How bad is it?"

"It stings." I take a couple of shallow breaths to work through a wave of pain that moves up and down my arm.

"It's from the coral," Kai says, frowning. "You must have hit the reef when you fell. You're going to need to get that cleaned up."

"It's just a scrape. I'm sure the saltwater will clean it out."

"Coral scrapes can be serious. They can get infected really quick," Kai says. "First thing you need to do is wash it out well with soap and water, then you need to see a doctor, okay?"

"Shit." I glance at my elbow again. "Well, that sucks."

"I'm sure it will be fine once you get it cleaned up," Gabe says.

"You'll have to take a few days off," Kai adds. "Just to make sure it's healing."

"But tomorrow is the last class." My voice quivers, and I hate that I'm so emotional.

"It's okay," Gabe says. "It's only one class."

"How about this. I'll do a private class when you're fixed up, okay?" Kai says.

"Okay, thanks." I grimace again at the stinging pain.

"That's awesome, thanks, man," Gabe says.

"No problem. Think you can paddle yourself in?"

I nod. "I'm okay."

"I'll get you the name of a clinic once we get back to the shop," Kai says, maneuvering his board toward shore.

"See?" Gabe says. "It's all good."

I sigh and paddle the best I can around the pain, the waves helping me get to shore more quickly. I thank Sara when she takes my board from me, and head toward the shop.

"I'm just going to wash this," I say, holding my elbow out. "And then grab the clinic name from Kai."

"Need a hand?" Gabe says.

"I'm good. I'll be back in a minute."

Inside Kai helps me scrub my elbow with warm water and soap, which actually makes it feel a bit better, then gives me the name of the doctor. I open my locker and take out the necklace, then get changed out of my wet suit.

"Thanks again for the offer of the private lesson," I say, coming out of the change room.

"Happy to do it," Kai replies. "Just make sure you go to the clinic today."

I wave and start back toward the door.

"Hey, Tegan?"

"Yeah?"

"Listen, my dad has a café in town, the Banyan Tree? Maybe

you've seen it?" I nod. I noticed it the other day when we went into town for lunch—the café is built around a giant banyan tree. "The whole group is invited for breakfast after our last class tomorrow," Kai says, pausing before adding, "Anyway, just wanted to pass the invitation along."

I smile, my hand on the door. "Thanks, wouldn't miss it."

The doctor says I've done the right thing by washing out the scrape right away. "Which school were you surfing with?" he asks, holding my elbow and looking at it closely under the light. He seems almost too young to be a doctor, his dirty blond hair falling just below the tops of his ears in soft waves. As he turns his head to get a better look at my arm, his hair moves and I notice a tan line on his temple, probably from sunglasses. I wonder if he's a surfer. He looks like a surfer.

"Surf the Swell?" I reply.

He looks up from my arm with a smile. "Ah, Kai's school. He taught me when I moved here three years ago." So I was right. A surfer. "He's the best. Anytime someone asks for a recommendation I always tell them to go to Kai." For some reason this makes me proud, which is ridiculous because I don't even really know Kai.

"Okay, so this looks pretty good to me," he says, swiveling around on his chair. "I'm going to give you an anti-inflammatory cream and an antibiotic, just to be sure it doesn't get infected." He pulls out a prescription pad and clicks his pen. "Any allergies?"

"No."

"Are you taking any other medications?"

"Um, I have an estrogen patch," I reply, then clear my throat. I'm nervous to admit the antidepressant, wondering what the surfing doctor might think, but remember my promise to Gabe. "And Lexapro. Fifty milligrams a day."

The doctor whose name I have already forgotten just nods and writes on his pad. “Here you go,” he says, handing me the prescription. I look down at it and see his name, Dr. Mark Darbinger. “There’s a pharmacy downstairs where you can get it filled. Do you have insurance?” I nod. “Okay, good.” He reaches out a hand. “Nice to meet you, Mrs. Lawson, and I hope that arm behaves. If you notice any swelling, or if it gets hot and red or there’s any other sign of infection, come right back, okay? We’re open seven days a week.”

“Thanks, Dr. Darbinger.” I shake his hand. I get up and gather my purse, then remember about Kai’s offer of a private lesson. “One other question. When can I go back in the water?”

“If you start the antibiotics today I’d say day after tomorrow, okay?”

I nod. “Thanks.”

“Enjoy the rest of your vacation,” Dr. Darbinger says.

I say I will, and then walk out of the office.

“All good?” Gabe asks.

“All good. Just some antibiotics and a day or so out of the water.”

“That’s not so bad. What do you want to do for the rest of the day?”

“Hot shower first,” I say, getting into the rental car—a canary-yellow Mustang convertible that had been the only one left on the lot when we arrived. Gabe joked the bright color made the car seem “needy,” but I liked it. “Then maybe shopping? I want to pick up a few things for our parents and Anna.”

“We also need to get more of that banana bread,” Gabe says. “I’ve been dreaming about it.”

“Me, too, but that requires a trip back to Hana.”

“What about tomorrow? You can’t go in the water anyway.”

“I was thinking maybe the bike ride down Haleakala in

the morning? The hotel said they still have space," I say. "It's supposed to be amazing, even though you know how I feel about mixing fast bikes with steep pavement."

"That I do," he says. "Think you'll be okay with your arm?"

"I'll be fine. And the ride is finished early, so maybe breakfast with the surf class at the Banyan Tree after?" I add the last part breezily, as if I don't really care one way or the other.

"Sounds good to me," Gabe says. "I'm easy. As long as they have banana bread, of course."

I smile and turn on the radio, humming along to a top-forty song I recognize but don't know the words to. As I hum, I try to brush away the small ribbon of guilt that wraps itself around me. I don't really think there's anything to it, aside from him being a nice guy and enjoying his company, but I find myself looking forward to seeing Kai again.

# 48

It's cold at the top, like Chicago in late fall kind of cold. And it's drizzling, which makes me glad for the quite ugly, oversize but practical two-piece yellow rain suits they give us when we get out of the van. I wiggle my fingers and blow into my hands, trying to warm them. I long for my supersoft cashmere gloves that are back in Chicago, and for a brief moment I feel homesick.

Along with the chilly, damp weather, it's also incredibly crowded at the summit. Everyone says it's a Maui must-do, watching the sunrise from the top of Haleakala, but so far I think we've paid a lot of money to get drenched and chilled, before riding mountain bikes down a winding, busy road to the base of the volcano—which, for the record, feels like a bad, potentially injury-producing, idea. And it's definitely not an intimate experience; vans and buses full of sleepy tourists line the parking lot like canned sardines.

We climb up to where we'll watch the sun rise, and follow the crowd into the Haleakala visitor center to warm up a bit. I don't feel tired despite the hour, not even five o'clock in the morning, or the fact that the wake-up call had come at two in the morning.

I peer through the windows into the darkness, along with

two dozen or so similarly outfitted strangers. Seems the color of your rain gear depends on which tour you're with. The bright yellow, red and blue suits remind me of when my kindergarten class was let loose with primary-colored finger paints to make a mural in our classroom. Along with the vibrant colors inside the brown-walled building, there's a distinctly unpleasant smell of wet rubber. "It's so foggy," I say. "Think we'll see anything?"

"I hope so," Gabe replies. "Otherwise we got up at the crack of crazy to snap pictures of Hawaiian fog, which for the record, looks a whole lot like Chicago fog."

The sky is changing, lightening ever so slightly, and I stare into what has now become a dove-gray, fluffy sea of nothingness. "It's strange up here. Like we're suspended on the clouds."

There's an announcement that it's time to move outside again, and a line quickly forms by the exit. I'm jostled by a group of eager tourists and I force a smile when one of them turns to apologize. Our rain suits offer a bright contrast to the black pavement we stand on as we jockey for position around the metal railing. Frequent flashbulbs light up around me, reminding me to pull the camera out of my backpack.

And just like that, the sun begins to rise. It's amazing to go from an inky-black sky to one full of fire, so quickly. Now that the sun is warming the sky, the view is spectacular. We are above the clouds. The sharp peaks of the volcano's crater reach up into the sky, which is filling with layers of hot pinks and deep oranges. Wispy clouds, like tendrils of smoke, swirl around the crater. It has stopped raining and it's very quiet, all of us in awe at the scene.

I am overcome, and for a few seconds, forget everything that has brought me here.

I go to reach for Gabe's hand, and instead feel unfamiliar fingers against my own. They're thick, and cold, and belong to a man who is equally as surprised to find me reaching for his hand as I am to have done so.

"Oh, I'm so sorry," I stammer, pulling my hand back and jamming it into my pocket. "I thought you were someone else."

He's at least a few years older than me, with a kind smile and a young child standing on his other side. "No problem," he says with a laugh. "I was just thinking how cold my hand was."

I laugh, too, and then we both go back to watching the sunrise.

I don't know where Gabe has gone, and I start calling his name. Quietly at first, but then a little louder when I don't hear him. A few people look my way. Irrational panic sweeps through me.

"I'm right here," Gabe finally answers, beside me again. "What's wrong?"

"You just disappeared," I reply, taking a deep breath, trying to calm down. "I couldn't find you."

"Where would I go?" he says, laughing softly, which doesn't help. I'm in no mood for joking. He senses it, adding, "Tegan, I don't want to be anywhere but here. With you, and this."

There is an almost simultaneous contented sigh from the group as we watch the sun come up over the crater. It's the most beautiful thing I've ever seen. As the fiery globe continues its rise, the sky changes from deep purple, to fuchsia pink, to lighter shades of both, until soon my face warms with the rays that reach it.

"Everything is going to be okay, Tegan." I feel Gabe's fingers lace through mine. "You'll see."

# 49

*Three months before the accident*

"Everything is going to be okay, Tegan," Gabe said. "You'll see."

He wrapped his arm more tightly around my shaking shoulders and kissed the side of my face, which was wet with tears. I wiped my eyes with the tissue Gabe took from the box at the triage desk and tried to relax. Deep breath in through my nose, deep exhalation through my mouth. Repeat. Repeat. Repeat.

The waiting room was packed with barely an empty seat. An older woman beside me had a dishcloth, which obviously used to be pale green but was now deep red, held to her bleeding forehead. A concerned younger man sat with her, talking to her in a loud voice every now and again. A young girl, maybe five or six, was across from us looking quite green in the gills, with a plastic bowl on her lap and a bored-looking mother flipping through a magazine beside her. There were also a few people with ice packs on various parts of their bodies, and a couple others who looked like me—seemingly healthy, but obviously here for some reason.

The triage nurse opened the Plexiglas partition. "Tegan

McCall?" Everyone in the room looked up, as if hoping she had just called their names, then went back to their waiting.

Gabe helped me stand, one hand on my elbow and the other on my back, and the nurse gestured for us to come and sit down at the desk.

"It's actually Tegan Lawson," I said. "I just haven't had a chance to get everything switched over yet. We've been married for a month."

"Congratulations," the nurse said, barely looking up from the chart she was writing on. I took a seat in one of the cheap wood-and-vinyl chairs in front of her, and Gabe sat in the other. "So, Mrs. Lawson, it says here you're thirteen weeks pregnant?" It felt strange, being referred to by my married name, but I loved the sound of it.

I nodded. Then Gabe replied, "Yes, it will be fourteen weeks on Saturday, I believe."

At that the nurse looked up at us and offered a smile. "We'll put thirteen and a half weeks, okay?" I smiled back, though all I wanted to do was cry. "And you're having some cramping and bleeding? How long has that been going on?"

"About three hours." I wrapped my arms tightly around my midsection. "It started around ten o'clock, right, babe?" I looked at Gabe and he nodded. The nurse glanced at her watch, and wrote something down on the chart.

"Is this your first pregnancy?"

"Yes," I whispered, close to tears. "We just had our ultrasound last week. The doctor said everything looked perfect." I trembled and Gabe rubbed my back. I glanced at him but couldn't make a smile come to my lips. He looked nervous, too, his face pinched and tired, but I knew he was trying to hide it for my benefit.

"Okay, Mrs. Lawson, let's check your temperature and then we'll get you into a room to see the doctor."

A few minutes later I was settled on a cot in the emergency room, wearing a gown that despite its oversize nature, seemed to not cover the parts I wanted it to. Gabe stood beside me, leaning down every minute or so to kiss my forehead, and lips, and to ask how I was doing.

"I'm okay," I said. "I just want to know our baby is, too." Then I started crying. I'd been holding it in so long, I couldn't help the sobs. I was embarrassed at the sounds I was making, but not enough to be able to stop.

"Shhh," Gabe said, bending down to take me in his arms, where I shook with my tears. "The baby is going to be just fine. You'll see. You'll see."

I had never wanted anything more badly in my life. Though I was not one of those little girls who dreamed of becoming a mother one day—apparently my mom said I wanted nothing to do with dolls as a child, though I blamed that more on having two brothers—the moment I saw the positive pregnancy stick I couldn't think of anything I wanted more.

Another cramp seized my belly and I took in a quick breath. Gabe promptly released me, watching my face.

"You okay?"

I pressed my lips together tightly and nodded. He kissed my damp cheeks, then wiped my eyes with a tissue. He was going to make the most amazing dad. I prayed fiercely he wouldn't have to wait any longer for his chance.

The curtain was swept aside by a youngish woman in scrubs, with a long blond braid running down her back and a face that looked great without makeup. She had so many things hanging off of her—a stethoscope around her neck, with a roll of white tape held in place by the tubing; three pens clipped into her scrub top's pocket, which held a small wire-coiled notepad; a hospital identification card and a cell phone attached to the waistband of her pants; a necklace that held a gold wedding band; and a wrist full of plastic braided bracelets, which told me she either had a daughter or a niece. For some reason that row of colorful bracelets made me feel better.

"I'm Dr. Megan Foster," she said, reaching out the hand without all the bracelets. She shook my hand, then Gabe's, and then pulled the curtain back around the three of us, the small room suddenly quite crowded. "Why don't you tell me what's been going on?"

She listened carefully while I described my symptoms, with Gabe chiming in every now and again.

"How much bleeding would you say you've had?"

"Not that much," I said, looking up at Gabe. "More than spotting but not enough to fill a pad." I watched her face for any clues, desperate to hear positive news. "That's good, right?"

She smiled kindly. "Bleeding is common in the first trimester," she said. "It doesn't mean it's normal, but it is common. And what about the cramping. Can you describe it?"

"It actually feels a lot like the cramps I get with my period," I said.

"On a scale of one to ten, with ten being the most painful, how would you describe the pain?"

"Maybe a six?"

"Good, good," she said. "Okay, Mr. and Mrs. Lawson, I'm going to send you for an ultrasound so we can get a better picture of what's going on."

"Thank you," Gabe said.

"You're welcome," Dr. Foster replied, opening the curtain. "I'm not too concerned," she added. "Try to relax and I'll be back shortly."

After she left, pulling the curtain around us again, Gabe let out a long breath. I grabbed his hand and squeezed it tightly. "It's going to be okay," I said with a confidence I wasn't sure was warranted given the situation. I knew how precarious early pregnancy could be. One of my coworkers, who was in her thirties and had been trying for five years to get pregnant, had recently found out at her twelve-week ultrasound that her baby had no heartbeat. My ultrasound had only been a few days before hers, and the news had filled me with cold dread. I felt so sad for her, but also grateful it wasn't me.

And now it might be my turn to learn just how tragic and unfair life could be.

Gabe kissed me on the lips three quick times, and gave me a big smile. Twenty minutes later the doctor had a portable ultrasound machine beside the bed and I shivered uncontrollably as she applied the cold gel to my stomach, which still showed no signs of what was growing inside it.

"I know, sorry," Dr. Foster said. "The warmer is on the fritz."

"It's okay," I said, my teeth chattering a little. Gabe took off his scarf and wrapped it around my neck. But I knew it wasn't the cold that was making me shake; it was the nerves.

"Okay, let's have a look." She moved the ultrasound wand in a circle, making sure it was well covered with the opaque blue gel, and watched the screen closely, which I couldn't see from my vantage point. I stared at her face, willing her lips to open and give us good news.

*Please, please, please, be okay.*

"There we go," she finally said, taking one hand and turning the screen toward us. "Mr. and Mrs. Lawson, here's your perfect little peanut."

Gabe whooped, then clapped a hand over his mouth. I grinned through my tears, impatiently brushing them away so I could see everything more clearly. I pressed my fingers to my lips, delirious with joy as I watched our baby kick and punch and roll about on the screen.

"Thank you," I whispered to Dr. Foster.

She smiled, I'm sure happy she wasn't delivering bad news to us this evening. "It looks like everything is just fine," she said. "It was probably a clot that you passed. But as you can see, your baby is doing great. Looks like you're going to have a little boxer on your hands." She raised an eyebrow, and I laughed.

"Does that mean we're having a boy?" Gabe asked, slightly breathless.

"Still too early to say," she said. "But girls can box, too, you know. My second one moved like that in utero, and let's just say she can take her older brother down any day."

Gabe laughed, saying, "Fair enough."

Dr. Foster wiped the gel off my stomach, then put the gown back down over me and pulled up the blankets. "I'd like you to stay here for twenty-four hours or so, just to make sure the cramping and bleeding subsides, but I'll see if we can get you a bed upstairs so you can get some sleep, okay?"

"Thank you so much," Gabe said, holding my hand so tightly I almost had to tell him to loosen his grip.

After Dr. Foster left the room Gabe wrapped his arms around me, burying his head into my neck.

"See?" I said, trying to talk and breathe through his embrace. "I told you everything was going to be okay."

"That you did," he said, letting me go so he could pull up my gown and kiss my naked stomach. I lay my hands on his head, taking the moment to silently express my gratitude. Then he covered me back up, gave my belly a sweet pat and kissed me deeply. "I need to remember you're always right."

# 50

Much to my surprise, I survive the ride down Haleakala without a single fall off my bike. There are a few spontaneous stops to take photos, each one more picturesque than the last, but by the time I'm at the bottom I feel amazing and full of energy, my cheeks flushing and my hair flat to my head with sweat and the helmet's tight fit. My legs are rubbery, but at the same time I feel strong. Like I can do anything.

"Look at you go," Gabe says, after the bikes and rain suits have been returned. "Not even a scratch."

I laugh, trying to fluff up my hair. It doesn't do much, so I pull it back into the elastic I always keep around my wrist. My hair has grown a lot these past few weeks of traveling, and my ponytail grazes my shoulder blades. It's hot, so I take off my sweatshirt and wrap it around my waist, grateful for the tank top I'm wearing underneath. The breeze feels incredible on my skin.

My stomach growls and I rub it through the thin cotton of my top.

"Hungry?" Gabe asks.

"Starving," I reply. I look at my watch. "Breakfast is starting in about an hour."

"We should be able to make it," Gabe says. "Come on, let's get seats on the van."

An hour later, my ponytail still wet from the shower, we walk through the door at the Banyan Tree café. It's larger inside than I expected, with the beach-side wall completely open thanks to the garage-door-style windows that have been rolled up to the ceiling. A fresh ocean breeze floats into the café, filtering through the banyan tree's large glossy green leaves. It's busy inside, and I scan the room looking for our group.

"Looking for a table?" a man about my dad's age says. He's quite fair, with pale green eyes surrounded by the lines of advancing age. Laugh lines, which grow deeper with his smile.

"No, well, yes, sort of," I say. He raises an eyebrow, still smiling.

"Sorry, that didn't come out right." I laugh. "Is Kai's class here?"

"They sure are," he says, beaming as he holds the menus to his chest. He's wearing a brightly colored Hawaiian shirt, open at the neck where some gray chest hairs poke through. "I'm Kai's dad, Bud Edwards," he says, holding out a hand.

"Oh, right," I say, shaking his hand. I'm surprised Kai's dad isn't Hawaiian, though I hope my surprise isn't evident. I assume Kai must get his Polynesian coloring from his mom and wonder if she works here, too.

"Nice to meet you," Gabe says, a lot more smoothly than I do.

"I always love meeting Kai's students," Bud says, pointing to the step at the front door. "Watch the step there. Come on, come on, I'll take you to the table."

The class is sitting out on the patio, under the shade of the banyan tree. There's some hugs and shifting of chairs, but soon we're all settled. There's a faint smell of wet-suit stink around the table, but I don't mind because it reminds me of being out on the water. Bud takes our orders and then grabs a stainless-steel carafe. "Coffee?" he asks, holding it up. "It's our special Kona blend."

"Oh, yes, please," I say, turning the mug in front of me right side up.

"None for me," Gabe says. "I'm still buzzing from that ride this morning."

"If you guys haven't done Haleakala, you really should," I say, adding a thank-you to Bud when he fills up my cup with the dark, steaming coffee. I bring it to my mouth and inhale deeply before adding a touch of cream. No sugar, though. Between the espressos in Italy and the fragrant Kona coffee in Maui, I finally get it—if you have to put sugar in your coffee, you shouldn't be drinking coffee.

"Oh, you did that this morning?" Lauren, previously known as Mrs. Gold Bikini, asks. "We're going tomorrow."

"It was amazing," Gabe says.

"Definitely an experience not to be missed. But take warm clothes to the top. Trust me, it's freezing up there before the sun comes out."

"How's the arm?" Kai asks me. He butters the half piece of banana bread in his hands, reminding me of my dad, who up to this point is the only person I know who likes a thick layer of butter on baked goods. My chest tightens. I miss home. But I'm not ready to go back there, not yet.

I do a few bends of my elbow and push thoughts of Chicago out of my head. "Good as new," I say. "Dr. Darbinger said I'm going to be fine."

"Not even a grimace of pain on this beautiful face during the ride," Gabe says.

"Glad to hear it. Those coral rashes can be superpainful," Kai says. "You missed a good class this morning. Think everyone had a great ride." He sips his glass of orange juice before adding, "The waves were kind to us today."

There are a few snorts around the table. "You're the one being kind," Roger, Lauren's husband, says. "I think I still spent more time in the water than on top of it." Everyone laughs and digs into plates of pineapple spears Bud sets out. The pineapple is tangy yet sweet, and so juicy some dribbles down my chin. Bud says he'll be right back with the rest of our food.

"Let me help you, Dad," Kai says, pushing his chair back.

"Nope, you sit." Bud waves him back to his seat. "Nadia can help me bring the plates out."

Kai ignores his dad and follows him to the kitchen, telling us he'll be right back.

"He's a nice guy," Gabe says.

I nod, watching Kai head through the kitchen's double doors.

After breakfast—I have the Maui Wowie French Toast, generous slices of egg-battered coconut loaf covered in brown sugar and butter-fried bananas—the group begins to break up as everyone makes their way to the next activity on their vacation roster. We say goodbye and hope to see each other again, though that's more about being polite than anything else.

"So, you want to do the lesson tomorrow morning if the weather holds?" Kai asks. Apparently we're supposed to get some serious rain overnight, but Bud says it will be fine by morning, joking that Maui is dry, hot and sunny when the tourists are awake, like she knows it's time to put on a good show.

"That works," Gabe says. "We have nothing planned for the morning."

I nod in agreement. "What time?"

"How about nine o'clock?" Kai says. "We can always do

breakfast here again after. I'm helping Dad out tomorrow for the lunch rush."

"Perfect!" Gabe says, and I think he must be missing the way Kai is looking at me. It's been a while since I noticed that look from anyone but Gabe, and it both unsettles me and makes me feel good.

"Okay, well, see you tomorrow?" I reach for the door and in doing so forget about the step at the front. I trip over it and end up flying through the doorway and landing on my side.

"Tegan!" Gabe shouts. "Are you okay?"

I jump up and brush the dirt off my no longer white tank top. "I'm okay," I say, and start laughing. "P.S., watch out for that step."

Kai is on my other side and has a hand on my arm from helping me up. I look at my arm, then at his hand, which he drops before taking a step back. I clear my throat. "Well, at least I know how to make an exit, right?"

Gabe laughs, and all I want to do is get out of there. I don't like the way I'm feeling.

"Okay, then," Kai says, heading back through the door into the café. He seems uncomfortable, or maybe I'm just projecting. "See you tomorrow?"

"See you tomorrow," Gabe says, and I just smile.

"Thank your dad again for a delicious breakfast," I say over my shoulder.

"Will do." Kai gives a small wave before letting the door shut.

"Told you." Gabe sounds smug.

"Told me what?"

"He's sweet on you."

"He is not," I say, but feel a blush creeping into my cheeks. "You said it yourself, he's just a nice guy."

"I'm not jealous or anything." His tone tells me it's the

truth. “I know exactly why he looks at you like that. That’s how I look at you.”

It’s true. Gabe can make my knees weak just by the way his eyes hold mine.

But it has been a long time since he’s looked at me like that.

And I suddenly realize how much I miss it.

# 51

“I’m a teacher,” I say, feeling the burn in my arms as I paddle out through the waves. The waterproof bandage I have on my elbow tugs at my skin with the movement but seems to be staying put. Kai suggested a full-sleeved suit today, just to make sure the seawater stays out of the scrape. But I’m finding it a lot harder to move my arms through the water with wetsuit fabric down to my wrists. “Kindergarten,” I add, working harder to catch my breath with the effort.

“And a kick-ass one at that,” Gabe says, which makes me smile. A few years ago we ran in to an old high school friend of Gabe’s at a music festival, and this guy had clearly spent too much time in the beer tent. He slurred out a sarcastic comment about how tough it must be to “teach” kindergarten, what with “all the finger painting and summers off.” The experience irritated Gabe far more than it did me, and he has since developed a habit of proactively defending my career choice even when it isn’t necessary.

“Oh, yeah? My mom was a teacher, too. Grade eight, though,” Kai says, looking over from his board without breaking his paddling. He smiles, but his eyes carry something else, which is explained a moment later when he adds, “She passed away about ten years ago now.”

Gabe and I offer Kai the requisite platitude, the I'm-sorry-for-your-loss line that I've personally heard too often these past few months. But I understand why people say it—it's a fast way to close out a potentially awkward and emotional conversation no one wants to have.

"Thanks," Kai says. "It was quick and she didn't suffer. That's about the best you can hope for in a situation like that, right?"

I look ahead and try to squash the nausea that threatens my breakfast. My arms slow and I take a few deep breaths.

"What's up, Teg?" Gabe asks as I lag behind.

"Nothing," I say quietly, and try to work my arms harder. "My arm is just a bit sore." I feel guilty lying, especially since I promised Gabe I wouldn't do that anymore. But I don't feel like explaining things to Kai, who is now straddling his board about fifteen feet ahead of us. He turns back, a questioning look on his face.

We give a thumbs-up back, then I slice my hands through the water, quickly making up the space between us.

Straddling my own board, I let my breath return to normal from the paddle and feel my stomach start to settle.

"So when are you heading back to Chicago?" Kai asks, keeping his eyes on the waves farther out. The muscles in his forearms twitch as he adjusts his position on his board, and I suddenly remember how strong his grip was when he helped me up yesterday. I quickly look out to the waves instead.

"A few more days."

"Three, actually," Gabe says, and shock settles over me. I know the trip is coming to an end, but it's hard to believe it's been almost six weeks. I'm not ready to go home. Actually, I'm scared to go home, because I don't know who to be when I get there. I'm not the Tegan everyone knew before the accident, but I'm also no longer the broken shell of myself I was when I left.

Kai nods and keeps his eyes on the waves. "You'll have to come back and visit again," he says.

"For sure," Gabe says.

"Definitely," I add. Then we're all silent.

The waves move our boards a little sideways, and we occasionally have to lie down and paddle to get back in position. The sun is getting strong, and as Bud predicted, despite torrential rains the night before, this morning everything is clear and dry. I pull a sunscreen lip balm out of my wet suit's pocket and apply some to my lips and nose.

"Don't worry, it's eco-friendly," I say, when I notice Kai glance over. I turn the tube to read the label. "Actually, it says it's dolphin-friendly. Guess they weren't too worried about the rest of the ocean critters?"

Kai laughs. "I wasn't worried. I was just thinking that's a good idea, the sun is pretty fierce today."

"Do you want some?" I ask extending the tube toward him.

"No thanks, I'm good. My skin was made for this sun."

"Not Tegan's," Gabe says with a laugh. "Last time we were in Maui her shoulders got so burned she couldn't wear a bra until we got home."

"Really?" I say, quietly, but with a smile. I can almost feel the pain in my shoulders, remembering the burn. I bought coconut oil from the gift shop to "just get the tan started" and then went for a two-hour walk on the beach to hunt for shells. By the time I got back to the pool, Gabe's olive skin had soaked in the sun beautifully and I looked like a boiled lobster. "Must we share that?"

Kai looks my way. "Sorry?"

"Nothing," I say, shaking my head. I tuck the lip balm back into my pocket. "So, what are you looking for out there?"

"The perfect set." Kai's attention is again on the ocean's waves. "There's a pattern to the waves, and if you can get ahead of just the right set, you'll have the ride of your life."

"How long have you been surfing?"

"All my life. My mom used to say I came out on a surfboard."

"Ouch," I say, the three of us laughing. "Your poor mom."

"When you grow up in Hawaii you learn to surf the second you can walk. In fact, my mom used to surf when she was pregnant with me, so I guess I've technically been surfing since before I was born. Oh, hey, there we go..." Kai's voice trails off and his arms flex again as he adjusts on the board. "Okay, get ready. We've got a beautiful set coming."

I scan the waves and don't see anything different, but follow Kai's lead and turn my board around so it's pointing toward shore. We lie down and when he starts yelling, "Go, go, go!" I paddle like my life depends on it. There's a feeling of speed picking up that isn't coming from my paddling, and when I hear Kai shout "Jump!" I anchor my hands to the board's edges and hop my feet into position. A second later I'm up, my shoulders facing the shoreline the way Kai taught us.

The wave catches up to me and I shriek, the board lifting to ride the crest. I pick up speed and for a moment think I'm about to lose my balance, but then relax my knees and know nothing is going to knock me off this board.

I feel strong, happy and capable—three things I haven't felt in a long time. "Yes!" I shout as loudly as I can, luckily closing my mouth just before I smack face-first into the wave and go under the water.

Sputtering and whooping with joy, I break the surface. I throw an arm over my board and shoot the other arm high above the waves to give the all-okay sign.

"Thumbs way the hell up!" I shout, laughing as I wipe the

water out of my eyes. The saltwater stings my eyes, and the scrape on my elbow burns, but I don't care.

All I want to do is get back on the board, and ride another wave, and then another, and another. Until the happiness fills up every bit of me, leaving room for nothing else.

# 52

*Two and a half years before the accident*

"What is that?" Gabe asked, looking around. He had one hand on the door and had just put the ukulele he bought at the general store on the convertible's backseat. I was already in the car, my seat belt buckled, when we heard the high-pitched sound.

"I have no idea," I said, turning in my seat. "It sort of sounds like a baby crying." But it was hard to pinpoint exactly what it was, as the sound of revving motorbikes suddenly filled the air. I pulled on the seat belt to get some slack and glanced behind me, following Gabe's gaze to see at least a dozen motorcycles coming up the hill toward us. The sound was deafening.

Then we heard it again, the high-pitched squealing. "There." Gabe pointed halfway down the gravel parking lot. And then I saw it: a very small black-and-white potbellied piglet, running back and forth in the parking lot, squealing in terror.

"Oh, no, Gabe!" The bikes were about to storm into the driveway, and the piglet was directly in their path. I'm sure the bikers didn't see the tiny pig—with the miniature pink-

and-white flowered lei around its neck—as it was no larger than a kitten.

But Gabe was way ahead of me. As he ran toward the piglet, I screamed at him to be careful and tried to get my seat belt unbuckled. "Fuck, fuck, fuck!" I shouted, the push button sticking on the belt lock. I finally got it undone and scrambled out of the car just in time to see Gabe standing with his arms and legs out to his sides, in a starfish position, shouting at the bikers to stop. The piglet continued running in circles squealing, but at least Gabe shielded it now.

I had no idea how the bikers stopped before running Gabe or the pig down, because it all happened so fast, but they did. Gabe threw his head back and brought his hands together, looking up to the sky. "Thank you!" he said, then repeated it to the biker at the front of the line, who was still confused as to why Gabe had blocked their path so dramatically.

The contrast between Gabe, standing amid the swirling dust from the bike tires in his khaki shorts, grass-green golf shirt and clean-shaven face, and the bikers, dressed head to toe in black leather with beards long enough to braid, was hilarious. And now that I was no longer worried about Gabe getting run down by a bike gang, I laughed and snapped a photo with my phone.

Along with the help of a couple of the bikers, we cornered the little pig and Gabe managed to grab it by the lei as it tried to run past him for the tenth time. The squealing piglet bucked in an attempt to get out of Gabe's arms, but he held tight, and thanked the bikers again.

Fifteen minutes, five loaves of homemade banana bread and one recipe for said banana bread later, we left the general store again and walked back to our car.

"Petunia is lucky you were here today," I said, reaching my hand into the back pocket of Gabe's shorts and pulling him closer. "Even though you could have been killed, that was supersexy what you did back there."

Gabe raised one eyebrow. "Sexy, huh?"

I nodded demurely, and was about to give his butt a squeeze when he suddenly disappeared from beside me.

"Fuck!" he yelled, from the ground. He was sitting, one leg stretched out in front of him, but the bag of banana bread still safe in his hand. He grimaced and held his ankle with his other hand. I saw a large pothole in the ground beside him. "Shit, shit, shit, that hurts."

I kneeled down in front of him. "Let me look." I tried to pry his fingers away. I could see his ankle was already swelling.

"No, don't touch it," he said, moaning.

"Gabe, let me look," I said again, using the patient but firm voice I generally reserved for my students.

His face was scrunched in pain, but he released his ankle and lay back on the gravel, his arms resting over his eyes, plastic grocery-bag handle still clutched in the other hand.

I gently took off his flip-flop, forcing myself not to comment on how I had suggested sneakers might be a better option for today, and chewed the inside of my cheek. His ankle was fat, double the size it should be, and it looked like he had a golf ball tucked under his skin, which now had a bluish tint. It didn't look good.

"We're going to need some ice," I said, knowing better than to touch it. Jase had broken nearly every bone in his body as a kid, and I knew a broken bone when I saw one. "Think you can get up if I help you?"

Gabe nodded from behind his arms and he managed to stand on his good leg, though he leaned heavily on me. His face was pale and his mouth tight. I could tell he was in a lot of pain. "You okay?" I asked. He nodded again. "Okay, let's just get you to the backseat and you can stretch your leg out."

He hopped, moaning with each step, and together we got him to the car and settled in the backseat. "I'm going to get some ice and then we'll go to the hospital."

"It's just a sprain," Gabe said, but I could tell he knew it was worse than that. He'd sprained his ankles plenty of times playing basketball with his college friends. "I don't want to sit in a waiting room for hours."

"And I don't want to hear another word about it," I said. "I'm taking you to the hospital when we get back to Lahaina. But first, I'm getting a bag of ice."

He glanced down at his ankle, then nodded. And then he looked up at me quickly, dismay clouding his face. "Shit, the surf lessons."

"It's okay." I leaned down to kiss him.

"You can still go without me," he said, but he couldn't help the small pout that took over his mouth.

"Forget it," I said with a wave. "We have our whole lives to learn to surf. No way am I missing the chance to kick your ass on a surfboard. And this wouldn't be a fair fight."

"I'm sorry." He shook his head, not interested in making light of it. "I can't believe this. What a way to ruin a vacation."

"Nothing to be sorry for," I replied. "It would take a lot more than you on crutches to ruin my vacation. Just stop talking and let me take care of you, okay?"

"Okay," he said. I smiled and turned back toward the store.

"Teg?"

"Yeah?"

"Think we can tell everyone I busted my ankle saving Petunia?"

I winked. "Isn't that exactly what happened?"

"I love you, Tegan Jane McCall," he shouted after me.

"I love you, too," I replied, adding, "You're a hero, you

know. And not just to Petunia." I gave him a smile and headed inside to buy a bag of ice. It was at that precise moment that I knew when Gabe Lawson asked me to marry him, I would say yes.

# 53

Kai stands in front of the table at the Banyan Tree café, one hand on the chair across from me and one holding a swinging, delicate chain from which two rings and a silver pendant hang.

A pendant, the size of a quarter. Half an inch thick.

My necklace.

My hand flutters to my neck and sure enough, it's bare. I try to swallow, but the bite of coconut cake sticks in my throat and I cough. Kai asks if I'm okay, then pats my back a few times as I sputter until the cake makes its way down.

*How does Kai have my necklace?*

Then I remember. I took it off before we went surfing this morning, like I did every time, and put it in the locker. But I forgot to lock it up, distracted by Kai talking about switching up wet suits to one with full sleeves. To protect my coral-rashed elbow. After surfing, still on a high, I forgot about the necklace altogether and left without it. We walked around downtown Lahaina, picking up souvenirs for our families while I enjoyed the feel of the sun on my face, without my necklace. Without noticing its absence. Then we came here, thinking only of how hungry I was from shopping and my deep craving for coconut cake.

I left my necklace behind.

And Kai has it in his hand.

I have tunnel-vision focus on the necklace, and it takes me a moment to realize Kai is asking me a question. "Tegan? This is yours, right?" I nod, feeling uneasy though I'm not entirely sure why. My stomach twists uncomfortably around the coconut cake, and suddenly I know what's coming next. Panic shoots through me, along with a sense of desperation. I stand up quickly, though I'm not sure what I'm planning to do. Kai holds the pendant in his fingers, and the rings slide to the bottom of the chain. I hold my breath as he squints at the pendant's flat surface, reading the inscription I chose months ago, before looking back at me curiously.

"Who's Gabe?" he asks.

The café tilts, and an electric shock moves through me so quickly I feel weak. I should have stayed in my seat, because a second later my legs give out.

Kai somehow catches me before I hit the ground, and gets me back in my chair where I slump down. His arms are strong against mine, and I know he's singlehandedly holding me upright. He's talking to me, but I can't hear the words over the blood pounding through my ears. I close my eyes, taking shallow breaths. Someone is asking about an ambulance. There's commotion, and too many voices all at once, but none of it matters.

*Gabe.*

As I sit in the chair, Kai so close I can smell the ocean on him, the meticulously crafted world I've created over the past few months begins to break apart. The seams stretching to the point where the threads no longer hold the pieces together. The pictures move through my mind, bright and painful, like flashbulbs in the dark.

*Sitting alone at the kitchen island, cutting up the biscotti Gabe's grieving mother kept bringing over out of habit, even though he would never again eat it.*

*Only my hand dipping into the glass vase, choosing the three squares of paper from our past.*

*The empty seat beside me on the plane to Bangkok.*

*The photo at Torre dello Ziro, me standing alone against the stone wall, the brilliant blue ocean and sky creating a spectacular backdrop.*

*My hand clutching nothing but the misty, cool air while watching the sunrise on Haleakala.*

*Only one passport scanned, one backpack checked, one side of the bed slept in.*

*Me, alone, for all of it.*

Though it sounds like it's coming from deep in a well, Kai's voice finally reaches me.

"Are you okay?" Kai asks, over and over, his voice low but sharp with concern. There are too many faces around me, and I try to tell everyone to move away. But all that comes out is a low moan.

The more I focus on my breath, the harder it becomes to breathe, and soon I'm hyperventilating. I close my eyes again, dizzy from the lack of oxygen, and try to shake my head.

"Tegan?" Kai says, close to my ear. "I'm calling an ambulance." He's trying to hold me while reaching for the phone in the pocket of his board shorts, and I grab his hand, shaking my head.

"Don't," I manage to say, though my breathing is uneven. "I'm okay." Kai's not convinced, I can tell.

Then, Gabe's voice. *It's time, Tegan.*

"No," I reply, eyes squeezing shut. "No...it's not...time." My lungs fight so hard to fill, and I suck at air around me in desperation and focus on Gabe's face in my mind. On the eyes I know so well, I could draw the tiny flecks of navy that dot the otherwise crystal-blue irises. On the mouth that knows my lips, and the curves of my body, intimately. On the cheekbones I hoped our son would inherit.

"Time for what?" Kai asks, and I open my eyes to see his own, confused and concerned, and very close. "Take a few deep breaths, Tegan." I do as he says. "There you go. That's better. Just slow down your breathing." As I force my lungs to fill more slowly, the pinpoints of darkness ebb.

I keep my eyes on Kai's, noticing not for the first time how long and dark his eyelashes are. They're pretty, his lashes, like he's wearing mascara; surely not how a man would like his eyes described, but beautiful nonetheless. After another few breaths I ask for some water. Someone hands Kai a glass and he holds it to my lips while I take a small sip.

"What happened, Tegan? Are you okay?"

I can't speak, tears falling to my cheeks.

"What's wrong?" Kai asks, holding me tighter. That's when I realize I'm shaking. Quivering like a turned leaf, barely hanging on in a gentle fall breeze.

*Tell him*, Gabe says.

# 54

*One week after the accident*

There was something wrong with my eyes. I wanted to open them, but they seemed to be glued shut.

And it wasn't just my eyes. Every part of my body was heavy, as though my veins and bones had been filled with cement. I tried to think, but couldn't hold a thought for more than a few seconds at a time. There were unfamiliar noises all around me. Beeps and alarms, and a low hissing noise that was relentless. Finally I got my hands to move and placed them on my face, where I felt plastic tubing wrapped around my ears and going into my nose.

*Where the hell am I?*

"Tegan, sweetheart?" My mom's voice. Blurry, but definitely close by. I felt someone take my hand, pulling it away from the tubes in my nose, which I had been trying to pull out. Everything felt wrong. All wrong.

"Rick, go get the doctor," Mom said. Footsteps echoed on the floor, rubber soles squeaking with each step. He was moving quickly, my dad, wherever he was going.

"Tegan, you're in the hospital."

*The hospital? Why?* I tried to speak but no sound left my parched throat.

"You…there was an accident, sweetheart. But you're okay."

*An accident? What happened?*

Snapshots landed back into my memory. *Rockin' around the Christmas tree…have a happy holiday…* The strong scent of peppermint. Twinkling lights everywhere. The wine, falling off my lap. My lap…the bottle leaning against my pregnant stomach…

I groaned, and my mom shushed me, holding my hand tighter.

With my other hand I frantically grabbed at all the bedding, at the starched gown that covered my body. My movements were clumsy, but determined.

"Tegan, stop. It's okay, honey. It's going to be okay." My mom was crying, and the fear inside me blossomed.

A moment later I had my gown pulled to the side and my hand landed on my stomach, on what felt like a large piece of gauze. I didn't know what it covered, but the flatness of my abdomen told me all I needed to know.

There was no baby inside me anymore.

"Tegan, look at me. Look at me," my mom said, her voice firm despite the emotion it carried.

I looked at her, her face swimming in and out of focus. She looked horrified.

"There was an accident, sweetheart. A terrible car accident," she said. She took a deep breath, so I did, too. My chest hurt. "You had a lot of internal injuries and they had to do surgery to save your life."

I wanted to tell her to hurry up, to get to the part I knew was coming. But I still couldn't find my voice.

"Tegan…the baby…the baby is gone."

*The baby is gone?* That made it sound like he was simply

missing, gone from me but coming back eventually. Frustration flooded me, along with a sensation I had never felt before—a horrible mix of rage, sadness and disbelief.

My mom was ghost white, no longer bothering to wipe away her tears. She sat on the narrow bed beside me, somehow finding a spot amongst the tubes that seemed to come in and out of a number of places on my body, and wrapped a hand around the side of my face.

"I need you to listen closely, my love. This is going to be the hardest," she said, her words catching. "I'm so sorry you have to go through this." Her voice lowered to a whisper, and I focused in on her lips so as not to miss anything. They looked dry, with only a hint of the soft red lipstick she always wore around their edges.

"Gabe…sweetheart, our Gabe…" She pressed her face to mine and I felt her tears transfer to my cheeks. "Gabe died in the accident, Tegan. I'm… Gabe is gone, honey." She sobbed, and I opened my mouth to tell her that was ridiculous.

I wanted to tell her Gabe was just down the hall, getting a coffee or taking a work call. That he'd be right back and she should stop saying all these awful things, because he'd be right back and he wouldn't be happy to see me so upset. *You'll see*, I wanted to say. *You're wrong. He'll be right back*.

Gabe was not dead. I was just sitting beside him in the car. He was singing his favorite Christmas carol. His hand was on my leg. We were laughing. He was eating candy canes.

I'm about to tell her she and Dad can just go home now, because surely they have a lot to do. That I don't need them here because Gabe would be right back.

He would be right back.

I opened my mouth to tell her all of this.

And instead, I started to scream.

# 55

I didn't mean for it to happen. I knew Gabe was dead. How could I not? His side of the bed was empty, cold. His clean laundry was still folded in the hamper, unworn.

His ashes were in my necklace.

But the sadness, the despair at being left all alone, was too much. So at first, I just pretended he was still with me. Soon, when I imagined him speaking to me I could hear his voice clearly, and when I thought about the feel of his touch, my skin responded. It wasn't long before I didn't have to pretend anymore.

Keeping him alive in my mind was the only way I knew how to stay above the surface. Of not joining him in a place I could never come back from.

Later, when I finally confessed the truth to Dr. Rakesh—that Gabe was as real to me now as he ever was—he explained it as a sort of psychotic break, brought on by grief. Apparently it's not uncommon for people who have suffered such a loss to try and recreate life with their loved ones—in essence, to bring them back from the dead—as a coping mechanism. Though it may sound strange to be grateful for any kind of psychosis, I'm happy such a thing exists. Because it meant I had Gabe back, at least for a short time.

I guess you could say I became crazy with grief. Seeing him, hearing him, feeling him…it was as though I'd resurrected him.

At least until the moment Kai read the inscription on my pendant. And then, something broke inside me and I could no longer ignore the truth.

Now, Kai and I sit on a smooth, hollow log on the beach a few steps from the café. The log's surface is so polished by the salt spray and wind it feels almost man-made. The wood is warm, soaked with sunshine, and I press my palms firmly down onto it to try and transfer some of the warmth to my shaking, clammy hands. The dizziness has ebbed, but emptiness has taken its place. It's as though I've been cast out into the ocean waves in front of me, drifting anchorless.

"Oh, my God, Tegan," Kai says, exhaling deeply when I finish telling him what happened. He kneels in front of me and wipes the tears from my hot, sun-kissed cheeks. And with that simple gesture, I come undone. The seams, under so much strain for too long, unravel simultaneously. I have nowhere to hide.

Gabe is gone. And he's never coming back.

"I didn't even get to say goodbye," I say, my voice straining.

Kai nods, but says nothing, leaving it up to me to break the silence when I'm ready. I listen to the birds sing in the massive banyan tree that shelters us somewhat from the sun, and try to sense Gabe. I hold my necklace tightly, rubbing the pendant like a lucky talisman. Still nothing. I'm terrified that I can't hear him or feel him anymore. I'm not sure I can cope in a world without Gabe.

"At first I was so angry," I say. "I hated him in a way I didn't even think was possible when my mom told me I lost the baby." I swallow hard and the tears fall. I don't bother wiping them away. My voice comes out so quietly Kai has to lean in to hear me. "And for one moment...one horrible moment, I wished... I wished Gabe..." I can't go on.

"It's okay, Tegan," Kai says gently. "I'm just here to listen."

"I wished Gabe had died instead," I say. "And then when Mom told me... When she said Gabe was dead, I felt..." I squeeze the pendant tightly and take a deep breath. "Like somehow wishing it had made it true."

The songbirds fill the silence, and something releases inside me, like an overfull balloon that's been untied. I put the necklace on and pull on the chain to make sure the clasp is secure.

"I hated everyone for a long time after that. Not just Gabe, for leaving me. I hated my family, and Gabe's, and our friends, even though they lost him, too. Basically, I hated everyone else who got to carry on living, who wasn't faced with losing everything they cared about, you know?"

"I understand," Kai says. "I was really angry when my mom died. At the world, at the doctors, at God. She found out about the cancer in January and was gone three weeks later. I never imagined how little time we'd have with her."

"I'm so sorry, Kai. I'm sure you miss her a lot."

Kai nods. "I do. But I try not to think about the tragedy of it all now. I try to focus on how lucky I was to have her as my mom for as long as I did. And that she didn't suffer, when her time came. She basically went to sleep one night and didn't wake up. They said it was the chemo, it just stopped her heart." Kai wipes the corner of his eye. I reach out and hold his hand, squeezing his fingers tightly. He smiles and squeezes back.

I take a deep, shaky breath and look out over the ocean. "Do you think you could help me with something?"

"Anything you need," Kai says.

I tell him what I have in mind.

# 56

The water is warm, its waves gently lapping at my shins as I sit on the surfboard, feet hanging below the ocean's surface. I rotate my legs in small circles, not because I'm trying to get anywhere, but because the movement helps focus me.

Though I know it's time, letting go isn't going to be easy. I have filled the hole Gabe left behind with a memory of him so tangible it's almost as though he's been brought back to life. Like when you read a sentence missing a word, but your brain fills in the word regardless because it knows it's supposed to be there. That's what these five months of grief have been like. My brain working hard to convince itself Gabe isn't really missing after all. Early on, I pretended he was just at work during the day. Nighttime was harder, but it wasn't long before I tricked myself into feeling his presence. Convincing myself that he didn't die in the accident along with our baby, and any hope I had of the future I still crave so fiercely.

But once I told Kai the truth, I saw the hole clearly. Saw the missing link between the sections of my life, and now I can't stop fiddling with it. Making it bigger. Things have begun seeping into that hole, disappearing into the black void, the way things do. It's becoming more difficult to hold Gabe's smile in my mind, to remember the sound of his voice. The gentle touch of his hand on my neck.

It's happening so fast, Gabe's disappearing act, that it takes my breath away.

I shield my eyes and glance at the shore to where Kai sits on the beach. Waiting for me to come back, when I'm ready. He opened the surf shop and let me take his board out, the one he spent the past year building. Its black-and-white surface is glossy and beautifully smooth, aside from the two panels running the length of the board, which are rough, like a cat's tongue. Just textured enough to ensure my feet don't easily slip off.

Kai paddled out with me in a kayak, carrying the glass bottle that now stands safely between my thighs. With a warm smile that crinkled his features in a way that reminded me of Gabe, Kai left me to it and made his way back to shore.

The necklace is clutched in my other hand, the pendant and my rings digging in to the sensitive skin of my palm. I'm afraid of it falling into the water too early, before I'm ready, so I'm holding it tighter than I need to. I rub my thumb along the inscription on the back of the pendant, on the letters too small to be deciphered. It's a line from an Edgar Allen Poe poem I studied in high school English class, and it made me cry the first time I read it.

Gabe,
We loved with a love that was more than love.

While the lazy waves move the board closer to the shore, still a long way away, I hum. Nothing in particular, just notes to help me stay clearheaded and give my brain something else to focus on for a few minutes. The birds squawk around me, diving into the ocean periodically for their supper of small fish and other sea life. The sun sinks even lower, getting ready to say goodbye to the day.

There are so many things I want to say.

Nothing I can say will be perfect enough.

"We loved with a love that was more than love," I finally whisper, adding, "Thank you for loving me, Gabe." The tears come fast, hot against my cheeks, but I don't heave with their force. They just drop, new ones quickly taking their place.

I let my hand sink into the water, then pull it back up and clutch it to my chest.

"Fuck." I'm crying harder now. "I can't do this. I can't do this, Gabe." I sob, clutching the necklace with both hands, chin resting against my chest. I stay like that for a few minutes, fighting the panic that threatens to take over. Then with shaking hands I undo the clasp and let the rings slide off the chain into my palm, putting them back on my finger, where they belong. At least for now.

But I understand now that the necklace won't keep Gabe with me. Nothing can do that. He's gone. Has been gone for a long time.

I let my hand drop again, the water rising to my wrist. My breath comes fast, unsteady. The pendant is still clutched in my hand and I close my eyes, willing my fingers to open. To let go. *Just let go, Tegan. Let go.*

I let go.

The necklace slips through my fingers and is gone so fast I barely have time to register the moment it left my hand. My heart hammers in my chest, as if marching to the frantic squawks of the hungry birds around me. I feel light-headed and hang on tightly to the edges of the surfboard until I'm sure I'm not going to pass out.

A few minutes later my heart rate slows, my head clears and I'm feeling stronger. I wrap my hands around the bottle, into which I stuffed the squares of paper from our wish list—*Buy a piece of art painted by an elephant…in Thailand; An authentic cooking class in Ravello, Italy, for Tegan; Hang ten in Maui*—as well as another paper with the song Gabe proposed with, rolled in a scroll. I kiss the corked bottle and toss it into the waves, where it sinks quickly thanks to the handful of stones Kai suggested I put at the bottom.

I sit on the board for a while longer, until the birds quiet and the sky becomes filled with deep pink and burned orange swirls of another perfect Maui sunset.

Then I paddle back to shore.

# *five*
# Chicago

# 57

"I knew I loved Gabe from nearly the moment we met, but it was when he made me his dad's Dutch pancakes for the first time that I knew I'd be crazy not to marry him." I look out into the crowd, a sea of black suits and sad faces, and connect with Gabe's dad, who is seated in the first row directly in front of the podium. He gives me a smile and I rub my palms together, feeling the sheen of nervous sweat between them. My black heels, bought especially for today, pinch my toes and I wish for my comfy ballet flats in my closet back home.

"Yesterday would have been our first anniversary." I'm unable to look at anyone as I say this. "And while I wish we were having a very different kind of event today, I'm honored to celebrate Gabe's life with all of you." My hand shakes as I pull on the microphone, adjusting it down to better suit my height. It creaks as I do, which is when I realize just how quiet the church is despite how many people pack the pews.

"First, I want to thank Gabe's family for their patience, and for waiting until I was ready to have this memorial service." I lock eyes with Rosa, and she gives a stoic smile though I can't miss her tears. She lets them fall, despite the tissue in her hand. Lucy sits beside her with her family, and my parents and brothers round out the rest of the row. I run my eyes across each one of their faces, silently thanking them for loving Gabe, and loving me. We're all stronger now, the passage of time the only true healer, but the pain is still raw.

"I'm not sure our parents know this," I continue, glancing down at the small stack of note cards in front of me. I don't need them because I've essentially memorized the words, but it gives me comfort that they're there, just in case. "But our first date wasn't exactly legal, or, um, traditional." I smile and look at Anna, who is chuckling behind a carefully placed hand over her mouth. Samuel, the new boyfriend she has fallen head over heels for in a matter of weeks, holds her other hand tightly. Though part of me is jealous she has him beside her while Gabe rests beside me in an urn, I'm also grateful Anna has a chance to experience what I had with Gabe. Everyone deserves that.

"It was our first year at Northwestern, and there was a floor crawl at my dorm. Basically every floor hosted a different kind of cocktail, and, yes, I know we were underage, Dad." I glance at my dad, who's laughing softly. "Anyway, my floor's drink was Purple Jesus." I swallow uncomfortably, realizing that probably wasn't appropriate to share, being in church and all. I imagine Gabe, laughing at my gaffe, but saying, *You're in it now, so just keep going.* I smile, and do exactly that.

"Gabe knocked into me and my drink spilled everywhere, all over both of us. The next thing I knew, I was drinking shooters with him in the women's washroom. It was pretty clear he was trying to get me drunk..." I look down at my cards again, taking a needed break, and a small murmur of laughter moves through the otherwise somber church. "So that was our first date. Eighteen years old and doing shots with a boy I just met on the disgusting, linoleum floor of my college dorm bathroom." Another round of soft laughter echoes through the crowd.

I take a deep breath and shift my feet, feeling blood move back into my pinched toes. "Now, this is not the story I wanted to tell our grandkids when we were old and gray and they asked how we met," I say, looking up again. "So I told Gabe we needed a do-over. A proper first date, full of great stories for generations—" My voice falters, and I clear my throat. "Excuse me. For generations to come.

"Gabe was more than up for the challenge, which probably won't surprise any of you," I say, smiling again. And as strange as it sounds, I feel excited to tell the story in spite of my black dress, too-tight shoes and terrible reason I'm standing up here.

I get to be with him again—back in a time where being happy was easy—even if just for a few minutes.

"We were on the phone one morning, about a month after the shooters-in-the-bathroom incident, and I told him I didn't think it was going to work out..."

# 58

*Eight years before the accident*

Gabe said nothing. I tried to muffle my laugh, turning the handset away from my mouth, which I covered with my other hand.

"Oh, okay..." he finally said, and I pressed my lips together, thinking how mean it was to trick him like this. "But, what happened?" He was confused and surprised, which made perfect sense because up to this point our conversation had been flirtatious. Also, I'd only left his bed a few hours earlier.

"I'm sorry, but I'm just not that kind of girl," I said, then pulled the mouthpiece away again so he couldn't hear me laughing.

"What kind of girl?" He sounded perplexed.

"The kind whose first-date story starts with bathroom shooters and ends with walking back to her dorm the next morning in the same clothes," I said, my tone teasing and light. "That's a story I can't repeat to my grandkids."

Gabe exhaled with relief. "Grandkids, huh? Think you might be getting a bit ahead of yourself, McCall?"

I smiled and twirled a piece of hair around my finger. "Do you think I'm getting a bit ahead of myself, Mr. Lawson?"

A brief pause, then… "No. No I don't."

My stomach flip-flopped. "Okay, then, it's settled," I said. "We need a do-over."

"Oh, I'm happy to do that night over again, and again, and again…"

"Stop it," I said with a laugh. "I want a first-date story that will still be romantic fifty years from now, when we're so old we can no longer see without pop-bottle glasses or cataract surgery, and our sweaters smell like mothballs."

Gabe laughed. "You would look adorable in glasses," he said. "With one of those beaded librarian strings to keep your glasses around your neck? So hot."

I rolled my eyes. "Do you have some kind of librarian fetish I need to know about?"

"I hadn't thought of it before, but now that you mention it…you, in a short skirt on a stool, reaching for a book on a high shelf…"

"Hey, focus, mister. Can we get back to the real issue? You giving me a swoon-worthy first date?"

"A 'swoon-worthy' date, eh? Yeah, I think I can do that."

I smiled, lying back against my pillow. I wanted so badly to see him right now, to crawl through the phone and let him wrap his arms around me the way he had the night before, and then…my body tingled and I sat up, trying to cool things off.

"Perfect. So when should I be ready?" I imagined which dress I would wear. Probably the black halter-top one. Or the red silk one, whose skirt rested well above my knees and hugged my body like a second skin. There would be dinner, somewhere with candles and overpriced steaks and a leather-bound wine menu, even though being underage meant we'd have to order sparkling water with lime instead. Maybe Gabe would cook me dinner at his place so we could enjoy something a little stronger with our steaks, if he could kick his roommate out for the night. We might dance a little, or walk down to the pier, where we'd make out by the water, under the stars. Then we'd…

"Can you be ready in an hour?"

"What?" I asked, the daydream spell broken. I looked at the clock on my desk. It was eight in the morning. I had class at nine. More importantly, I was a disheveled mess in my sweatpants and ponytail. "An hour? Like, an hour from now?"

"Yes," Gabe said with a laugh. "Wear something comfortable. And tennis shoes, okay?"

Comfortable? Tennis shoes? I frowned. This wasn't exactly the romantic first date vision I had in mind.

"Oh, okay," I said. "I'll be ready at nine. But what are we—"

"Ah, ah, ah, no questions," Gabe said. "I'll pick you up in an hour. Get ready to swoon!"

I threw down the phone and grabbed my toiletries bag, running to the washroom so I could grab a shower before the morning rush. Fifty-five minutes later I sat on the bench outside my dorm, my hair washed, dried and straightened, and wearing a long, belted navy blue turtleneck sweater with my jeans and tennis shoes. The mid-October air was crisp, but it was a blue-sky kind of day. I pulled out my sunglasses and put them on just as Gabe pulled up.

Jumping off the bench I headed toward the passenger side, but Gabe had gotten out of the car—which had been a high-school graduation gift from his parents and was nicer than any car my parents had ever owned, but I decided not to hold that against him—and quickly came around to open my door. He held it open for me and I grinned, giving him a kiss before getting inside.

"Well, this is a good start." I buckled my seat belt.

"One of my dad's theories on life," Gabe said, leaning in

and tugging on my seat belt to make sure it was secure. He gave me a wink. "The moment you stop opening her car door is the moment you fell out of love."

I blushed, probably reading too much into his words.

"So, where are we headed?" I asked as Gabe pulled away from the curb.

"First, back to my place," he said, keeping his eyes on the road.

"Oh, really?" I rested my hand on his thigh, his muscles tensing under my touch. "Is that how you're planning to make me swoon this morning?"

"Get your mind out of the gutter," Gabe said. "This isn't that kind of date. Remember, we need to be able to tell the grandkids about this one." He took my hand and put it back in my lap, and I pretended to be annoyed, crossing my arms and giving a huff.

"Good things are worth waiting for," he said, and I dropped the act and smiled. I couldn't have agreed more.

# 59

For a moment I forget where I am, lost in the memory of our do-over date. Then someone coughs, and my eyes refocus on the rows of people sitting in front of me. Black clothes. Mournful faces. The gold urn, still beside me. A wave of nauseating sadness moves through me and I look down at my shoes, willing myself not to buckle at the waist. Suddenly, I feel fingers lace through mine and I look up to see Anna standing beside me, holding my hand tightly. She smiles and steps a little closer to me, her fingers warm and strong. My lungs fill back up with air and I whisper a thank-you to her before continuing.

"First he made me his dad's Dutch pancakes, which for those of you who haven't had them before, are amazing. Like a crêpe, filled with real maple syrup." I smile, remembering the moment I took the first bite of pancake and thought, *Don't fuck this one up, Tegan.* "I think I ate five of them, no joke. Then he handed me an envelope. I opened it up and inside was a scavenger hunt list of ten things I had to find downtown. He said he'd been a bit rushed, so he'd pulled up the first scavenger hunt he found on Google, which was one from some parenting magazine. 'I tried to make it easy for you,' he told me, 'to make sure you get the prize at the end.'"

My mom wipes her eyes and gives me a nod and gentle smile. This is her favorite story about Gabe, and the one she's proudly repeated so many times, saying it was the moment she knew her daughter had found "the one."

"Over the next few hours we ran around the city, chasing the clues. Of course he knew exactly where everything was, and set up a system where a very public display of affection, like a long kiss in the middle of the sidewalk, earned me hints." I turn one of the cue cards over with my free hand, though there's no need to. I'm not following the cards; I just need another moment to gather myself. Anna squeezes my hand again and I squeeze back, thinking that of all the moments she's been beside me, this will be the one I'll never forget.

"The very last one was at the Bean. I had to get a photo taken with exactly twenty-one other people, all of us smiling. Gabe just laughed while I ran around, begging some people to get in the picture and asking others to step to the side. Finally, I managed to get twenty-one people willing to help me out, and we stood in a group, me shouting at everyone to smile and yelling at a few stragglers to get out of the shot, and Gabe went to take the photo, and—" My throat catches, but I push on. "Nothing happened. His camera battery was dead." The church fills with laughter, and I join in, wiping away the tears with the balled-up tissue in my hand. "So he gave me that one, and let's just say the prize was well worth all the effort." I look at the mangled tissue in my hand, and close my eyes. Needing a second to be alone with my thoughts, and Gabe.

I look up, willing myself to finish without breaking down. "We didn't have enough time together," I say. "Not even close." I press my lips together, tears streaming down my cheeks. Anna is crying softly beside me, and I rub my fingers gently over hers. Even though my grief is like a scab that's been ripped off too soon, it feels good to not be alone with it up here. "But I wouldn't change a thing. I'm grateful he was mine. I'm grateful he chose me." Everyone is quiet now, and I choose to keep my eyes away from the faces in front of me. "Thank you for listening."

Anna takes my arm, leading me by my elbow, and we step down from the podium.

I let my eyes rest on the urn for a few moments, then I take my seat beside my mother. She gathers me in her arms, where I cry as quietly as I can for a long time.

"He was perfect," I say, laying my head in my dad's lap like I used to when I was little. We're on the couch in the Lawsons' library room, far away from where Gabe's friends and family enjoy canapés and wine, and reminisce about him. "I'm not going to find that again." My nose is plugged, my eyes swollen. It has been a long day. After the memorial service we went to the cemetery, where Gabe's urn was buried under a headstone in the Lawson family plot. Beside Gabe's stone is another marker. A small, marble plaque, which reads, *Harrison Gabriel Lawson, beloved son of Tegan and Gabe Lawson.* There's also an empty plot beside the marble plaque, which I know Rosa specifically requested be held, though we have never discussed it. Lucy told me Rosa said that while she prays I find happiness again, she wants me to know I'm always a part of their family. And as morbid as it may seem to have a dedicated cemetery plot at the age of twenty-seven, it brings me comfort to know it's there.

Dad shakes his head and brushes my hair back from my face. "Oh, he wasn't perfect, sweet Tee," he says. "He was just young."

"You're wrong." I sit up and look at him. "Even if we'd had an entire lifetime together, I would still think that."

"I have no doubt that whether it was the year after you married or on your fifty-year anniversary, you would have loved Gabe no deeper than the day you married him. I loved your mother from almost the first moment we met. But I didn't know her then like I do now." He smiles gently at me. "Do you understand what I'm saying?"

"I think so," I say, though I don't, really. I'm too exhausted and drained to focus on much aside from staying upright.

"I don't love your mother any more than I did all those years ago, but the way I love her has changed."

I close my eyes and take a few deep breaths. I just want to get out of my uncomfortable black dress and sleep for an entire week.

"We all have our flaws, Tegan, and you and Gabe..." Dad pauses, sighing deeply. "Well, you just didn't get the time to figure out what those were."

I look at him with surprise. "It's sad we didn't get to know each other's flaws?"

Dad laughs. "That's not exactly what I meant. It's more that those flaws become part of you, as a couple. And they make your strengths shine brighter, which is what allows that love to change. It's knowing someone deeply, and loving him or her in spite of the things that drive you crazy. And that, my sweet girl, takes time."

I nod, my head bent. Dad reaches to the side table and pulls out a couple of tissues, which he hands to me.

"As your dad, more than anything I hate that this has happened to you, that your life is so much harder than it ever should have been, and that I can't fix any of it." He clears his throat and I know he's holding back his own tears. "But I'm grateful for Gabe. For his presence in your life, however brief. Because no matter what happens now, or who else you decide to give your heart to, Gabe has helped shape who you are. And you have a beautiful heart, Tegan. The heart of a survivor."

"I don't feel like a survivor," I whisper, leaning my head against my dad's shoulder. The material of his suit jacket is rough against my cheek, but I don't move.

"I know, baby, I know." Dad kisses my cheek, and then leans his head against mine. "That will take time, too."

# 60

The local weather channel says we might get snow tonight. But it's only the ninth of November, and my mom is beside herself.

"Snow before Thanksgiving?" she says, when I pop over for a morning coffee with her and my dad. It's become a Saturday morning ritual since I've been home, with Connor and Jason often joining us, too. "It just isn't right. It's all the plastic we're using. Rick, remember that documentary we watched the other night? About the plastic and global warming?" Mom tops up my coffee, the Banyan Tree's Kona blend. I brought home so many bags of it I had to pay a fee for my luggage being overweight.

"I do remember," Dad says calmly, continuing to read his paper. His glasses perch on his nose, and he catches my eye and gives me a knowing smile. I remember our conversation at Gabe's memorial, the one about loving the flaws. He clearly knows what's coming next.

"Well, I'm going to stop buying anything in plastic," Mom says, sitting at the kitchen table with her coffee in her hands. "Paper or glass from now on, that's it." I hide my smile behind my own mug, loving my mom for believing if she stops buying plastic it won't snow before Thanksgiving.

Dad murmurs, "Okay, Janet," and I try to help by changing the subject.

"I'm going to the cemetery today," I say, taking a sip of my coffee, which transports me back to Maui. I miss the rainbows and endless sunshine.

"Oh?" Mom says, lightly. I haven't been since the memorial, over a month ago.

"I have a few things I want to show Gabe," I say. "From the trip."

Dad folds his paper and looks at me over his bifocals. "Do you want company?"

I shake my head. "No, thanks. I need to do this alone."

"Of course," Mom says, reaching out and holding my hand. "Dad and I went last week and left some flowers for Gabe and Harrison." My heart swells at the mention of them, and I'm grateful to my mom for not shying away from speaking their names. I don't want them to be forgotten, but I've found people don't like to talk about Gabe much anymore. At least not with me. As though not mentioning him, or our son, will somehow make it easier on me, when in fact, the opposite is true.

"They probably need to be replaced. Rick, why don't you run down to the market and get some more flowers for Tegan to take with her?"

"Great idea," Dad says. "Anything else you need?"

"A quart of milk," Mom replies. "But not a plastic jug. Get it in the glass bottle, in the organic section."

Dad smiles, then kisses my mom's cheek and mine and heads out the door.

"I have to apologize to you, Tegan," Mom says, once we're alone.

I look up at her. "For what?"

"I never thought it was a good idea, that trip," she says, stirring a little more cream into her coffee. "But everyone else told me it was exactly what you needed. That you were strong enough to do it." She shakes her head and looks into her cup. "I didn't think you were. And I'm sorry for not trusting you." She looks up at me. "For not believing in you."

"Mom, it's okay," I say, putting my hand on hers. "I wasn't sure I could do it, either. To be honest, I'm still amazed I did."

She nods and smiles at me, relief on her face. "Well, I just wanted to tell you. Because I'm so proud of you, for how you've handled everything. I don't think I could have been so…" She pauses, then locks eyes with me. "Brave. You have been so very brave, Tegan."

"Thank you," I say.

We drink our coffees and chat about Thanksgiving, and she asks if I'd like to invite Gabe's family over for dinner. I say I think that would be nice, then Dad is back with the flowers and glass bottle of milk, and I say my goodbyes.

Twenty minutes later I grab the heavy, reusable shopping bag from the trunk of the car and walk across the well-tended-to grass until I'm standing in front of Gabe's headstone.

"Sorry it took me a while to get back here," I begin, crouching down to unpack the bag. "But it's taken me a few weeks to perfect this." I hold up a Tupperware container, then set it down beside me. I also remove a small bottle, and a few other items from the bag, including a large wool picnic blanket, which I lay on the ground in front of the stones.

I sit on the blanket, cross-legged, and pull out a rolled-up piece of canvas from the cardboard tube.

"First things first," I say, unrolling the canvas and then turning it around to face the headstone. "One painting, by an elephant in Thailand named Phaya." I glance at the painting, the elephant's self-portrait. "I think it's exactly what you had in mind and I've already bought the frame and hammered in the nail. Right beside the front door, so I'll see it every day." I roll it back up and put it safely inside the tube again. "You should have seen what those elephants could do with a paint-brush. You weren't kidding—they really were awesome."

"Next, Italy," I say, taking the lid off the Tupperware container. Inside long spaghettini noodles swim in the thick tomato sauce, made from the recipe I learned in Ravello. "You were so right about Italy and Ravello. It was magical. But you know that already, of course." I take a bite of the pasta. "And this sauce?" I slurp up an errant noodle and then chew and swallow it. The pasta is lukewarm now, but the flavor doesn't suffer any from the cooling off. The sauce is sharp and rich, with a perfect balance of garlic, basil and a touch of heat. I lean toward the headstone, lowering my voice to a whisper. "I think it's better than your mom's. But let's keep that between us, okay?"

The lid back over the top of the dish, I wipe my hands on a paper napkin then pick up the small bottle beside me, its cap tightly closed. I shake the bottle and golden grains of sand float inside, buoyant in the saltwater. Unscrewing the lid, I pour the contents over the grass growing directly at the base of the headstone. "I wanted you to feel this," I say, shaking the bottle to make sure the sand comes out. "This is from the beach in Maui where I caught my first great wave." I screw on the lid and place the empty glass bottle back inside the bag, along with the painting, dish of pasta and napkin.

Placing the bag to the side of the stones, I pull out a crumpled envelope—greeting-card-sized, with fresh tape holding the flap closed. "This was supposed to be your Christmas gift. Actually, it was going to be epic, the joke I had planned. I still have the other gift, the gag one, and maybe I'll bring it next time. But I wanted you to have this." I lean the envelope up against Gabe's headstone, and let my fingers gently caress its edges, softened by my daily touches over the past few months. "I hope you'll sing it to him, okay? I don't know if you have a guitar where you are, but I expect you do."

Lying down on the blanket, I turn my face to the sky. I shimmy my body up a bit, so my head is close to the stone. Reaching out my right arm, I lay it on the grass beside me, where our son rests. The ground is cold on my back, even with the blanket.

"I named him Harrison by the way," I say softly. "Harrison Gabriel Lawson."

A bird whistles from one of the nearby trees, and it makes me smile, its timing perfect.

"I know, I know," I say. "It wasn't your first choice, but I think you would have come around. If it makes you feel better, Anna admitted she was on your side, at least when it comes to the name Harry." I watch the few clouds in the sky float quickly by. I have a chill, and wrap one arm over my chest, hugging myself tightly. But I keep my other arm on the grass beside me. "I hope you're with him, Gabe, wherever you are now." I rub the blades of grass between my fingertips, and picture Gabe holding a swaddled baby. Holding Harrison in his strong arms.

"Even though I know it wasn't real, you were with me the whole time. Every day." My voice strains, and the bird whistles a short tune again. A black-capped chickadee, by the sound of it.

"Maybe one day it won't hurt so much, thinking of you. Imagining what our life could have looked like. But I'm never going to forget how much I love you."

I wipe my eyes and sit up, pulling open my coat to retrieve another envelope from inside—this one crisp and bright white. I'm shivering now, but I don't zip my coat back up. Kneeling on Gabe's grave, I place the sealed envelope against the headstone, beside the other one.

"I wrote you a letter." I lean back on my heels. "For you and Harrison actually. Will you read it to him?" I adjust the envelope a little and push it down into the grass, making sure it's secure enough not to blow away. On the outside of the envelope's surface is a quote from a card Rosa gave me after the memorial service.

*Death leaves a heartache no one can heal, love leaves a memory no one can steal.*

She told me it was from a headstone in Ireland, and to me, it says everything.

I run my fingers one more time over the deeply etched names on both the headstone and plaque, then replace the flowers with the fresh ones my dad bought, pick up my bag and head back to the car.

# six

# Home

(Two years later)

# 61

"You should see the board," I say, my feet doing a lazy figure-eight motion in the water. I run my hands over the rough top of the surfboard, my fingers drawing outlines with the drops of water on its surface. "It's white with these amazing gold and pink flowers. I feel like a superstar when I'm riding it." I smile, looking back to the beach where Kai waits for me. A small speck moving across the sand, waxing the school's surfboards so they're ready for tomorrow's class.

The sun is starting to lose its strength, the shadows from the palm trees on the beach growing longer. "Kai made it for my birthday." I turned twenty-nine the week before, and along with the surfboard, Kai threw me a surprise party at the Banyan Tree. My parents, the Lawsons and Anna and her fiancé, Samuel, had flown in to surprise me, and it was hard to say goodbye to all of them this morning when they left.

"And you won't believe it, but your mom put me in charge of dinner next time I go back to Chicago." I laugh. "Your dad said my pasta sauce was better than your mom's, and Lucy backed him up. Looks like I'm finally being brought into the Italian family fold."

The wind whistles in my ears, and the ocean swells under my board. I look out at the waves, reading them as they roll in the way Kai has taught me. Now it feels instinctual, recognizing the wave that will bring the best ride. Not seeing the set I'm hoping for yet, I turn my attention back to the warm, deep blue water my legs dangle in.

"Your mom and dad are doing really well," I continue. "I even got your mom on a surfboard." Rosa finally agreed to the surf class when she realized everyone else was doing it, and I had to give her credit; she only barely grimaced at the wet suit's stench when I zipped her into it. "It wasn't pretty, but she did the whole lesson without complaining. You would have been really proud of her."

The wind moves my board out of position, and I lie on my stomach to paddle myself back around before straddling the board again.

"Dad looks amazing," I say. "He's lost so much weight he looks at least ten years younger. Mom, too, actually. And Anna, oh, my sweet Anna. She's turned into a bit of a bridezilla." I laugh again and shake my head, remembering the formal wedding meeting she insisted I be conferenced into, where the floral arrangements discussion took a full two hours. "I'm not sure our friendship will survive the next five months." Of course I'm joking. I'd do whatever Anna wanted, even wearing a lemon-drop yellow halter dress with a taffeta tutu skirt… in the middle of a snowy, Chicago March.

"My kids are so great this year," I continue. "They made me the sweetest birthday card, using their handprints as flowers and their birthday messages written in lines like the stems. Very creative." My current kindergarten class is my favorite to date, and I'll be sad to see them go at the end of the year.

"Oh, and I almost forgot the best news," I say, slapping the board with my palms. "Kai's dad added your Dutch pancakes to the breakfast menu at the Banyan! I made them for him about a month ago and he loved them. Your dad was beside himself, all puffed up like a peacock when he saw it on the menu. They're called 'Gabe's Sweet Cakes' and apparently they're a big hit already." Talking about the pancakes makes me realize it has almost been a month since I chatted with Gabe out here in our usual spot. I still dream about him often, but now, when I wake up, I feel happy for having spent the night with him rather than heartbroken at the reminder of what I've lost. Plus, I know wherever he is our son is with him. And that settles me in a way that's hard to put into words. It makes me able to carry on, a little bit more easily, each day.

I look out at the waves again, quietly counting the crests. Then I see what I'm waiting for—a double set. I lie down on my board and look behind me, paddling with my arms to keep me in line.

"See you later, love," I say, moving my arms like a windmill to get ahead of the wave. I'm strong now, and my tanned and muscled arms cut through the water easily. "I'll be back soon." Then I hop onto my feet, with the smooth grace of someone who's ridden enough waves to know what she's doing, and whoop as I feel the ocean swell pick up my board.

He's always on my mind when I surf, like it was our thing somehow even though it was something we never did together. When I first moved to Maui over a year ago now, I spent a lot of time in the spot where I dropped the necklace, straddled on a board Kai loaned me whenever I needed it. Sometimes I'd sit, floating for ten minutes, having little to say, and sometimes I'd be out so long my waterlogged fingers and toes would turn to prunes. Though Gabe's buried in Chicago, under a handsome dark gray granite headstone, this is where I feel closest to him. On the water where I said goodbye.

Gabe never talks back anymore, but that's okay.

I know he's listening.

★★★★★

# Acknowledgments

The idea for this story came from a conversation at my uncle's funeral (thank you, Dana Sinclair), and grew its legs thanks to my husband, Adam, and date night at Indie Ale House.

However, it wouldn't be where it is today without a lot of help. Thanks to my agent, Carolyn Forde, for your support and determination, and for responding to my (many) emails with enthusiastic exclamation marks. To Michelle Meade, my editor, you make this look so easy—thank you for loving this story as much as I do. To the rest of the MIRA team—your excitement and hard work has made an impression. When they say it takes a village, they aren't kidding.

I wrote much of this book between the hours of 5:00 a.m. and 7:00 a.m., and I couldn't have done it without my Twitter #5amwritersclub crew, or copious amounts of coffee. To my early readers, and critique partners—Kim Foster, Roselle Kaes, Abby Cavenaugh, Kristi Shen, Rachel Goodman, Julie Green—your critical eyes and kind words have made all the difference. Thanks Chris for the coffee chats, and Scotty for the pancakes. To my writing community, and friends, pinch me—the day is finally here! And because you have always told me I can do whatever I put my mind to, and would be the first to sign up for my fan club, thank you Mom, Dad and the rest of my family. Nana—I'll leave you a signed copy on my bookshelf.

Finally, to my husband and daughter—everything I do, I do for you.

# COME AWAY WITH ME

KARMA BROWN

Reader's Guide

1. Tegan carries a lot of anger toward Gabe after the accident. Did you feel she was unfairly holding Gabe responsible, or was she justified to blame him for what happened?

2. Grief has many stages, including denial, anger, depression and acceptance. Discuss Tegan's experience of these stages along the course of her journey.

3. Do you think traveling and the experiences helped Tegan accept her loss and deal with her grief, or was it simply having time away from the spotlight of her family and friends that helped her heal?

4. By the time Tegan meets Kai, she and Gabe seem to be getting back on track. Before the truth about Gabe is revealed, how did you feel when Kai's character showed up? What did you think it meant, if anything, for Tegan and Gabe's future?

5. Tegan struggles with her mental health throughout the story. How did you feel when you realized the truth

about Gabe, and understood what Tegan had fabricated in order to cope with her grief?

6. While it was an incredibly difficult thing to do, Tegan is eventually able to let go of Gabe and their baby during a beautiful moment out on the ocean in Hawaii. How did you react to her dropping the necklace in the water? Have you ever experienced a similar moment of letting go?

7. Do you have a wish list or bucket list for things you'd like to do or places to travel? What's at the top of your list?

**Come *Away with Me* is as much a story of grief and loss as it is about hope, healing and love. What inspired you to write such an emotional story?**

*So many stories focus on the experience of falling in, or out of, love, and I wanted to explore what can happen to a great marriage when tragedy strikes—does it pull people closer, or force them apart? Also, I was inspired by my cancer diagnosis at age 30 to write a story about how to move forward, and how to find happiness again, when your life changes overnight.*

**The love between Tegan and Gabe is palpable from the early pages of this story, and their journey is heartbreaking to follow. Were they based on real people, and did you find yourself more attached to any character in particular as you wrote?**

*My husband will definitely see parts of himself in Gabe, and some of the scenes between Gabe and Tegan are fictionalized versions of experiences we've had. But while I fell hard for Gabe, probably because he reminds me of my husband, it was Tegan who stole my heart. I put her through a lot in this book, and at times when I wrote scenes I'd whisper a quick "I'm sorry" for where I was taking her story. After spending months with these characters, they feel like people I know in real life. That's one of my favorite parts of writing.*

**Tegan goes through an extremely emotional journey throughout the course of the novel, and by the end she's managed to face her loss and begin to build a new life for herself. What do you hope readers will take away from watching the evolution of her character?**

*That the uncertainty of life is not something to be afraid of, and that the best way to not be crushed by the bad stuff is to always keep moving forward. One of my favorite quotes is the famous one from Winston Churchill: "If you are going through hell, keep going." It's simple and direct, yet says so much about resiliency and determination, both strong themes in* Come Away with Me.

**Throughout the novel, the exotic locals Tegan visits truly come to life. What made you choose Thailand, Italy and Hawaii? Have you traveled to any of the places described in the novel?**

*I wanted the travel aspects to feel authentic, so I chose places I've traveled to, as well as ones that have an emotional connection for me (for example, my husband took me to Amalfi for my 40th birthday!). It was so much fun, reliving my travels through this story, and I think the added elements of culture, food and setting truly enrich the journey Gabe and Tegan are on.*

**Do you read other fiction while you're doing your own writing or do you find it distracting?**

*I read more when I'm writing! For me, reading—especially in the genre I write—offers an outlet when I'm feeling uninspired by my own prose or stuck on a particular plot point. I never fail to find inspiration in others' words, and I love the opportunity to be transported to another world even for a short time. I typically come back to my own work more motivated and excited.*

**Can you describe your writing process? Do you outline first, or dive right in? Do you have a routine? Do you let anyone read early drafts, or do you keep the story private until it's finished?**

*I have a young daughter, and deadlines for my freelance work, so I get up at five o'clock nearly every morning when I'm working on a book. It's usually quiet (as long as my daughter doesn't get up with me, which she often does as she's also an early bird), and armed with a pot of coffee I find it the most creative time to write. I also write every day when actively drafting a book, and stick to a daily word count. As for sharing my work, I have done it both ways (sharing as I write/holding off until the first draft is complete), and for me it works best to share in chunks with my critique partners—a few chapters at a time. I find it helps keep me on track and accountable to getting the story down.*

**What was your greatest challenge in writing Come Away *with Me*? What about your greatest pleasure?**

*The most difficult part was dealing with the emotions while writing* Come Away with Me*—there are dark themes in the story, and I had to absorb those fears and get close to them* *to write them well. The easiest was getting the story down—it was one of those books that just flowed out of me. I wish it always happened like that!*

**Can you tell us something about your next novel?**

*Like* Come Away with Me, *my next novel explores the themes of friendship, marriage and parenthood—this time dealing with a family who uses a surrogate to have their first child. It's an emotionally charged story about a family desperate to protect both their unborn child and a longstanding friendship after things take a tragic turn.*

Back
~~Front~~: 275/40 ~~3R20~~ 20
3R20

Front: 245/45 R320
~~Back~~: